I WAS BORN ON THIS WORLD,
MY BODY IS BUILT OF ATOMS THAT HAVE
BEEN PART OF IT SINCE IT COALESCED.
WHAT RIGHT HAVE I TO SCATTER THEM
ACROSS SPACE AGAIN?

"Ye lucky—where'd you be goin', then? Orbital station?"

"Further."

"The Moon? The Martian settlement?"

I shook my head, which must have been just about visible, because I heard a sharp gasp in the fog.

"No, the . . ."

I could see her silhouette gesture away into the infinite distance of the mist.

"The Colony, yes. I've a place option on the second Ship."

"No wonder ye're wanderin' round in a dream!" She sounded oddly breathless and shocked. 'How'd ye manage that?"

"Just asked. Wasn't hard. The Ship's got room for thirty thousand people but last I heard they'll be lucky to get twenty K the way it's being undersold."

"Might be other reasons," said Kirsty neutrally. She leaned against the wall, and I could hear her kicking idly at the earth. "How many folks want tae go on a journey like that? Ten, eleven years in the Ship and never comin' back—how can ye face it?"

I grunted. "That's one of the things I need to sort out . . ."

Also from Orbit by Michael Scott Rohan

MICHAEL SCOTT ROHAN

Run to the Stars

Run to the stars:
Stars won't you hide me?
All on that Day . . .

The Lord said:
Sinner Man, the stars'll be a-fallin',
All on that Day . . .

Futura

An Orbit Book

ISBN 0 7088 8312 5

Printed and bound in Great Britain by
BPCC Hazell Books
Aylesbury, Bucks, England
Member of BPCC Ltd.

Futura Publications
A Division of
Macdonald & Co (Publishers) Ltd
Orbit House
1 New Fetter Lane
London EC4A 1AR

A member of Maxwell Macmillan Pergamon Publishing Corporation

For Deborah, without whom…

Acknowledgments

Many people helped me in writing this novel—one or two without realizing it. I have no room to list them all, but I am especially grateful to Richard Evans of Arrow and Susan Allison of Berkley; to all the Pierian conspirators, particularly Alan "Berserker" Scott, also Andrew Stephenson, Rob Holdstock and Dave and Hazel Langford; to Dermot and Perdita Dobson; to Dave Raggett of Research Machines and nearby solar atmospheres; Philip C. Gardner; Dr. Christian Lehmann; Michael Skelding, M.B.; and, most of all, to my parents and to my wife, Deb. The relativistic weapons concept at the heart of the book also occurred more or less simultaneously to my friend Dave Langford, and is touched on in his *War in 2080*, by far the best (and funniest) factual guide to Armageddon. I am grateful to ICL for computer training which allowed me to model some astronomical and socioeconomic points, and to Beam Office Equipment for spare-part surgery in time of need.

ONE

IN the mists at the edge of the world, a red eye opened. It blazed angrily at me across the black Atlantic for a second, then it was as if its gaze had shifted skyward, tracing a line of flame on the darkening sky. I watched it climb higher, grow thinner. Now it was no longer a line, but a blade of flame, stabbing upward against the stars. Was it imagination, or could I hear a low grumbling roar across the long sea-miles? It passed before I could be sure. I knew well where it came from, what it was, but not where it was going. I didn't give a damn about any of it—I was on leave, I should be forgetting all that. But why did it look so sinister? I smiled wryly at myself. *Because any day now that could be you . . .*

The Earth was firm beneath my feet. I felt rooted in the very solidity of it; the sea-breeze was light and cool, hardly stirring the thickening mist, but if it grew to a tornado it couldn't blow me away. *I was born on this world, my body is built of atoms that have been part of it since it coalesced. What right have I to scatter them across space again? Isn't that a kind of entropy?* I stood there on a twilit plain in Galloway, knee-deep in grass that rose and fell in gentle waves, grey as the sea beyond it. A little beach separated them, a strip of clammy

1

sand, home only for cockles and other cold fish.

Beyond that the sea, the dark Scottish sea outstretched to the horizon. Somewhere in the mists would be Ireland, but it might as well have been on the other side of the world. I'd come here to fill my mind with emptiness, loneliness, silence. But there was no silence here, nothing to compare with the void between the stars. Sea hissed and bubbled at the beach, grass rustled, trees creaked, the seagulls could still be heard. *(Will there be seagulls there? Only if we take them.)*

I stood there as night and mist closed in, staring out at the inhospitable universe. It got colder and danker, but I didn't mind. I couldn't get the fiery eye out of my thoughts, and I realized why at last. It was an unscheduled take-off, outside the Station's daily routine, which had practically ground itself into my subconscious by now. And it had been big ... It certainly hadn't been a normal ferry, or cargo carrier—and if one of the really huge special carriers was due to go up I'd surely have heard about it long before I went on leave. I dropped the shutters on it, hard. That was another life, and one I knew damn well I ought to be getting out of, fast. But to where? Was this the right, the only opportunity? So still I stood, and let time drift past me, flowing, flowing....

I came back to myself with a jolt, cold and stiff. How long had I been standing there? The mist gathered itself in front of me, hiding the rising moon, and closed suddenly over my head. The stars were blotted out, the land and landmarks had long since gone. I turned and stumbled heavily over nothing. I was adrift in a uniform pale glow, unable to see my own hand stretched out in front of me. Somewhere out there, a kilometre or two back along the peninsula, was a comfortable old farmhouse, between it and me a mass of little fields with drystone walls and thorn hedges, and the sea awaiting my wrong turns on either side. I looked down and couldn't see my feet beneath me. Luckily there were no cliffs to fall off; the land here rose only a metre or two above sea-level. I pulled up the collar of my heavy jacket and set off in what ought to be the right way. If anything could get me tired of Earth, this might. Even the sound of the sea was muffled and directionless, no help at all. The gulls had gone and all I could hear was my own breath and the dull clomping of my own feet. The rich damp earth caked onto my boots, weighing them down with every step. Weren't there cattle out along here, a bull maybe? Or would they have been taken in? I stamped heavily along, like one of the Irish giants in the old legends, and tried to listen for a bull's breathing, or heavy tread. I amused myself by wondering if any of my unarmed combat training might be useful on a bull. Why wasn't there a section in the manual about it? "First grasp the right horn firmly in the left hand (or vice-versa, as is preferred) and pull firmly back and to the side, at the same time striking upward sharply with the heel of the other hand at . . ." I stopped abruptly. Had there been footsteps, somewhere ahead? If so, they'd stopped when I did . . . I began to walk again, then stopped in mid-stride, a good jungle trick. Sure enough, a foot definitely hit the ground when mine should have. That was no bull; someone was stalking me. An amateur. Now who the hell . . .

I let my foot down softly and began to step sideways quietly, but not too quietly, trying to make it sound as if I were walking forward normally. My outstretched hand touched something cold and damp, and I froze. Nothing happened. I relaxed my hold on the chill stone of the drystone dyke, invisible even at arm's length, and inched along it, raising and lowering my feet absolutely silently. There were definite footsteps ahead now, evidently doing their best to be quiet. Whoever it was wasn't very large, but then neither am I. I came to a corner in the wall, evidently the right-hand corner of the field I was in. The wall stretched off to my left and on the other side to my right was a large holly tree. I had a fair idea of where I was now. There should be a gate in this wall, somewhere. I began to inch along towards it, keeping low and tensed to spring at the least sound.

There was a scrabble, a swishing sound, a solid thump on the ground a metre or so in front of me. I'd lunged forward and grabbed in the instant I heard it. There was a yelp of surprise, and I let go hurriedly. Unmistakably female . . . There was a low mischievous chuckle not too far below my nose, and a pleasant warm scent that was very welcome in the dank night.

"Mr. Bellamy, I presume . . ."

My immediate reaction was flaring irritation.

"It had to be you, of course. Vaulting walls in the fog!"

Giggle. "Ye might be a bit more grateful! Here I've come a' this way out in the haar 'cause I thought ye might be lost—"

"In the what?"

"*Haar*. Mist tae you. Sounds like an old viking word, eh?"

"If you say so. They never taught me that kind of thing. Look, it was kind of you to come out, but why? Now there's two of us lost—"

"*I'm* no' lost! I *live* here. D'ye think I canna find my way about in a wee bit of ha—mist like this? Thought ye might run intae the bull, is a'." Sharp sniff of disdain. "Should've let ye."

Kirsty O'Neill. Daughter of the farmhouse where I was the mysterious and solitary guest, eighteen and waiting anxiously to hear about a college place. Bright, brunette and good to look on when there wasn't a mist in the way—all I could see of her now was an outline ruined by a heavy anorak—but surely not my type. Too intellectual, and anyway I'm no cradle-snatcher by nature.

"So now we've settled why I'm here, how about you? What was it brought ye out on a night like this?"

"I'm an African spy. Gone a bit pale with fear—handy, that. I was watching spacecraft take off."

"Oh aye? From the Sea Station? Much good that may do ye, Mister Spy. We see 'em all year round here, but the station's way down below the horizon. If ye'd eyes tae see that ye wouldna get yourself lost—" She stopped abruptly. "Hey! The last launching I saw was just after nineteen!"

"What's the time now? Left my procom—"

"Near midnight when I left the house. Have ye been standin' there for five hours?"

"Looks like I have. Didn't feel that long."

Kirsty whistled. "Ye've got something on yer mind, a'right!" Expectant silence. I didn't say a word. Eventually she burst out "A'right, so I'm bein' nosy! So ye don't have tae tell me about it, or about you, or about. . . . about anythin' else! What d'ye want tae talk about then? Weather? Fine night for the fog, isn't it?"

I chuckled. "Since you ask . . . Yes, I have got something on my mind. Those launchings—give them a wave when you see them, from now on. I might be on one of them."

"Ye lucky—where'd you be goin', then? Orbital station?"

"Further."

"The Moon? The Martian settlement?"

I shook my head, which must have been just about visible,

because I heard a sharp gasp in the fog.

"No' the..."

I could see her silhouette gesture away into the infinite distance of the mist.

"The Colony, yes. I've a place option on the second Ship."

"No wonder ye're wanderin' round in a dream!" She sounded oddly breathless and shocked. "How'd ye manage that?"

"Just asked. Wasn't hard. The Ship's got room for thirty thousand people, but last I heard they'll be lucky to get twenty K the way it's being undersold."

"Might be other reasons," said Kirsty neutrally. She leant against the wall, and I could hear her kicking idly at the earth. "How many folks want tae go on a journey like that? Ten, eleven years in the Ship and never comin' back—how can ye face it?"

I grunted. "That's one of the things I'm here on holiday to sort out."

"But what'd make ye want tae leave in the first place? I mean, I'd never think of it—"

"Are you that fond of the world the way it is? Under the BCs' thumb—and other areas?"

"Well—no, since ye put it like that... But things may change—"

"Not in my lifetime, except for the worse. I'd rather take a chance at a fresh start—the only chance I can see. And there's more to it than that. It's hard to explain—but it's like this feeing some of the pilots have told me about. There are times when they take off, they just want to head outward and keep on going, never mind if their air runs out—"

"Hmph. Any o' these pilots actually *tried* sailin' away? Thought not. Romantic enough but it's still just fancy suicide. But how were these pilots tellin' *you* about this? Was it the pilots at the Sea Station?"

"Right."

"Go there often, do ye?" She sounded positively sly.

"Often enough. Why'd you ask?" As if I didn't know.

"Would ye take me along some time?" And then, breathlessly, the inevitable. "Could you get me intae space?"

"For a joyride, you mean? Or more permanently?"

"If there was any chance o' a job—"

"Only if you get yourself some kind of scientific or technical qualifications—which you don't want to—"

"Can't!" she said miserably. "Never any good at fashin' science. There's no other way?"

"'Fraid not. Unless you join the police or military—" I didn't insult her by suggesting a Department Guard.

She shuddered. "I've heard about that. Reports an' dossiers an' psychoprofiles on your every move. BCs breathin' down your neck night an' day—"

"Some people survive OK. But you might not, I'll agree. Does you credit. But I can get hold of an airspacer, so I could arrange the joyride, at least. Why so eager to get out there, anyway?"

"Cause it's about as far away from here as I can get!" she snarled. I hadn't heard that kind of venom in her voice before.

"Is it that bad, then? I like it. Not many open fields left these days. This place has room to breathe—"

She snorted scornfully. "Aye, ye can do that a'right. No' much else, though, 'cept eat an' sleep an' freeze in winter. Only excitement last year was when a harvestin' machine went daft in a greenhouse—barley everywhere. Stop here an' I'll go fat an' daft like my ma or dried-up and dour like my old man. Or just out o' my mind wi' boredom."

"Space loses its excitement after a while. A short while. You sound like another candidate for the Colony."

"No' me!" she said decisively. "I'll stick tae the Solar System, thank *you!*" She made a low shivering sound. "So cold, so far. Take a quarter of your life tae make the round trip . . ."

"Twenty-two years? More like a sixth—"

"Whatever. And no way back if everyone else didn't want tae go as well. Away from family an' friends an'—brrh! How ye can even think o' cuttin' yerself off like that . . . ? Is there nothin' tae hold ye here, nothin' that's too important tae leave?"

"All the relatives I know of have been dead for years. I've got friends, all right—but none I couldn't bear never to see again. Wouldn't blight their lives much, either. And there are plenty of enemies I'd as soon be away from—seems like half the human race at times."

Kirsty gave a great guffaw. "Paranoids are after ye, are they? But ye've nobody at a'—no really good friends, no girls? I mean there wilna be much wine, women an' song on the other side o' the Divide, will there?"

"Why not? There'll be no BCs to restrict it, after all. Anyway," I added severely, "I've had my share of them all, except maybe singing—can't have too much of that, as long as it's folk. But I've had enough of hangovers and half-baked affairs—they're both terrible in the morning. Maybe I'm just a loner..."

That was definitely the wrong line to take. I knew what she was going to come up with before she said it. "Maybe ye just havena found the right one yet..."

"Maybe," I said discouragingly, "I could die trying. Life's too short and sex is hard work, thanks to modern medical science—giggle if you like, it's true! Two centuries ago I could have given it up at seventy. Now I've no let-up until I'm ninety or a hundred. More than half a century of loused-up emotions! Not to mention pulled muscles, bankruptcy and—" The fog betrayed me. Slender but solid arms wrapped themselves firmly round my neck before I'd even finished talking. I don't often envy two-metre men—too easy to dodge and overbalance—but I did then; my neck was too accessible. She was practically swinging from it, pulling my head down to her. Protest was stifled at birth by her generous lips, with a sweet hot taste on them that countered the chill mist. Perhaps I should have shouted rape, but my mouth was full—of tongues—and who'd have heard me anyway? So I landed Kirsty with the tongue problem, letting mine scribble short sensuous paragraphs on the underside of hers while my hands gently scratched the punctuation on her back. Even through the anorak it felt hot. I stood with feet apart to come down to her level (and take some of the weight off my neck). She crushed hard against me, shifting weight from one foot to the other so that her legs rubbed against the inside of mine. Hotter and hotter—We came up for air.

"This isn't fog," I decided, "it's steam." She slumped against the wall, giggling helplessly. Not too helplessly to pull me with and against her, though, but by then I'd given up minding. However, not being a cradlesnatcher has its responsibilities—such as giving fair warning.

"Listen, you," I said as soon as I had the chance, "don't think I'm not enjoying myself, but take an old man's advice—don't be in too much of a hurry. Save something—oh, not for the love of your life or anything, just for better places than against a wall or the back of the cowshed—"

"Back o' the byre's no good," she mumbled, keeping up the death-grip. "Too popular most nights. And ye can see the most o' it from the house. Well, if ye lean out the backstairs window and twist tae the right a wee bit ye can——"

"What I'm trying to say—mmmp!—is, don't waste it on me. You're young and fresh and I'm twenty-five years older——" A whole set of nails dug into the nape of my neck. I caught my breath sharply, and the sudden strong scent of her made my nostrils flare.

"Young n' fresh, eh?" she growled. "Makes me sound like chicken breast or somethin' when a' he means is I'm no' experienced enough! Young n'raw, that's what you mean, isn't it? For your mature taste! I'm so bloody sorry I could cry! Maybe I'm only fit company for the great muck-maulin' gowks round here! Maybe if I could've got away tae college or a job I wouldna be needin' your learned advice—or anythin' else!" I heard her turn on her heel and stamp away off down the wall, muttering hot wet things.

"Listen!" I protested, striding along to keep up, "I like you young and everything, you're not like most girls your age——"

"Who're either uptight Social Morality freaks or tarts, aye. Well, you can keep 'em both. But did it no' occur tae ye in your vast experience that I might just occasionally get a wee bit tired o' youth and etcetera? Not, o' course, that I've any say in the matter——"

"You're behaving like an eight-year-old——"

She stopped dead and rounded on me. "Listen, you!" she mimicked. "Ye were stranded out here before I came. If I ran off ye'd likely end up in the sea or playin' tag wi' the bull!" There was a rustle of fabric in the mist. "And there's only one way you'll keep me by ye——" And she sprang at me, swinging from my neck and biting at it, catlike. The scent of her, headier than any mere perfume, rose around me like the smoke of a prye, and when my hands reached her waist they touched warm flesh where anorak and slacks had parted. She wore nothing underneath. That did it.

"I'm caught, I wilna' run," she murmured. "Weigh me down. . . ."

Anything to oblige. Her weight was a burden round my neck, so I went searching for handholds. Her clothes slid away to provide them. I gave gently at the knees and sank back, pulling her on top of me.

"Grass's wet," I explained.

"Sounds fun——"

"Then we'll take turns——"

We finished facing each other on our knees, rocking in the smooth ancient rhythm of the sea. Her breasts were hardness crushed against me, and the sea somehow got louder and faster and saltier and smooth as wet velvet and went roaring away through my ears in a pounding cascade. Kirsty's fingers stopped tracing out my spine and grabbed desperately at my hips, her breath came in hoarse strangled gasps, and our bodies slammed and battered at each other as if in fury. Then her body arched violently back and she screamed aloud as all of me rose to meet her in an electric, emptying thrill that went convulsively on and on. Distant thunder rang in my ears as we collapsed gasping against one another, and seemed to build up into a whistling howl that had nothing to do with the thumping of my heart. Kirsty clutched me tight again as the sound grew louder, then she shrieked in horror as a thunderous shockwave ripped the concealing mist away from us in a mad scattering whirl. With a roar of dragonfire something enormous blazed by overhead, as if the Moon itself were dropping onto us. The trees bent before its passing and hurled up their leaves to its fires. The long grass was blasted flat by a single sweeping wave of hot wind that left us huddled half-naked in each others' arms, terrified as field animals when the harvester goes by. Then there was a terrible impact offshore, an incandescent roaring splash that blasted up a wall of steaming water. A fine boiling rain splattered down over the field, stinging points of agony on our exposed skins. Kirsty was sobbing hysterically against my chest, but I detached her gently and stood up, staring out to sea through the passage carved in the mist. Sizzling, smashing, creaking sounds came from a great shadowy bulk, wallowing in the erupting sea a kilom or so offshore. Parts of it shone with a sullen furnace glow that set the sea seething into bubbles and steam. Larger bubbles, huge ones, were gulping up as it settled. Then I realized what might happen, and flung myself heavily on top of Kirsty, knocking her flat. There was an instant's awesome gargling, as if the ocean were draining away; I raised my head cautiously.

There was a concussion, more than a sound, and the trees bent back again and lost the remainder of their leaves. The night glared red for an instant, then there was more hot rain interspersed with blast-shredded leaves. A broken tree fell smouldering into the wet undergrowth. Something large went swishing slowly by overhead and fell into the field beyond; the solid impact almost bounced us off the ground. There was a rattle of smaller debris, some in our own field. When it stopped I rolled off Kirsty, who was too winded to move, and struggled to my feet, pulling my trousers back on as I went. Fortunately the skeletal trees still hid us from the farmhouse, though I could hear dogs barking and doors slamming, and a gabble of excited bird cries and hoarse human voices. Not so far away the bull was bellowing hysterically. A rising breeze thinned the mist and in the restored moonlight I could just make out the remains of the object, dull and dark now. It looked as though the blast had broken it in two, but large chunks were still visible above the surface. I became aware of Kirsty hanging onto my arm, trying to pull herself upright on unsteady legs. Once I helped her up she'd no trouble staying there, but her face was pale and bloodless and blank.

"Move it, girl," I muttered, retrieving her slacks, "your old man'll be down here soon with the farm-ops. Want them to catch you bare-assed?" She didn't answer, just looked at me with wide shocked eyes. I couldn't blame her for that—having the ceiling fall in is no way to begin your sex life—but I was in a hurry. I bundled her back into her clothes, dusted her down as best I could, and bolted for the beach. If that thing was what I thought it was there might still be a life to save.

The sand was littered with little bits of hot wreckage and assorted sea-debris hurled up by the explosion. Stumbling and slipping through piles of lacerated sea-wrack garnished with shredded crab and fish and jagged chunks of metal, I stared hard out to the moonlit sea, churned-up and foaming, for the least sign of a human form. At first I'd thought a big airspacer had come down in flames, but then I'd remembered something. That first thunderclap had been a sonic boom, but by the time the thing itself passed over it was below soundspeed. What decelerates as it falls? Answer: something under power. I had a strong feeling I knew what, although the hulk out there was hardly recognizable. It boded ill for the pilot.

"Mr. Bel'my! Come away frae there!" It was Kirsty's father, the Land-Manager, in an overcape and boots over vile-coloured sleeping gear. He came skidding down among the grass tussocks, stomping through the sand to grab my sleeve. "Come on! She might go up again any second! We can call the Emergencies—"

"They'd get here too late, I think. Anyway, she's unlikely to go up again."

"Too late for what? And how're ye so sure?"

"I know a bit about these—well, what I think that thing was. Did you see it go over?"

"Aye, a'in flames. I was feart it'd explode overhead!"

"It wasn't on fire. It's not an airspacer or zep or anything like that. Those flames were the exhausts of bloody great chemical motors, being gunned for all they were worth to slow it down; they were blown back round the hull by air resistance, so it looked like a fireball."

"What was it, then—a missile?"

"Oh, no. I got a look at the hull before it went up—couldn't place it at first, I haven't seen one for years. It was an old orbital launcher, the kind they used for large payloads before the big special carriers came in. They still keep a few for emergencies and awkward jobs, like sending up something big that can't be assembled in space. The only thing explosive about them's their fuel, and any there was would have gone up in the first explosion. There couldn't have been much or it'd have been larger. Way the motors were being flogged I'm not surprised."

"But then—"

"Yes. There was someone at the controls. That thing could have creamed anywhere in Central Scotland—your house, for example. But he managed to brake it enough to bring it down harmlessly in the sea. That's why I'm here. I didn't see anyone eject, but there's still a chance he might have. He could need help. I feel I owe him a bit of trouble, don't you?"

"Aye," said the old man dourly, "suppose we do—though after that bang I wouldna haud out much hope. Still—I've a boat at the jetty back by the house, if a piece of wreckage hasna' stove it in. If I get some o' the lads—"

"Right. Shouldn't be any danger as long as you keep clear of the wreck itself. I'll cover the beach, if you can spare some men."

"Aye, I'll see tae it!" I heard him puffing and panting up the slope, and then a collision at the top and some ripe swearing.

"Kirsty girl! What're ye doin' out here?"

"Scared outa my wits by the bang!" I heard her say quite steadily. "Came tae see if I could help—"

"Aye, ye can. Get back an' tell yer mother it's a'right, and call up the Emergency. Tell 'em there's some kind o' spacecraft come down..." Voices and hurrying footsteps trailed off into the distance. I began ranging up and down the beach, stopping from time to time to listen for a sound other than the disturbed sea slapping and grinding the sand. I tried calling out, but only managed to collect some fellow searchers that way. It looked bad. I heard the boat putter out beyond the point, a long blunt-bowed dory whose little hydrogen motor flogged away as it hit the churning sea. Powerful flashlights swept the water on either side.

"Keep off the wreck, remember!" I shouted.

"Wi' pleasure!" bellowed a voice in return, raising coarse laughter all round—not that it was at all funny, but we needed something to laugh at. Any of those blackened fragments lying about in the shallows or washing to and fro further out could be all that was left of the man we searched for.

"D'ye really think he coulda got out in time, Mr. Bel'my?" asked one of the farm-ops with me as he prodded dubiously at a scorched and twisted fragment of metal at his feet.

"Yes, any time before the bang. Ejection systems have come a long way since Gagarin and the Wrights. Even an old voice-activated system would've got him out and beyond blast range in time, even from underwater. I was looking for him when the blast went off. Didn't feel so observant then."

"Aye, I ken. Staggered me as well."

"Ah, get on, McBride, ye're allus staggered!"

"Aye, blind as a burycrat!"

"Haud yer yaps!" hissed the maligned McBride. "Who's callin'?"

A girl's voice—"Yer auld man's oot wi' the boat, Kirsty!" yelled someone. "We're doon here wi' Mr. Bel'my!"

I half expected her to scream and run at the mention of the name, but she didn't. She appeared atop a sand-ridge, leapt down off it into a gorse-bush without seeming to notice and came thumping across the sand towards us.

"Ma an' I called—" she gasped. "Emergency-police—Sea Rescue—everyone—wouldna come!" There was an angry babble of voices. "Said they'd had calls from all over," she explained when she'd caught her breath. "But they'd had word from Glasgow Interdep that this was Eurogov business, and there were Department men comin' tae handle it—" That did it. The magic word "Department" seemed to empty any sense of responsibility out of everyone. The ops began to drift off down the beach, heading back towards the house. I didn't bother trying to keep them; I wasn't so far from giving up myself. Maybe the boat would have better luck.

There was a small awkward cough from behind me. I turned to find Kirsty still standing there. It was high time to say something; the trouble was, what?

"Look—I'm sorry I had to just rush off like that, then. But—"

"Oh aye," she said tonelessly, scuffing the sand with her shoe. "Ye couldna help it." She gave a brief, artificial laugh. "I'd heard o' the earth movin', but that was too much . . ."

"Spectacular, at least."

"Oh aye. Grand finale wi' fireworks. But—" She sounded anxious. "It was all a'right? For you, I mean . . ."

She sounded altogether too serious. At that moment I was wishing myself halfway to the Colony or almost anywhere else. What had I got myself into? I'd come here to shake off entanglements, not add to them. But this wasn't one of those times I could just brush that question off with a dirty chuckle and a swat in the right direction. *There are responsibilities* . . . I dropped an arm around her and squeezed affectionately. It wasn't too difficult.

"An adventure in space and time," I quoted, and got a genuine giggle this time.

"It was great when ye—" I shushed her abruptly, and felt her stiffen with annoyance. But then she heard it too. A faint hail was coming from seaward, hard to hear against the rush and scrabble of the water. We pelted down to the water's edge, not stopping until our feet sank into the sand to be soaked by the more adventurous waves. The darkness was unyielding.

"Can't be the boat," I decided. "They're too far away, round the other side of the wreck—" Kirsty grabbed my arm and pointed to my right. Bobbing up and down in the waves, not far offshore, was a feeble orange light. We stared for an instant, then dashed along the beach and through a stand of stunted trees onto a sandspit covered in coarse scrubby plants that tangled round our ankles as we ran. At the tip of the spit the light was still too far away. I hesitated for a moment, then strode out into the water. My feet were already wet, but when the sea chill bit at my calves I had to stop and get my breath back. I wished I'd thought to get rid of my trousers, the water was deeper than it looked. I pushed on, though, as Kirsty caught up with me, puffing and swearing and half-swimming already. The swell rose to my chest now, trying to lift me off my feet. At sea-level like this I couldn't make out the light any more, and in desperation I let a big wave bear me up so I could see further. At its top a heavy weight cannoned into me, knocking me off balance. I heard Kirsty yell, then light and air vanished. I tumbled head over heels in bone-chilling blackness, striking an arm a hefty blow on a rock. Rather than sprout gills I kicked out, feeling my water-logged clothes go leaden around me, and came back to the surface. Spitting out gritty water, I saw Kirsty struggling with what looked like a headless body. I swam clumsily over to her, and together we maneuvered the gasping object into the shallows, where by the feeble orange light on its back we saw that the headless effect came from a flotation jacket that enveloped head and shoulders, clamping a breathing mask over the face. I knew the design, though I'd never seen one in use outside a demonstration tank. We half walked, half dragged its exhausted occupant onto the beach and collapsed all three, wheezing and shivering. Our clothes settled dankly about us as the wind rose, blowing clouds over the moon. The newcomer was the first to speak.

"Thanks! Speak English? Good! Hey—I hit anyone, anything expensive? That my goddam boltbucket out there—you guess?"

"We guessed. And no, you didn't hit anything, except maybe a few fish. What happened?"

He made a noise like a surfacing whale. "You tell me? Attitude jets, gyros, everything, go whoof! Secondaries, everything, out like light! Main throttles, too. Drop like stone, but I manage to get manual control of fuel feed and gun main motors to brake! Sheeeh—" He fell back on the sand with a great sigh. His accent was strong, and sounded North European—Norwegian or Swedish, maybe. And it reminded me of someone . . .

"Brave of you to stay at the controls," I said.

He gave a deep chuckle. "Ah, decided I could use medal or two! Eject only just in time, you know? And get ass burnt by blast as I'm coming down!"

"Lucky ye had the lifejacket, though," said Kirsty brightly. There was a choking noise in the darkness, which eventually turned into a rich Swedish oath.

"*Lucky?* Not so bloody lucky! Better they hang shark round my neck than this thing! Twice as dangerous, you bet!"

Kirsty evidently took this a bit personally. "Got ye ashore, didn't it?"

"Kept me afloat," grunted our catch ungraciously. "'Bout all it did. Crappy design—have to haul mask off your yap to yell!"

"Don't you have flares?" I chipped in. "You shouldn't have to shout—"

"Flares I've got. Full set. None of 'em work. Nor voice transmitter, nor locator beacon, nor loudhailer, nor siren. And this light is supposed to be so bloody bright, eh? From how far away you see it?"

"A hundred metres or so—"

"On a pitchy-black bloody night. What fashing good that? And my rebreather's full of salt water—busy generating strong alkalis instead of air! Come down in rough sea and I drown!"

I chuckled. "Well, it's as well you hung on then, isn't it? You've really got yourself a lemon there—every common fault, plus the rebreather, that's new. The old design was better."

"Yeah, much. Not so pretty, and less fancy medical gear. But never went wrong—" He paused, considering. "You know old design?"

"I fought to keep it, Captain Carlsen. Remember me?"

It didn't take him long, considering. "Hey-hey-hey! Hail to Chief! Long time no see, Mister B! So what you doing here—which is where, by the way?"

"Galloway—Western Scotland. I'm on holiday, nobody knows me and I'd like to keep it that way. OK?"

"Sure, sure, you just one of rubes for all I know."

"Great. But meet your co-rescuer, Kirsty O'Neill."

I heard Carlsen turn on the charm. Good going, after an hour in salt water but he wasn't strong on finesse. He was just what you'd expect someone called Carlsen to be—stage Scandinavian, big, blond, dumb. Well, no pilot is entirely dumb, but Carlsen did his best. His dossier rated him high on concentration and accuracy, low on energy, initiative and imagination. He never showed any sign of irritability or strain, though anyone he worked with usually did. And he had a solid respect for his own skin, too noticeable to make him hero material. I'd have expected him to bale out the moment trouble struck and forget those below; his psych-profile would have guaranteed it. And yet he'd hung on, at vast risk—you never can tell.

"You weren't hurt at all?"

"No, no. Wouldn't lie here so peaceful if I was!"

"Have you checked your monitors, though?"

"Too busy staying alive!" He sat up hastily and began scrabbling at the monitor panel. Evidently his dossier wasn't *that* wrong. When we eventually got it open the readouts beneath were activated automatically and began methodically ticking off the data from the little bodyscan and other monitoring gear built into the jacket.

"Coming too fast to read!" he complained. "They damaged too?"

"Don't seem to be," I told him. "That's normal as long as there's nothing to report. When there is—See?" The readout slowed to a crawl. Carlsen glared anxiously down at it, but all it said was that he was a little chilled.

"Otherwise you're healthier than I am, you great oaf. Let's get back to the house, my feet just died of exposure."

"Mine too. Can't ye get up, Captain?"

"Legs asleep. Ass too. Give hand, eh? Stay here longer and I became clam, eh?"

"It'd be an improvement," said Kirsty dryly as Carlsen hauled himself up via some of her more sensitive areas. Once on his feet, his circulation returned mysteriously, and he did a sort of war dance, contorting violently to free himself from the dripping jacket. It was quite a sight. Finally he ripped himself loose and flung the object, still flickering dispiritedly, far out into the waves. It washed slowly back in towards the shore.

"Leave to rot!" he barked. "We walk! Why they give up old jacket?"

"The usual, from what I hear—interdepartmental infighting. Sea Survival & Rescue (Design) at Kiel are on the wane, Marine Safety (Design) at Toulon are on the up, so they immediately have to edge out the other's best work. You know how it goes. Kiel got one of the interdepartmental economies subcommittees to guillotine the production budget for the Toulon design. Toulon had either to lose face by withdrawing the design and causing a shortage, or cut the costs by pruning safety factors. The only ones they left were on their selling point, the medical gear."

"Nobody do anything 'bout this?" howled the pilot as we climbed the sandy slope. "I maybe get drowned!"

"My objections," I told him, "along with a million others, are on file somewhere. They'll be investigated in due course—"

"Sure, in about twenty years!" Carlsen snarled. "Maybe I make some noise sooner! I go to Toulon and stuff their design flair right up—" He guffawed richly. "Up where they maybe keep my flares, eh?"

"I'll say this for ye," said Kirsty, clambering over the low wall of a field, "Ye're no easy tae damp!"

"Water off my back!" he called, and roared.

By maniacal shouting we managed to call the boat in, and then set off up the long path to the farmhouse. Carlsen stepped out briskly, and Kirsty and I had to hurry to keep up with his long stride. I realized with some annoyance that he'd hardly be wet at all inside his flight suit, while we were weighed down and chilled by our soaked clothes. Carlsen greeted the boat crew with noisy anticipations of drink, and I hoped he'd remember my incognito once he got going.

We all crowded into the kitchen of the farmhouse. It was an enormous place, like all old buildings, and nothing but the other farm buildings within a kilom. For all its sparseness there was a weird air of luxury about living in a house with eight rooms, no less, and three of them separate bedrooms! And each was bigger than my entire quarters, which had never felt small— not, at least, until recently.

Kirsty's mother plumped past bearing a bottle of something. I gave chase, but was firmly headed off and pinned in a corner.

"Just what are ye, Mr. Bellamy?"

"Lots of things, Kirsty. Cold and thirsty, for example. You had in mind?"

"Carlsen knows you," she pressed on inexorably. "Pilots tell ye things. Ye spend a lot of time in space . . ."

"Not so much these days."

"Whatever. Ye're something tae do with the Sea Station."

"I'd rather not advertise it. I'm still a prime target for the African terror campaign, even though it's mostly died now. The fewer people who know what I do, the better."

"But ye can tell me, surely—"

A giant arm descended round my shoulders and another round Kirsty's. One hand contained a bottle of scotch, which

I deftly removed and swigged at. I managed not to choke. It was one of the generally available blends, a weird mixture of the rough and the synthetically smooth. As a Department man I'd got used to better, but at least it stayed down.

"What 'bout Kirsty, she save my life too! You leave some of that for her!"

"Maybe later," she said, firmly removing a ham hand from its resting place. "Go easy on that stuff or we'll have wasted our time!"

"Can't hurt me!" he boomed. "Drink all night if—" He stopped suddenly and raised his head, listening. I heard it too, the howl of an airspacer coming in on hover. The farm-ops went streaming out to see it didn't land on the bull. Carlsen looked troubled.

"That's big buggers," he announced.

"Who?"

"Department men! Didn't someone say they coming?"

"Right—but which department?"

"SpaceDep, of course," grunted Carlsen. "That's who launch was for. This'll be HQ heavies, you bet! Now they haul me back out in freeze-ass cold to examine wreck—"

"Maybe not," I mused. In the state he'd soon be in Carlsen was capable of slipping up and giving away who I was. Then I'd get roped in as well, and also get torn off a strip for not coming forward in the first place. Altogether it would be better to get him out of the way . . . "Why don't we—"

I watched Carlsen and Kirsty disappear upstairs, and was obscurely pleased to see the hand that landed on her rear once again removed. Obscurely, because by rights I should be glad to get her off my hands; I couldn't quite manage to feel that way, though. Maybe she just deserved someone better than Carlsen. That would be it.

I was glad she'd taken the whole thing so well. This wasn't the 2000s any more. There was a creeping self-righteous puritanism abroad these days, not only in Greater Europe but throughout the world; it seemed to be based on the feeling that pleasure shouldn't, as our disgraceful grandparents thought, be there for the taking. It should be the reward reserved for the virtuous citizen by the benevolent State. It was the moral philosophy of the bureaucrat, given an ethical shell and christened Social Morality to make it sound respectable. In practice it was anything but; it simply gave the BCs another stick to beat humanity with. Anyone with enough pull did as they liked, and the only crime was being found out. In fact, whipping the covers off a rival's sexual indiscretions was fast becoming the ritual *coup de grace* in bureaucratic power struggles. Human nature being what it is, indiscretions could nearly always be found—or arranged. Sex, not lending itself to being collected, graded and doled out to approved recipients only on completion of the proper forms, came in for a particularly hard time from the SM movement. And, lowly as I was, I'd enemies who'd just love to use Kirsty against me if we quarrelled too openly. About my career I gave only the faintest of damns, being on the point of giving it up anyway, but I didn't want to leave my job wide open for takers. If I went, I intended to choose my successor—carefully.

Voices drifted past the window, and I listened intently. Kirsty's father, plus a couple I knew only by type—accentless European English, with the faceless smoothness of the senior bureaucrat. Behind them two others, harsh and clipped. I knew none of them, so they'd be unlikely to know me. Safer in that case to stay and meet them. Feet clomped on the worn stone flags of the passage.

"—and you can be sure that the Department is grateful for your assistance, Mr. O'Neill," one of the smooth voices was saying. "Our memo to AgDep will be couched in the most favourable terms—" The owner of the voice looked much as I'd expected, a cool sleek man with grey hair and a long poker face. His companion was a younger, fatter variant on the same type. Senior, but not the top; they were projecting an image in a way top BCs never needed to. But they'd be close to the top, coming from Oliviera's office, or van Huijk's, or Thorborg's, or any of a dozen others. I got a smile from them, free of the slightest flicker of recognition. The other two didn't smile. They didn't look capable of it, big square men in the uniform of SpaceDep HQ Guard—known for some reason as the Marching Morons, though they didn't march much. They'd been formed soon after I entered the Department as a special bodyguard for the high-ups, a job they still did; they'd expanded, though, to take over all of HQ security, which set them well on the road to being secret police. They certainly recruited some unsavory characters, and these two could have been their recruiting posters.

"This is Mr. Bel'my," said the Land-Manager, murdering

my name as most of the locals did. "It was my daughter'n him fished out yer man." The smiles were a centim or so broader, but still with no trace of recognition. I'd been confident about that. I wasn't a familiar face at HQ—no Station staff were, except the Commander—and my own mother would've had a job recognizing the half-drowned rat I looked at the moment.

"Well, that was very brave of you," oiled the plumper BC. "We were very worried about him, to tell the truth. Ah—was he much hurt?"

"Didn't seem to be," I avowed, with a look of innocent concern. "But when we got him in he just keeled over. He'd had a wee bit Scotch first, but not enough to—er—"

"Quite so," said the other BC gravely. "Concussion, perhaps. Did he say anything at all? Was he able to talk, I mean?"

"Not much. He was exhausted. Just said his controls had failed, but he'd stayed with the ship to stop it hitting anyone. We packed him off to bed—"

"I'm sure you did the right thing. We didn't have time to pick up a doctor—I'm afraid we hardly thought we'd need one—but our pilot, Heinz here, has paramed experience. He can take a look at him. We'll wait down here—"

I ushered Heinz to the worn stone stairs. "Big old house!" he observed perceptively as he clomped up. "OK if you like history, but give me—"

"Shhh!" hissed Kirsty abruptly. "Watch those great feet o'yours, you'll disturb the poor man in there—" She was overdoing it a bit, but Heinz seemed impressed. I was annoyed to see she'd deposited Carlsen in my bed, but I should have thought of that before. He lay sprawled now, doing a magnificent imitation of a casualty. Perhaps that rotgut whisky helped; I could see the end of the empty bottle under the bed. Our experienced paramed strode over to the bed and poked briefly about Carlsen. He evidently knew some anatomy, enough to check whether major bones were broken, but he behaved as if he were examining a cut of meat. I've caught myself doing that on occasion, checking that I haven't actually killed someone. The pilot straightened up, turned away and headed briskly downstairs with the most casual of nods. I followed him down.

"No danger!" he announced firmly as he strode into the kitchen.

"I'm glad to hear that!" exclaimed the older man as if he meant it. "Well, Mr. O'Neill, I think we might go and examine the wreck now, if you've no objection. We can take Captain Carlsen straight to hospital when we've finished—"

The voice oozed out of the kitchen. I was surprised it didn't leave a trail. The others followed, and when they'd gone out I obtained another bottle and made my way back upstairs. Carlsen was sitting up in bed, practically purple with indignation.

"Fashing scummy bastards! What kind examination they call that, hah? For all they care, might as well be at bottom of Atlantic!"

"Count your blessings," I told him. "You might not have malingered well enough to fool a real doctor." He didn't query that, just grabbed the bottle and took a considerable swig.

"Hangover," he said with an air of satisfaction. "Have to give doc something to do, eh?"

"We could always crack you on the skull," I suggested, "if you're so worried."

"Use the bottle," said Kirsty, "or ye'll hurt your hand. Let go o'that whisky a minute, Chris, ye canna hatch it. I havena had any yet, remember?"

She produced a tumbler from somewhere, and took a healthy quantity. We sat and talked for a few minutes, then Kirsty announced she was off to bed.

"All very well for you," I complained, "but I've got this great gook in mine. Where do I sleep?"

"You have this back and I go share with Kirsty!" guffawed Carlsen.

"Wouldna be good for yer concussion!" she retorted. "I'll find ye somewhere."

We left Carlsen loudly demanding to be tucked in.

"It's no tuckin' he's after," Kirsty commented as she shut the door firmly. "What a night!" She leant back against the doorpost and sighed. Even half-drowned and salt-encrusted she was a beauty, large dark eyes gleaming out from under heavy lids and a dark chestnut fringe. The effect, on top of a pert nose and full lips, was stunning.

"You look like a mermaid," I told her. "Or one of those Celtic things, you know, silkies, like in the ballad—a seal-woman. You'd make a nice seal."

She shook her head lazily. "Nearest I want tae get tae water's a shower. And ye'll need one before we let ye near our nice clean beds."

"My shower, like my bed, is back in there with Carlsen —"

"Aye, but mine isn't," she said firmly. "C'mon, if we don't want tae sleep a'night in the passage!" Her room was at the back of the house, set off from the rest of it by a long narrow corridor along which I was more or less dragged. Not that I was resisting too hard. Hadn't that been a twinge of jealousy when she'd used Carlsen's first name? Perhaps. Come to think of it, did she even know mine? Ah well. So much for detachment.

There certainly wasn't any room for it in her bedroom shower-stall. I looked at it dubiously, but Kirsty just twitched her anorak off and stepped out of her slacks into the stall. The water and foam came on as her foot touched the floor, and she twisted to meet it, stretching an arm out to me. She looked more slender out of her chunky clothes, and it wasn't only her nose that was pert.

"You look more like a silkie than ever," I commented.

"How about givin' me a chance tae see what you look like, then, *Mister* Bellamy?"

"Mark," I told her, and pulled my own jacket off. She stood there in foaming turmoil with her arms folded, watching me the way I'd seen her father watch livestock. I stepped in with her, and she ran her hands across my chest. The stall was overfull, but the controls angled the sprays neatly so that little landed outside.

"Muscular," said Kirsty approvingly, "But no' too much, no' like yer friend back there. Built square, but ye're no sae fat for a man o' your age—"

"Of my age?"

Her bed, fortunately, was a bit wider than the shower. We lay back to back, and the air was rich with that special scent that age and art takes away from women. I didn't feel much older than her and not much in need of sleep; her insulator was set at a higher temperature than I liked, anyway, and I was too warm. The sound of the clipped voice and clumping boots on the stairs jerked me awake at once. I swung out of bed and tiptoed over to the door. Voices from Carlsen's room carried clearly down the passage.

"Doesn't look very healthy, does he, sir?"

"No. Has Lyon been warned to expect him? Good." There came the familiar creak of an emergency stretcher unfolding.

Lyon? The Department's special hospital facility was there, that made sense. But even in an airspacer it was pretty damn distant, when we were less than a hundred kilom from Edinburgh, still one of Europe's top medical centres. Were they afraid to let Carlsen into a public hospital? My mind filled suddenly with thoughts of radiation and weird viruses, but if they'd been around his jacket monitors would have registered something. And the BCs wouldn't be standing around him so casually even if they were inoculated up to the eyeballs. Then why this desire to keep it all in the family? Their reason seemed to be worth risking Carlsen's life; for all they knew he was dangerously injured, and yet they were taking only token care of him.

I heard the stretcher being manhandled down the narrow stairs, and wished them well of Carlsen's bulk. Muffled curses resounded in the passageway, so I shut the door quietly and stole over to the window. They'd landed the airspacer in the paddock behind the house, and I could see its tail projecting from behind the farm building, an absurdly anachronistic contrast. There was Kirsty's father, damn near fawning over the BCs. There came the two goons with the stretcher; the weight didn't seem to faze them. I was impressed. Carlsen looked as if he'd succumbed to the drink at last, or was it the grey northern predawn that gave his face that greenish cast? Odds on that vile scotch, any day. The stretcher was bundled in through the rear door, the BCs took gracious leave of the old man, and the motors began a throaty warm-up. They rose to a grumbling howl, and I saw the tail of the machine vibrate and suddenly leap up. The whole machine appeared over the byre roof, and I saw the louvered jets in its belly tilt and swing back, turning its vertical lift into an arcing leap that carried it over the house and out of view. I heard its motors rumble away into the distance as I slid back under the insulator. Its warmth was a little more welcome now. Kirsty, disturbed, mumbled and drew her legs up into a foetal crouch. It made her look young, too young. But not, fortunately, too innocent. I heard her father stumble up to bed, too tired, it seemed, to care where anyone else might be.

All in all the room looked much as it might have in the nineteenth or twentieth centuries, except perhaps for the shower-stall and the large holocom that took up a corner table. It had a keyboard as well as the usual vocal controls and at least three hundred program capsules under it, things with titles like *Elizabethan Dramatists: Complete Works* and *Nineteenth Century War Documentation*. It was strange, seeing that last monster here; I'd sweated through it at command college, back in the days when I was still thinking of a military career. I wouldn't have found many of her other programs at college—they were mostly literature, politics, arts, philosophy, all the unfashionable studies. The science was mostly pure, not applied. That boded ill for her college prospects—the number of non-tech places was strictly limited. What there was went mostly to future stars of the bureaucracy, the shining ones being groomed for their eventual roles. Did Kirsty appreciate that? Almost certainly. But those programs showed no sign of any concessions in her studies. I felt a wash of real affection, looking down at her, peaceful for a little while. I wished I could believe in a better reward for her determination. I'd had English literature as a seven-day course, arts from a course of ten lectures recorded forty years earlier and showing it. Music I'd taught myself, and I'd never got beyond folk; modern stuff left me cold. Kirsty seemed to have all the serious stuff ever written plus, at the end of the rack, some ethnic folk. Good, we did have something in common then, beyond keys to fit locks and so on.

The sky was getting lighter now, dawn almost upon us. In another hour or so the farm machinery would come on, feeding and releasing the animals. The human ops would be up not long after; livestock work would never be wholly automated. Why waste the time asleep? I slid down under the insulator and stroked my hand down Kirsty's spine, right down and round to waken her pleasantly. We were together before she'd quite collected her wits, my arm across her warm waist clamping her to me. She twisted her head round at an impossible angle to kiss me. *Banzai! Arrigato!* And the dawn came up like thunder.

I'd tottered back to my room to dress when I heard the low hum in the sky. It sounded big, but it certainly wasn't another airspacer. I joined Kirsty on the shore in time to see a massive carrier zep hovering above the wreck, trawling it up in a wide mesh scoop protruding from its hold. It snared the smaller half and began lifting, water, weed and small debris pouring away as the mangled launcher was hoisted up.

"Like a sea-urchin," commented Kirsty. "The ones that don't bother wi' a mouth, just stick out their stomach round their dinner. To get it while it's hot, eh?"

"Yes," I said. "While it's hot. You know, love, this is indecent haste for the Department; they usually spend months wrangling about salvage costings while whatever it is gets rusty and in everyone's way. The newsmeds should have the official line on this by now, I'd like to go see—"

"Wait till they've finished!" pleaded Kirsty. It was certainly impressive. The scoop had snagged around the other, longer, part now. Instead of using their winch, the zep crew locked the line and boosted their whole craft upward as a flying crane. With an anguished creaking groan like a fabulous sea monster the remains lifted clear of the sea, disgorging half the sandbar it had landed on. Free of the weight of that and the water, the winch was able to reel it in. Magnetic nets were lowered to pick up smaller pieces. Close to shore the sea boiled, and a little submersible appeared with what looked like a motor fragment clasped aloft in its grabs. The nets scooped it up as well, wreckage and all, and the hold doors closed behind it. The big zep turned on its axis and headed out to sea, its motors blatting flatly with the inertia of its load. Kirsty and I strolled back to the house, hand in hand. That kind of thing was coming just too easily now. It wasn't as if I was in love with her or anything—fond of her, yes, but nothing I couldn't break off when the time came to make up my mind at last. Why had I been so impatient to decide? I'd months yet . . .

We sat drinking tea in her room, in front of the holocom. It was on a continews channel, running through a government report on some incredibly boring supply problem in West Russia, for which East Russia and Pan-Asia in general were being held responsible. It ran down into a quick snap on the new course structure for junior schools—more "political orientation" and SM—and then gave us the headlines.

LAUNCHER CRASH OFF SCOT COAST over a map, then a mug-shot of Carlsen—PILOT SURVIVES BUT DIES ON WAY TO HOSPITAL—

Kirsty's tea spilled onto my lap. I hardly noticed, I was concentrating on the wording of the report.

"—pilot Captain C. Carlsen stuck at controls to save lives below, ejected too late and caught in craft's explosion. Reached shore alive, died of internal injuries undetected during flight to hospital. Found to be dead on arrival at SpaceDep hospital facility, Lyon, France—" The staccato machine voice rattled on to the next item. I hardly heard it. Kirsty's breathing was ragged, trembling on the edge of a sob.

"The-the-monitors must've been faulty too—"

"No," I said flatly, "they weren't. The failsafes were left on them, remember? Those things are quintuple-checked. They're incapable of rendering a consistent result at all if they're damaged. I know—though I wish to hell I didn't. They were OK—and so was Carlsen, when he left here."

"An accident—they might've dropped him—" She was half hunched down, shrinking away from the com, from me, from the world. It was such a defensive crouch it almost invited me to unleash the gathering fury I felt. I had to hold myself back wanting to shout it in her face. As long as that airspacer was all right, Carlsen would have been. The stretcher was designed to shield him against being jolted or dropped; it was a standard model, one that worked. The flight to Lyon would have taken an hour at most, more like forty-five minutes. What could have happened in that time to kill a healthy brute of a man who'd come through a serious crash unscathed? Lyon was a Departmental hospital. Nobody there would be free to inquire too closely into a death the BCs wanted kept quiet. That perfunctory examination—*no danger!*—of what? Of him waking up and talking? He'd shown no signs of having any secrets, and he wasn't good at concealing things—his smuggling attempts had been amateurish. Something he might find out, then, if he ever got to thinking about it? He'd not been a particular friend of mine, but he was part of a community it was my job to protect. And he'd done one brave, uncharacteristic thing that had earned him better than this.

"Carlsen was murdered, Kirsty," I said, and it sounded like someone else in the room talking. "I'm sure of it. And only you and I happen to know it. I've no idea how—"

But as I said it my memory echoed the ring and clatter of those heavy boots on the stairs, those boots and a man pinioned helplessly in a stretcher. *Internal injuries undetected!*

"—or why. But the whole affair—the crash, the way they shifted that wreck so fast, everything—stinks of cover-up. Nothing provable, though. Not yet. But if there's anything to be found—"

Kirsty sprang up and grabbed my arms. There were huge tears rolling down her face, but it was set like flint.

"Aye! We'll find it! Any way we can—"

"I can't think of anything you could do, not yet. Except keep quiet, act as if you don't suspect a thing, and keep that superior brain of yours on the boil. The legwork should be mine—"

"It should, should it?" inquired Kirsty, with seething calm. "And you'll tell the wee lassie all about it when ye're done, eh? And just what makes ye think—"

"Eight years of theory, twenty of practice," seemed a good enough answer to me. "Professional training, you see. Any legitimate inquiry into this—and if they hold one I'll join the SM Movement—I'd have had to be in on. My job. So—"

She let go my arms abruptly and stared at me, wide-eyed. *"Your* job?"

"That's right. I'm Chief of Security at the Sea Station, Kirsty. If anyone can find a way into this muckheap, and sort out just who killed Carlsen, and why—well, could *you* do it any better?"

TWO

MY zep picked up the guidance beam from the Station while it was still a dot on the horizon, and from then on the controls were out of my hands. They needn't ever have been in them, but I like to fly myself when I can; zeps can't go much over a couple of hundred kph, so long flights can get tedious otherwise. I'd hoped I'd miss the afternoon ferry launch, but no, there it was, squatting in the outermost launch bath on East Arm, held up for minor repairs. There would have been ample time to land, but the beam, mindlessly obeying safety regs, sent me circling around the Station in a holding corridor, along with a couple of other personal machines and a huge airfreighter. They'd been there for fifteen minutes already and weren't feeling conversational, so I settled back with what my dispenser called coffee and enjoyed the view. At times like this I was glad I'd left my cockpit floor transparent; it gave the little craft a much more open feeling, especially over the sea. On sunny days like this I could often see far down into it, watch great fish shoals moving there. I'd definitely seen a giant squid once, and what I'd swear was a sperm whale, even though the only ones officially left were cloned cells in the Peking Life Bank. Of course it could have been just an oddly shaped submersible.

28

Modern sea-monsters were mostly man-made.

The Station had a distinct look of Kraken or Leviathan about it, a strange warty head with fat flattened tentacles. But it was too man-made, too regular to be really convincing. An irregular swastika shape, with a ziggurat at the centre—a floating remnant of Atlantis, maybe, adrift on the ocean named for it. Central Building, broad and square, looked a lot like an exotic temple, with its ten stepped floors crowned with weird antennae and other coms and tracking gear, plus four very unexotic beam cannon—air defences. From each side of the square an arm stretched out to the four points of the compass. East and West Arms, each fully two kiloms long, were flat and featureless until you got to the right-angle bend about four hundred metres from the end, containing the three huge launch baths. The nose of that infernal ferry, sticking out of the bath like a pyramid drowned by an irrigation project, was the highest point; its motors would flatten anything too prominent. The vast automated hangars and workshops that housed and serviced the ferrys and various carrier craft were all out of harm's way, underwater. Even the railcar system that took freight and passengers out to the baths was recessed; vital antennae were either bubble-domed or retractable. Otherwise the arm surfaces were as bleakly empty as the sea, and flatter. North and South arms were a complete contrast, shorter and more L-shaped, just over a kilom each with the bend in the middle and surfaces cluttered with buildings. North Arm had a seaport with sub and surface facilities; South had a passenger and freight airpad, boxed in by terminal buildings, various hangars and maintenance sheds, and the surface levels of the main warehouse complex. From each armtip massive rigid cables ran out to the seawall which surrounded the whole Station like a coral reef, creating the four calm lagoons in which incoming craft could splash down safely. It was a self-contained little world out there, anchored to the Mid-Atlantic Ridge; for twenty years, since its smaller, cruder predecessor was moved out from the southern Baltic, I'd been achored to it almost as firmly. It was no small storm that threatened to shake me loose.

My zep's fixed orbit was wide; I felt like an incompetent fly buzzing round the Kraken's head. Around the distant launch bath tiny figures, inhuman in outline, scuttled around the submerged ferry. I didn't have to use my scope screen to know they were robots or waldos; no human was allowed to get that close to the outside of a spacecraft once motor warmup had begun. They seemed to be concentrating on the main cargo lock. Reasonable enough; locks are the weakest and most stressed part of any hull, and the smallest fault has to be treble-checked to see it's not going to become something worse. Just then, though, the ungainly crowd broke and scattered for cover, into hatches, lifts, anywhere. A fuel top-off line withdrew slowly, dripping obscenely into the water of the bath, and retracted into the wall. At this distance I couldn't hear the launch klaxons, but I saw them scatter a great cloud of gulls from the arm and the surrounding lagoons.

My orbit brought me slowly round once again, and as I neared the end of East Arm I could see the water of the bath beginning to bubble. Immersing the massive craft increased the efficiency of the motors and drained off some of the heat they generated in the strain of liftoff. In case of real trouble—say an impending motor explosion—the craft involved could be hastily dumped into the ocean beneath. We'd never had to do it, so we didn't like to worry passengers' heads about it. Even so, I kept a careful eye on the rising steamcloud that hid the bath now. But even at this distance I could hear the motor rumble, and it sounded very strong and steady. Nothing to worry about there—

A great column of steam blasted up suddenly and fountained out at the apex. Out of the spray came a blinding red glare with a heart so white the front of my cockpit darkened to shield me. The roar grew louder, the fountain higher and broader until out of its summit rose the great squat cone of the ferry. I could feel the weight of it in the thunderous vibration that shook my cockpit. Through the smoky window it looked as if a tree grew beneath it, red with an intolerable glare at the heart. Then on a rippling wash of heat it passed by and vanished into the late-afternoon sky. Almost at once the beam was pulling me in, so I missed that flash of daytime starlight when the fusion drive was turned on. I'd seen it a million times before, but it had lost none of its magic.

The zep circled lazily round to windward, passing through drifting wisps of steam, then dropped motive power and let the fresh breeze waft it gently in across the lagoon. With the merest whisper of steering jets the little craft dropped like a leaf onto its appointed white circle on the airpad perimeter, alongside all the other middle management status symbols. It looked like a convention of those UFO-things people were beginning to see again—how they could tell they weren't just looking at zeps beats me. Clamping arms embraced the craft, the motors grumbled a little and then it settled down onto its skids. Fuel and maintenance lines hooked in at once, for a change.

"Welcome back, sir," said a disembodied but human voice. "Fresh breeze with a bit of spray in it, getting by the wall fields. Light shower just coming up. Want a shelter?"

"Belay that! I'll walk and like it. What's with the VIBC treatment?"

"Well, good to see you back from holiday, sir . . ."

"Thanks! But compared to where I was this is dry as an SM dinner. Tell Commander Herincx I'm back and I'd like a word at his earliest etc. *Don't* tell Lieutenant Simoneau. I'll give him the goods news myself. Later."

Herincx, commander of this floating fragment of Earth, accepted the bottle of bootleg Armagnac I'd brought him with a good grace.

"Landing taxes," he intoned solemnly, and poured me a hefty one. We warmed the beakers in our hands and let the brandy scent fill the room. In his brusque Belgian accent he welcomed me back and held forth at length on the sins of my number two, the unspeakable Simoneau, and abused the Department high-ups who had impounded the wreckage of the fallen booster.

"Someone's up to no good, Mark, believe me. Cover-up of some kind. You know the score as well as I do—our job, not theirs, to look into this kind of accident! You were in Scotland, weren't you? Shame I couldn't get in touch with you; you could have gone and had a poke around before the brass got there."

"If I had," I said carefully, "I might not have spread it around. Can be uncomfortable, getting caught up in a whitewash job—*if* that's what's going on . . ."

"*Rien d'autre!*" snorted the commander. "They've even impounded Carlsen's body—it's being cremated and buried in the Department gardens, apparently. Full honours, of course. Once he's safely out of the picture it can all be put down to pilot error and not all those substandard parts from somebody's uncle's department. Hah! More brandy?"

"Never say die. So you think that's all it is—just graft?"

"Might be a plot to rule the world, for all I know. And I don't think we've much chance of finding out—unless it happens again. *Then* we jump on them before they're ready. Maybe then the pilot survives, or the launcher drops on somebody too big to write off. *Fieu,* might've dropped on you, mightn't it?"

"Don't sound so disappointed. What was it launching, anyway?"

"A DESprobe, would you believe?"

"The hell you say—don't they send those away from the Moon these days?"

"Sure, when they send them at all. There's hardly been a major one for—oh, ten years? What do I know? Not my specialty."

"Nor mine. Last one I remember going up must've been back in '02—"

Or some such date, I couldn't be bothered remembering. Years ago, that was for sure. It gave me enough to think about. So Carlsen had been killed launching a plain old deep-space probe? So much for about half the mystery I'd expected. I'd thought the key to the whole business would have been in Carlsen's payload; I'd expected top-secret packages, some mysterious device—maybe some of that new Infall-drive research that ought to have got around to fifty years ago. Something mysterious, anyway. There wasn't anything much less mysterious than a Deep Space Probe. They were made up of an instrument package, a guidance system—good but not revolutionary—a crudely powerful antimatter drive and an Infall-type friction shield to slide them through interstellar matter. A high-acceleration fusion motor banged them to the edge of the system, then got vaporized when the a/m drive lit up. That hellish device then accelerated the rest away to examine whatever area of space the guidance system was programmed for, the instruments (hopefully) did their stuff, and the whole assemblage came barrelling back in a mere two or three decades, home time. Such is the relative joy of an acceleration rate that would squash a human being to a monomolecular layer. We poor fragilities had to travel by Infall drive, vastly more complex and expensive.

DESprobes were public domain, schoolkid stuff. They'd carried the instruments out of the solar gravity well to develop the Infall system; they'd looked at every star within about three parsecs, and found us the Colony in the process. DESprobe design hadn't changed radically in a century. If anyone did improve the model they couldn't call it a DESprobe, so fixed was the image in everyone's mind. As soon call a ferry a Lunar Excursion Module. So the payload wasn't the secret. But then why had they launched it from here and not from the Moon? Because in the cramped lunar bases there was no such thing as a secret? Maybe—

"Mark," observed Herincx kindly, "there is steam coming out of your ears, you dumb cop. Have another, and cease thinking. Otherwise you will burst your brain and leave me alone with that little shit Simoneau—"

"Now *that,*" I said, cracking the beaker down on his desk, "really is your own goddam business. Thought you *wanted* a military man in my seat? It's what you've been aiming for long enough—militarize Security. And all you achieve is losing me a good subordinate and getting that booted berk instead. You made your own bed, so go—"

"I know, Mark, I know. But he was the only candidate the Department would wear—"

"Because he's got connections, yes, great. You should never have tried it on in the first place."

"No choice. Nothing against you, my boy, you know that, don't you? But who chooses your successor? The Department, of course. And if you're off to Epsilon whatever I've just *got* to get it out of their greasy talons—haven't I. *Foi de Louis,* Mark, I would never try to oust *you!*"

"No, I know that. And I don't trust the Dep any more than you, not these days. But the military's just as bad—"

"*Comment?*"

"Present company excluded, of course. Anyway, you've not seen the last of me yet. I've decided."

"You're not going? Now that's the best news—"

"Hold the party. I'm hanging on as long as I can, is all. I've more unfinished business than I thought. When that's done, or my time runs out, *then* I'll decide. In the meantime I've some poking around to do. I'll find you a good replacement, even from within the Dep. Reform from inside, that's what's needed ..."

Herincx looked at me keenly. "Sounds as if you're taking up Department politics. Play not with fire, my friend. I'd sooner you just sailed away and left it to me. I'm out of their reach. Don't you trust me?"

"Sure," I sighed, standing up and stretching, "the military's lucky it's got you. But it's got Simoneau as well. Every day he's on my back I like it that much less. Ditch him—any way you can—and I'll believe Security's safe in your hands. But I somehow don't think you can, eh, Louis? Sorry, but that's how it is. I'd better go pry him loose from my chair now."

"Sooner the better, Mark. I'm sorry, too. But take my advice—keep your nose out of Department shitpiles. We've always kept a kind of independence here on the Station—don't let's throw it away now."

I didn't waste time telling him his independence had been half the trouble. He came from outside the Dep, he'd never see why. But I could remember a time when Station staffers used to wield a lot of influence in it. We were front-line men, like lighthouse keepers or airfield controllers in the old days, people you listened to if you'd any sense. Where were we now? In self-imposed see-no-evil exile, our voices drowned by policy-makers competing to jack up traffic volume and shave away vital operating costs, by feuding sub-deps and branch offices who'd have pulled the sky down to do their rivals a bad turn. At best we were just one more piece on the Department chess-board. So much for that independence Herincx was so proud of. He didn't know as much as I did about the Dep—among other things. The crash, for example. One extra piece of knowledge blew his theory about graft right out of the lock. Who kills just to cover up a little bit of graft? More to the point, who'd kill someone like Carlsen? Someone just born to be silenced by other means, the carrot or the stick or a fine blend of both. A hefty bonus, the promotion he well knew he'd no chance of otherwise—set that against a threat to post him to the back of beyond till he tripped over his beard, and you'd have him. Any competent personnel or security officer could have told you that from the psych-profile in his dossier. Whoever ordered the murder must have had Carlsen's dossier at his fingertips, as near as a desk or pocket screen—they must have known, whoever "they" were, and they would have been in a position to give Carlsen almost anything he wanted. And yet they'd not only risked murder, but had made no other cover-up attempt, leaving the world to mutter, like Herincx, "Graft again!" and pass complacently on. They couldn't have minded this—or maybe they even preferred it. Maybe the real facts were so sinister that graft just made a good cover story by comparison.

People waved in the corridors, I waved back and didn't stop. This I had to chew over. If it really was that big it didn't fit into any of the current rackets and scandals I knew of, and what I knew could have kept the independent media agencies busy for years if I could only have rustled up a little evidence. There were times I devoutly wished that people still used paper or punch cards or something else material—a policeman's lot must've been so much easier when he wasn't just chasing flickers on readouts. Pull the power cord and not a trace was left, zap! That old familiar grouse brought me back to immediate business. My quarters were on the top floor, like Herincx's, so I'd been headed there. Unlike him, though, I didn't keep my office there too; that was down on Sea Level, where the action usually was. It was Security's business to be on hand and accessible; I'd insisted that Simoneau stay there too, however degrading he found it. My quarters could wait; I headed for the elevator.

Sea Level was the lowest and the broadest, and the antiseptic corridors lacked the softer decor of the higher levels. This was the most public part of the Station, spacious but strictly utilitarian. Even here, though, you hardly knew you were at sea; stabilizers smoothed out the motion of the water, air conditioners scrubbed out the salt smell and replaced it with that infernally sickly scent everyone but me seemed to adore. In my quarters I'd installed an opening window, getting a reputation as an ascetic tough nut, or just a nut; my office, though, was deep in the windowless bowels of the building, beyond help. My reputation had been further enhanced by the sulphur stench that resulted from my first and last attempt to gimmick the air-conditioning; I got tired of folk asking to see my horns and tail, and tried to like the sweetness. It was embracing me now, slimy and enticing, not improving my temper; maybe I'd sprout the horns any minute now. What had people got against clean sea air? It was things like that that made me want to get right out of this world, far out. I stalked straight through my office door before it had finished sliding open, marched past my secretary without a word, and opened the door of my inner office. A pair of boots, resting nonchalantly across my desktop, stared me in the face. They appeared to have polished soles. I may just possibly have breathed out a little sulphur then.

"Lieutenant Simoneau!" I barked. A peaky brown face peered

out past the boots. "Thank you for taking care of things during my absence. You can work at your own desk again now."

Simoneau unfolded himself languidly and stood up, gazing good-humouredly down at me from a considerable height. "Mr. Bellamy!" he smiled. "Now we weren't expecting you back for another day or two, were we? Have a good time?" He chuckled with all the kindly contempt of military for civilian. "I guess you'll find things were pretty much under my thumb while you were away. Nothing much happened—"

"Oh? the Commander was telling me about a crash—"

"Oh, that, yeah. That stupid big bastard Carlsen dropped a launcher into the sea. None of our business. The Security check forms are OK, so we're off the hook—"

"I see," I said, settling back into my chair. "A weight off my mind, that. And there was nothing else? No smuggling, no cargo pilfering, no drunk pilots, no freighter crew squabbles? Well, what an unusual few weeks it's been. You seem to have struck it lucky."

"There's always less trouble with a military presence at the helm, sir." He didn't really have a hide like a rhino. The *sir* showed I'd rattled him.

"That would be it, right enough," was all I felt like saying. "Well, these last few weeks may look good on the crime figures, but now I'm back I'm afraid things'll just have to go downhill again. Make a *thorough* check on the bonded drug depot, lieutenant. And on the liquor consignments that came in last week. And the load of components for Montevideo, that'll have come in on yesterday's ferry—but of course you know about all that . . ."

"Yes, sir. Tomorrow, sir? I'm off duty tonight."

"Then do it now. Tonight there'd better be a raid on one or two people's quarters. I'll make a list, but you should be in charge of the raids. More in your line, as a military presence. But you won't be looking for stolen goods—"

"No, sir?" He sounded genuinely surprised.

"No sir. But you might just find some incriminating traces. The lads'll have had weeks to get the stuff out and onto the market, after all. Nice quiet weeks."

And so much for Simoneau. He meandered off in the direction of his own office, practising his ill-used expression. What really infuriated me about him was that he wasn't half as stupid or lazy as he pretended to be; his psych-profile said as much, and I'd seen him in action when he thought he'd a chance of showing me up, or had a personal stake in the action. Then he turned energetic and devious. The way he caught the sailor who mugged him one night—But he knew well enough he was irremovable, and just sat there and bided his time, figuring that as he was twenty years younger than I he could afford to. I worked him as hard as I could, and thought about him as little as possible.

But right now I was stuck with him. His incompetence was the last shred of hope for my payload theory. The payload couldn't hold the secret—unless . . . unless the security check had somehow been fudged or evaded, and what went up wasn't a DESprobe at all.

I went out to the outer office—large enough for men to report, prisoners to be booked, visitors to wait—and formally announced my return to my sec. The pleasant female voice greeted me with a huge load of unfinished business, most of which Simoneau could and should have handled. I shoved what I could in his direction and settled down to sort out the most urgent stuff. To add to my irritation, he'd brainwashed my sec into using crawlingly obsequious speech patterns which I had to countermand one by one as they appeared. I've never felt the need to have humans fawn over me, let alone machines; they call me Mr. Bellamy, or "sir," at most, and that's fine. Odd, though, that so many people don't feel that way. A hundred years ago *sir* and *mister* had gone the way of *seigneur* and *bwana,* until they were built back into the machines; that started folk using them on each other again. So much for progress. Really *I* should have been deferring to the bloody sec, which wouldn't let me alone until I'd at least worked out a timetable for dealing with the most urgent business. I'd only myself to blame for programming it to do that, but it was still irritating; it left that all-important security check itching maddeningly away at the back of my mind. But when I saw the most urgent item I quite forgot it.

"Clearances for *how* many emigrants? For tomorrow?"

"One thousand seven hundred and fifty-two persons, due to depart on the 14:50 ferry run tomorrow."

"I see. How long's this been outstanding?"

"Eighteen days, sir."

"I'll *kill* Simoneau!"

"Yes, sir, shall I inform the honourable sir and lieutenant?"

"No, why spoil the surprise? And cancel that mode of reference to him—and any others; substitute "Mister Simoneau" for all. Understood?"

"Yes, sir."

"Does anyone know anything about this fashing emigrant party, then?"

"Yes, sir. The party leader arrived the day before yesterday and is waiting to see Mr. Simoneau, when he has the time."

Now that was a laugh for a start. "Belay that. I'll see him—page him now. What's his name, by the way?"

"The Reverend John Whittaker, sir. Paging now."

That was all I needed. Seventeen hundred clearances to cope with before bed, and only a goddam priest to help. With competent help I could get through it all in a few hours, but what kind of help could a priest give me? I'd never met one before, and I wondered which of the media stereotypes to expect, the slimy hypocrite or the half-wit. On balance I'd rather work with an intelligent hypocrite, but I couldn't help thinking that most of those would have found a more rewarding front than religion these days—the SM movement, for a start.

I used the minute or so before he arrived to take a quick glance at that security check and settle that itch for the moment. It didn't make me any happier; Simoneau had carried it out personally, but with Ziz Brazda, an old friend and sometime bedfellow of mine. And she, blast her, was absolutely reliable. If there'd been anything but a DESprobe on the end of that carrier she'd have spotted it at once. So much for that. And before I'd a chance to read on the door opened and in stepped the priest.

He didn't look half-witted. He had to duck through the door, for a start, and not even Simoneau the human stringbean did that; it wasn't low. Whittaker was well over the double metre, an aristocratic height; only people with well-fed ancestors usually reached it—like Simoneau, for example, or Carlsen, son of the black sheep of a family that traced its ancestry back to the League of Nations. The common man tended to be much shorter, like myself. Whittaker had the face that went with BC blood, too, broad and smooth and cold as a snowdrift under a thick crown of white hair. Only his clothes ruined the impression, battered general issue trousers and tunic under an old green work jacket. Or did they? That jacket was a Viennese *Loden*, unmistakably so; even second or third hand those things cost a fortune on the black market. He could have swapped his for two good suits and a month's square meals, which he seemed to need. This could be more interesting than I'd expected.

I waved him to a chair, which creaked, and met that wintry look head-on.

"It's good of you to make time to see me," was all he said though, with not a trace of sarcasm in his tone. After a forty-eight hour wait, that showed uncommon control—or just good tactics. He'd dumped the ball firmly in my court, but not given me any chance to take offence.

"I'm only sorry you had the long wait," I said. "But I'm literally just back from vacation, and my number two—well, he's got calls on his time—"

"I understand," said Whittaker, and sounded as if he did, too. He didn't look as if he'd eaten much during that unexpected wait.

"These clearances could take a while, it'll be quicker if we work through dinner. I'll have some sent up—no, on my expenses. What'd you like?"

I guessed he couldn't afford much for himself, but he accepted unwillingly and politely, no gushing. Nothing oily about him, certainly. And over the next hour and a half I decided there wasn't much naivety, either. Because an hour and a half was all it took us to get through a job I'd allowed a good three hours for. Whittaker had every last detail of his party at his fingertips—who was related to whom and how, why some dossiers had gaps, what the background was to the vague cautionary notes and endorsements that seemed to turn up on so many dossiers. He'd anticipated just about all the major problems, and all my forays into the databanks couldn't fault him. And he ploughed ahead with such methodical ruthlessness that I began to get the feeling *I* was holding *him* up. He was obviously ravenous, but he ate almost automatically, as we worked. By the end of the session I'd decided two things about him— he was used to dealing with BCs, and he'd handled dossiers before, often. What he'd decided about me I didn't know, but the snow showed signs of thawing just a little. I took advantage of that.

"These people of yours, Reverend Whittaker. They surprise me."

He looked up from his coffee-beaker. "How so?"

"Clean as a whistle. No major crimes—no significant crimes, really—no troubles, no definite black marks. Nothing."

"Is that so unusual?"

"Yes, it is. And that's not just the policeman's paranoia. There are no outstanding good points, either—just these odd little cautions and sour notes. But they're all very vague. Your people are all pale grey, low profile—*no* profile, in fact. Featureless landscapes."

"So?"

"So—it's very unusual. Most emigrants are running away from something—oh, I don't mean they're fugitives from justice, anything like that. But they're usually some kind of misfit. Too much failure. Or sometimes, too much success. If that doesn't sound stupid."

"No," murmured Whittaker, "it makes sense. And we don't fit into either category?"

"Not by a long way. This is the dullest batch of dossiers I've seen for years."

Whittaker gave me a wintry smile. "You're not a religious man, Mr. Bellamy."

"Since you ask—"

"I didn't. You aren't religious, and you don't know anyone who is, or you wouldn't have had to ask about the dossiers. In a way you were right—we are running away from something."

"Which is—"

"Persecution," he said explosively. "Religious persecution."

"Fascinating," I said through my professional poker face. Who the hell would bother persecuting religion these days? Not even the African Junta; it was too insignificant even for them to bother about. Whittaker must think he was some kind of Pilgrim Father—

"You're wondering," said the priest grimly, "if I think I'm a reincarnated pilgrim father." I don't believe in telepathy, so I shut up. "I've heard that before. And worse things. I've even heard it said—sometimes by well-meaning people—that religion isn't significant enough to persecute any more."

"Since you put it that way—"

"I didn't. They did. They were young, like you, and they'd never had a chance to study history properly. Also like you. Or you'd know just how powerful a force religion, even minority religion, can be in human affairs—for stability, or for disruption."

"How? How could religion threaten a modern state?"

He didn't answer at once. He just sat there, swilling the coffee dregs in his beaker round, and looking at me with a slight frown. The freeze seemed to be coming back. I realized suddenly I was being sized up; he was wondering if I might be an *agent provocateur* out to trap him, wondering if he hadn't said too much already. The way my last question sounded— So he really was used to being persecuted, eh? But maybe it was all in the mind. Even so, it was flattering when he did give me a straight answer.

"By being an alternative source of values. By teaching people that they are people, not just statistical units, that every one of them, each individual, matters. That they're not just part of the masses. It teaches them that their horizons are wider than their masters want them to think. That's why the bureaucrats are afraid of us—"

"*Afraid* of you? Wild. Mind telling this particular bureaucrat why?"

He stared at me contemptuously. "You're no BC. Don't lower yourself by borrowing the name. If you really were one, you'd know enough to be afraid. Oh, I don't mean you'd walk in terror of us, but you'd remember what happened in Poland, for example, and the USSR ... it was just about the earliest modern bureaucratic state, a crude prototype. Lots of reliance on propaganda and secret police, they hadn't cottoned on to the power of apathy then. Poland was a satellite state, more or less a colony. Anyway, a Polish priest was elected head of the largest segment of the Christian Church—they still meant something then, the different churches. Anyway, when he became pope—that was the title—there was a tremendous religious revival in Poland. They stopped swallowing what the BC government fed them, they challenged and questioned and held out for individual rights. They were still a minority, they suffered some pretty savage reprisals, but they were the beginnings of the movement that tore down the BCs and won freedom from the USSR. And that in turn made religion the focus of dissent within the USSR itself. And that dissent began the struggle that tore the Soviet system apart a century later." He sighed. "Even in my day that wasn't the official version. The censors were creeping in then. But there were still a few of the old books around, if you looked . . . I should have kept them. It's too easy to wipe information now. Anyway—" He pulled himself together. "That's why they're afraid of us. They've got better at repressing us since those days, though, subtler. And that's why all my people have to lead model lives. They're safe enough as long as they do; they'll never do well at work, no promotion or anything, they'll never have much luck with holiday allocations, housing, you name it. Occasionally they might get transferred suddenly and inconveniently, maybe even demoted or given some kind of degrading job. Ambitious friends, relatives even, tend to drop them—that kind of thing. It wears them down. But they don't actually suffer. Not unless—" He grimaced. "Unless they're stupid enough to commit an actual crime. Then they suffer, their families too. Lots of ways. And the media hurl it in everyone's face . . ."

That much was true. You couldn't help noticing some of the extra attention the headlines got in the newscasts—MUSLIM DRUNK CHARGE! BUDDHIST PRIEST GETS RAPE RAP! PRIEST AS-SAULTS OFFICIAL! But I'd always thought they were just distracting people from the important news. A sudden shock of recognition brought me up short.

"Mr. Whittaker," I said, "there's one clearance we haven't discussed yet. Yours."

Another wintry smile. I tabbed up his dossier.

"Trying to lead me away from it with the history lecture, weren't you?"

"Yes," he sighed. "Till I got so damned interested I led you back again. Well—is an old assault charge a bar to emigration?"

"No—but the outstanding one is. Why the blazes hasn't it been brought to trial yet?"

"It might have to be thrown out, is why. It's more use to them hanging over my head."

I'd encountered that tactic before, but I wasn't about to tell him that. Let him sweat for a minute or two. "So what are these assault charges about?"

"I imagine the dossier—"

"In your own words."

"The old one—simple enough. Shortly after I became a priest . . . It's a spare-time occupation these days. You have to work to live, jobs are hard to find all of a sudden. I began working in a public catering dep; its manager hadn't any more sense of hygiene than a sewer rat, I told him so, he hit me, I hit him back and drew a year in jail. End of story."

His dossier was oddly short at the beginning, but I didn't stop to see why, I just called up the account of the charge. Whittaker had missed out three interesting details. First, his victim had been unconscious for a week; second, soon after he woke up the said victim had been dismissed on theft and hygiene charges; third, Whittaker's wife had died while he was in jail.

"End of story, as you say. The new charge?"

"Stupid. A street brawl. I was barged, I—did my best to keep my temper. I didn't quite manage it. Stupid of me, as I say; the man was drunk, I think."

"It doesn't say here whether you actually hurt him."

"I only hit him once, he was too fast."

"A light-footed drunk. Very interesting. And that was five years ago. Just before you applied to emigrate."

Whittaker's smooth face creased into a heavy frown. "You're saying—"

"A little official harassment."

"I hadn't applied yet, but naturally I'd asked how I could apply. I've often wondered if it was a set-up—and why—"

"Just a precaution. Something to hold over your head, if the need arose. The dossier report as good as says it, for them that have eyes to see. But you've never seen that, of course."

"Who has? Seen their own dossier, I mean." I had, and more, but you don't tell chance acquaintances that. "What are you going to do?" he added, wearily.

"File a request for instructions on your case."

"How long will that take to come through?"

"Anything up to five years."

"Five *years*—"

"If I use the right procedure. By then Earth time won't have much meaning for you, you should be well on your way."

"But you—"

"That's my worry. But I could well be with you. I've a place option on the Ship as well."

"Take it," said Whittaker earnestly. "Take it. You're wasted down here. I don't know how to tell you—"

"Don't bother," I said dryly, "it might get to the wrong ears. Come in, Lieutenant," I added, wiping Whittaker's dossier hastily off my main desk screen. It was hooded, so people on the other side of the desk couldn't see it, but Simoneau was tall enough and snoopy enough to just accidentally lean over. In he shambled, pointedly ignoring Whittaker, and gave me a perfunctory salute.

"Those checks you wanted—with all this other bumf—"

"—you've no time. Tell you what, Lieutenant. Why not just keep going till you drop—then we'll see about what's left."

"I'd better be going, then," said Whittaker hastily. "But thanks for everything you've done—"

"You couldn't have been more helpful yourself. Tell you what—maybe the Lieutenant would like your place on the Ship. Then I'll give him his job—"

"Catch me going off in that thing," said Simoneau murderously. "Waste of valuable resources, all this space travel shit. Should spend the money on more weather satellites and asteroid mining. Solve the Solar System's problems before rushing off to the stars—"

"I was in my twenties when the first Ship went," said Whittaker briskly as he reached the door. "Only a little younger than you are now. It was the most exciting thing my generation ever saw—I'd have sold my soul for a place. But you, all the other moaners—have you souls left to sell? Goodbye, Mr. Bellamy." He ducked through the door, then checked and turned back as if he'd suddenly meant to say something else. But he looked at Simoneau, hesitated and stepped out. The door slid silently shut behind him.

Simoneau grunted "Good riddance." I hardly noticed him. Whittaker had been about to say something, all right. Only Simoneau's presence had stopped him. Well, he could call me, or come back in. But after my experience with his dossier I was sure of one thing—if he hadn't told me what it was by tomorrow, I was fashing well going to find out. I quite liked the old man. But trusting him—another matter entirely. There wasn't much naive about the Reverend John Whittaker.

I threw Simoneau out, and settled down to take a really good look through that Security form. It scrolled across my screen in the form of a long dissected diagram studded with smaller detail panels and captions to show where special checks should be made. And, infuriatingly, they all had been, from the squat base of the launcher to the nacelle of the probe. Its shape was unmistakable, streamlined not against air but free particles and gas clouds, impossibly tenuous until you began moving at significant fractions of lightspeed. Then no mere matter could stand such friction; a shieldfield, derived from fusion containment shields, would flow back over the surface and smooth its passage. Speed was in the very profile of the thing, like a flung dagger—the blade the nacelle, integral part of a massive instrument package; guidance motors and instrumentation the wing-like crosspiece; and the stubby, sinister hilt the antimatter motor. This was basically the same design as on the earliest probes of more than a century ago: a simple device for the storage of antihydrogen and its commoner counterpart, and their gradual introduction—all done with more shieldfields, which took the terrifying result and channelled it into a drive flame of awesome power.

It was these fields, spawned by the search for better containment for fusion reactions, that had in their turn given birth to the Infall fields. Infall offered a much safer and more large-scale means of interstellar travel, but after the first explosion of interest that resulted in the Colony project its development had languished. It was easy to see why; Infall—named for a mistaken association with black holes, on the basis that both have some kind of event horizon—was so energy-thirsty that only large scale and long distance made it economical, and so complex that it needed a human crew to nurse it along, adjusting, redesigning' and redeveloping as they went. The raw power of a/m, on the other hand, still depended on acceleration to reach interstellar speeds, making it too slow for humans; only at accelerations no flesh and blood could possibly stand could it reach reasonable interstellar speeds. So it could carry robots and freight to develop the resources of the outer system, keeping humans nicely penned up in grinding old fusor-driven ships that took months to cross the system and couldn't possibly reach even the nearest stars. Which suited the present generation of BCs very well indeed. Apart from old experimental craft with range no greater than half a lightyear, there was only one Infall craft left, the Second Colony Ship. Soon, when it had gone, there would be none. Simoneau had parroted the official line on space travel word for word; a waste of time, and there'd be no more.

It made a weary background to the check, that thought. I

read it again and again, and could find no flaw in it anywhere. Perhaps Ziz had put Simoneau on his mettle, for once. Where could there be a secret about this straight-forward craft, something Carlsen had to die to conceal? Not graft, I'd decided, and nothing immediately obvious about the thing itself. Its purpose, maybe? What it was to do, and where? Possible. The launcher pilot would have had to have at least some idea of its eventual course; so would Flight Control, but not its human part—fed directly to the machines, the course could be read, allowed for and filed without them being bothered. And files can be secured, or wiped. But not the pilot.

I stopped abruptly, and swept the Security form off the screen. That'd be a can of worms to open! Because if Carlsen had been murdered for knowing the course, then—I slid my chair along my desk to the com bank and called a familiar room number. HOLD, said the screen, then cleared to show a heap of bed-insulator with a bare arm reaching out to the bed-side console. It sagged sleepily, so I turned up the volume and cooed "Ziz my love? Zdzislawa?"

The heap growled and stirred. It only looked large enough for one, which was as well; calling Ziz could be embarrassing at times. She surged up suddenly like a surfacing dolphin, shaking long auburn hair out of her eyes and setting her small breasts dancing beneath it. Ziz had a serpentine body, long-limbed and supple with no flesh to spare, only wire-cable muscles under skin tanned like delicate leather. Except in one place, a white splash between the ribs where a' bullet had passed. Experience had left a few lines on her lean features, but the huge brown eyes were deceptively young and doe-like. She was a year or two younger than me, unbeautifully attractive and tough as nails. Once we'd nearly lost her, recovering evidence from a lagoon onto which an incoming ferry was presently descending. She got out with her wetsuit smouldering, and the makings of a murder charge. Right now we were headed for another. "So-o-o, my Chief's back, hmm? My dear dishy little Chief who abandons me to that bastard Simoneau for weeks and then comes waking me up when for the third time in succession *I'm due on watch at midnight—*"

"Easy, *liščička*, easy! Just one thing and you can sleep. That security check you ran on the DESprobe launcher, Carlsen's job, you and that long streak of—well, never mind. Tell me about it."

She shrugged, which looked pleasant. "What's to tell? He let me do all the mountaineering bit at the top, but I didn't mind—"

"The top? The probe itself, you mean?"

"Sure. Suited me, I'm lighter'n more limber than him, and I was through quicker. Whole thing's sealed up solid, not much to check. He really got the worst job. Did it thoroughly, though. Only got through about five minutes before it was due to go."

"I see. Thanks, Ziz. And there was nothing unusual about the probe? You didn't catch what it was for, where it was going?"

"No, and no. Hellfire, my Chief, what do DESprobes usually get up to? Finding somewhere else not to colonize, I suppose. Sleep, hmm, please? Since you've gone and woken me, least you could do is come over and stroke me to sleep again, hmm?" But Kirsty was still a warm taste on my lips, and I was able to plead the huge Simoneau backlog as an excuse. She did manage to extort a promise to waken her again at 23:45 in person. I hoped I'd be a little safer then.

I was glad I'd backed down when another call came through the moment I'd cut her off, this time from Kirsty. She was between shower and bed, wrapped in a very skimpy towel; the view was amazing, and I transferred it to the huge wall screen behind my desk. When I told her that she began to play the tease, quite subtly, with the knot of the towel. She was developing a considerable talent for that kind of thing, blossoming out in all kinds of unexpected ways. I still made reluctant noises about cradle snatching, but I knew well enough I was only the worm wriggling on the hook.

The last seven nights had been turmoil—heady and addictive, a sprawling, sweating battle of limbs that pitted youth against experience, agility against strength. A potent mix, unstable, explosive. If there'd been nothing more than sex it mightn't have lasted longer than that week. But Kirsty was as fascinating out of bed, bubbling with other enthusiasms, pouring out all the hard-won education and culture she couldn't share with anyone else. Not that I was up to some of it, but her own intense pleasure caught me up even in what I didn't understand, spicing it with her peculiar personality. And I did have things to offer in return, the wider world I knew; the travelling I'd done while I still had the heart to, and my experiences on the Station—sometimes edited, sometimes not.

Travel excited her; I could see her eyes sparkle in the wide image as she asked me about a trip I'd promised her for some weekend soon, to Austria. Apparently her parents didn't mind; I hadn't expected they would. At first we'd strained to make love in silence, hands jammed over mouths bursting with laughter. But when Kirsty had got it across to them that I was an official of reasonable rank we were damn nearly given breakfast in bed.

One thing she didn't mention, as we'd agreed, our shared secret. I'd long ago made sure the Station's coms couldn't be tapped without Security knowing, but I couldn't do much about outside calls. I was glad enough not to have to share the thoughts I was having, anyway. I pushed them aside and thoroughly enjoyed myself until Kirsty saw how late it was and decided she needed sleep; we'd been talking for hours. She bounced to her feet, blowing me a goodnight kiss, and at long last the overstrained towel collapsed to the floor. It had my deepest sympathy.

Channelled air, sanitized and scented, wasn't what my over-heated mind and body needed just then; something sharper and rawer was called for. In only a few minutes I was right at the apex of the Station, stepping out onto the roof of Central Building, where the weather was certainly obliging. Driven rain-clouds drew grey curtains across the horizon, drawing closer; the wind whipped their chilly advance-guards into my face. I threaded my way among the tangled roots of the antenna jungle, the metal and plastic slick beneath my feet, until I reached open space at the southwestern corner, clear for the traverse of the great beam-cannon towering overhead. By now even the end of the long launch arm out there was invisible but for the halo of the launch-bath lights, and the wind and sea were drowning the Station sounds. Only the deep incessant rumble of the chain of wave-power generators making up the sea-wall was louder. But their shape would simply catch and translate the sea's violence; the more it rocked them the more power they would generate for the wall's radiating damper field. Another stablemate of Infall, it lay on the sea surface in a shallow lenticular shape that flattened waves into slower, smoother crestless surges the wall units could cope with easily, leaving hardly enough kinetic energy to rock the Station on its anchor cables. "Gravity oil," someone had christened the field. But it couldn't stop the rain that raced across and turned the lagoon surfaces to ground glass. No more than I could avoid my own thoughts. Like the rain, they flung themselves in my face.

I was sure that Carlsen had died to cover up something about the mission, not just the crash; it simply wasn't big enough. But that would mean he had always been meant to die, at some point. When, then? After he returned the launcher to the Station? Too public, too risky, too many chances of him letting something—the course, say—slip, before his mouth was closed. Before that, then. Which cast an interesting new light on the crash.

A mysterious control failure that develops on reentry, just at the point where the pilot can forgivably save his skin by baling out. There weren't that many qualified launcher pilots in Europe, and I'd had dealings with them all at one time or another. Run computer checks on their dossiers and psych-profiles to choose the single cert to bale `out, and you'd be handed Carlsen on a silver platter. He would eject, driven not by panic but by cool self-interest, and land in the open Atlantic, from which he would soon be picked up, as people always were these days if their survival gear was in good order. Only his had every notorious fault in the book, plus a leaky air rebreather that fed him poisonous alkalis, and was hard to keep off your face without getting out of the lifejacket altogether. And with SpaceDep keeping the usual rescue services discreetly out of the picture, the result was as good a death-trap as any I'd heard of. A certainty, if you believed, as most people did, that psych-profiles were infallible; it was a particularly understandable belief for the BC high-ups, because they seldom dealt with their inferiors on any other basis. So, suppose there'd been no leak in that rebreather, that salt water had been added in advance? And that there'd been no control failure, just some skillfully-timed sabotage?

The shower howled it in my ears. Small natural glitches, maybe, but that security check couldn't possibly have missed the single thing it was specifically designed to detect. And the man who had carried it out had been the last man aboard, leaving only when Carlsen himself was settled in and ready. I thought of a tall lean shadow, a weird blend of casualness and determination, of inefficiency and martinet precision, of laziness and ambition, a military man with strong BC connections...

There was Simoneau, right at the heart of my department,

irremovable while I had so little proof to leaven so much certainty. And with him there to keep an eye on what I was doing, getting it would be that much harder.

I pounded my fist onto the cannon-mount in sheer frustration. Maybe I'd already gone too far.

THREE

By next morning, though, I felt better about things. Even if Simoneau was somehow involved in this—and I was pretty sure he was—I hadn't said or done anything I couldn't wriggle out of. It was natural enough to be curious about the crash; it was still the high point of Station gossip. And as the man who'd have chaired the preliminary enquiry, if we'd been allowed to hold one, I had some legitimate excuse for showing an interest. Blaming me for that would only draw extra attention to something the BCs evidently wanted people to forget. The risk of less official retaliation—up to and including murder—wasn't that great, for similar reasons. At least, not yet. And I could look after myself well enough, living in a tight little island community like this. Let Simoneau do his worst, as long as I was onto him.

Last night's black mood had worked itself out in dreams, dark, turbulent and strange. I remembered little except a sense of falling slowly down through endless ocean depths, and later images of Kirsty and of Ziz that seemed somehow to merge and blend. I'd escaped from Ziz with only light tooth and claw marks, feeling virtuous; evidently my subconscious had had other ideas. I reached out to the well-worn bedside panel and tapped the control that slid my special window open, letting in the early morning mix of pallid light and cool air. I slumped back with the insulator moulded luxuriously around me, listening as always for the descending thunder of the day's first ferry. Newcomers to the Station tended to flinch at it, as if the sky were falling on their heads. I liked it. The vibration massaged me gently, and I felt ready to take on the world again.

By the time I'd caught breakfast in the mess the lagoon was just clear undisturbed sea once more, sparkling bravely in the wan sunshine. The ferry had been unloaded at one of the underwater docks before being scooped into the automated service and storage bays. Another ferry craft would be on its way to the launch basins now for the mid-morning take-off. Simoneau had left half of its cargo clearances for me to handle, meaning a heavy load of both terminal work and legwork, so I bolted the last of my toast and coffee—higher ranks still ate well—and stomped away to my office. I'd enough red tape to keep me walled up there for a week, but I took time off now and then to have Whittaker paged. He was curiously hard to find, however, and I didn't want to waste my staff's time searching; I'd catch him when his party arrived. Meanwhile I took a longer look at that dossier of his.

It was a weird affair, almost as if life for him began at forty. Before that there was his birthdate—he was eighty-five now—his stats and medical record (rude health), date of marriage and wife's dossier code, and not a single fashing thing more. No parentage, education, background, nothing, as if he'd spent his first four decades in a fairy-tale trance. And, strangest of all, no psych-profile, that compound millstone strung from cradle to grave around the neck of every citizen, save those more equal than others, the princes of bureaucrat kind. I took a full ten seconds to stare before hurrying on to other work.

As a result, when 1400 hours came around I had enough time to supervise the arrival of the emigrant party in person. I felt I should, because it was the largest party we'd ever had through the Station. There were already around ten thousand people aboard the Ship, but they'd mostly gone up in dribs and drabs, two or three hundred at a time, over the last couple of years. Most had passed through the Station, joining the normal ferry run; this lot, though, was going to fill an entire ferry, between bodies and baggage—little of *that* as there was. It had already arrived by zep, in pre-checked flight containers;

all my men had to do was check the seals. I wished we could pack people that way instead of overstraining our resources. Space was at a premium on the Station, and our passenger traffic relatively small compared with freight. So all we had was one rather under-sized passenger processing system consisting of the usual approach corridor filled with screening gear for bombs and other weaponry or the more usual contraband items, a hall with two identification and clearance-check machines—senile turnstile models I'd been trying to have replaced for years—and beyond them a departure room that simply could not hold seventeen hundred people. If we shunted people systematically onto the rail cars out to the ferry, though, we could manage—just. It all depended on how orderly they all were.

I thought for a while and then, on the basis of their dossiers and the kind of man in charge of them, decided not to issue electric goads to the guards. I carried one myself, though, in case of emergencies and as a badge of office, swagger-stick style. If there were going to be any trouble, it would help if people knew who to listen to. With neither Ziz nor Dubucq, my two most senior staffers, on watch it would all be down to me. I made my way down to the South Arm airpad, and as I crossed over to the rather shabby passenger reception area of the air-transport terminal I saw Whittaker standing at the salt-spattered window, staring out at the ant-like procession of self-powered freight pallets filing out of the warehouse complex opposite. That would be the return load for the zep bringing his people in.

In the time it took me to get through the terminal doors, though, Whittaker had somehow dropped out of sight again. I knew well enough when I was being avoided, but I bided my time; the later he left the little chat I had in mind, so much the more inconvenient for him. And his time was running out, for here was the zep rumbling down from the clouds in a sluggish parabola. It was a huge cargo affair, with less of the saucer outline than smaller craft; wide tail-vanes turned it into a bulky dart. Its steering jets toppled a rubbish-basket and whipped its contents across the terminal frontage as it settled with a long-drawn-out moan onto the undersized freight pad. Transit officers scuttled out to book in the new arrivals like so much livestock, and there was the priest deep in conversation with a couple of them. I moved out after him, but he was already shepherding the first outpouring of people into Arrivals. Once through there they were the responsibility of my guard detail, so I strolled down to keep an eye on things.

They looked like an ordinary enough bunch of people as they came chattering and bustling through the gates, perhaps a little shabbier than usual. They were battered and crumpled after their uncomfortable ride in the zep's cargo hold, and more than once I caught the tang of vomit from breath or clothes, but they seemed to be in high enough spirits. A group of the younger ones even started to sing, some clapping in time as they walked. I knew the tune, but I was surprised they did; it was at least three hundred years old. One line repeated three times in a rising crescendo—

> Run to the Stars—Stars, won't you hide me?
> Run to the Stars—Stars, won't you hide me?
> Run to the Stars—Stars, won't you hide me?

—and then a falling line full of grim relish—

> All on that day!

An odd thing to be singing, I thought, considering it was just what they were doing. They sang it authentically enough to satisfy a folksong freak like me, in the old slurred diction, the natural way folk used to speak before we all began trying to sound clipped and precise like machines. There was a pretty girl, a much-freckled blonde with a small child on each arm, who had a great voice, as dark as she was light. She caught me looking at her, sternly heavy in uniform with goad, and faltered uncertainly, obviously afraid voices were against regulations. I grinned at her and joined in, picking up the second half of the verse—

> Lord said "Sinner Man, the Stars'll be a'falling!"

—and she almost fell over with surprise. I strode along beside them, giving them the benefit of my sea-ravaged baritone; I enjoyed it, and it made it easier to keep an eye out for Whittaker. He wasn't with them, so I saw them into the processing system and went back along the swelling line. He wasn't with the Transit men, either. I was beginning to get intensely irritated, and plunged right down the middle of the line towards the system entrance. Halfway there my procom squawked an alarm, and I began to barge ahead, pushing people out of my way. At the corridor entrance I vaulted the rail to the staff walkway and ran down into the processing hall.

It was escalating pandemonium, a shuffling, milling, impenetrable mass of people. No more singing, just the low grumble of a bored crowd. There were far too many people piling up in this half of the hall, though the stream through the turnstiles to the other side seemed quite steady. In the enclosed space the air was becoming rancid with humanity. My guards were invisible at first, till I saw one elbowing his way desperately round the wall towards me.

"They're fucking lunatics, Chief!" he wailed. "One of them got into some sort of idiot screw-up at the machines, the line backed up and they just kept on coming, we tried to hold them back but the others just kept coming on like fucking *sheep—*"

"The flow seems all right now—give me a hand, Rebrov!" I jumped up onto the walkway rail with him steadying me. A surprising number of elbows banged at my feet, but I could see right into the centre of the hall. There was a little oasis of calm around the machines, people filing up to them in good order and providing fingerprints, voiceprints, blood samples and the rest without a moment's hesitation. I'd cleared them to pass, the machines' job was to check that the people fitted the clearance details. Old or not, they worked well, just slowly. But not slowly enough to account for all this. Even though the guards directing them had been crowded aside, people seemed to be passing through as quickly as could be expected. That one, in fact—

I sprang down from the rail, right into the crowd, and plunged towards the centre. I'd seen Whittaker's broad back there, but that wasn't the only reason. A sudden milling movement of the bodies packed ahead threw me outwards and back like the ball on an illegal gambler's wheel, hard against the wall. That did it.

"Call up the duty squad!" I shouted to Rebrov. "And a stretcher team!" And not for me, either. Flicking the goad in front of me, I lanced out into the throng. I left the power off at first; rapping a few heads and elbows, jabbing the odd kidney, cleared the way without more serious damage. But an angry buzz rose round me, and I thumbed the contact. I was angry myself, now, almost angry enough to turn out the guard and fill the place with gas or foam; many security men would have. It was written on all the faces round me that something was going on; some looked desperate, ready to start a fight as I neared the machines. In this little hall it could become a riot, and there were children and old people about. I'd no choice. One burly man raised his fist, another turned to spring. I stiff-armed him in the face as he leapt, and whacked my goad into the other's biceps. Nails swung at my eyes, a knee at my groin; I ducked aside and jabbed the goad between their owner's shoulder blades as she passed. She fell writhing. That blonde, and in front of her kids, yet. Someone was going to regret this as much as I did. A thin man swung a hard kick at me, knocking the goad from my hand, then toppled aside with a yell. Whittaker stood over him, face suffused with fury. I ignored him, slapped my pass to the machine and hurtled through as the whole turnstile assembly clanged aside.

The man I was after, the one who'd passed the machines too quickly, was tugging at the far door of the departure room, leading to the rail halt. My guards, being properly trained, had locked it again before rushing back to the melee in the hall, so he had no way out. He spun to face me, and I got a brief impression of black hair and heavy scowling features as he dropped into karate stance. It wasn't the brightest thing he could have done.

I dragged him back to the machine gate by one ankle; he was taller and broader than me, a considerable weight. Silence had fallen on the hall, except for children crying. The duty squad, another ten guards, had arrived, but nobody was resisting them. The girl I'd goaded was sitting up, retching; I waved the stretcher team over to her, hoping she'd only need first-aid. I stabbed a finger into Whittaker's chest.

"You! My office. Help me with this one—move!"

Whittaker bent down and scooped up the groaning body as if it was an infant's. I blinked; he must be as strong as a gorilla. He didn't move. "What about the others?" he asked quietly. "They're not involved—"

"Balls," I said, and turned to the duty squad. "Clear them through, as many as possible onto the cars, but nobody further than that till you get the word from me. Stack 'em three deep if you have to! Any that don't fit, my office on the double.

Just one cheep of trouble, flood the place with gas and call me. Right?"

By the time he was dumped on a chair in my outer office the body was coming back to life. Whittaker was looking concerned. "He'll be all right," I told him, rummaging in my desk for a pack of antistun. "He just rattled his head off a battle-plastic door, that's all."

"You're unnecessarily violent," said Whittaker sharply.

"Balls," I said again, squirting the antistun up the body's nostrils. "He had a good go at me—good for an amateur, anyway. And your people started the really rough stuff, too. I was just tapping them aside, before that."

"I know," sighed Whittaker. "I don't know if you'll believe how sorry I am—"

"I might. I saw you pull that type with the feet off me."

"They panicked. Stupid, but with so much riding on this, so much planning about to go wrong—"

"Pretty stupid planning. Might have worked with your average mainland cops, but not us. We don't have quite that low opinion of people; when we see 'em suddenly start acting like panicky sheep we don't assume it's natural, we wonder why."

"Yes," said Whittaker. "I thought that was a possibility when I met you yesterday. I had half a mind to tell you, to ask you to help, even, but—Too big a risk, I thought. I chickened out."

"Well, you'd better start talking now. That ferry's due to go in forty minutes, I can't hold it longer than five. And I'm not at all inclined to let your people on board. Hellfire, man, don't you know what smuggling a stowaway onto a spacecraft can *do?* It can make hay of safety margins, load tolerances, millions of other factors—"

"We allowed for all that. We had a veteran pilot advising us. Weight's the main problem, so we sweated off enough between us—"

"It's still a serious offence. Who is he, anyhow?"

"Ryly, Chaz Ryly. An American, citizen of Illinois, I think."

International repercussions, marvellous. I tapped up a request for any form the European files had on him. "What is he, anyway? Some kind of political refugee?"

The desk screen answered me. *Ryly, Charlze Bron* was indeed an Illinois citizen, now domiciled in Praha, Czecho, as an accredited representative of the Chicago-World Free Media League.

"He's an acrep? A medman? I see. But he didn't get by the machines that quickly on any press pass. I'd have been consulted before one was issued, anyway. So how did he get through?"

Whittaker hesitated, then delved into his pocket, pulled out something and tossed it onto my desk. A slim blue-and-gold plaque. My hair almost curled as I picked it up; it was only the third or fourth I'd ever seen. It opened down one long edge, rather like an old-fashioned paper-type book, to reveal a complex, swirling pattern on its inner surface, silver on black and fantastically detailed and intricate. Palm and fingerprint patterns interwoven so completely that the human eye couldn't separate them. But each separate network of lines was easily distinguishable by a machine, and so inlaid into the structure of the thing that any attempt to alter them would ruin it completely. A simple and elegant way of making a universal pass for that rare elite who could come and go as they liked on the strength of their identity alone; no doors were closed to it and no prior clearances needed. There were only a few thousand pass-holders, a tiny percentage even of the BC elite. They'd been using this kind of pass since the last century; this particular design was recent, a reintroduction of an elegant model of half a century or more ago. Or was it? I looked more closely, and saw I was wrong. It was one of the old originals.

I glared at the priest. "You can't jinx these things, you know? Not with pattern-prints, skin moulding or overlay, not even the holder's severed hand—they tested for that, the machines can tell. There's only one way it can be done, and that's if the holder cooperates. If he's got unusually long arms, long enough for someone to slip by underneath while he keeps his palm on the machine's reading plate. And then the holder's stuck, himself. He can't use his pass again, the machine will notice. And sooner or later he'll have to explain why he's one place while the machine says he's another. It's assumed that people with these passes don't need to resort to high jinks like that, anyway." Whittaker smiled faintly. "But you—you've already got your second clearance, haven't you? In another name, on another dossier—"

"All perfectly official," said Whittaker, a little sadly, and left it at that. There was a lot more I wanted to know—such as what and who he'd been before the BCs decided to write him out of their script half a century back, and how he'd

managed to hang onto that pass. And that was just for starters.
But just then Ryly began waking up, in the usual fit of coughing
and sneezing antistun brings on.

"Sweet fashing—" Then his eyes focussed, and he recognized me. "You sonuvabitch, I'll—"

"You'll sit tight and answer his questions, Chaz," said
Whittaker severely. "He can block the whole departure if he
wants. And we could never afford a second lot of ferry fares.
We'd be ruined, destitute." The words were for Ryly, but the
message was a challenge to me; did I really want to do that
to a group of potential fellow-colonists? I looked over at Ryly,
gripped by another attack of coughing and wheezing, and
wondered. His heavy, rather wooden features looked Caucasian-
Afro-Oriental, a common enough mix in the North American
countries, but his skin was pale when it wasn't going purple.
Recovering, he glared up at me.

"Oh, hey, no, Rev, don't go overboard—don't be so naive!"
The voice was gravelly, the accent peculiar, Standard European
over something harsher and slurred. "There're other ways round
this sort of thing, aren't there?" He was asking me. "So you
can hike the price a little 'cause I came on rough—"

"Are you trying to bribe me? D'you want another little nap
or something? And every fashing charge in the book, when—
if—you wake up—"

Whittaker jerked the medman back into his chair. "That's
enough, Chaz! You can't handle him that way, and you can't
fight him, either! I'll do the talking—"

"For the moment," I said. "Well?"

He looked down at his fingers, twisting and twining. "This
concerns the colonists on the Ship, as well as my party. It was
agreed some months ago that as the largest single group we
were best placed to smuggle Mr. Ryly aboard—"

"Why? He could apply for a press pass."

"You're jokin'!" sneered Ryly. "From a Free Agency? Only
the official mob get onto the Ship, and handpicked hacks at
that!" I could believe that. I wasn't quite sure how I felt about
the Free Agencies myself. There were five of them, all
American-based and backed by agricultural combines, the last
news media operating without official control or censorship.
That was valuable. But they were also a load of muckraking
sensationalists, spending most of their time digging up and
inflating queasy little scandals to titillate the public. As such

they were a useful ally to the keyhole-eyed Social Morality Movement and powergaming BCs. But from time to time they did come up with some good investigative journalism.

"You say the Ship people were involved. The officers as well?"

Whittaker smiled thinly. "Since they're coming with us, the problems are theirs as well. But let's say they have no official cognizance of this particular approach." Meaning they were in it up to their necks. I could guess where that veteran pilot's advice had come from.

"Let's say that, for the moment. What did you need Ryly for so badly? Twenty-five minutes left."

"*I know, damn you!*" snarled Whittaker, then caught himself and went on. "The Ship is in trouble. Serious trouble. Do you remember the message from the first Ship?"

"The Presentation? Sure."

Which was putting it mildly. It had been part of my life for ten years now, and it could still give me the odd sleepless night, excited as a kid over his New Year presents. It had burst upon a world grown dull and introverted, and a humanity growing tired of trying at last. It seemed to me at least, then, that my horizons had finally closed in, that the relative stability of the BC states was the best we could hope for and that we would just have to live with the mess man had made of his home-world. I could only struggle on in the crowded sty, and get my nose as far into the trough as I could. Why not? Where else was there to go?

The Colony then was a dream forgotten, the kind that you awake from miserable with loss. It had been twenty-two years before I was born that the first great Ship had departed, attenuated by Infall to a needle of hot blackness that arrowed out of the system and, it seemed, the minds of men. Officially, it had never been heard from again.

That wasn't so surprising. Even its most fanatical adherents had admitted that the whole venture was a dangerous gamble, only handled the way it was because there were no obvious alternatives. The Ship design, for example, was nothing if not chancy. It was based on the old concept of orbital colonies, self-contained artificial ecologies that were once expected to extend local *lebensraum* more or less infinitely. An attractive prospect, a built-to-order Eden in a giant pressure flask. Until, that was, they discovered that such self-contained ecosystems can't be made to last longer than a decade or so without extensive restocking, of raw materials mostly, from a planet's surface. That made them uneconomic for Earth—all present-day manned orbitals had small ordinary lifesystems; but for the journey to and gradual move onto a colony planet their advantages far outweighed the cost. There was just one problem: Infall misses out on both the swings and roundabouts of relativity, and most notably on time dilation. The subjective length of the journey to E Eridani would be just under eleven years, and essential halts to readjust and overhaul the drive would add a few months; that meant cutting it pretty close with the eco-system. At best it would be declining by then, at worst dead, and the crew with it.

The planet itself was another element of risk. The early DESprobes sent out to nearby stars were equipped to look out for planets and life, but only in general terms. When one of them found *both* while orbiting E Eridani, however, it was followed up by a barrage of more specialized machines, fitted out with scanners, landers, and whole laboratories looking for everything from amino acids to the common cold. Their reports had been overwhelming in terms of quantity, quality and sheer good news. The planet was marginally larger, but otherwise shared every major characteristic with Earth—density, composition, and a substantial satellite to form a barycentre with an orbit tracing a path through the star's liquid-water zone that gave it a broadly similar seasonal pattern to Earth. And it was the same age as the Earth. All those factors, said the experts after they'd hurriedly rewritten a few theories, made it almost inevitable that life should have developed there. And since the conditions were so similar, so—equally inevitably—were its chemical reactions. And once that was settled, straightforward evolutionary convergence, the same force that made fish, icth-yosaurs and dolphins look alike, did the rest. The likeness wasn't perfect; for a start, an age difference that was astronomically insignificant made a lot of difference to life, which hadn't been out of the sea for long out there. And while it was also based on DNA chains, they weren't in the least compatible with ours. The two forms couldn't interbreed or catch each others' viruses, though there was nothing to stop either digesting at least some alien forms. If we took along whales, we wouldn't need to take plankton as well.

All of which seemed like a gift for colonization, a world

on which we could live, onto which we could ease ourselves gradually with the minimum of disruption, not repeating the blunders and destruction we had created on Earth. Our life forms would probably block the alien evolutionary progression, but hopefully not extinguish it altogether. It seemed almost too good to be true. But man had known since the early days of the Viking probes that machines can only find what they have been designed and programmed to look for. The probes had been made as independently intelligent as was possible in those days, but they could still have missed something beyond their designers' experience or anticipation, even something potentially deadly.

The first colonists thought that a risk worth taking. But with so many other risks as well it was easy enough to believe that at least one hadn't paid off, and that the whole venture had come to a dark and distant end. From time to time there were rumours that something had been heard, but it never amounted to anything. The media, and especially the Free Agencies, would occasionally fill slack time with nut reports, claims that messages from the colonists had been received telepathically or encoded in com static or by religious revelation. I remembered one man, claiming to be some kind of Christian archcardinal or something, who was a particular favourite with the main European agency. With them around any genuine messages were all too easily buried. Until the Presentation, that is.

At staff college we'd discussed the Colony's fate officially, nodded our heads in wise agreement with the official verdict— bold, foolhardy, wasteful and foredoomed—and then sneaked up to the maser receivers and trained the antennae onto Eridanus in pure rebellious hope. Of course, we got nothing but mush, which we sieved through amateurishly in illicit computer time, drawing, of course, a total blank. I gave up, graduated, and with no family pull was glad enough to find an unglamorous but independent posting on the new embryo Sea Station, then moored off Rügen. I grew as it grew, forgetting all the wilder dreams I'd once had and quite happily occupying myself with laying hands on deserving petty criminals, thieves, frauds, killers, saboteurs and even the odd spy. And yet all those years, though I didn't know it, I was only marking time, and waiting.

The change came suddenly, when one day a maser beam of spectacular power—I hated to think of someone crossing it nearer the source—lanced abruptly through Earth-Mars com links. That in itself was impossible to overlook, and when the boys up there at Jomsborg-Marinères began to get pictures out of it, they raised such a howl that soon every spare maser set-up on Earth was headed the same way, drinking in the repeated message. It was a skilful bit of work; there must have been some good PR men among that first thirty thousand. And more than that; to send so powerful a beam the colonists must have bled themselves of all but their most essential power supplies for months, diverting most of the Ship systems plus whatever they could pick up from their new sun. Their Ship must have become a cold shadowy vault in which plant life struggled to live against the cold of space creeping in. But it was worth it. It was a *shout*.

It was the visuals that did it, good though the words that went with them were. They made the best possible case for sending men rather than robots into space, because there was a whole new aspect to the Colony that those joyless machine minds had never bothered to comment on. It was almost impossibly beautiful, a treasure chest of a world that the Colonists spilled out in front of us. Viewers trapped in an airless land-scape, overfarmed, overcrowded and rank with centuries of pollution, were suddenly confronted with scenes that might have come from ancient photogravure or even paintings, or simply out of their dreams. And yet there was nothing alien about them, and paradoxically that was the most alien thing of all. Wild empty mountains reared high against an impossibly blue sky, a sight we were hardly used to, and yet to most of us it seemed instantly right that their slopes should be uninhabited and the air against which their snowcaps blazed be so clear. Our own world, the only one we'd ever seen, began to look shabby by comparison. Below the mountains, along the gorges and across the floodplains of the great rivers, tangled jungle grew. Its dominant colour was green, but more summery and yellowish, freed by slightly different chlorophyll reactions from the heavy emerald darkness of terrestrial rain forest. Young rock stained the rivers different colours in different parts of the world, reds more vibrant than the Amazon and yellows brighter than the Huang He, and in the north a strange dark blue, a marriage of steel and midnight, that I had once seen a ghost of in Iceland. Beyond the riverine areas vegetation was less exuberant and sure of itself, still picking a careful way into the raw new soil. The plants were mostly sophistications of water forms, not unlike Earthly ferns and cycads, though here and there trunk and leaf analogues had developed. There were no flowers at all, though the innumerable tiny creatures who scuttled and hopped and even flew among the foliage were enough like insects to make use of them. They, too, were adapted water forms, and commonest closest to the sea.

The film followed a great river there, foaming almost scarlet through rapids and cataracts, until it plunged down an enormous chain of waterfalls, higher than Iguaçu and the lowest step almost as wide as Niagara, straight down into steel-shaded ocean with a force that churned and turned its waves as if they were pond-ripples. To one side the high rock-wall stretched out into a promontory, sheltering and calming a bay-sized pool. Here the sun struck down on long lean shapes that flicked and darted in and out of the rougher water, snatching at food it whirled up and returning to bask in the calm. Eight to ten metres long, they had primitive but serviceable endoskeletons, massive armoured heads and toothless jaws that splintered the shells of the things they fed on. Shaped by a fishlike ecological niche, these were just about the largest native lifeforms; next came their principal diet, exoskeletal objects not unlike two-metre crayfish. A brief glimpse had been caught of something potentially larger, a huge humped mass surging uneasily out of distant wavecrests, and then disappearing in a writhe of pale tentacles, but it was thought to be a deep-sea creature like the *Architeuthis* that had once or twice surfaced around the Station.

After the richness of the sea and the coastal swamplands, the uplands, seen from a zep-mounted camera, looked relatively barren; native life hadn't adjusted to the thinner air and extra ultraviolet over a thousand metres or so up. Only smaller, scrubbier variants of the more advanced plants had spread there, crouching among weird windsculpted rock formations. The zep took us through some of the upper river valleys, where there was usually little except lichen-analogues or mere organic films on the waterside rocks. Then, without warning, it plunged us headlong over the rim of another valley and into a vision of greenery. After yellow soil and pallid scrub the sheer richness of it was breathtaking—and so were the implications. For at this altitude conditions were closest to our own temperate zones, and as far as the eye could see the valley brimmed over with the dark greens of Earth. Familiar trees dipped in the wind, and flowers blazed around their roots; terraced fields of grass or grain rippled in the zep's downdraft. Any buildings were lost in the expanse of living growth.

It was the Colonists' showpiece, and the crux of the Presentation. This much they had accomplished in a relatively short time, with only the limited equipment the first Ship had carried. The original plan had sensibly specified that the second Ship should wait until the first Ship was heard from, confirming that the voyage was worth it and detailing what the new Colony would need. But as the years passed and it seemed increasingly likely that the whole venture had failed, the second Ship was allowed to languish. Its expensive ecosystem was not renewed, and its support systems failed or were turned off; darkness, death and decay swallowed all its higher lifeforms, and only micro-organisms which could stand the airless cold survived. The magnificent Ship became an orbiting tomb. Its automated factories were used for some years, but they too were shut down. Before the Presentation arrived plans were well in hand to convert the hulk to "more productive uses."

All that changed. It seemed that the Colonists had been sending messages, after all, from not long after their arrival—messages, at first, with nothing but good news. The voyage, long as it was, had gone without a hitch, the world was even better than the DESprobes had suggested—but the proper equipment was urgently needed, if it was to be approached properly, and not despoiled as Earth had been. This time it was to be seduction, not rape. But only stony silence came back to them, the echo of an empty universe. The messages grew more urgent, more desperate—so much was slipping away from them. Soon they would have to choose—expand onto the planet's surface with inadequate technology and revert to the Industrial Revolution or earlier in two lifetimes; dwindle and fade within the restricted world of their Ship; or return to a homeworld that sent them out with cheers but greeted them now with silence. Perhaps they guessed what was happening, and why. If so, they didn't labour the point, tactfully blaming the apparent non-arrival of their messages on "interstellar conditions." But they did make damn sure this one couldn't be ignored.

It certainly raised a great stormcloud of suspicion on Earth—though maybe not as great as it would have fifty years earlier. The BCs met it with bland regret, the official equivalent of a shrug, and many references to the convenient interstellar conditions. They soon found it wasn't going to be enough. Political rivals sharpened their claws on public outrage and demanded further investigations. With surprising speed the powers that be not only fell in with the popular will but raced ahead of it. In a series of spectacular and well-publicized gestures a bracing message of love and hope was beamed off to the Colony, and a ten-year plan begun to recommission the second Ship and restore its ecology. But many things can happen in ten years. A surprising number of worthwhile projects suddenly found themselves with swingeing cuts in funding, poor areas lost out on promised aid and remedial measures, and even in the most prosperous areas living standards began to look slightly grey round the edges. Not all of this was blamed on the expense of reviving the Ship, of course—not overtly, not at first. But there were still people alive who could remember the economic ruin the Ships had brought on their creators, and the story was given plenty of media exposure. And there were sudden, infuriating, shortages of the commonest essentials, often local, sometimes continent-wide; ration quotas went up and down like people's blood-pressure, so that the wastrel, the hoarder and the reasonable citizen all did equally badly. Officially, just one of those things; unofficially, you always heard "needed for the Ship, I suppose. Can't grumble . . ."

The fanfares sounded rather tinny by the time the place applications were opened, five years on. Just a few months short of departure the Ship was less than two-thirds full, with only half the experienced crew it should have had.

"All because people think of it as wasteful!" blazed Whittaker. "They're afraid to encourage it any more in case their clothes are stripped off their backs and the food snatched out of their mouths—"

"They can't help rememberin' America," said Ryly, a little on the defensive. "Only reason Europe's where it is now. They don't want to go the same way."

"But they don't have to! Cleaning it up and restarting the ecosystem, that was expensive, yes, but not *ruinous*. And you know what they've done since then? Damn near nothing! Cosmetics, that's all! Remember all those media items about beautiful new equipment being installed? It was just about what was there already, left in store or dismantled while the Ship was waiting!"

"I see," I said, and thought for a moment. "And you claim this under-equipping is enough to endanger the Ship?"

"Not the Ship," snapped Whittaker impatiently. "There's nothing to stop it making the voyage—I'd say that's deliberate—except the pointlessness of it. The way it is now, it couldn't do a damn thing when it gets there except double the first Ship's problems. It's got damn near none of the stuff they wanted, the list of things in the Presentation, *none!* Bellamy, for the love of—for pity's sake, man, there's only five minutes left—"

"Six," I said. "And what's your stake in this, Ryly?"

"A story, an exposé, what'd you think? Graft's my speciality."

"Not sex scandals?"

"Another department," he said, quite seriously.

"Wild. What've they got on their door?"

"Bellamy!"

I smiled seraphically and leant over to my sec. "Get onto Flight Control would you? Ask them to hold the ferry lift, my authority. Just till I can sort out a small security hitch and get their passengers loaded. Not much point in lifting without them, anyway. Say, about half an hour, all right?"

"Confirmed, Mr. Bellamy," was the immediate reply. I turned to face two icy glares. "I lied," I explained.

"We noticed," said Whittaker. "But I don't suppose we can throw stones, either."

"Right in one," I said, and tapped my procom. "Rebrov, any problems?"

"None, Chief. Crowded, but they're cooperating. Not happy, though."

"No. Well, start shovelling them on. That'll clear the air a bit."

Whittaker crumpled in his chair, breathing out a great gust of relief. "Bellamy, I—"

"Save it a minute," I told him. "In these particular very special circumstances I'm going to let you go with them." Whittaker stared unbelievingly. "Don't think it's the kind of thing I do regularly. But you're no threat to the security of the ferry or the Ship, so my main brief isn't affected. I'm even going to let the master of martial arts here go with you." That fixed the pair of them, till I added "But it's going to cost you."

Ryly shot Whittaker an *I-told-you-so* look, and turned back to me with a satisfied smirk. "Sure. Your personal account is—?"

"Try to bribe me again and I'll brig you on the spot. Thanks to your little touch of macho, I've got to account for attempted assault and violent arrest, right in front of my own men. I can't just let that go, the way I could have if you'd come along quietly. But I do have the authority to levy fines for minor offences. So—that'll be a hundred and fifty for being drunk while boarding a spacecraft, another fifty for fifth-degree civil disturbance, another two hundred for those people who attacked me. Fair? Four hundred in all."

"No wonder you're not on the take," groused Ryly, fiddling with his procom. "The fines racket must—"

"Guess again. That account number's SpaceDep Penal Account 450. A receipt goes into your personal files and a record of the charges and your guilty pleas into your dossier." I enjoyed watching him bubble with impotent fury over that. "It's the law," I pointed out. "And it is your own fault, after all."

"I'm afraid he's right, Chaz," said Whittaker sadly. "But couldn't you credit those charges to me? Put them on my dossier? I won't be here to worry about them, after all."

"Well—" I'd no reason to be doing either of them any more favours, least of all Ryly. I'd stuck my neck out a mile already. But I'd already been thinking about the Simoneau problem, and the limitation he could be on my activities. I might have uses for Ryly yet and so much the better if he owed me one. Besides, I wasn't in the business of humiliating people. "All right. It should be possible. He was using your pass, after all. Which reminds me—get the thing out of here, will you? I don't want to know about it. And whatever you do, don't ever use it again! Burn it, chuck it in the sea, take it off to Epsilon Eridani, I don't care."

"How'm I supposed to get back?" howled Ryly.

"Easy. Apply for a pass to visit the Station. Won't matter which way you're coming from. I'll see you get it. In fact . . ." I tabbed up a form. "Fill that in now and I'll have it waiting for you. Use the fingerprint window there, voiceprint there, forget the bloodtype and so on. Purpose of trip—say, the increase in smuggling over the last few weeks. You want an interview, I'll give you one." And Simoneau would have kittens. "Well, Rev, while he's doing that, why don't you go up and help sort out your flock? But save the glad tidings until you're on board and my guards can't hear, right?"

Whittaker began woofing thanks, but I cut him off as sharply as I could. He stopped at the door. "That's twice. If I can ever help you—But I hope we meet again, anyway."

The form was as long as forms usually are, and it was getting close to time when I bustled Ryly up and through the open turnstile again. All the emigrants were aboard and my guards just hanging around in the empty departure room. With a crush like that they'd done well, and I let them go, saying I'd take Ryly out myself. On the halt platform I tripped over something repellent, a child's stuffed toy animal of no known species and about as appealing as a zep accident. Still, somebody probably cared about it. I picked it up by one appendage, and saw Ryly convulsing with silent laughter. The railcar's polished flank showed me why.

There I stood, a short blocky figure scowling out from under a thatch of thick chestnut hair. That much I was used to. But it was the expression that did it. A face like anybody else's, but set in fixed lines of chill diabolical distrust and suspicion, the eyes narrowed and opaque above cheeks that were hard planes, the mouth set and rigid. The very intensity of it was almost alarming. And yet my face was quite relaxed; that was its natural expression.

The animal made it hilarious, of course, as if I'd arrested it on suspicion of being an enemy alien. But I was quite shocked. It wasn't the way I thought of myself, the face I remembered in the mirror. I looked like somebody else altogether—a specific somebody, one I disliked. Simoneau! I'd seen him drop that suave smile often enough, and look like—me. Whether the imitation was conscious or otherwise, I wasn't flattered. I told Ryly to stop braying, chucked the beast down beside the driver's seat and thumped the control buttons. The railcar rose on its magfields and slithered off, but I drove in a daze.

Ferries seldom carried so much human cargo; the workshops had had to fit out two holds with life-support and extra seating. It was all a bit rudimentary, but the emigrants were chattering cheerfully enough as they strapped themselves into their crash-webs. I off-loaded Ryly, and someone who recognized the toy directed me up to one of the proper passenger lounges. Silence fell there, too, until my prize was vociferously claimed by a small girl strapped in in one corner. As I leant across the blanket-wrapped form next to her to hand it over, the body stirred, looked up and nearly jumped sky-high when we came face to face. It was the girl I'd flattened with the goad, unmistakably the little one's mother. Fortunately she didn't scream, so I was able to explain my rescue mission and get tremulous thanks instead.

"No problem. But make sure she doesn't leave it on the ferry, eh? I'm damned if I'm coming that far with it, then! Er—how are you feeling?"

"Pretty bloody," she said weakly, clutching the blanket at her throat with nervous fingers. "Not looking forward to take-off . . ."

"It's smooth, don't you worry. Not like on the fliks. You'll be fine in half an hour or so, anyway; antishock works quickly. I'm really sorry I had to—"

"No," she said, with a faint smile, "don't worry about it, I was being stupid. I panicked. I should've known you wouldn't mean us any real harm, you've a kind face . . ."

"You've *got* to be joking—"

"No, really," she insisted. "When you smile it makes all the difference. And your eyes—"

I couldn't help myself, I had to kiss her. She didn't scream then, either, just looked at me with wide eyes. At that moment, though, the launch lights flickered on, and I realized I was in danger of getting carried away in several senses.

"What's your name?"

"Maurya—Maurya Merikanto. You're—"

"Mark Bellamy. Happy new world, Maurya. Take care."

Flight Control, annoyed at the delay, sounded the launch klaxons before I was halfway back. I had to drive like hell, and all I saw of the launch was the cloud of steam that enveloped me. But I didn't need to see more. I knew they'd be all right.

FOUR

"AND so died Carlsen..." Ryly's voice was quiet, almost lost in the soughing of the trees. Autumn came to Vienna on a cold wind off the steppes, and the sun, dipping behind the hills, was taking what warmth and colour there was with it.

"That's it." I said, when he didn't go on.

"And just your word for it? No other evidence?"

"The word of the girl who was with me. But nothing else."

"I didn't tell him Kirsty was with me in Vienna. Not that I didn't trust him—I'd done some very thorough checking on him while he was in space—but I didn't want her a millim further into this than she needed to be. I'd wangled her a pass to the city's museums and galleries, and left her to get her cultural rocks off while I contacted Ryly. That suited her right down. As the daughter of a minor land-manager, she'd never been able to set a foot outside Britain—no money and no perks of rank. With her mind that must have been torture, like being in the Middle Ages, or in prison. Now, as the new mistress of a middle-ranking official, she was grabbing at life with the same single-mindedness she'd directed at me that eventful night in the fields. It was a little exhausting, but I reckoned I could stand the pace. In fact, doing so had somehow become rather important to me, and not just because she'd provide a good cover for my trips ashore.

After having hardly stirred off-Station for three years, though, I did need one, especially if my plans for Ryly came off. I'd hauled him in as if for interrogation when he came back from the Ship a fortnight later, and set up this meeting. It was convenient for him, based in Czecho. He'd been quite eager then, scenting a useful contact if nothing more, but now he was looking distinctly uneasy.

"Nothin' else," he repeated, his odd accent deepening for a second. "Just two accounts, unsupported. . . . Listen, you bein' what you are, you must see I can't touch this, not now. Not that I don't believe you. Our local stringers picked up on the crash, as you'd expect; got nothing beyond some local colour the official reports didn't bother with, nothing interesting. But I remember their reports comin' in, and some of the details tie in with your story. Maybe if I'd heard it at the time. . . . But Carlsen's just ashes in a wall-niche by now—who can prove what killed him? And that jacket's with the Department, or with Davy Jones. And the probe's near as far away's Carlsen is. So how can I help you?"

"The murder's hard to prove, yes. But it's got to be part of something bigger, much bigger. Something centering round that goddam probe—where it came from, where it's heading, what it's meant to do. It's got to be something along its timeline—hasn't it?"

"Sure it has. But—"

"I want to trace that timeline. Back into the past and forward into the future. The future means finding out the course it was launched on, for a start.. That's mostly a matter of finding a way into X thousand files, or even tracking the thing if we still can. I guess I can do that. But tracing the thing to where it came from, finding out who made it, what they built into it—I can't spend enough time off-Station to do that properly. And you've more experience of that kind of inquiry, anyway."

"Meanin' muckrakin'," said Ryly, thoughtfully. The wind whipped the hood of his coat up round his ears, and he tugged it on, shadowing his face. "I don't know, Bellamy, I don't know . . ."

"I'd help you, of course. Any way I could. And if this thing breaks, it'll give you the story of the year, the decade maybe."

"Think I need you to tell me that? We could use somethin'

like that, I'll admit. Big stories mean more money from the backers; some of that floats my way, fine. But I don't know. . . . It means trying to crack SpaceDep for kickoff, and that's bad news. Too full of sonovabitching security men—*aren't they?*" There was a sudden glint of teeth in the parka. "Hell, why'm I even *talkin'* t'one? Must be mad!"

"Not to mention freezing your ass off in the Vienna Woods. OK, so it's difficult—"

"It's more'n fashin' difficult! You're so damn right I've more experience with this. Just to get one small lead I usually have to go through twenty, maybe thirty contacts. In SpaceDep? When all it takes is one that won't play along? 'Cause one's all it takes! One bleat to Security and me and the Agency are in deep—"

I held up my hand to interrupt. "Suppose you could be sure your contacts were reasonably safe to approach? That they were the kind of people who'd be likely to be bribable? Or, if you had some hold over them, so they'd be unlikely to squeal?"

Ryly cocked his head to one side. "Big Rock Candy Mountain," he grunted. "You're talkin' about where the good investigators go when they get found out. Or you're talkin' about dossiers, psych-files, security records—"

"I'm not talking about anything. If you have that information, will you help me?"

Ryly scuffed the ground with a toe, kicking up a swath of rotting leaves. The wind grabbed them and sent them whirling down the steep path. He turned to watch them go, and said nothing.

"It wouldn't quite be this whatever-it-is mountain of yours," I went on. I had him hooked, I was sure of it. "Staff who blot their dossiers don't get the sensitive jobs, they don't know much. But then you won't be wanting people who know *too* much—"

"Right," said Ryly, "or they'll have a fair idea why they shouldn't be tellin' it to me. Just the little people, with the little bits of info that they can't see the harm in givin' me— doormen, cleaners, data-poolers, despatchers—"

"Go along with me and you might be able to aim higher than that," I told him. "You'd be amazed the jobs some people can get, these days . . ."

"If they happen to be somebody's nephew? Hell, Space-Dep's gettin' to be just like everywhere else, isn't—" He turned, caught sight of my face, and didn't finish.

"It is," I said wearily. "And that's one reason I'm doing this. I don't expect you to share my reasons, but there's just got to be a good story somewhere in it for you. And I'm sticking my neck out an astronomical distance to give it to you—*Sod you, Ryly, are you going to do it or not?*"

"Oh sure," he said soothingly, "sure. Didn't I say?"

Actually I wasn't sticking my neck that far out. He'd get the dossier data he needed in various anonymous ways, through untraceable data transfers or dataprom memories left at various drops for his local stringers. They were going to make unsavoury reading.

"—and any other sexual deviants approaching treatment level; alcoholics, practising and incipient, ditto; petty thieves and fraudsters; gamblers, compulsive or just plain stupid; dope addicts, known or suspected, all levels; political unreliables—"

"There won't be many of those," I told him. "And most of them are innocents with African connections; they're usually just itching to show how loyal they are, preferably by turning in someone who isn't."

The medman shuddered. "Right, I've run into a few of them myself—too close, once. How about gospodies?"

"Religious? Who cares about them?"

"Not everyone. Enough, though; at the higher levels mostly, but it's filtering down gradually. Guess it hasn't reached you yet. Where you work you'd never have gospodies to deal with. They'd never get that far. Whittaker said somethin' about that."

"And that I didn't believe him? Score one to him, then. But I won't be setting them up for you; they've got troubles enough."

"OK, I guess," said the medman unconcernedly. "Unless I get desperate. Which I may."

He had one more suggestion to add, and it was a good one.

"In among the addicts—single out the weedfreaks. Especially if we're goin' that little bit higher—young office management, that kind of thing."

"Right, they're the classic addict pattern—young, ambitious, nervy, half in love with stress. And the tobacco habit doesn't impair them much—can even help them, in the short term. But it'd be a black mark against them—" I stopped short. There was a slight extra chill in the dank air, something the gathering gloom couldn't quite account for. Ryly's heavy features stood out against it, startlingly pale. And there was the wind, and the distant sounds of the city, and the faint sigh of his breathing. I shouldn't have been able to hear it, but I could. I remembered him coming round after I'd hit him, wheezing, rasping, coughing; I'd though it was just a severe antistun reaction. And he was young enough, and ambitious, and certainly nervy, the way he'd lashed out at me then. Not just fear of being found out; he must have been carrying, if he was going away for a week or two. And so the poor bastard would die young, between fifty and eighty most likely, of cancer or gangrene. Better than the psychochemical rot of other drugs, maybe, but still—

Still, it shouldn't make him less useful. And it gave me another small hold over him, not that I expected to need one.

The wind was biting now, and there was a drizzle working its way to us across the city below. I could see it glisten across the roof of the Stefansdom Museum, and hoped Kirsty was enjoying herself; I'd have to go pick her up soon. But there was one more thing to settle with Ryly, the most dangerous. Personal contact was going to be chancy, even in spots like this one, sheltered by trees from long-range mikes and easily checked for local police monitors. But meet we must, to report, compare notes and brainstorm, the only way to get the best out of our scraps of data; face-to-face is always safer than the best-shielded comsystem. So we worked out rendezvous points at regular irregular intervals, with covers, dummies and fallbacks; these would fit into my long weekends with Kirsty.

"Edinburgh, Athinai, Praha—kind of close to home, that . . ."

"I've a good cover reason." Kirsty, so help me, for the opera.

"Oh, OK. Rio—*Rio?* If you want sun, what's wrong with Split or Yalta?"

"Everything, I've—"

"I know, I know. A good cover reason. Mr. Securicop. Rio it is."

And that was a kind of prophecy, because in a number of ways, Rio it was. We left the Wienerwald by separate paths; mine ended at the high cityside fence. I scaled a tree with no detectors in it, and swung down onto a sidewalk emptied by the rawness of the evening. I decided to walk a few blocks before registering on the cameras in a *Strassenbahn* car. The night was chill, but I could scent warmer things ahead—Kirsty, yes, and *Glühwein,* and something else, hotter and spicier. Like blood.

But over the next couple of months that scent cooled. It was hard to feel like a hound on the track when I had to spend all my time tethered to a console, weaving an incredibly delicate path through vast and intricate information structures. Sometimes, concentrating furiously, I seemed to see them looming over me like a skyscraper city of infinite heights and depths. The glowing dot of my screen cursor wove a strange, roundabout path along back alleys and little-used pathways, snatching at what scraps it found. A lot of the time I was running two or three borrowed or bogus (but carefully established) identities at once, working through a chain of them with one or two neutral clearing-houses interspersed. As often as I could I would split the data up and route it into unsecured clearing areas where I could draw on it unchecked, or into safe dumps such as regular reporting files that came my way automatically. To some extent the effort paid off; I was able to compile lists for Ryly without leaving enquiry records that could be traced back to me, even in departments such as Supply and Personnel, where I had less direct authority. I'd planned to do what Ryly was doing myself, but with Simoneau around I had to watch my step; in any case Ryly, with experience, time and his agency's money to add carrot to the stick I provided, was doing it much better. By our second meeting, on a wet icy day in Edinburgh's Leith dockland, he had found out which SpaceDep workshop the probe had been despatched from; all I had to offer was confirmation that someone had been doing heavy checking on all SpaceDep pilots around the time they would have been planning the launch. My real objective, the course, was as far out of reach as ever.

The carrier's launch run was on record, of course, looping out to a fairly wide orbit. The probe itself could have been fired off at any point along that, in just about any direction that didn't cross main traffic vectors. Then there would have been records of it everywhere, marked out in large red arrows. As it was there was nothing. Normally Carlsen would have entered his flight orders in Station files, which would automatically copy to HQ databases, and from there to every Flight Control in the world, even Africa. Space safety transcended national rivalries, almost. Now, though, there was something in the way, a flat security block as unyielding as anything I could construct myself, that simply stood there and referred you to HQ Security, Duty Officer. That was at the first access I tried; when I attempted to bypass it by cross-reference from another secure file I hit a security trap I only just backed out of in time. Someone less experienced would have been caught. It was nothing terrible in itself, but there was no way out of it without leaving proof of identity and reasons for inquiry; if you tried to break contact your comlink would be held and traced in a millisecond. Since, for obvious reasons, you couldn't access secure files through public coms, that would have put me right under the official eye, where I could least afford to be right now. For the next week or two I worked on various ideas, progressively madder, for by-passing block or trap. None of them worked; the trap turned out to be a virus program, a virtual entity in the files which simply recreated as many copies of itself as were needed to meet each stimulus. Creating any kind of gap supplied the stimulus that put a trap in it.

So, when I scrunched through the grimy snowdrifts that had built up in Praha's winding backstreets, I was almost as empty-handed as before. "It's got to be well away from almost every standard route, or they wouldn't dare keep it this quiet. But that still covers a hell of a lot of space, I can tell you."

"Well, d'you have to depend on the files so much? Couldn't you track it?"

I stared down at the greasy little tabletop—typical Supply diner—and wondered if Whittaker's old boss, the hygiene charges one, could still be in business. "That's difficult. Tracking gear's sensitive stuff; what the military don't keep clamps on, the BCs do. I've sounded out one or two Station people— you know we can turn the whole goddam place into a radio-telescope, using the damper fields and the lagoon surface? Fact. But I'd have to come up with a really good reason for using it, and I don't know where I'd find any other gear I could use. Hellfire."

Ryly did his best to sound sympathetic, but it was clear he was beginning to cast himself as the Great Detective, with me in the role of Idiot Cop. I could hardly blame him; he'd been busy tracing back the various components of the probe to their points of manufacture. "Even got to see a requisition for part of the guidance system—*deep-space research, unspecified,* it

says. Shee, cheer up, Bellamy! You look haunted, or somethin'."

I was haunted, by a number of things. For a start, my
professional pride was taking a beating. That I might have
shrugged off if I hadn't been so acutely aware of other things:
passing time, and the other problems it was carrying nearer.
My place on the Ship, for one; I had till next June to decide
on that, no longer. And, interwoven with that, my relationship
with Kirsty. I'd gone to Scotland to try and shrug off a few
ties; instead, I'd acquired my single most important one. One
thing I knew; she wasn't interested in coming with me. How
easy would I find it to leave her behind? This afternoon she
was off on one of her little literary pilgrimages, in the footsteps
of a classical writer. She'd made me read some; I had to admit
he was good, but right now Kafka was hitting me just a bit too
close to home.

A week or two later I was desperate. It was evening, my eyes
bleary from hours at a desk screen achieving precisely nothing.
Ryly had left me with one solid suggestion, but I didn't like
the idea at all. "Listen, if you can't break this block, maybe
someone else can. What you're givin' me works like a charm—
why not do yourself a favour? Find a Flight man you can bend?"
I'd already thought of that myself of course, but drawn a blank,
as I'd expected. Flight Control men tended to be sound and
stable, or they ceased to be Flight Control men. I did have
influences other than fear and coercion; it was just that I hesitated to involve someone else. But now I had reached the end
of my tether. I stood, stiffly, and hobbled out into the corridor.
I would have liked to go outside to clear my head a little, but
it was blowing a fine winter gale; I'd risk being brained by a
flying icicle. The nearest lift scooped me upwards more comfortably. It wasn't far to Khalid's door, but I took my time
getting to it, and hesitated before I pressed the doorcom. I
nearly didn't.

Khalid, after all, was a friend of sorts. He was also a security
problem. He was an nth-generation English Arab, descended
from someone who'd had the sense to take the money and run
before the oil ran out. His ancestral homeland had gone the
way of all the other oil sheikhdoms, a savage decline and fall
abetted by all the enemies they'd made in wealthier days. Khalid

still had relatives there, and sent them money when he could. He had even been there once or twice, and as they were practically African colonies, riddled with Junta agents, this sent eyebrows through the roof in HQ Security. Khalid knew he owed me several for fending them off, and that made it paradoxically harder to ask him for what I wanted. But he was the only Flight man I dared ask, and so I did.

He was in the middle of dinner with some poor girl at the time—she had to take refuge in the showerroom while we talked—but he was ready to go rushing up to Control to file an inquiry right away. He was definitely the enthusiastic type. I managed to talk him out of that without actually telling him why I wanted the course information—it would be far safer for him if he didn't know. He would just be making a routine inquiry, that would be all. The worst authority would do would be to pin his ears back a little, and that he was ready enough to risk. I could only hope he wouldn't start talking out of turn in his sheer enthusiasm; he was far too open and easy-going. It made him a good controller, and an awful spy. He was to take his time, bring the matter up casually next time he was talking shop with his contacts at HQ Flight Control, see if he could get them interested enough to start nosing around. That would obscure who was actually doing the asking. And HQ controllers had high Security clearances, because they had to have access to military spacecraft movements; they might be trusted where Khalid wouldn't.

I knew it would take time, but at least I had something to report to Ryly while we strolled around Athinai. It was a late drizzling January, only a little warmer than out in the Atlantic, and the Acropolis wasn't worth a second look since the last African raid. This time it was Ryly's turn to be nonplussed.

"You know, I thought seein' that budget outline would be the biggest break yet—just a skeleton outline of some departmental costs, a dump copy that hadn't got wiped yet. But it has a budget with the same number as the requisitions for the probe components. . . ."

"And?"

"It's too goddam big, it's ten times too big. And that's only over a year, but it's obviously ongoin'. They could be buildin' a whole fleet of probes for that! Either it's carryin' costs for somethin' else, or that probe is just the tip of the iceberg— some iceberg! And there's somethin' else. I thought I'd accounted for all the main components of the probe, where they were made and so on. But a little guy in Transport found me a transit notice to the probe's assembly workshop, dated the same time as all the others, for somethin' really huge, bigger than half the other pieces put together. I'm goin' to have to trace that too . . ."

I got Khalid's answer more than a month later. At half past three in the morning, in fact, when the rasp of the com jerked me out of a dream about Kirsty.

"Mark, hey Mark! You awake?"

"I am now—"

"Good, good, afraid I'd be disturbing you, but Mark, I couldn't sleep with this, it just came through! You know what those shit-stupid bastards in HQ have done? They've gone and filed a fashing fake course, is what the fuckers have done—"

If I'd been more awake I might have been able to stop him mentioning the course over the com. Also, if I hadn't been distracted by the sight of his girl Marsha disappearing hurriedly into the showerroom again. Khalid was so hopping mad he'd forgotten to dim the video. As it was, the damage was done; it would look more suspicious if I shut him up hurriedly. Small chance of that, though.

"A friend of mine filed an official request with Security, and this is what they gave him—look!" He tapped out the figures all over my screen. I ground my teeth, and did my best to look unconcerned.

"Well? They're viable vector coordinates, even I can see that—"

"But they are not, not for the present arrangement of the System! I checked, and you know what they are? The course one of the early DESprobes took, is what! To Alpha Centauri!"

"Couldn't they be sending another?"

"No!" howled Khalid furiously. "When that probe was launched they would have been meaningless! Someone just looked them up and copied them, someone who doesn't know outer-system navigation, someone who thinks the bloody Earth stands still! Probably some bonehead securicop! You don't go giving controllers fake courses, *ever!* We're hopping about it!"

"So I see," I said wearily, and yawned to get time to think. Angry or not, Khalid had been damn silly to spread this all over the com, but I wasn't too worried; I'd made sure over the years that it was impossible to tap the internal system without the cooperation of the Sea Station Security, me. But I wasn't planning to take any chances, and I wanted to get him and his HQ friend off the hook if I could. I gave Khalid as direct a look as I could manage at that time. "If I were you," I went on carefully, "I'd tell your friend to forget all about it. I agree, it probably was sent from Security or somewhere—as a way of telling you to mind your own business. Didn't I say that's what they'd do? Serves you right, you nosy bugger!"

Khalid's brown features went an incredible shade of purple, and his eyes, bulging at the best of times, looked ready to up stakes and go, but he caught on quickly. "Security men!" he grunted. "You're as bad as the rest of them! Why'd none of you ever give a straight answer?"

"Maybe," I said cheerfully, "because we're never asked straight questions. See you in the morning!"

I turned over, wide awake now, and thought. We had to keep this looking like sheer curiosity and not organized investigation; I'd brief Khalid on that in the morning. My mind was more on the course that wasn't. It proved one thing; the real course was the secret, or a large part of it, enough to warrant absolute secrecy even to trustworthy people who had a real right to know. If the HQ controllers couldn't get the course, very few other people could.

That left only tracking the beast. The Station wasn't up to it, and I couldn't think of any better outfit I could use. Then how on Earth. . . .?

And that was it. I sat bolt upright in bed. A good idea, an amazing one as it developed. It could solve a whole load of my problems, and it would let me keep a promise to Kirsty, at least. I'd keep it as a surprise for her. It would be Rio next, wouldn't it? Then maybe I'd have a surprise or two for Ryly, as well.

"Oh, there ye are!" snorted Kirsty, not sounding overjoyed by her discovery. "Listen, you, I've been huntin' about all over this place for you! Why couldn't we meet at the Dumfries zep station same as usual?"

"What's wrong with Prestwick Central?"

"About two thousand Glaswegians, plus you, is what! I was only standin' there ten minutes an' I was propositioned three times—"

"Accept any?"

"I should have! What's got intae ye? Ye're daft enough as a rule, but no' this bad—"

"The effect you have on me. . . ." I purred, and scooped her up. She was about to fell me till she noticed the outraged little man with the Social Morality badge, and flung herself into the embrace with total enthusiasm.

"Seriously, pig," she said when we came up for air, "why here?" Then she stiffened suddenly. "Ye're in uniform! Ye're no' in trouble—no' the—"

"Trouble? Hellfire, no." I laughed, I'd tantalized her long enough. "Come on, grab your gear and let's go!"

"But the zep park's over there!" she protested as I led her down a much quieter corridor off the main Prestwick concourse.

"I didn't come by zep. Transatlantic takes forever in a zep. We're going in style—" A heavy door in front of us sighed aside as I flashed my landing pass at it, and the human sentry inside gave me the full salute treatment, all clenched fist and clicking heels. He also gave Kirsty the eye, so I returned the salute with the kind of smug smile that sparks off mutinies. I couldn't really blame him, though; my extra clothes rations and credit had done a lot to enhance Kirsty's natural outline. Neither of us liked the overtones of this—"too much like the usual wee burycrat an' his tart," as Kirsty put it—but it made sense, and it kept her parents quiet. And Kirsty, despite herself, was impressed by the trappings of authority we were passing through now. It was nothing like the concrete jungle outside; the walls were decorated, the flooring was soft and silent underfoot, there were plenty of empty seats and it was quiet. And when I led her through into a smaller, quieter lounge that was actually carpeted, and had an automatic bar, her eyes popped.

"What've ye done, blackmailed a BC prince? Or screwed one?"

"Nothing so crude. Just applied some tact, discretion and back pay in the right quarters. This is the departure point for personal airspacers."

"Personal—" It took a lot to make Kirsty speechless, but she didn't say a word while I flipped our passes into an ultra-modern P-P terminal. I had to fight off the urge to rip it up and take it back to replace my Station machines. It bounced the passes back respectfully, and the sentry here did an even snappier salute, and ignored Kirsty completely. I hurried by in

case he eyed me instead, and onto the moving floor that led
to my parking bay. Kirsty was just getting her voice back when
we arrived, and she saw the sleek outline, gleaming the colour
of old burgundy, sitting quietly in its stall. Her eyes gleamed
and her grip tightened on my arm, but I knew it wasn't because
she was impressed by the looks or the price or the prestige of
the thing. About those she didn't give a damn, and that suited
me. It was the potential of it that was making her breath shorten
and her body quiver the way it did in the first stages of love.

"Then ye hadn't forgotten!" she breathed. "I didn't want
tae remind ye—it'd be so expensive—oh, ye fool, fool! It
must've—"

"Nothing I couldn't afford," I assured her, fumbling with
the unfamiliar lock. The door hummed aside, opening straight
into the little cabin. "A sort of airlock tent inflates in here when
you need it—I didn't blow my credit, Kirsty. I rate equivalent
to a police chief or a subdep head, that's quite good credit and
I haven't been spending it. Fewer overheads on the Station, to
make up for the isolation. So—this is registered out in the
name of a higher official, who has unofficially leased it to me
for a month. Quite a common arrangement; I reckon I could
afford it once a year."

"Then—we can just go out into space? Just like that?"

"Any time we want, within this toy's range. But Rio first,
mo chride, and via the upper atmosphere only. I want to get
used to flying this before I try anything fancy, OK?"

Our seats strapped us in, although Kirsty was bouncing
around and squeaking so much hers had a hard job. Still, I was
able to taxi out and take off without too much trouble. Once
we were aloft and on course, though, I switched to autopilot
so I could go back to the tiny bunk space to change out of my
uniform. Kirsty decided to assist, so we stayed on auto for
nearly an hour.

There wasn't much room for luggage in the little cabin, but
in Rio at that time of year we didn't need too many clothes.
Moralidade social had reached the South American Federation,
but even with government encouragement, or perhaps because
of it, it wasn't catching on as fast as it had in Europe. After a
hundred years of near poverty, followed by another of pure
poverty, the Brazilians were still too busy enjoying their relative
prosperity. Even so, the scars hadn't all healed yet; on our way
in to the Galeão station we could see the masses of *favela* towns

crusted like a rash on the flanks of the surrounding hills, from
Pão de Açúcar up to Corcovado itself. They flowed down like
lava around the feet of the few huge hotel blocks still standing
along the Ipanema beachfront, and were spreading along to
Copacabana itself.

"Some of the *favelas* are state-licensed, or even main-
tained," I explained. "They were becoming a tourist attraction,
for the kind of tourists who get kicks out of squalor and violence—bargains in the *favelado* markets, cheap sex down every
street. Great for repressed Europeans. But when the violence
started to include them they squealed. So some of the shanties,
the ones round the hotels mostly, they're just tourist traps."

"What, a' quiet an' sanitized?"

"Hellfire, no! Spoil all that picturesque filth? Just no violence, not to the tourists anyway. And the local BCs sell the
approved markets their bargains wholesale, sometimes at a
subsidized price. Then they cream forty per cent off the top,
with another ten for the local police. That keeps the shanties
looking the way they ought to."

"Wish ye hadna told me that," sighed Kirsty as the Galeão
beam took over, swivelling our jets downward for landing. "I
was hoping I'd like this place."

"Nowhere's perfect. And the real *favelas* keep some human
dignity, at least. Many of the shacks are spotless inside, and
you can even find little cafés. You'll see for yourself soon
enough before we meet Ryly on Tuesday."

Her eyes got the unholy gleam. "We? Ye mean, I get tae
come, for once?"

"I don't like getting you involved, you know that. But, after
dark or anytime, this is one place I'm not leaving you alone
for a minute."

After a day sunbathing and swimming *au naturel,* Copacabana
being one of the few beaches in the world where you could
still do that, our clothes felt harsh and slightly sticky as we
moved through the market. Real, not protected, it was held,
or rather it materialized out of the brief dusk, along one of the
impromptu streets that wound crazily along the slopes of Corcovado. There were a few tables and stalls, but mostly the
vendors just spread their objects out on a cloth in front of them,
ready to be bundled up for a quick getaway into the maze of

sheet iron and plastic hutches behind. Up here there were actually good things for sale; Kirsty found a scarf of real silk, something I'd never seen before, and a very old edition of Shakespeare, probably stolen from some official's villa. I was looking for a guitar, and found several, but none as good as my two and a half century old Sevillia. What I did come across was a rarer treasure, not displayed but offered to me in a tattered food box by two young thugs dressed in parakeet colours and flying high on something. It was an ancient photochemical camera, an engineered jewel half the size of my palm; it dated back to the late 1900s or early 2000s, just before the final triumph of electronic image-making. The price was high, but worth it, with a roll of reusable phototape thrown in. The sellers faded into the evening, giggling happily, and Kirsty and I moved on to a café I remembered from my last visit, run by a full-blooded Quechua Indian called Huascar. By the time we'd drunk tiny cups of his bitter coffee it was abruptly dark outside; I'd forgotten how short the tropical dusk was.

Even in the moonlight the steep street surfaces, rubbish-strewn, unpaved, unlevelled and undrained except for a vague central gutter, were very slow going. It was getting later, much later than I had intended to stay up here, and I was worried. Apart from the occasional whore and/or client, there were few people about. Contrary to dikflik tradition, I had no mysterious sixth sense that we were being followed, but I had no need of one to make me stop, listen and check at times. So the sudden swift patter of feet out of a side alley didn't catch me unawares, and at the first gleam of a knife I had flicked Kirsty aside and against the nearest wall. This was no hold-up; the first attacker grabbed my arms, giggling, and the other's knife swept up straight at my thoat. Using the grip on me as an anchor, I kicked out a foot and scythed the legs from under the knifeman, then twisted in the grip and kicked off the pavement, toppling the other man over on his back with me on top. I landed with an elbow in his diaphragm and a hand on his chin, slamming his head down onto the ground. It was too soft to knock him out properly, but the knifeman was almost on his feet and too close to Kirsty. I kicked hard up into his armpit; the arm convulsed and the knife flew sparkling away. He sprang, body-blocked me into the wall near Kirsty and struck out at my face; I moved, he missed and punched his fist straight through the rust-thinned metal sheet that was that part of the wall. His scream was echoed from inside, but cut off as I slammed him against the wall and broke his throat with the edge of my forearm. I dropped him as the other scrambled up, but he took one look at the wall and ran off straight up the road, yelping. I have mixed feelings about guns; they clutter up your hands, and are too easily taken away and used on you, and in a fast fight could clip bystanders, such as Kirsty. But now I had time to aim; the muzzle flashes lit up the little street. Two bullets at the base of the spine bowled him into an untidy heap blocking the central ditch.

I looked at the other man, hanging motionless from the wall by his wrist. Even by moonlight I recognized him; the blood from his mouth hadn't quite obscured the coarse gaudiness of his shirt. In the shadow next to him I could see the whites of Kirsty's eyes.

"I wonder how many times they sold that camera?" I asked her, and took her by the arm. "C'mon, we'd better be elsewhere quickly."

She didn't move. I pulled her, and she stumbled after me like a sleep-walker. That slowed us, but it was not so far now, and the streets had somehow emptied in front of us. But it was only when we were back on the main streets that I put my gun back in my waistband holster, and I kept my hand near it till we were back at our hotel.

Kirsty, pale and staring, had not said a word. She stripped and tumbled into bed without showering, which was unusual. I got in beside her, stroked the smooth dark hair and down across the soft curve of her back, hot as if it was radiating back the sun of the day. She flinched, and for the first time I heard her sob, faintly.

"You know I had to do that," I said, quietly. "They'd have killed me. And you—eventually. And if one had got away he could have brought lord knows what down on us before we were halfway out of there—"

Kirsty's voice shook. "Ye could, ye could've knocked them out, tied them, called the police—" I laughed, though nothing seemed very funny just then. Kirsty twisted round violently to face me and sat up, eyes blazing. "A'right! A'right, so I'm just a wee country girl who's not knocked ..ound the world like you. So I havena' your sophistication, aye, go ahead, laugh! But ye know what's upsettin' me most? It's that someone I thought I knew—that I thought I could love—

can kill two men, even for the best bloody reason in the world, an' not be a bit worried about it! That's what! Ye're just a cauld-blooded—" She choked on her own fury.

"Not everyone wears their feelings on their sleeves." I wiped away the largest of the tears rolling down her face.

She didn't flinch, but sniffed violently and inelegantly. "Aye, but there's somethin' missin' in ye, ye're too *calm*, Mark! The first time I killed someone I'd—It isna' the first time?" Her face was going grey under the sunburn.

"I'm a cop, Kirsty. You know that. I've killed four people before tonight—three who'd have killed me otherwise, one who was going to kill one of my officers. All in the line of duty; it's one of the things I've been trained for. But not the main thing! Don't ever think that. Or that I ever even remotely enjoyed it, tonight or any other time." She'd drawn up her knees, sunk her head down on them. I laid a tentative arm across her shoulders. They were steady, not shaking, and she didn't flinch. "If you can still—" She flung herself at me like an uncoiling spring, clinging with bruising strength. Now she was crying, certainly. I stroked her hair till things subsided a little.

"Tomorrow," I said, after a while, "we head for space . . ."

Kirsty looked up at me blackly. "A treat tae get the wee girlie's mind off things, eh?"

"No. Tomorrow, because I have to be back in time to meet Ryly. And because after all this ugliness *I* badly need, well, something else . . ."

She murmured something indistinct, and an instant later lips branded my chest, and the warm body in my arms stirred and sank down. So I slept, that night, after all.

When the sun rose the next morning, we were already rising to meet it. There was a climbing corridor right over the summit of Corcovado, where the gospodies had put up a big statue, and I took the little airspacer spiralling up it. City and hills slipped away beneath us, and we could see right to the continent's heart, a great red plain with a few darker areas. That was all that remained of the Mato Grosso, a few patches of rain forest ringed by exhausted farmland, its topsoil ruined by clearance and monoculture, dried and blown by the wind into the red dust that reigned over all. I snorted in disgust, and steppened our climb as much as I dared; there were far fewer official eyes here than in Europe, but I still preferred not to attract attention by hurrying. But when we were well past the tropopause I called to Kirsty to hold on, tilted the nose back and gunned the jets till they screamed. Heavy fingers plucked at us, the sky changed from blue to black in a breath, and Kirsty shrieked with excitement as the navcom cut in the fusor and the thinning air about us erupted into an auroral cloud. Its glory faded swiftly, and we climbed over the world's rim on a needle of intense light.

The navcom chose us an orbit, and I cut acceleration. We had plenty of time, and the longer this looked like just another jaunt, the better. Kirsty sighed, tilting her face languorously to the sunlight spilling fiercely into the little cockpit. "Can I get a tan up here?" she laughed.

I lowered the fieldshield the merest fraction. "Now you can. And so will I." Her chair unstrapped her and she floated free, gratefully peeling clothes off yesterday's sunburn. Drifting there against the sun, her hair a corona, she looked like something mythological. I kicked free of my clothes and surged up to join her.

Love in free-fall is amazing if you avoid corners and hard edges. In this cockpit there didn't seem to be any, and I began to wonder about the design philosophy of these executive airspacers. The navcom rolled the craft gently to keep us in the sun, and all was excellent as on the first day. At last, though, the navcom chimed reprovingly at us, and I regretfully unwound Kirsty's legs from around my neck. In a few minutes the drive-flame grew longer and brighter and our orbit began to widen, climbing sharply outwards. Probably no tracker here or below would pay us any more attention now than they did to the other darting fireflies that shared the sky that morning. I had a cover story ready for our little trip if I needed it, but the chances were I wouldn't. I gunned the drive to its limits, and weight settled dully on us as we accelerated.

Our destination was in geosynchronous orbit in one of the least desirable localities out here, the inner Van Allen. It had been shifted there for a number of reasons; the company of vast amounts of energetic charged particles didn't worry it, it was so big it would be in the way in more popular places, and it suited the BCs to have it out of sight. Which it certainly was.

"That's it? That sort o'black triangle thing?" Kirsty peered at the screen, set on 'scope. "I thought it was a cylinder shape . . ."

"It is. That black outline—it's a broad-based cone, by the way, if you look carefully—that's the Infall fields it's generating. They collect and focus the sunlight on the agricultural greenhouses in the two outer toruses—they're for food production, and restocking the main hull ecology if something goes wrong. So they're completely separate life-systems, they even rotate independently—"

"Aye," said Kirsty absently, peering into the screen as if her eyes could burrow through the blackness created by the Infall fields. I don't pretend to understand the things, but apparently any radiation entering them comes back out more or less randomly dispersed; everything else bounces off. Ships generate them like the walls of a bubble, and communicate with the outside universe on interferometric principles. Calls would be hard to overhear, and that suited me. As we moved outwards we saw more of the flat base of the cone, looking somehow less black than the walls, almost smoky. I trained the com maser on it, and pressed down the microphone button.

"Colony ship from private airspacer approaching. Will identify more fully later. I want to speak to one of your colonists, most urgent—Whittaker, John, er, the Reverend."

"Idiot in the airspacer from the Colony ship," came the quick reply, in a peculiarly lilting male voice. "Hope your fieldshield's in good order, then, coming out here. Categorically deny we have anyone on board of that name or title. What would you be wanting to talk to him about, just bye-the-bye?"

Kirsty giggled. "Colony Ship from perfectly competent airspacer pilot," I said severely. "Tell him it's about that old assault charge . . ."

Twenty minutes later a beam from the Ship was guiding us through what I devoutly hoped was a gap in the Infall shadows. Faint irridescence shimmered about them as we approached, caused by light refraction between them and their weaker cousin, our fieldshield. It intensified for an instant as we passed through, and then Kirsty gave a great wondering gasp of delight.

It was like entering a vast shell, with a strange pearl at its heart. A long cylindrical metallic shape with two slender rings around it turned with ponderous, gigantic ease. The light directed onto the toruses sparkled with almost unbearable brightness. From outside the blackness had conveyed little real sense of scale, but now the stars, the moon, the Earth were blotted out completely. We were alone in the vaulted shadow with the mightiest-ever work of man.

They'd built two of them, then. An international consortium, headed by what was then the single richest nation on Earth, the United States of America and Canada. They couldn't have seen much financial gain in the project; my history courses had mentioned political prestige and the concentration of research that produces so many invaluable spin-offs. But at the root of it all I'd always seen a huge helping of America's original sins: relentless altruism and the frontier ideal. It was as if history hadn't taught them a thing. Costs mounted, lesser nations slid in and out of the project, leaving the burden on the USAC; delays mounted, and public enthusiasm everywhere slowly soured and stifled. People who'd hoped to see the Colony established in their lifetimes died embittered; enthusiastic teenagers became disillusioned fifty-year-olds, capable fifty-year-olds became incompetent centenarians. And meanwhile the Federal government had become so entangled in the project it could hardly run the country; states had to shift for themselves, and the States Rights movement grew. It won enough power to abort the project—and then found that, ironically, it had become the last remaining mainstay of the USAC economy. A hole, in effect, that you had to keep filling or it would grow larger. At least keeping it up brought in a little foreign money and a little time. But it had to end someday, and it did. So, with amazing suddenness, did USAC.

The former superpower fragmented, just as its old rival Russia had in the previous century, into a welter of little states. Federation and central government, blamed for the disaster, became dirty words; the states subsided into a mire of local politics and squabbling, ignoring the world arena. In a quest for individual self-sufficency their economies became increasingly agrarian; industry, no longer national, dropped back. And they cursed the two fat specks of light in the night skies, embodying the wealth that had flowed away from them. The first Ship sailed with a complement of thirty thousand people, a thousand of them fully trained crewmen. They were hand-picked from a thousand times as many applicants. Between official and public disapproval—which could add up to lynch mobs—not one American was among them.

The Ship swelled awesomely above us as the beam guided us in. We were moving towards the flat leading edge of the cylinder, to a point nearer the axis than the rim. As we came closer I could see what had looked like a smooth surface resolve into a bewildering maze of details. The sheer size of that single flat end-piece distorted your notions of direction; we suddenly seemed to be doing a slow-motion crashdive onto some kind of industrial installation, a jumble of pipes, tubes, lights, scaffolding, and other less identifiable things. Some of the scaffolds I reckoned at thirty metres high or more, but they hardly stood out from the surface.

Kirsty was gaping. "The size—I'd seen the pictures, but this—just the end of it's like an island or somethin'—how wide? I canna guess . . ."

"From the figures I remember, the hull's about 33 kilom long, about 5.5 across, and that looks like a straight vertical section. So, yes, not a bad-sized little island, about 23 square kilom—look there!"

Ahead of us a tiny slot, looking about big enough for a hand, had opened, and we were actually accelerating in towards it. The navcom sounded a warning beep, and our chair harnesses embraced us affectionately as the control beam fired our attitude jets to rotate us in line with the slot. It was an individual landing bay, the smallest doorway in a row of about twenty, but still too large for our little craft; the largest was a fullsize freight carrier dock, as large as the Station's largest launch bath. The cradle we settled into was a great clanking affair, old-fashioned and immensely solid; it clasped the little craft as if it was a blown eggshell.

"Evenin', folks," drawled the com, in an accent not unlike Ryly's. I was glad a few Americans were making it this time, anyway. "Welcome to heaven, 20:50 hours, Ship's Time. No bullshit, no BCs, no securicops. Just real hard work. We'll be runnin' a dock tube out to ya any minute, might as well check your clothes 'cause it leads ya straight to the delouser, and it's not worth doin' 'em if y'ain't stayin'. We'll issue ya coveralls at the other end, OK? Someone'll meet ya there."

"Delousin'?" Kirsty was outraged.

"Primitive humour. In a miniature enclosed ecosystem like this you've got to be damn careful what micro-organisms you let on board. That was another trouble with the old space colonies—you couldn't keep things out forever. Sooner or later something got in or mutated, and things degenerated from there. Well, hardly worth getting dressed, was it?"

The quaint-looking sign on the doors said *D-Con*, but the

MEN and WOMEN labels on the inside doors were new; the original builders evidently hadn't cared much about sex segregation. The process consisted of a belt-ride through successive chemical showers, each fouler than the last; this close to the Ship's rotational axis the pseudogravity was less than on the Moon, and the droplets, blasted out at high pressure, hung in clouds around me till they were sucked away through vents. At one point I stood while a filament probe wormed its way under my skin, and drank a cup of something horrible a dispenser pushed out at me. Finally there was a cleansing shower, a hot-air drying and a choice of recyclable coveralls from a dispenser. All of which took five minutes. I was reunited with Kirsty on the other side, at a door which opened onto a wide hall, low-ceilinged and softly lit. A cheerful shout greeted us, and a massive figure strode forward, bouncing absurdly for lack of weight.

I hardly recognized Whittaker at first. His white hair was longer but tidier, he had grown a neat beard to match it, and he had filled out quite considerably. A lot of the reserve and suspicion had gone, too, although he still looked tired and harassed. His greeting was happy enough, though, especially for Kirsty, of whom he evidently approved.

"And so," he said, after the introductions were complete, "what brings you all this way, just for a visit? Still not sure you want to come with us? Or are you thinking of persuading Kirsty to come too?"

"Oh, no' me, thanks, Mr. Whittaker," said Kirsty fervently. "No' me!"

Whittaker was evidently ready to launch into a sales spiel, so I began to outline what Ryly and I had been up to for the past few months. Whittaker's face grew grimmer and grimmer as he listened, until finally he looked quite terrifying, a mixture of pain and anger.

"You're right, of course," he said when I'd finished. "There's definitely something going on, something thoroughly evil, by all the signs. That peculiar budget, especially. In my day there was something—well, never mind that. What can I, what can the Ship do to help you?"

In his day? But I let that drop, and told him about the course problem. "The Ship has better tracking gear than I could ever get access to down on Earth. And the Infall field can be used like a gravity lens, can't it, when the Ship's at rest? I want you to find that thing for me, to track its real course. That'll be the best clue to its purpose we can get!"

Whittaker thought for a moment. "I see no reason why not. . . . Come along, we'll go down a few levels and get some decent weight back. And we can have a word with the first officer—he's in command while the Captain's away."

"Ekkela's away? That's a pity, I was looking forward to meeting him."

Whittaker ushered us onto a little electric runabout. "Yes, he's a remarkable man," he said, steering us towards the shadowy depths of the huge hall. "He's away trying to get something done about the supply problem . . ."

"You've still got trouble with that? After the roasting Ryly's report gave the authorities?"

"Yes, after that. We got a lot of promises, a few minor concessions, and a heavily orchestrated campaign in the official media about 'armchair pioneers' and 'greedy colonists,' that sort of thing. Suggesting that we were just out for what we could get, and not worth wasting valuable resources on. That killed what public feeling there was stone dead, and things are as they were. Or possibly a little worse, because they're trying to claim we've already used up an impossibly large allocation—" He paused, biting his lip. "You know—I wonder if that mightn't be connected with that extra-large budget of yours. That settles it, Mr. Bellamy. You'll get your help."

We pulled up short—very short, Whittaker drove badly— at a large elevator door, which opened as Whittaker approached. I couldn't help adding "If I can persuade the first officer. And if he'll take the responsibility in the captain's absence . . ." We started down.

"*I'll* take the responsibility," grunted Whittaker. "You wouldn't know, of course, but the Ship has an elected governing council; the captain still commands—he and the officers are all members—but it can advise him. And he's the sort to pay it due attention. *Not* the command structure the BCs planned, but the blazes with them."

"And ye're a councillor?" asked Kirsty.

"I am, Miss O'Neill, yes. In fact I'm the president. So I have a little pull, and I don't mind using it in a good cause— not to mention discharging a heavy obligation, both personal and on the Ship's behalf."

"Forget that, Rev. I only wish it'd done more good. But I

won't deny it's good to have a friend in high places."

"Yes," grinned Whittaker. "I know what you mean. Though I think I've got a better one. Well, this is Bridge Deck we're coming to—" There was the familiar feeling of increasing weight as the elevator slowed, but not all of it went away when it stopped. "Feel it? We're much nearer the ground—the rim, that is. Just about normal weight."

Bridge Deck looked impossibly luxurious when the doors opened. The lighting was soft and indirect, the floors were deeply carpeted and the walls were panelled with a fortune in wood veneer. "This is Officer's Row, as well," said Whittaker as he led us down the wide corridor. "They've got quarters and offices along here, to be near the Bridge—"

"A'right for some, eh?" commented Kirsty, looking around quizzically.

"You think so?" chuckled Whittaker. "This was all made in happier times, remember? Compared to the Ship proper, North End is rather functional. You should see my house, it's palatial by comparison, and it's by no means the best—but here we are!"

The double doors ahead were four metres high, and looked more like solid wood than veneer, though I wasn't sure that was possible. I expected some kind of security, an identity scanner for cochlear vibration maybe, or at least a pass-lock, but Whittaker just pushed one massive door slightly open, poked his head round and beckoned us to follow.

In the corridor the doors had looked large; in the Bridge they looked almost insignificant. It was an enormous open space, rising to a great vaulted roof; the effect was very like European cathedrals that Kirsty had insisted on dragging me round, but airier and less massive. Three of the walls were covered with large screens, beginning just above the tops of the doors. The fourth—

There wasn't a wall, just a low barrier of blue transparent stuff with a black rim along the top. Above that was emptiness. The Bridge was a great balcony that looked out onto the landscape of a dream. At first it was just a jumble of details your mind couldn't accept, hills at right angles, concave woodlands, the gleam of a lake on an impossible slope, a dim blue sky with clouds swirling along its centre in an unnatural formation, as if they were held in a fine glass cylinder running from over our heads into the dim distance. At the cylinder's centre, half-hidden by the cloud patterns, was a long streak of blinding gold, the colour of the evening sun. On either side the land rose in walls and faded into the depths of the sky, until overhead there was only the occasional faint suggestion of another landscape, a mirage-like reflection that eluded the eye. Here and there a bright light winked, like stars.

Vision adjusted to it, but not mind. It was like looking down a tunnel into the past; there was no landscape like that left on Earth. It was rich, pastoral, temperate country that could have come from a dozen different regions; I thought of old England or Ireland, with Vermont in the hillside forests and Scotland and Norway at their peaks. As if some god or legendary giant had cut himself a piece of turf to save it from the mistakes of man, and rolled it around a sunbeam.

"It's beautiful," said Kirsty in a small voice. "But it's . . . unreal. Like a set for a flik, a backdrop, an image construct—"

"That's right," said Whittaker in sober agreement. "It's splendid, but it's artificial. Like most things man makes, it's a bit fragile, it needs patching up, and it won't last very long. That's why we have to find ourselves a proper planet for a home. . . . Well, our two chief officers are on the control tower, so let's go and have a word with them, eh?"

The floor of the Bridge was a maze of control desks, set in all kinds of arrangements—circles, sometimes around a raised central desk, long straight lines, ranks of two or three, all separated by colour-coded lines on the floor. Few of the desks were manned; one or two were covered, others were dismantled. The whole thing had a relaxed, harmonious air about it that owed a lot to the design and colour scheme, and to the cool evening air that came flowing in. But I wondered how they managed during even a mild rain-shower or a snowstorm, if they had them.

The control tower didn't seem to rate its name; it was a railed-off area raised about a metre off the Bridge floor, lower than some of the desks. There were only two men in it, and they turned towards us as we climbed the two short steps. One, a burly man about my height, stepped forward; he had thick dark hair and wholly Oriental features, but his skin was paler than Kirsty's. He had a round, rather fierce face intensified by a bristling moustache and sidewhiskers; I tagged him as upper-crust Chinese.

"Commander Liang Wu, our First Officer," said Whittaker. In the course of introductions I found out that Liang was a former military pilot, that he was from Sechuan, that he sounded as fierce as he looked and that I rather liked him. The same went for the Second Officer, a big blonde fellow in his mid-twenties called Owen.

"Full name's Owen Owen, as it happens," he said seriously. It was unmistakably the voice we'd first heard over the com. "But I don't like folk using my first name, see? Got our dignity, we Celts." Owen had been a seaforce combat pilot in Europe, and we turned out to have some casual friends in common. That came in very useful when I began to tell my story; he'd met Carlsen once or twice, and had heard about the crash. Whittaker didn't have to do much persuading; Liang had been sputtering and fizzing during the telling, and exploded in wrath at the end. The gist of it seemed to be that he'd be happy to help and who dared doubt it, but that it would take time.

Owen nodded agreement. "We're only just getting by as it is, Bellamy. Five hundred crew, when we should have twice that and be training up as many colonists. And a degree-by-degree sky sweep takes time."

"Do it piecemeal," barked Liang. "Work it into training program, if we can. But still—one month, two even? And soon after that we leave. But I cannot promise you better."

"I understand," I said unhappily. "I'd hoped to be able to see some results before then—so I could make up my mind about coming with you more easily. But it's good of you to help at all, with your problems."

"One last kick in the ass for the BCs," chuckled Liang. "An ideal parting gift! Hey, cheer up! Come along anyway, think like colonist and leave Earth to stew in its own juice—no? Then maybe we get lucky and one of our navigation classes spots it first time—" He stopped, stiffened and smacked one hand into another with an alarming crack. "Navigation classes! Bellamy, this thing is usual DESprobe, eh? Squirts out of system on fusion stage, then lights up antimatter—"

"*Iesu Grist!* Yes! The flare!" yelled Owen. "The records, boy—when was that bloody probe launched? Last September? Somebody got the speed figures on those fusion stages—"

"High acceleration, sure," said Liang distractedly, bent over a desk screen and hammering keys. "Look in pilot's file— those stages are standard jobs for unmanned outer-system—"

Kirsty and I looked at each other in bewilderment; Whittaker seemed to be trying to remember something.

"Maximum three burns," reported Owen, rattling off a string of figures. "What's that come to, Liang? Two months?"

"More like one and a half?" said Liang. "Don't have to get right way out to Pluto, just. . . . Ah! Here it is."

"And it fits, damn it!" breathed Owen. "Here, Rev, Bellamy, Kirsty, look here—no, don't, let's give 'em the works, Liang. Navigation, can you run this on the simulator?"

"If you insist," said a bored Australasian voice from Liang's desk screen. "Gimme a minute to kick some life into B-Com."

"Hold onto your hats, people!" grinned Owen. I heard a whine from the end of the Bridge, and saw that the blue railing at the window was rising rapidly. It was actually the upper edge of a huge window, which rose to cover the whole open space, the black rim acting as seal at the top.

"In case of bad weather!" said Liang. "Or depressurization of the main hull. Now, be careful, please!" That was mostly for effect. There was another faint hum, and then the floor under us began to lift, entirely smoothly. I couldn't see much point in this, except to bring the big screens nearer eye level— so why not have the tower the right height to begin with? Then Kirsty looked up and pointed excitedly. In the middle of the roof, directly overhead, the vaulting formed a kind of dome, and we were rising towards this. I wondered if it was one of those old-fashioned planetariums. But we stopped well short of it, about thirty feet off the floor; a metal staircase, well railed, had quietly unfolded out of the tower as it rose. The light up here was dim, and it grew abruptly darker. Even the faint light of the desk screens below faded out, as if smoke passed over them, and suddenly I could see nothing beyond the rim of the tower. There was a moment of isolation. And then the unreal stars came out.

"Good trick, eh?" laughed Owen. "And very useful, when you're shut deep in an Infall field. It's a synthesis of all the little bits of data we get through from outside. Lifelike, eh?"

It wasn't perfect, but he was right. Presumably they hadn't quite got the graphics technique down pat when the Ship was built, but it was far in advance of anything I'd seen elsewhere; the stars had just the slightest square-edged look about them, and the colours were not quite as pure and subtle as they really look beyond the atmosphere. And Earth, visible below and to one side, was much smaller than it actually would have looked from where we were.

"Well, don't want that thing cluttering up all our lovely sky, do we?" said Owen. "We'll go back a bit in time, to late October. See? When you and your medman friend were just getting going, we'd got your answer all ready for you. Should've come to us sooner, boy..."

Liang didn't look half as pleased with himself. He was just standing there, arms folded, face twisted, as if he was trying to remember something worrying. Whittaker was looking rather the same. The stars shimmered sickeningly and changed, and a large orange arrow appeared, indicating a spot dead ahead.

"See this...?" whispered Owen. It didn't look very dramatic, unless you considered the distance. A spot of light appeared, swelled, intensified and faded in about three seconds. Something persisted, bright but not exceptionally so. "Not visible from Earth, not even most of the orbitals," Owen added. "But we saw it during a navigation training class, when we'd moved further out, see?"

"That's it," I said. A single moment of dissolution, when matter met its opposite and vanished in a climactic moment, a stream of energy that utterly annihilated the spent carrier and left no trace within the system of the probe's passing. "And your computers can extrapolate the course from that, can't they? Then that's it! A hell of a piece of luck you happened to be looking that way—"

Owen was shaking his head, and he, too, was beginning to look worried. Liang looked at Whittaker and shrugged.

"Not luck, boy," said Owen. "Though just as well you came to us, maybe. It's clear enough where that bugger's headed—don't you know your constellations? That's Eridanus up there. And we were looking that way 'cause that's where the Colony is. Where we'll be, soon enough..."

"So that's it, Ryly," I said, scanning the distant beach. Where was Kirsty? I should have been able to make her out, even among all the other naked broiling bodies; she'd only gone a delicious red-and-cream colour so far. "The bastards are out to spy on the Colony. Pretty good espionage vehicle, a DESprobe, if you don't know it's about. It can sit around on the fringes of the system and monitor every communication they—"

I stopped short. Ryly had been wearing an odd stifled smirk for some time but now he was laughing so hard he bobbed up and down in the water. "Hey, I'll really bet you and the Ship guys got all hot under the suit about that—" He vanished with a howl, and came up spluttering and coughing, hanging onto the float to get his breath. Kirsty popped up beside him.

"We meet at last, Mister—oh hell, wrong foot! I hadn't a mask on, ye see—I'm so sorry, Mr. Ryly—" But she spoiled it by giggling helplessly.

"Count yourself lucky," I told him. "Think what she might have grabbed. Anyway, it was about what I was going to do; what's so funny? OK, they should be able to shoot the thing down, it won't get there till after they do, but—"

"But they could just leave it be and it wouldn't make one good goddam bit of difference," laughed Ryly, still spitting out water between times. "Or the best thing would be if they could turn it round and send it right back home!"

"How'd you mean?"

"Well, I guess somebody somewhere may think it's going to be their spy, but it won't! There's more than one scam here. See, that extra part, the big one—I traced it. Back to Sweden, back to where it was made. A small Manufactures Department iron foundry, a hole of a town called Gällivare. I even saw a fragment of the mould, they'd no idea it was important. A solid iron castin' the size of the probe's instrument package. I traced it through Transport to a security warehouse, that castin'. Or I thought I did. That warehouse isn't so secure, and there's no castin' in its case now. Just one very genuine instrument package, ready for handy strip-down and recylin'—at a very handy price, no doubt. Graft. My speciality. Now am I a genius—"

I grabbed him. "Ryly, you idiot, are you sure? Sure they launched that thing, that casting—instead of the—"

"All umpteen tonnes of it, yes, the idiot's sure. Don't rush to thank me, but I found traces of spray plastic on the case, and some filings. They'd been shapin' an' coatin' that thing to look real. Fire it off to nowhere, and who'll ever know? Technical fault, please fund a replacement at once. Looked like they left on the field shield, though—suppose it'd be noticed if it wasn't there. It's just a lump of iron, Bellamy, that's all— rust potential."

"Iron, cold iron—"

"—is the master o' them all!" quoted Kirsty, then nuzzled

up to me. "Mark, now it's you not sayin' what's wrong..."

"Everything's wrong! Kirsty, a DESprobe's guidance system turns it over to decelerate halfway through the trip. What'd happen if it didn't?"

"Well... it'd just go on past its target. Unless it hit something—"

"And?" Something was beginning to dawn on Ryly, it showed.

Kirsty knitted her brows. "It'd do some damage, that big an' that fast..."

"It'd do more than that! It's not travelling in Infall, Kirsty! Its velocity's real, a significant fraction of light-speed! On the end of an antimatter drive it could reach something amazing eventually, eighty or ninety per cent or more, depending on how the thing's set to burn; it's been technically possible for years, but who needed it with Infall? And you know what would happen then?"

"Well, time—"

"No! I mean yes, but what else?"

"The mass—oh my god! The mass increase—that thing'd mass—but it's a' right, they sent the guidance system so it'll still slow down like it's meant to—"

"It isn't meant to." The sea was warm here, but it was the same ocean at whose cold heart the Station floated. "At Staff College somebody brought the idea up. I still remember it. The instructors laughed him down. Not an efficient weapon, they said. However massive it is, it's still physically small, its impact point would be too small. Just heavy localized destruction, not a planetwrecker; it'd just crack a tectonic plate, maybe, and the liquid core'd absorb the shock. Planets are soft, really. But here—"

"This is insane!" muttered Ryly.

"I'd agree. But here, with a soft head that spreads on impact—"

"Like a dumdum bullet?"

"More like a HESH head. An armour-piercing principle, centuries old but still used from time to time. Soft metal splats on the outside of the armour in a wide circle, the shock smashes out shrapnel inside. This thing'd spread out on the upper atmosphere. The shockwave alone—Ryly, that thing's got to be a missile. A relativistic missile, man! They're not out to *spy* on the Colony—"

Kirsty and I argued all the way back to the Station. We were stopping off there, ostensibly because she'd never seen it, actually because I was too much on edge to stand the whole flight back with her just yet. I wished I could share her view of the human race, not being capable of things like that. It would have been so tempting to believe she was right; Ryly did, but he'd gone off to read up on the principles. But just as we were coming in to land, Kirsty, half in tears still, made the sensible suggestion I needed.

"Look, ye don't have to carry this on your own shoulders, damn you! Just find a way to tell the Ship before they go! They'll have specialists, they can make up their own minds and find something to do about it! Leave it to them!"

That I agreed with, and she cheered up mightily. So did I, after a while; she was right both ways, and it wasn't all my worry.

I soon acquired another, though. My sec buttonholed me over the com the moment I opened the door of my quarters.

"Mr. Bellamy, there is a message for you. From the private office of the Director, Research Coordination Bureau, Headquarters, European Department of Space—"

"Yes?"

"You are cordially requested to call, at your convenience, for an off-the-cuff discussion. At any time that suits you in the next few weeks, quite informally. The time will count as duty and expenses will be credited. Simply call Director Thorborg's office when you have chosen your time. That is all. Do you wish me to reply?"

"Using the prescribed forms of reply, add that I will be happy to call on her at the earliest time my duties permit. Send that, all right? Out."

Kirsty was shaking with terror. "Mark, what'll we do? They've found ye out! Don't go—"

"Have they hell! That's soft soap, they wouldn't waste it if they even suspected me of anything substantial. They'd have a goon squad here in half an hour and I'd never be heard of again—don't cry! No, this may have nothing to do with our business. But if it does, experience suggests they're going to try smothering me in cream. That's what I'd try, going by my dossier."

"*You?* Your dossier suggests that? That you'd let yourself be—be bribed into silence?"

R.T.T.S.—6

"If it was official and not too illegal, yes. Protecting state secrets at all costs, that kind of thing. I'm rather stolidly loyal, you see . . ."

"You?" She was shaking her head in sheer confusion.

If there was one place in this world that couldn't be bugged, it was my quarters; I'd seen to that, and checked it recently. Still, I whispered in her ear. "Yes—according to my dossier. Because dossiers are my speciality, you see. And over the years, by a combination of sneaky information work and living the part, I've managed to work some slight misinformation into mine. A bit like writing your own obituary, really. You can't put in pure untruths, exactly, just—biases . . ."

"Ye mean like you being loyal, a' right—but not to . . ." She stared, burst out laughing, and hugged me hard enough to bruise. For the rest of that evening she hardly took her eyes off me, and that night she coiled and clung like a vine. I stroked her sleeping back, and thought. I'd leave her with Ziz, an explosive mix but the safest for her if I didn't come back; Ziz could be trusted, and was capable of looking after her. It would be up to them and Ryly, then, to warn the Ship. By and large, I believed what I'd told Kirsty about that invitation; I wasn't too worried. But there were precautions enough I could take.

FIVE

I was in no hurry at all to get to HQ. I let the zep dawdle along on the Bordeaux-Stuttgart beam, and signalled the ETA it gave me to Thorborg's sec. I was startled when it replied that the Director would be pleased to see me as soon as I arrived. No two-hour wait? That was practically unheard-of, and I didn't like the sound of it at all. If a high-up like Thorborg was so eager to see a relative nobody it meant she'd something pretty important to deliver—the chop, for example, in one form or another. Not that I cared much about that, as long as it didn't stand in the way of my Colony place, but the whole feel of the thing was disturbing. I'd know soon enough though, so I forced myself to relax and watched the countryside of the Massif Central flow by beneath my feet. This was still mainly livestock country, especially in the fertile uplands, and so relatively little was greenhoused in; I liked that, you could get some idea of the actual landscape. Most grainfields the world over looked alike: row after row of plastic tubes, with only weeds or a few old neglected hedges growing between them. The French varied this with the great straight rows of poplars that grew along what were once their major roads; now most roads were minor, but the poplars were still there. They looked pretty hypnotic from the air as I skimmed past; they must have been a positive danger to ground drivers back when, providing both a distraction and something to collide with as a result. Watching them made my eyelids heavy, and I began to yawn. Why resist? I'd need to be fresh this afternoon. I slept, and when I awoke the cluttered slopes of the Harzgebirge were rising before me. I like mountains, but I like them even better when they're not lousy with chalets and cliff-face apartments. Living halfway up a mountain was a status symbol these days; the view was reflected in the prices, and you positively had to rate a zep or other personal air transport. Not that public transport was actually shot down on sight—not quite.

Space Department Headquarters was on low rolling countryside, a good few square kilom of incredibly pricy Schwarzwald. The wide grounds within the perimeter wall had been landscaped to look like the original Black Forest—conifers, deer, eagles (from the life banks), the lot. I'd been to conferences in the two luxurious hunting lodges at the north and south extremities of the grounds, and I'd heard rumours of the other two, fenced off at east and west. Apparently they represented the two extremes of Department hospitality. The western one, for Department high-ups and VIP visitors, was a cross between a health farm and a harem; the eastern one was called the Lubianka, not after that hotel in Moscow, but after the grim jail it used to be. It had got crowded during the last African blowup, when most sabotage and espionage suspects ended up there for interrogation. I'd had nothing to do with that, beyond trying to keep people out of it when I could. However efficient and humane you can make modern interrogation techniques, they seem to attract sadists who back them up with traditional methods—"just to be sure," as one guard said to me. He was explaining, if that's not too strong a word, the deaths of two girls suspected of diverting military materials to the Africans. I was sorry I'd ever caught them.

I flew low over the western lodge as I came in, catching a glimpse of bodies roasting in the spring sun, under glass like the cornfields; some of them suffered from official flab or VIP angularity, but others had some very interesting curves indeed. The HQ beam guided the zep neatly through the narrow mouth of the underground hangar, and dropped me neatly onto a shelf halfway up a parking stack. I quickly changed out of my coveralls. Full uniform, with a reasonable sprinkling of silver here and there about the midnight blue, was the rule in HQ territory, the exception outside it; I wore it rarely enough to enjoy it, and even Simoneau would have approved of my boots. The fit was rather spoilt by some bulges in my pockets; he wouldn't have approved of those. In fact, if he'd known what they were, he'd have had a fit. Taking them where I was going was practically sacrilege, so I was sure I'd enjoy it even if I didn't have to use them.

I could have taken a walkway from the hangar to Admin Central, but I'm not a troglodyte by nature; I took the surface elevator and walked along the tree-lined paths. The air was fresh with the pine-scent, and breathing it was like drinking Niersteiner. I tilted my face to the sun as I walked, pulling off my cap to feel the warmth on my forehead. It was about the worst mistake I could have made, as it turned out.

Admin Central was the usual tide of people when I arrived, but the moment I checked in the reception processors swept me through ahead of an enormous queue and printed out a route card direct to Thorborg's suite, via the executive transit system, no less. I floated over soft and silent floors to wide, uncrowded elevators, rubbing shoulders with higher BCs from this and other Departments. The man in my dossier ought to have been in seventh heaven, and even the real me couldn't help being a little impressed. But smothered in cream or drowned in Malmsey, you're no less dead.

Most of HQ was underground; nobody below middle management level ever saw the light of day in their offices.

"The higher the fewer" rule prevailed. The surface buildings were mostly long and low, but they had a few towers around the edges. Thorborg's new bureau had evidently got off to a good start; it topped its particular pinnacle, and only two or three others rose much higher. I let her private elevator waft me up at the relaxed pace that BC high-ups can afford, and enjoyed the view while I could. At last, though, it disgorged me into a large and empty hallway. My feet made no sound on its thick soft carpeting, a very old-fashioned thing to have these days. But of course Thorborg was old, wasn't she? The walls and ceiling were panelled in dark glossy wood, and that was unusual too. I felt the impact of a strong personality here, and I wasn't so sure whether I liked it or not. The hall was gloomy, making the walls look blank and featureless at first. But there were doors, set almost invisibly flush with the panelling. Four of them were marked—a conference room, a library, a lavatory and at the far end of the hall the emergency stairs. One was blank and unmarked. I showed it the route card, and it studied it for only a second before sliding open soundlessly to reveal a small waiting-room, furnished much like the hallway. I expected to be greeted by a secretary, but it was a human voice I heard. To my right a door stood open, framing a tall man. It closed behind him as he stepped forward and held out a hand, an archaic gesture that caught me on the hop. I had to think before taking and shaking it. I half expected him to bow and scrape.

"Chief Security Officer Bellamy? I am Andrei Philipovich Yermolov, personal assistant to Director Thorborg. She will be ready for us in a moment—may I offer you some refreshment, a whisky perhaps? I can recommend this, although it does not have the advantage of being black market, of course." I looked in vain for a trace of a smile. He was solidly built, but his face was lean and ascetic. About my age, I estimated, and not soft— probably quite dedicated, in his way. He didn't wear the gloss of corruption that so much of the Department did these days. The whisky level in his glass wasn't half that of mine, which annoyed me. Was he trying to soften me up? Some security chief I'd have been if it was that easy. We sat in overstuffed chairs and weighed each other up.

"Bellamy?" he inquired amiably. "English? Or Irish?"

"Mongrel British crossed with American, also mongrel. And brought up in half a dozen places throughout the world, passed through a hell of a lot more. Kind of complicates my sense of nationality."

"A service background?" mused Yermolov. "I thought so." His smile was a bit wintry, but definitely there. "I myself am from an entirely bureaucratic family—West Russians, you know. Not that the bureaucracy is entirely hereditary there, but an outsider might be excused for thinking so. Well, Mr. Bellamy— you are of course wondering why you have been invited here. Perhaps you are even a little worried? Don't be. Although I can tell you it concerns the unfortunate accident to the recent DESprobe launching—but the director is ready for us now. Will you come along? And please bring your drink."

My innards had tightened, but with excitement, not fear. At least it didn't feel quite like fear. I didn't need Yermolov's little assurance, interesting though it had been. The unfortunate *accident*—they could blow that out of their motors, for a start. What kind of a line was I going to be handed this time?

It was Thorborg's main office we stepped into as the door sighed to behind us. It was a big room, and even more gloomily opulent than the hall. Only three walls were wood-panelled, but the wood here was carved in uneasily intricate geometric patterns. The carpet was the exact shade of fresh arterial blood, the hangings by the tall narrow windows were the same, only dried. The air had a hint of perfume about it, as if incense had been burned before the dark old icon that decorated the end wall. And yet in the middle of all this Gudrun Thorborg radiated vitality. She stood up from behind one of the data-screens that littered the wide central table. Taller than I remembered her, she topped me by at least half a head, bringing her nearer Yermolov. Her casual black jumpsuit showed off a figure as lean and healthy as a greyhound's and her glossily tanned face was made of nothing but bone and corded muscle. Ice-white hair was the only indication of age about her and that, the easiest thing to change, was a mockery rather than an acknowledgement; it was spattered with metallic black flecks to create an ermine effect. She shook hands warmly and firmly—Yermolov would have caught the habit from her, or even imitated it to prepare visitors—and waved me to a deep armchair, settling herself slowly into its twin. Yermolov carried over a severely functional chair, an obvious antique, and perched on its edge in virtuous discomfort.

"Chief Security Officer Bellamy!" smiled Thorborg. A large whisky had somehow materialized in her hand. "I'm so glad you could come! We don't manage to lure you Station hermits over here very often. And you and I just *have* to have a talk before things go any further. Has Andrei—good, you have a drink! I'm afraid I asked him to keep you entertained while I sneaked another look at your dossier. We haven't met for years, have we?"

More flattery. Her tone suggested it was just one of those little accidents, rather than the result of an astronomical status gap. Even a senior security officer was one with the worms under those particular feet. I did my best to sound deferential.

"Not since you came out to open the new maintenance complex on the East Arm, fifteen years ago. I'm surprised you even remembered. . . ."

Her chuckle was warm and throaty, but not unmusical. She

could have been a young fifty, without modern geriatrics; I knew how close she was to double that, and still going strong. Especially her sex life; according to Department rumour that was aimed mostly at young girls and middle-aged men, so I felt safe enough in that area. Not in many others, though; she was very cat-like. Big, not domestic; and both of them toy with their prey. We chatted over my career at the Station, how I'd ever been able to stand twenty years of it, and why I was thinking of emigrating. I had the feeling of being catechized. *Another look at my dossier?* Either her memory was inhumanly perfect or she'd read nothing else all day. No, all week. I did my best to live up to it. Yermolov stayed silent, sipping his whisky with bland concentration, but I caught the faintest flicker of meaning in a glance she passed to him just an instant before the talk wound its way around to the state of affairs on the Station at present—

"—which has a bearing on my reason for inviting you over, Mr. Bellamy. I want—" she gave me a roguish grin—"I want to *pump* you. Not about working or living conditions or staffing levels or that kind of thing; the Department has Herincx's excellent reports to cover those. But he's the Old Man, isn't he? Isolated, in his own ivory tower whether he wants to be or not. It's people like you who really know how the land lies, if that's the right term here, eh? So I need your help. And I'm sure you won't refuse me. . . ."

She actually managed to look a bit helpless. I was meant to be charmed.

"How could I?" I grinned gallantly back, thinking of ways to. She gave me the kind of smile one gives a bright child.

"This is a sore point. We may have handled things badly. The recent DESprobe launching—the crash, the death of that poor pilot. It's caused a lot of ill-feeling, hasn't it?"

Well, here we were at last. Did they suspect I'd been snooping? Maybe. But they surely didn't know how much I'd found out, or the claws would be out by now. Nothing about Ryly, certainly.

I took a minute to think before answering, which was natural enough. "Not so much the crash as the mystery around it. That pilot, Carlsen, he was an experienced man, able enough in his own sphere. The clampdown on information, cutting out the usual Station inquiry—naturally that worried people. A clear cover-up like that just encourages everyone to assume the worst.

They bitch, they grouse, they worry. . . ."

Thorborg pounced. "And dig around to find things out?"

I nodded calmly. "Everyone does. Two theories per person on average, and some of them pretty wild. Sabotage and graft are the favourites."

"Your favourites?" asked Yermolov quite neutrally.

"I'm a security officer, not a medman," I said stolidly. "A professional investigator. I don't theorize without facts, and I haven't enough of those."

Yermolov was going to say something, but Thorborg choked him off with a wave.

"What did I tell you, Andrei?" she snapped, cracking her tumbler down on the chair-arm. Another fragment of a glance, a very enigmatic one. "We *have* handled it badly! No doubt about it! I should never have let you and the rest of the Committee talk me into it. Mistrust breeds mistrust, and it rebounds onto us!"

"But Director," protested Yermolov gently, "as you yourself have said, we have little choice. We cannot tell just *every-one—*"

"Not everyone does not mean no one!" snorted the old woman. "Some people will have to know. Oh, it was my decision in the end, I do not blame you. But I am learning. From now on we will put our trust in those we know to be worthy of it, eh?" She grinned in my direction. "They will be able to quell the spread of disturbing rumour. Chief Officer Bellamy here is a prime example. Because we failed him, he's had to poke around for himself, eh?" A look of indulgent amusement needled me. I looked natural and discreet and honest and a little hurt and the kind of good servant who'd have no truck with medmen.

"I'd have headed the investigation, normally. I was choked off, without the least explanation. Naturally I looked around."

"Yes, it's natural. Though Andrei and a number of others didn't think so. They do not make sufficient allowance for human nature. And did you find out much?"

Crunch time. If they knew more than I admitted to I was in trouble. But then if I told what I knew I was in deep anyway.

"Not a lot," I lied happily. "Nothing secret about the probe or its functions. But as to where it was going, and why—well, that course was a real mystery. What's out that way that we haven't seen already?"

Yermolov's wintry smile warmed up a little, unpleasantly. "Not a thing, Mr. Bellamy. As I'm sure you suspected. The course we released was not that which the probe is actually following. Another blind, intended to distract the unduly curious—" I looked hurt—"until the probe was far enough away on its real course to be beyond easy detection. We did not wish to draw attention to that area of space. It was, in fact, that course inquiry that alerted us to your, ah, *interest* in this matter . . ."

"Oh? Mind if I ask how?"

He looked slightly embarrassed. "Your friend's call to you—"

So it had been that, right enough. But then—"Were you running a general tap? On the entire Station? Every call?"

Of course they had. So all those steamy little chats with Kirsty—I didn't have to pretend to be furious, and I didn't mind letting it show. General taps were still technically against the European constitution, and were among the few issues that could still stir the general public out of its apathy.

"Small fashing wonder you're not trusted, then!" was all I needed to say. From my level to his that was stinging enough. I watched him bristle, then check himself and turn to Thorborg for support. As I expected, he didn't get it. They were playing hard and soft respectively, and it would have spoiled her role. He swallowed hard and changed tack.

"I can assure you that if you understood the issues at risk you would consider them serious enough to warrant—"

"Mr. Bellamy will have the chance to judge for himself!" interrupted Thorborg. "And when he does," she added, "I am confident he will agree with you, Andrei. You see now the advantages of my approach . . ." Yermolov nodded ruefully. I tried to look mollified, but it wasn't at all easy. The implications were just getting through. Hadn't I congratulated myself that the Station's com network couldn't be tapped without Security's cooperation? Obviously they'd not had mine! And any member of Investigation would have reported any such approach to me, I was sure of that. Which left just one candidate, an obvious enough choice. . . . I thought of Simoneau, smirking merrily over my private calls, and burned away inside. Other people than pilots could have accidents. If I got out of this with a whole skin. . . . But Thorborg was still talking.

"Of course we entirely understand your anger, Bellamy,

entirely. But we have done such things for the general good! Not just of ourselves, of the Department, or even of Europe. For the good of all humanity, Bellamy! Consider that!"

I did. And mentally reached for my revolver.

And yet, in a peculiar way, they seemed sincere. Thorborg's eyes were bright against the gloom, and Yermolov was nodding with self-righteous seriousness. They hadn't been sincere earlier. The man in my dossier might have been taken in by the little duet they'd staged, but the real me was wearily familiar with the apologetic sincerity routine. Most petty crooks could have given this pair acting lessons. Or maybe they just didn't feel they needed to try too hard for that dossier man.

Yet for all the mummery I'd caught undertones of a real dispute, a genuine disagreement between them. Over tactics, perhaps? Over what exactly to do about that damn-fool security man who was prying? Whether to liquidate him in another quiet accident, or transfer him to Corfu or Novaya Zemlya—or maybe even tell him the truth? *Don't be ridiculous.* . . . But miracles do happen.

"You must understand, Mr. Bellamy," said Yermolov, "I have not been questioning your loyalty or discretion; your record is adequate testimony of those. But as a policeman you will appreciate that the more people who know a secret the less likely it is to remain a secret. Hence my misgivings. If we tell you we must tell others. Where do we draw the line? What is safe?"

"Nothing is, Andrei," said the old woman crisply, "not absolutely. And the spread of rumour and gossip is a considerable danger in itself. Mr. Bellamy is in a position to stifle a lot of unauthorized snooping around, especially if the free media agencies take an interest. He, and others like him, must be our strong right arm—and how can we ask that of them if we are afraid to let them see what they have to guard? How else can they appreciate its importance?" The old vulture certainly had a way with oratory. If little words like *accident* hadn't kept coming up I might have been half off my guard now. She leant sharply forward and shot out a long lean hand that clasped my knee like a mechanical grab. "And you must appreciate it! What you are about to see is of momentous importance. It cannot, simply *cannot,* be released to the general public just yet! The governments and international administrations of the world—yes, even the African Junta!—are unanimous on this.

Now how often has *that* happened before?" Her fingers dug deeper into my leg. Despite myself, I was impressed. It tied in with those budgets of Ryly's. But it still needn't be the truth. "My department was created specially to handle the problem," she said with quiet pride, releasing my knee in a caressing sort of way. "And that too is unheard of, isn't it? With international funding, no less. We are only part of SpaceDep so we can draw on its resources more easily. The problem is that big. So you will appreciate why I make it an order, absolute and without limit or exception, that what you see here today remains with you alone, and is not repeated to any person not here present, however convincing the authorization they may have. Until such time as I, or any future holders of my office, personally cancel this order. You understand?"

I did. Official mumbo-jumbo made no difference; if they wanted my head on a plate they would get it. Thorborg relaxed into her chair.

"Understand," she said grimly, "if you try to break that we'll throw away the key. *And* blacken your name, and that of anyone you tell, enough to discredit what you've said. Harsh but necessary!" For a minute, although nothing about her changed, she looked her age. A haggard old weaver of evil destinies for those who offended her. Then she was all smiles again.

"Good! I think you may be very interested by this! We're going to watch a very unusual flik—" she gave a grating chuckle—"not *that* kind, of course! We could go through to the conference room, but it'll be more comfortable to just watch here. So you must move your chair over here by mine—yes, that little control there!—and turn it to face this wall, so. There!"

The table was already sliding silently back against the wall behind us, the draperies hitching themselves out of its way. Yermolov vanished through the massively ornate oak door they revealed, and the windows swiftly darkened to an opaque black. Our chairs swung to face the unpanelled wall, from which the draperies were also lifting. Its central section lost its rich smoky cream tint, lighting up from behind. It was the largest screen I'd seen outside a public theatre, and better quality than you ever saw there. The rows of infostore code numbers that began to form in its depths were sharp and crisply contrasted, and yet there was no glare. And the depth effect was unobtrusively natural, not exaggerated. Thorborg's chair bumped gently up against mine. She slouched comfortably back and drew her long legs up. Yermolov reappeared and carried over his skeletal antique chair; some human secretary had once looked a great deal better on it than he did, quarter of a thousand years ago. Maybe he liked looking like a beaky Slavic eagle on a perch, I didn't know. He waved a light pointer at one set of numbers, which moved out of the serried ranks, front and centre. Then they began to flash red.

A machine voice spoke briskly. "Restricted Information—no class or category, available only on pre-registered personal clearance. Warning! Any attempt to retrieve this information by improper means may result in—"

Thorborg cut it off. "Personal authorization is available. Mine. I am Gudrun Thorborg, and I stored this information for release only on my clearance or that of Andrei P. Yermolov. There! Is that enough for voice identification?"

"Yes," said the even voice. "Material clear for running."

Rather a childish security procedure, I thought, but then a lot of BCs were childish about such things—resounding titles, pompous procedures, the size of the desk. Their egos seemed badly in need of bolstering. For me, the most effective security stores are the least obtrusive.

"I've seen this before," the Russian whispered in my ear. "First time I had no idea what it was. You won't either. Better not to—it really hits you that way. It's the answer to everything you wanted to know, and it's not comforting." There was a hint of tremor in his voice. "In fact, it is probably the most disturbing thing I have ever—"

Suddenly and without warning the screen went from black to red, a deep burning blood-red spattered with black scars, in huge still blocks or smaller moving shapes. Red highlights seemed to glint off them, flashes of ruby light like beamfire at night. There was no sound, none at all.

My eyes burnt and watered as if I was looking into a low-g steel furnace. After a few seconds, though, I began to see traces of other colours besides red and black, and gradations and shades of these. And then as my eyes refocussed I began to see depth. The shapes and colours were so weird I'd hardly realized I was looking at a conventional holopic. Just as this sank in, a point of brilliant lemon-yellow light whipped out of one hulking black shape, hung in red emptiness for an instant, then turned sharp right and dashed into another, more distant shape. I'd still not the faintest idea what I was looking at, but it was entrancing. Dark things moved between the blacker masses, mostly in ordered rows; a few darted about at different levels, but the majority seemed to move across a flat plane. With alarming speed the picture zoomed in on one of these shapes, viewing it at a crazy angle. The object became more sharply defined, shape rather than shadow; fine points of detail began to appear, churning up the kind of queasy subconscious recognitions you get from a Rorschach blot. Queasy, because my conscious mind refused to match it up with anything I knew, at first. A familiar shape, an everyday function—the frame froze, the image vanished, to reappear an instant in isolation against a pure white background. A ghostly computer image lifted out of it like a departing soul, reducing its complex outline to a stylized shell of glowing lines that became more and more indentifiable as it turned and twisted about various axes. The screen ruined my moment of triumphant recognition by announcing "GROUNDCAR." And then it was instantly obvious to the merest idiot. It was weird, it ran on three spheres, not wheels or gas cushions and by the size scale next to it it was a dinosaur's town runabout—but groundcar it was. For an instant I marvelled. Then, explosively then, I began to think just whose. . . .

To complete my disorientation, back came the red and black glare, a different view this time; was it a landscape? One groundcar was identifiable, and what it stood on, that pale pink-grey line, would have to be some kind of road. And next to the groundcar—

Zep owners have a proprietary air as they stand beside their craft. *This is mine*, their attitude says, *I control it*. Something *was*, I couldn't say *stood*, by that warty abomination of a vehicle. And as I watched, appalled, it somehow seemed to flow inside it. The car, now visibly occupied, moved off. Above it *(above?)* lemon-yellow pinpoints sailed easily around the sky, the red, red sky.

"The colours are false, of course," said Thorborg in a precise, dry, tone. "So in a sense, is the whole image. Apparently the original transmission wasn't an image in light encoded for maser transmission. It seems to have been in microwaves all along—" There were other outlines on the screen now, three or four. They weren't exactly shapeless, but the shape did change, continually, and it never approached anything familiar or even describable. A size scale had been superimposed, presumably by us since it was marked in metres. I decided that dinosaurs had been on the small side.

"The size estimates are based on constants included in the original transmission," whispered Yermolov. He could as easily have spoken aloud in the silent room, but he seemed to be overawed by the whole thing, like a rabbit facing a fox. His fear spread out around him.

"Watch the horizon!" he hissed.

A thick white line picked it out, and below it appeared measurements for the arc. Another, more deeply curved line appeared beneath. I didn't need the label to tell me it was Earth.

"That makes their world a little smaller than Neptune," muttered the Russian thickly. "Gas-giant proportions. I had no idea a solid planet that size was possible—but then, perhaps it isn't. Look!" Another white line appeared, outlining what appeared to be the hills across which the road wound. The line held their image for perhaps five minutes, during which we sat in silence and the three shapes (four?) bumbled shapelessly about in the foreground. Then more figures ticked up under the line, followed by a flashing question mark.

"Our research team is doing its expensive little nut over that!" chuckled Thorborg. Her voice had lost the clipped control of a few minutes before; if the images had daunted her at all she wasn't going to show it. "They need a longer sequence to be sure—it *could* be picture problems, but they think the profile of those hills is changing..."

"Changing?" I boggled. "You mean, while we watch?"

"Yes. Sand-dunes can do that, in a high wind. But a road or causeway like that would soon be covered if there were such loose material around. Instead it seems to move with the hills, to ride them, almost. And the deformation is constant. As if they were incredibly low-frequency wave-forms—"

"In what, for Chrissake? Water? Lava?"

She gave a gurgle of laughter. "Why, man, how should I know?"

I summoned up a smile of sorts. "How indeed?" I felt disoriented, insecure, jarred. My eyes ached, my head pounded, and I had finished my drink centuries too soon. And yet for all this I was beginning to enjoy myself. All my life I'd wanted to play tourist on an alien world. And more alien than this I couldn't hope to get. I only hoped my eyesight would hold out. Thorborg saw me rubbing at my smarting eyeballs and made sympathetic noises.

"Those damn colours! Chosen for contrast, apparently. The lab team tell me that the extremes of light and shade, or whatever you'd call their equivalents, are so wide in the original that you lose detail if you cut them down. Even this is a compromise. The first version I saw, they'd rendered into yellow and black—like looking into a fusor, bah! I nearly went blind!" She gave a serpentine head-to-toe shudder that somehow brought her legs against mine. "Now I wish I knew just what *this* was all about!"

The scene had changed again as she spoke. I heard a slight, half-stifled choking sound from Yermolov, but his face was unreadable in the dimness. Onto the screen flowed a riot of those shapeless shapes, uncountable, indefinable, and furiously active. It was just possible to make out individuals colliding, staying together in a frenzy of change, and flying violently apart once more.

"Whatever it is, they seem to like it!" chuckled Thorborg in my ear. "Do you suppose it might be—" exaggerated whisper, tickling my eardrum—"*sex?*"

It looked more like a lynching to me, but maybe we were just reflecting our present preoccupations. Thorborg seemed to be leaning heavily in my direction, which was alarming. I began to feel very middle-aged.

In, out and roundabout wove the mass of dark bodies, in a dance, a parade, or just a busy street; there was a background, tantalizingly vague behind the alien, hypnotic rhythm of movement. Yermolov was muttering fragmentary obscenities in a variety of languages. Thorborg was edging so close I could hear her raspy breathing. I didn't give a damn for either of them. The sheer alien quality of it held me enthralled. It seemed like a door opening in front of me, a cell door perhaps. To a life-long prisoner freedom can be a bit alarming, but he gets to like it in the end. I was learning fast. So there were others, after all, other minds with other desires, other wisdoms, other stupidities. They could be quite like us, or they could be less comprehensible than bacteria. That didn't matter. They were there, and in a universe that contained them and us there must be others, too. Like and unlike, friendly and hostile, anything and everything, nothing predictable about them except unpredictability. The horizons of humanity had suddenly become infinite.

A light spidery touch on my knee jerked me back down to the foreground. Thorborg's hand had landed there with unerring accuracy, though she seemed not to have taken her eyes off the screen. I did my best not to shudder, although I'd almost sooner have had one of the aliens. It wasn't just Thorborg herself—it was the power and authority she represented, toying absently with me as if I were one of the hired hands at West Lodge. I stopped my flesh crawling by concentrating on the screen.

Scene followed scene, and all alien in the extreme. And yet as my eyes at last adjusted and the pain died down, I began to feel I could distinguish "people" from "animals" from "machines"—though the "people" seemed to differ more widely among themselves than we do. Completely forgetting I wasn't supposed to be too perceptive, I mentioned it to Yermolov. He looked sharply round at me.

"Quite right," he said, with an effort. "We think much of the material we receive has been tailored to suit us—as well as can be done at this stage. Some sequences obviously parallel what we sent them—sometimes quite exactly, groundcar for groundcar, for example. Of others we are less sure. Such as this!"

Change again, to a weirdly divided scene. Above the horizontal line, smooth shades of ruby, below it sparkling highlights that made it hard to see what produced them. Whatever it was, though, had a kind of regular, lurching motion to it that was tantalizingly familiar—

"The sea!" I exclaimed. "Sun on the open sea!"

The other two laughed, Yermolov sounding strained.

"I'm sorry, Mark—I can call you Mark, can't I?" laughed Thorborg, and didn't pause for an answer. "We were wondering how long it'd take an old seadog like you to recognize it! Actually, all we can say is, it's liquid of some kind. We sent them a pic of a big river estuary at this point in the sequence, and they sent this back. But those aren't waves; they're concentric ripples, radiating from somewhere over the horizon. As if something was continually falling into the sea—"

"Or perhaps a stream of gas bubbles was coming up," said Yermolov. "But they are moving very rapidly and evenly, as you see. We are sure of the speed because they sent us a constant to set it by, as we did with them."

"Who made contact first?" I asked innocently.

"They did," said Yermolov flatly, and turned back to the screen. Thorborg gave a luxuriant chuckle, and absentmindedly massaged my knee.

"Andrei is just an old chauvinist, he takes that to heart. He's foolish. All they did was send out a signal which we eventually picked up. Pure chance! For all they knew there might have been nobody there."

But they had sent the signal. It was more than we'd ever done. I decided to ask an awkward question, in all apparent innocence.

"How long ago was that?"

"A little over forty years—"

"Forty years!" I couldn't help the outburst, but fortunately Thorborg didn't seem to think it was too uncharacteristic.

"It is not as long as it sounds. The signals come from—"

"Director!" There was real hundred-carat fury in Yermolov's voice. Thorborg's fingers clamped down on my leg with startling strength, but her voice stayed steady and good-humoured.

"Easy, Andrei! Down, boy! I'm not so old that I don't know what I say, eh? You should know that!" Yermolov scowled at her but stayed silent. The convulsive grip on my leg turned into a playful squeeze as she turned back to me, ignoring him. "Always he worries! You see, Mark, we would trust you with our secrets, our lives, anything, but there is no need to weigh you down with things you do not need to know. I was just going to say that the signals come from about five parsecs away—that may mean more to you than to me, but I do know that it makes their travel time over sixteen years. One little exchange, therefore, has taken nearly thirty-three years. There, Andrei! I have answered Mark's question and told him no more than I should—"

I wasn't listening, despite the insistent grasp on my knee. Five parsecs! I struggled to hang onto my thoughts. I'd that sudden icy feeling of having the whole thing in my hands now, of having had it for a while and yet unable to see. Unable, I wondered, or unwilling? Or was I just dazed by that awesome horizon on the screen before me, daunted by the cold gigantic alienness of it? I tried to pull myself together. A minute ago

I'd been all for wider horizons, hadn't I? But this one was just too much, too soon. That eerie rippling was getting to Yermolov too, I could tell. I wondered how Thorborg could stay so cool. Either she was incredibly insensitive or she'd seen it often enough to be blasé. I didn't believe that for a moment; she'd have had to be a vegetable. Come to think of it, she *was* behaving oddly; the heavy pass she was making—and that near-slip. She *had* been going to tell me where those signals came from then, open the whole can of worms. I was glad she hadn't, though; it might have put me head of the line for an accident. For all this guff about trust and truth I suspected there were plenty of things man wasn't meant to know—common man, that is.

When a second later the screen darkened I sighed with relief. So did the others, and the grip on my knee relaxed, the taut arm slipped back to rest loosely on my thigh. For a minute I developed a little fellow-feeling for these two creatures; we were like small scared animals huddling together in fear of the unknown. But I beat that down. Why lose your head because something you've always wanted turns out to be more than you can handle? Learn to handle it, or you don't deserve it. I steeled myself for what the next scene would bring me.

It was as well I did. The darkness resolved into a glimpse of that unstable skyline, then there was a rush of blurred, indistinct images across the screen, a moment of speeding confusion, then—

"Sweet fashing hellfire!" was about the most intelligent thing I found to say, and in the circumstances I was proud of myself. The screen was awash with weird patterns, peculiar swirling shapes that swung round the screen in sickening slow motion. The patterns themselves, though, were motionless vortices, like frozen whirlpools, all shapes, all sizes, some brighter, some dimmer. They rolled across the screen like a tidal wave, only never getting closer; I couldn't get any idea at all of how near they might be. Thorborg was running her fingernails up and down the inside of my thigh, which doesn't do much for me at the best of times. I gritted my teeth and tried to concentrate on the screen. I couldn't see where the picture was taken from, not a trace of skyline, background, horizon, changing or otherwise. Just the slowly passing patterns—and again there was something peculiarly familiar about them. Something I'd seen often enough. . . .

And then the motion of the vortices slowed, and I could make out faint flickers in the smoky reddish darkness between them, moiré patterns that formed and vanished in almost the same instant. An arc of solid blackness at the lower left flared red along its rim; I'd just time to see it was the curve of a planet before an intolerable redness, a shapeless glare, seethed over the rim and scattered red across its surface, scouring the dark away before it. I knew what it was, all right, but words literally failed me. I turned wildly round to look at the others, and saw their faces clear in that hellish volcano-light. I saw fear there, even on the old woman's face, more fear than I'd expected. It was as if this somehow represented an even greater threat to them than anything else we'd seen, almost a personal threat. I'd seen that look on people at the business end of a gun, usually mine. Like the caged animal, hungry for its keeper's throat but scared of the sound of his voice. All this for a simple sunrise? Seen, of course from space.

"That's how it looks to them?"

"With microwaves, yes," Thorborg answered tautly. "You see that background pattern? Our people are not sure, but they think it may be the microwave background—"

Now *that* electrified me! "The uniform background? From the Big Bang? They can see it? They've always been able to see it?" The idea had almost religious intensity. To see the relic of the first moments of space-time all around you—it would make space into a museum, a cathedral. Or maybe to them it was just as ordinary as starlight is to us.

"They would have to have telescopes, I think," said Yermolov. "Or even be out in space, beyond their atmosphere." I'd thought of that, too, but I'd kept quiet, making up for my earlier slip. Now he felt secure, explaining that of course we hadn't seen it in their pix, so presumably their camera-equivalents couldn't register it, so therefore they probably couldn't either, normally.

"Maybe at night," he concluded, "but if they have a night they take no pictures in it—none to send strangers, anyhow." That thought seemed to jolt him out of patronizing complacency. "Who knows what they have and have not told us of? Anything," he muttered to me, "it could be absolutely anything!"

Thorborg just laughed. "Well, there's one thing we know of, anyway! Feast your eyes on this!"

While we talked the arc of the planet had been sliding round beneath us until we were looking straight down on it, an almost featureless red surface that couldn't have looked less like the Earth from above. The eye raced for the relief of the pinpoint of green that swelled up among the flat aching glow. Another followed it, and another, expanding, taking shape as they lifted out of that impenetrable atmosphere. Green oblongs, rough along the edges like tiny single-cell creatures under a microscope, rose towards the viewpoint, smoothly, quickly. Thorborg gave a harsh crow's cackle.

"Pretty, aren't they?" She leant heavily over into my lap. "But they're antiques compared to ours, crocks, junkheaps, rustbuckets before they've begun. They're about where we were a hundred and fifty years ago, no later!"

About fifty years before you were born, I thought as she waggled her ermine hair under my nose. The intensity of my loathing startled me. I needed Kirsty badly, or Ziz, or just about any woman who wasn't a power-tripping fossil.

"Of course they're *big,*" she said with mock ruefulness, "but as the old saying goes, size isn't everything..."

I wouldn't have thought a BC princess could have a gift for understatement, but I did when the size scale appeared on the screen, pacing the oncoming shapes. The frame froze and whitened around them, just as before, and the computers lifted the ghosts out of them and sent them spinning skeletally around. The relentless red of the screen turned to gray now, and showed me how hollow Thorborg's good humour was. Like a tide, it had run out, leaving her face the colour of sand. Yermolov's long face had drawn back into lines, a contemptuous smile that rang as hollow as waves in a cave.

And yet she was right. The captions that came streaming around the ship-images told a full story, and anyone who knew much about spacecraft could confirm most of them himself. They were primitive, all right, riding massive fusion motors and apparently nothing else. A bit like driving a groundcar with a flamethrower for an exhaust. But perhaps they'd lots of room down there. The drive flames, starbright to human eyes, showed only as a slight rippling disturbance to this viewer. The outlines of the craft were clear enough, though; they were all the same, as far as we could see, gaunt, irregular things with a spiny internal framework and a tight skin over them which flexed and pulsed in a very disturbing way.

"You're quite sure they're artificial?" I inquired nervously.

Yermolov grunted. "Most of them is, nobody's too sure about that skin. Nauseating things, aren't they?"

One day I might tell him how much I disagreed. Not now. They were as awesome as anything else about these aliens, and the same mixture of things familiar and things fantastically new. To measure them in human terms was a pointless exercise. Each of those ships was fifty-three kilom long, more or less, yet capable of atmospheric lift-off at a cool 15G acceleration—painfully slow to them probably. So what? An ordinary pursuit cruiser could vaporize them all; an Infall ship could be half a lightyear away before they were out of the system, assuming they had the range. Or could it?

"Do you think they've got Infall?"

Thorborg smiled thinly. "Those ships, definitely not. And from looking at the rest of their society we guess they haven't got it on any of them. They seem to have some kind of gravity tech just getting off the ground, pardon my expression, but nothing comparable to ours. At a guess they need a century or so, if their progress rate's like ours. We've reason to think it is, if we read their chronologies aright—but it's about the only thing!" Her skin still looked gray. The images, stark against the white, were almost filling the screen now. Free of their red background they looked more natural, less threatening.

"No apparent weaponry?" I read off the screen.

"No, none," said Thorborg. "Harmless as a stingless bee, except for the drive exhaust—and even that is not a combat design. And they have none of the elementary defences which even the most pacific human ship carries." She gave a sardonic chuckle. "It would seem they don't fight each other as much as we do—"

"Or maybe that is just what they want us to believe," interrupted Yermolov. "I think it is all too obvious, just laid out for us. You are a policeman, Mr. Bellamy, with a professionally suspicious mind—would you not agree?"

"Well, I wouldn't take them on trust," I said, scratching at my scalp with honest concern. "I'd want to know more, I guess—"

The muted buzz of a deskcom cut me off short. Thorborg barked a word I didn't catch and the frame froze completely.

"Oh, business, business," she sighed. "Answer that, will you, Andrei? And make sure the screen can't be seen—"

"Yes, of course," muttered Yermolov, swinging the heavy instrument around. The windows undimmed, and Thorborg stood up, yawned and stretched till the outlines of her small breasts flattened out. I stood up also, and she grinned at me. I smiled back as amiably as I could; I had a cold unpleasant feeling that it might be hard to get away tonight. Not that she was so repellent physically, rather the opposite in fact. What turned me right off her was the way she'd been using me as her amusement, her distraction, her defence against what she saw on that screen, what it awoke in her. Like a pet, a lap-dog. No, lower even than that. Like worry-beads.

"I'm sorry about the interruption," she said, glancing over at her assistant, engaged in a low-voiced altercation over the com. "But it was a good moment to take a break and let it all sink in. Frightening, isn't it?" She gave a sinuous shiver.

"Awesome," I muttered, looking at the static image in the screen. The whole thing had knocked me ass-over, it was so far from what I'd been expecting my mind kept on confusing itself, whirling around something indefinably important but impossible to pin down, a panic that obscured its own causes. I sat on it, hard, forcing myself not to think about it at all. Till later, when I calmed down.

"Personally," went on Thorborg, "I think they really don't fight much. They do have some kind of combat—I'll show you that later, if you'd like—but I warn you it's a bore. Ritualized, almost, and apparently not at all wholesale." She frowned over at Yermolov. "He could be right, of course. We cannot be sure. Meeting truly alien minds for the first time— a terrible prospect, terrifying! Can we trust our own understanding? Whatever fool thought that science, mathematics, would be a common ground? The facts, yes. But the attitudes to them, the subjective interpretations—"

"All right, all right!" the Russian barked suddenly. "If he's so damned insistent, let him through—"

It was as if my mind heard and obeyed. That thought, that realization I'd been fighting so desperately to repress, came plunging through every defense I'd put up, and the implications of it froze me in my chair.

"Which is why we had to keep all this a secret." Thorborg gave a brittle little laugh. "Can you just imagine the doubt, dissension, the outright panic, if this got out—prematurely?"

"Oh yes," I agreed. "I can."

"People can't be relied on, can they? If they were too ready to take our little friends out there at face value—perhaps even try to exploit their existence somehow—subversive ends—we cannot allow that, can we?"

"No," I said. "Of course not."

"We have to find out more, don't we? So we have sent out an interstellar probe, with as little publicity as possible—why, Mark, are you all right?"

"Headache, I guess." I smiled vaguely at her. I wondered if anyone had ever smiled like that at Stalin or Hitler.

She nodded briskly. "Understandable. A most disturbing film, in many ways. Sit back and relax, and I'll massage—"

"Perhaps Mr. Bellamy would like to rest by himself for a few minutes?" suggested Yermolov unexpectedly, over my shoulder. "Unfortunately this call has brought up urgent private business, Director. We will need to be alone for a few minutes—"

"Never a moment's peace!" laughed Thorborg. "You see what high office is? If I'd any sense I'd come and live on your Sea Station where nobody could get at me—well, almost nobody!" she added archly. "Help yourself to more scotch, Mark, and go and relax in—" She caught another flicker of gaze from the Russian, and the hand that had been waving me towards the waiting room now indicated the massive oak door, "—in my private office. Just for a few minutes. There's an *extravagantly* comfortable couch—"

I was wafted through the doorway onto cloud masquerading as carpet, into a much lighter, airier room than the outside office. Somehow it looked harder too, with a black infostore squatting in one corner. A lean hand brushed almost accidentally against my cheek, and I was alone with the closing door. I stretched out fingertips to the smooth surface and felt the almost subliminal hum of a security lock engaging. I was shut in.

I stood, leaning my forehead against the cool hard wood, trying to calm my racing brain. Too many things had become clear at once. What I'd been shown was real, there was no getting away from that. Image forgery had its limitations, and this was far beyond them. I'd been off balance for a while, bombarded with an awesome truth when I'd been expecting lies. How many others had they done that to, people who'd stumbled upon something awkward, but were a little too sig-

nificant to be quietly rubbed out? Plenty, I guessed. They'd
come, they'd gaped, they'd gone away willingly muzzled—
for the general good, of course, of aliens as well as humans.
Just as I would have, in my turn. If I hadn't happened to have
that extra little bit of knowledge—

So now I knew it was just their second line of defence. First
secrecy, then a gigantic half-truth, so big it overawes the most
determined troublemaker, making him shut himself up for fear
of stampeding the human animal. And all the time the beast
was loose, and at its ugliest. I remembered the granite grey of
Thorborg's face, Yermolov's lips drawn back in an ape's grim-
ace. Baboon reaction! Unthinking, murderous fear! Nothing
had changed. The probe was what I'd feared it was, a swelling
mass of destruction, a hammer to strike a whole planet from
the skies. Only its target wasn't the Colony.

There was no rest for me here. Why hadn't Yermolov wanted
me to wait in the waiting room? Because he couldn't stop me
getting out of there? In which case—

I plucked a small rod of grey plastic out of my pocket and
clipped it onto my procom interface. A thin spike stuck out of
the other end when I twisted it, and I drove that into the center
of the door's largest panel, leaning on it to drive it in. It didn't
penetrate far, but it was enough. I had to hear what that com
call was about, and I was in the best place for it. There'd be
every conceivable bug shielding against the outside world, but
between an inner and outer office? Surely not. Anyway, there
was only one way to find out. I clipped in the procom earpiece.

"—it's too ridiculous!" came a tinny squawk. Low quality,
but good enough. It relied on the door for resonance, and it
was thick wood. "Let me talk to the man! You—whatever your
name is—you say you saw this man *where?*" I couldn't make
out the reply; the com wasn't loud enough. I could have used
a better bug, but this was the only one I could lay hands on
without authorization. I'd confiscated it a couple of years ago
from an unsavoury little voyeur—I beg your pardon, an au-
thorized Social Morality investigator—who'd been using it to
pry into the ups and downs of our free and easy Station life.
I heard Thorborg clearly enough, though.

"But what the fu—what would he be doing there? You know
who he is? No? He's the Sea Station security chief, that's who!
No question of his being there officially—definitely not! So—
you're sure?" She was beginning to sound hysterical. "When

he took his cap off?" A long silence. I kept thinking about that lock. In a dikflik I'd have had a selection of logic-controlled lockpicks, but in real life those were hard to come by. Or a gun, but I'd never have got one past the scanners. I did have some stuff in my jacket lining that could take drastic care of the door, but in this confined space it would take care of me as well.

"I see!" said Thorborg suddenly. "Well then—you haven't mentioned this to anyone? Good! Then don't! It's more than your hide's worth, *verstehst du?* Good! Then you get your ass up here on the double! And bring your gun along—*ja, Kanone, sicher! Und halt's maul!*" I heard the blip of broken contact.

"Fashing Kraut!" she said harshly. "They never speak English properly!"

"Director—if this is true—"

"If?"

"But how could Bellamy have been there? He was supposed to be on the Station."

Even through the bug her voice sounded ragged. "No he wasn't! He was on leave, remember? That's how that little shit—what's his name? Simoneau—that's why he'd so little trouble fixing Carlsen's—" A great gusty sigh ended in a crash. She must have collapsed into a chair. "So, Andrei, it looks as if dear Mark is more than he seems. And you and I have come within an ace of making the biggest blunder of our lives. It must never get out, d'you hear? Never! Never! I'd be finished—"

"As would I," said Yermolov. "But it looked to be the best thing. He could not just disappear—and the film has always worked so well—and from his dossier he seemed just the—'

"Fokke det!" exclaimed the old woman. "He could be anyone—anything—an agent—but whose? The interrogation—careful, it must be, no sloppy sadism. I'll see to that . . ." There was a pause, then she asked, "How long till the guard gets here?"

"Ten minutes at least, Director. He was calling from Admin Centre."

"We can't trust him any more than anyone else. For the moment we need him, but . . . Well, that can wait. For the moment we have work to do. If they find out that we actually *invited* Bellamy here—The evidence must vanish. At once!"

"Well . . . If I get his route card from the door, it should be possible to override the Security controls and wipe it all out of the databases—" That was news. He shouldn't have been able to do that. Standards must be slipping with a vengeance. "But there is still his zep—I cannot do anything about hangar records while it is still in there..."

"We'll shift it later. Scrub the main records now, d'you hear? We're in danger every fashing second they're here!" You could tell she wasn't at all used to being scared.

"A minute's work, Director..." soothed Yermolov.

"Then do it!"

Silence fell, giving me a chance to look around the little office, for the slightest shadow of a way out. There really didn't seem to be one. The room was in one corner of the tower, and the two walls were mostly window, overlooking a pleasant pine stand. They evidently didn't open, and had the characteristic bronze sheen of modern battle plastic; nothing, not even the infostore or the light wooden desk, would be heavy enough to break them. The other two walls held only the one door, and seemed to be solidly built. Well, they'd just have to unlock it for me, that was all. And somehow they had to be persuaded to do that before the guard and his *Kanone* got here....

Which would be in just over six minutes, now.

Start a fire? Sure, by rubbing two bits of carpet together. Not being a tobacco addict, I wasn't carrying inflammables. The desk might have been full of them for all I knew, but it was solid and well locked. Something electrical? The room controls would be all properly failsafed and fireproof, and the infostore had intelligent protection.

I began stabbing at the control panel on top.

"Restricted Information—" began the brisk voice, then changed pitch as I gave the casing a solid kick. "Warning! Any attempt to retrieve information by improper means—" I hit another combination of tabs, not at random. I was trying out some standard service and maintenance codes. Useless without proper authority, but accurate enough to disturb the box-brain into squawking—"may result in the activation of security measures"—and its voice would be heard through the screen out there. How would they know what I was capable of doing to it? "—up to and including memory dumping and self-destruction of this unit!"

I left off at once, shaken. A dangerous toy for a BC princess! Anything that would destroy the static as well as dynamic memory units would mess up this room somewhat in the process. I'd have to think of something.

The lock hummed and the door swung open. Yermolov was moving fast, lifting an improbably large handgun. I kicked the couch across in front of him. He caught it across the shins and staggered, flailing his arms wildly to keep his balance. I chopped hard at his wrist, and the gun fell—but behind him, slithering away across the outer office floor. I springboarded off the couch and slammed into Yermolov, sending him sprawling backwards through the doorway. He folded under my weight and I sailed on over his head. I landed on my hands and rolled forward onto my feet, cutting Thorborg off from the gun, now lying half under the long table on the far side. She lunged at a nearby deskcom, and was almost too quick for me; her hand was on the panel when I reached her. The other hand clawed at my eyes; I ducked under it and gave her a roundhouse slap. I don't know why—no more merciful than a punch, when you think about it, and it left a tooth stuck in the back of my hand, something you don't see happen in the dikflicks. She hit the wall and bounced off, sliding down it like old coveralls off a peg, out.

Yermolov was on his feet now, and I barely dodged a vicious chop at my throat; he'd more science than I'd expected. Perhaps Thorborg liked her aide to have basic bodyguarding skills. He also had a much longer reach, and normally I'd have stayed outside that and worn him down. But now I'd nothing much left of time or second chances. I closed, taking a jarring thump on one temple, blocked the next blow, seized the arm, spun on my heel, dropped and yanked sharply down. For a millisecond or so the tall man's weight was pivoted across my shoulder. In that precise instant I snapped upright and heaved. He *flew*. And landed with a crash, and lay still.

I tried to run to the gun and scoop it up, but the blood was roaring in my ears; I missed my balance, fell and crawled. Surely the guard would try the doorcom first. He didn't. The door just sighed open and there he was in all his glory. Maybe he'd heard that last crash. I knew him at once, but I was surprised he'd remembered me from all those months ago at the farmhouse. After all, I'd been bedraggled by the after-effects of seduction, seawater, alcohol and exhaustion that night. And yet all I had to do was take off my cap in the sunlight and he knew me at once. Smarter than he looked, this guard—

Heinz's buddy, the other pair of boots on the stair. And he was reacting quickly enough now. *Wasted potential*, I thought as his gunmuzzle jerked around and down towards me. A *shame* . . .

The big gun was under my fingers. I scooped it up and fired from where I lay. There was a thin bright flash and a terrible sizzling sound, but I saw nothing, because I was rolling aside and onto my feet. I heard, though, a hard bouncing impact. I saw the guard's gun jerk up to follow me, but it was only reflex. There was no shot, just a grotesque dancing stagger before the headless body toppled backwards over the doorsill. The boots kicked viciously, at nothing now but the empty air. There was a stink of ionized air, and underneath that a smoky, greasy reek. The boots twitched again, and that was all.

To stop my stomach heaving I stared down at the strange weapon I held. Trust Thorborg to have the latest gimmick— one of those handbeams everyone was talking about. As well I'd only needed to fire point blank, or I might have tried to allow for trajectory. Gimmick or not, though, it had one useful quality, and that was silence. I could have been sliced into strips small enough to disappear down a kitchen recycler with never a sound. Once, of course, I'd had my brain wrung dry.

Somebody groaned. I hefted the gun and strode over to Yermolov. If he was waking up—But when I turned his head towards me I realized there was little chance of that, unless Whittaker's mob were right. The skull was as puffy and soft as bruised fruit, and the eyes bulged out horribly. A violent impact on the back of the head—textbook symptoms. He'd had an awkward landing.

I swore. I hadn't meant to do that. But anything can happen in an all-out fight; people survive worse, are killed by less. And it was a hell of a lot quicker and cleaner than what he'd planned for me. I turned away in disgust, with an urgent need to think about something else. There was plenty. I fumbled in my jacket and brought out my note-recorder, shaking it gingerly. Nothing rattled, which was comforting, because inside it was the stripped-down mechanism of that antique camera from Rio. There were ultra-modern cameras which could usually baffle a standard camera-detector, but these were hard to come by, for obvious reasons; anyway, this old fellow had them all beaten. Nothing, not even the basic image-making process, was at all electronic; it simply wasn't possible to detect such a thing. I flipped it out, and pivoted slowly on my heels, clicking the shutter mechanism as I went. A few stereo images of all this, however crude, would make some hefty evidence. I used up the first half of the photoreactive tape on that vast frozen image that filled the heights and depths of the screen. I took some more that showed both the screen image and the room around, to establish its location. These old chemical pix had another advantage; they couldn't be produced by image construction, not convincingly. I clicked my way through the tape methodically, calmly, then put it into develop mode and pocketed it again. I felt better; it had kept me from thinking about something really unpleasant, something necessary if I wanted to live long enough to get that evidence where it could be used. Well, I'd have to face it now. I picked up the gun from the table where I'd laid it, and turned unwillingly round.

And froze.

Thorborg was facing me, awake, upright and leaning on the far side of a desk. My numbed mind took in every little detail with clear, stupid helplessness, the tousled ermine hair, the trickle of blood from one side of the thin lips, the deskcom panel less than a foot from her outstretched hand, the cold malevolence in those eyes. She knew damn well I couldn't possibly reach her in time, that whatever I did to her after she touched the one necessary tab would be nothing compared to my own inevitable death. It had been her groan I'd heard, of course, but in my eagerness to stop thinking about Yermolov I'd blotted her out as well.

There was the gun in my hand, a jet of coherent radiation faster than any hand just waiting to bridge the gap between us. But my hands had the weight of two bodies on them, I could hardly lift the heavy object up and I knew I was wasting my time trying because I couldn't possibly fire it, whatever I'd been planning, and I was finished and would have everything I'd ever known ripped out of my mind and so in their turn would everyone who'd trusted me, Ryly and Khalid and most of all—

This time I saw the beam. It seared a hairthin line on my retina, stretching from the wide muzzle to the outstretched arm and the wall behind. The hand jerked convulsively away from the panel, and the sleeve smoked where she clutched at it, staggering. I set my teeth and fired again, and again, and again, hating myself and hating my need to do this and hating her most of all for creating the need until at last my finger clutched the trigger convulsively down and a continuous beam streaked through the greasy smokecloud and the ionized air puffed into a string of glowing globes along its path.

Then I dropped the overheated gun and was immediately, violently sick. When I could think at all straight I was on hands and knees, still retching. I tried to tell myself I'd have had to do it anyway, that I'd known that from the moment I'd thought of escape. But I knew equally well that if she hadn't wakened, if the need hadn't been so urgent, I might not have been able to kill.

Or I might. And, illogically, I was most afraid of that. I was more than glad it hadn't come to a test.

There was very little smoke, not enough to set off a fire alarm, but the room reeked of burnt body. That isn't the same as cooked meat, which is cleaned first. My stomach had nothing left to get rid of, but it was still trying. There was water in the drink dispenser, and I rinsed out my mouth and wiped down my uniform. A seam had gone here and there in the confusion, but it didn't look too bad. I swallowed a double brandy, and that wasn't too bad, either, so I had another. Then I found my cap, and picked the gun up, despite a strong inclination to hurl it away. There was no sign of a scanner pass on it, yet there was bound to be a gun detector in the waiting room or the landing. Puzzled, I searched Yermolov's body and found nothing. But a corner desk had an open drawer, and in that I found a combination holster and recharger, with the essential pass. It would have spoiled the cut of the Russian's clothes, but there was room for it under my uniform jacket. On top of the desk there was an activated data terminal, and I was startled to see my name on the main screen. Looking closer, I saw my route card slotted in below, and remembered the end of that overheard conversation. Naturally I knew my way round SpaceDep Security databases, and I was amazed to see how thoroughly Yermolov had done his work; they held not the slightest trace of my presence here today. I could have vanished in mid-Atlantic, for all the world knew, and left not a breath of suspicion on SpaceDep. Except for the zep, of course, and that wouldn't have taken long to dispose of. Superb work for an amateur—or maybe he'd had lots of practice.

It took a second or two to dawn on me just what he had done. In trying to shield himself and his boss he'd also shielded their killer. Till then escape had just been a matter of a few hours freedom for me, long enough to tell the world what had been done in its name. After that, a manhunt, and in this electronic age they never lasted long. Then the end, because to shield Kirsty and others I daren't be taken alive. But now?

If I could get out of here, half a day or more could pass before the hunters got on my tail. Long enough to make a clean getaway. Hope was almost painful, like blood flowing back into an unused limb. But it could be done. I could see how and where and with whom. Hellfire, it was worth a try!

I snatched the crimped piece of throwaway circuitry out of the slot, and scrubbed the details of it off the screen. Then I strode over to the guard's corpse and forced myself to rifle the pockets for his pass. I couldn't help seeing the ragged mess in which the neck ended. The gun had a needle beam; my hand must have been less steady than usual. At last I stood, grabbed his boots, and hauled him fully into the office, where his head already lay. Thanks to the beam's cauterizing effect there was only a little blood on the waiting room floor; shifting a chair over that made the little room look quite innocent, unless you knew what lay behind the inner door. It turned out that Thorborg, understandably, had privacy-blocked all the com lines, which was the last of the precautions I'd planned. There was nothing more to do. I stood at the inner door, and looked an unwilling last on what I'd done. I tried to remind myself that it was one of Carlsen's murderers that lay there, and two of the murderers' bosses—small fry relatively, but big enough to be in charge of the cover-up operations. Looking at it like that, nothing in that grim scene seemed anything less than just. No less sickening, though. I slid the inner door gently across, turned on the privacy sign on the main door and let it lock itself behind me. The air was cleaner out here.

The guard's pass got me down the tower and into the open air. It wasn't safe to rely on it after that, so I was in for a long walk. I didn't dare hurry too much—in a senior uniform that would be conspicuous—but there was the outside chance of meeting someone who knew me. It was a fine evening now, with plenty of people still about. The evening rush home was just tailing off, and the guard's pass got me into the hangar among a cheerful crowd of stragglers. It hadn't been too hard; no large office complex can be turned into a security fortress for more than short periods, and with the African emergency fading into history things had got worse than slack. Compared to the Sea Station—I chuckled, though it was gallows humour of a sort. Maybe it would go the same way, now, without me. Because there was no going back now. The only real home I'd ever known was lost to me.

That hit me hard, but not as hard as it might have. I was puzzled, pacing along the concrete walkways to my zep shelf. Underneath all the strain and horror and fear something kept on bubbling up, making me feel kilos lighter, putting a jaunty spring in my stride. Hysteria? It didn't feel like that. When my procom paid the toll without demur I almost burst out laughing. When I settled myself in the pilot's seat and freed the clamps I felt ready to float away by myself. I began to wonder if my mind was going, but I couldn't even worry about that. I was still a functioning pilot, at least. I took the zep up, turning it slowly to face the slot of blue sky that was my first step to freedom. When my turn came I gunned my motors and soared through into the untainted sunlight, up towards the lowest clouds and the Paris–Wien lanes. The wind was light, but I felt like a leaf it could whip halfway round the world, weightless and free. I understood myself at last.

I was happy. Whatever other weights I bore, I was free of the worst. The man in my dossier, my dark, dogged *döppel-ganger*. The man Thorborg had seen in me, the loyal creature she could trust and toy with, he'd died with her—and not a merciful moment too soon. I did laugh now, remembering a face set in lines of cold suspicion; well, Simoneau could have it now, that and the corner in hell that went with it. A bequest. I could be as dead as my dark twin in a few hours, but what did I care? However long I lived I'd be free of him, and home and security weren't too high a price to pay.

The Security Chief was gone.

For good.

SIX

THE thin mosquito-whine of the camera motor faded down into silence. Ryly lowered the viewfinder-viewer from his face, greyer now than the cold dawn light could account for.

"Right..." was all he said, and then "*Svatá pravda*, what a mess!"

Kirsty reached out and took the camera from him, clicking it into rewind. I wanted to snatch it out of her hands, but what was the point? I'd already told her what had happened; if she didn't see what the result looked like, her imagination would only supply something worse.

Ryly stared out through the steamy side window of the airspacer's cockpit, out to sea and the cliff-edge where Ziz Brazda was stalking up and down, trying to keep warm. I could see her casting longing looks at the cockpit of my zep, but she knew well enough why she couldn't go in; if I was wrong, if the countdown clock in the back of my mind was even a little bit out, she could find herself shut in and shanghaied by police beams latching onto the license sender. All she could do was shelter behind it, and not for long; it was too cold to stay still. I was sorry about that, but it couldn't be helped; the airspacer cockpit was the only place we could talk in—Ryly had landed

134

in nearby Quiberon and walked out—and Ziz just didn't want to hear. She'd gladly flown Kirsty, my guitars and other treasures over in the 'spacer, there being nothing illegal in it, but beyond that she wouldn't get involved. The Station mentality, just like Herincx and so many others—like myself, for the last twenty years. I couldn't blame her, not really.

The rewind clicked to a halt. Kirsty bent over the viewer. It was Ryly who broke the silence. "How 'bout you? You get anythin'?"

"The navcom says 40 Eridani. Hard to believe—it's a multiple, KOV-M5eV and a white dwarf—wild! But it's the only thing out that way at the distance she gave..."

"If she wasn't just feedin' you—"

"She wasn't. Remember, she'd no idea I knew anything about the probe's real course. Without that, distance alone wouldn't have meant a thing. About another five lightyears past the Colony, damn near beside it in our sky—might be how they cottoned on to us in the first place, picking up maser communications to a DESprobe out that way."

"Or to the first Colony Ship, before it officially faded out."

"Possible. Hence my little mistake. At kick-off, before course corrections, it'd be hard to say which of the two stars the thing was headed for."

"But *why?*" shrilled Kirsty, so loud we both jumped. "That's what I want tae know—why? The BCs and the Colony, aye, spyin' on it or wantin' tae smash it up, I can understand that! But aliens, *these* aliens—why the hell? Just xenophobia, baboon reaction, is that it? See stranger, fear stranger, hate stranger, *kill*—"

"Some of that, I'm sure," I said. "It used to be a popular debate subject, once. What do we do if *They* knock on the door? Don't answer, was what a lot of folk said. *They* might want our world, our natural resources, our slave labour or just us, as beef cattle or whatever. Don't answer, just hide under the bed, there ain't nobody here but us chickens!"

"Ever since H. G. Wells," sighed Kirsty, but all she got was our blank looks.

"That all, you think?" inquired Ryly.

"Of course not. Some of that, but there's more. They've got good reasons, good as they see them, anyway. They wouldn't want aliens any more than they want the Colony, or Whittaker's god. What was it he said? Something about encouraging people to look beyond this world, the one the BCs shape and rule. Reminding folk there are other concerns, other ways of life, things the BC state can never touch—alternatives. That's what the bureaucrats hate—that's what they want to kill! Baboon reaction, yes—but reasoned."

"Aliens," muttered Ryly, and coughed rackingly, unpleasant in the confined space. "The Colony—people, that was different, but—Bellamy, hey, hold on. Think a minute. So what you say's true—couldn't the BC still be right? I mean, these're *aliens*, man! Better we'd never contacted them, but now they've found *us*—hell, we can't trust them! We can't be sure! It's the human race at stake."

"Ye're sayin' that genocide—worse than that, even—that ye like the idea?" demanded Kirsty.

"Hell, no, think I'm Stalin or somethin'? Like I said—better we'd laid low, shut up, kept to ourselves, safe, Earth and the Colony both. But these things, we can't *afford* to take a risk with them! Better the missile cleans the mistake off the slate, things quiet down an' we're safe again. I don't like it, I *hate* it—but then I'm not so wild about some of the things you feel you were justified in doin' either!" He folded his arms, sat back and glared at me defiantly. "You goin' to smash in my head next?"

Kirsty was off the bunk in one fluid motion and in spitting distance of the medman's face. "Ye stupid sonuvabitch!" she raged. "D'ye think Mark enjoyed killin'—anyone? He was just tryin' tae protect people—me an' you among them!"

"Easy, Kirsty," I said, and sat her down gently on the bunk beside me. She clutched the camera as if she was afraid the scene inside it might burst out. "Ryly, you're no fool, but you're bloody well talking like one. That missile can be *tracked*, man! With the mass it'll have by the time it connects it'll leave a wake of gravitational disturbance—on interstellar radiation, for a start—pointing right back this way. That's why it's a one-shot weapon—no second chances! *Safe?* What's safe? As if we could somehow hide away from the rest of the universe. Not as long as we use any kind of broadcast communication, we can't. Think of it! Just round here, in our own little neighbourhood, three planets inhabited, two with intelligent life, two with roughly the same kind of life! There must be millions of inhabited worlds out there, whatever the experts spout. Some like us, some not. Sooner or later one of them's bound to track back our communications overspill and find us. What then? Under the bed?"

"If that missile hits its target," said Kirsty venomously, "we'll have tae hide. Shrink back into our own wee system, never make a noise, never stir outside it. What if any other race ever found out what we'd done? *Then* we'd never be safe. They'd never trust us. Not for an instant. There's bound to be some of them who think like you, Ryly. We'd be giving them grand evidence, wouldn't we? They'd wipe us out like plague germs and feel good about it!"

My own imagination was striking sparks off Kirsty's, and kindling an evil flame. "Unless..." I began, and actually had trouble shaping the thought. "Unless we got them first. At once, on first contact. A pre-emptive strike, before they could possibly have a chance to find out about us. Hellfire, isn't that a glorious future history for us! A race of paranoid killers, skulking in our own backwater system when we might have had the stars! Clamping down on exploration, communications, anything that might lead someone else to us and make us stain our hands again with the same old crime... Carrying that weight down the generations. What would that make of us?"

"Predators," breathed Kirsty, "Carrion-eaters—no, worse, ghouls, vampires, killing just tae carry on our own worthless shadow-lives."

"But the BCs—they must have thought of that..." protested Ryly, with the look of a trapped man.

"Aye, sure," sighed Kirsty, "they're no' all fools. I guess they like the idea—"

"Like it?"

"Yes," I said. "The same way their reasons look good, to them. What better for them, their dynasties, than a society that daren't look outwards except to strike? That has a fixed frontier over which nobody dare stray, because everything beyond it is by definition hostile? Like the Russians tried to establish, back when. A society that has to organize to protect its secret, that has to huddle around its own rotten core, keep strict discipline and order to shield it, that daren't even dream of change or revolt because a moment of relaxed vigilance might let the secret slip out—"

Ryly bunched his fists and smashed them down on the chair arm. "But that couldn't *last*—"

"They think it could. Remember the official line—life on other worlds is rare, civilizations like hen's teeth? Their experts have laid that down, their committees—and BCs rely on them to understand the universe, the same way they rely on dossiers to understand people. It's almost a matter of faith—take it away and their whole philosophy crumbles. The document's the thing: the established official fact, only to be altered by more of the same. So they believe—the BCs—that it'll be a million years or so before we get another contact. It's to their advantage to believe that, which must make it a whole hell of a lot easier. And if they're just a little bit wrong, they and theirs will be long dead anyway, so who cares? That seems like a good gamble to them."

"Aye," said Kirsty bitterly. "Ye were spoutin' about safety, Chaz. That seem safe tae you?"

A hand hammered on the lock alarm, and the door swung open at once. Ziz, her face a nasty leaden shade under her tan, vaulted in, slammed it behind her and squashed in between Kirsty and me on the bunk, wrapping chilly parts of herself indiscriminately around us. "You b-b-b-bastard, Chief!" she stammered. "Oh-oh-07:14, I've been out there two hours. And you wanted t-to be away by eight!"

I rubbed her back vigorously, feeling the spine and smooth lean muscle through her flight suit. She wriggled so I was rubbing her rear end, which felt equally muscular. I studiously avoided Kirsty's eye.

"We're just about through, I guess, Ziz. You can stop your ears, though, if you like. Well, Ryly? I'd cheerfully argue ethics and power politics with you all morning, but I've got this little countdown going in my head, you know? My getaway margins, and Kirsty's. Some time after 0800 they'll dig up the fact that my zep was there when apparently I wasn't, and tag it just on sus. When that gets them nothing they'll track down this airspacer. By that time I've got to be out of beam reach."

Ryly blinked sleepy scepticism. "Pretty exact timin', huh?"

"My business. Somewhere between twelve and fourteen hours it'll take them, allowing for discovery time and their damned inefficiency. If Thorborg hadn't blotted me out of the databanks to save her own skin—sorry, Ziz, you didn't hear that—it'd have been two or three hours at most. So—"

"So?"

"Hellfire, man, I'm not asking you to agree with every

fashing thing I say—just to take the story on, put the arguments across, your own, mine, anybody's! As fairly as you can. So it doesn't all happen in silence, so the human race doesn't go by default! It's too big a question, it's everyone's destiny. Isn't that what your goddam free agencies are all about?"

Ryly looked very directly up at me. "Now you're talkin'. If you'd jus' said that first we wouldn't have had all this palaver. Sure, I'll do that—" He stretched out his hand for the camera. Kirsty thrust it at him, but before he could withdraw his hand my own clamped down on it. I found myself glaring down into his dark sleepy eyes as if I could somehow sear my way through to what lay behind them—ridiculous, yes, but that was how it felt. "That's my only evidence, Ryly. You know it can't be duped, not without all kinds of crazy chemical baths and stuff. You take that and you'd better mean what you say. Fail me and I'll—"

The eyes narrowed in sudden fury, and he tried, unsuccessfully of course, to pull his hand free.

"Fail *you?* What the fuck do I care about *you?* So you can break my neck, what's that make you? I'm not doing this for *you*, you arrogant bastard, I'm doing it for everyone! Even the fashing BCs, they're human too! Like you said—that's what we're all about. But I guess you wouldn't understand that." He burst into an incredible paroxysm of coughing, and I let go of him in involuntary disgust. "I need some air," he said thickly, pocketed the camera and moved to the airlock. Ziz swung up to intercept him, but I shook my head. He stepped heavily out and down.

"You tell me if he lets you down, hmm, my Chief?" Ziz murmured in my ear. "Just that, not how or anything, and *I'll* kill him. Just drop me the word, hmm?" She sat back and smiled seraphically at Kirsty. Cold air and gull-cries drifted in, and the endless rush of the sea below. I smiled at the two women and stepped out after him. The Breton turf was soft under my boots, very like Galloway a lifetime ago. The air and the gull cries were the same, too. *So I come back to it again?* I thought. *All that worrying about my choice, when I never was going to have one, after all.*

"Point taken," was what I said to Ryly. "I'm sorry. But you know how much this means to me."

"Sure," he said. "I know."

"You can keep the camera. After all this is over, I mean.

Might come in useful, in your line of work."

"Thanks," he said, surprised. "You might need it, too—"

"Not if I can help it. But I do want something from you."

"Shoot."

"You usually pay for good stories, don't you?"

"Well—yes, in some cases. When we have to. Somehow got the idea cash wasn't your main concern. Since I had some trouble bribin' you. So what is your price, then?"

"Thirty thousand, in this account number, now. You can do that. You paid it for the land reclamation evidence, three years ago."

"How'd you know that?"

"Dossier."

"Shoulda known. But that emptied the agency's snake fund for the quarter. I can't just—"

"I've no time to dicker. It's for Kirsty, not me. To buy her an education, some kind of future."

"With your rank, your connections—"

"Not after this. For her, it'll blow over. For me, never. Understand?"

He nodded. "What's that number?"

He tapped the figures out on his procom. The minute the deposit registered in my account I shifted it, split it, fed it through a whole lot of other accounts to which I'd prepared access codes. In five minutes it looked as if the money had reached Kirsty from a whole range of sources. Highly suspicious, but hard to challenge.

"You could always take to data fraud," grunted Ryly admiringly.

"You should see the men who trained me," I said. "They'd skin me in a second. Not a word to Kirsty, remember? Thanks. And now you'd better be thinking about making tracks. How soon can you get the story out?"

"1800 slot. I held it just in case. No trouble with the agency, I can go right to the boss-man an' he'll jump at this, I know him. Risk any amount of trouble just to keep another agency's paws off it. And I would take it to another, too, if I had to. Kansas Interpress, just down the road aways."

"Thanks again. But it seems I'm trusting a whole lot of people . . ."

"That's the way the world works. Lone hero never did get anywhere, whatever the dikfliks say. You want to be heard, you've no choice. Gotta trust somebody."

"Suppose so. I'm just not very good at that." Kirsty and Ziz were climbing out of the machine behind us, deep in conversation. I looked at my procom. "0745, Ryly. And I've a couple of things to do."

"Sure. Well, it's been fun. I have this feeling I'm not goin' to see you again."

"We may be able to keep in touch, sort of. We'll see. Good luck!"

"Same to you, security man. Hey, lady! I'm splitting. You wanted a ride?"

"To Brno," said Ziz. "That'll be my cover. Home for a couple of days. So off you go, Chief, hmm?" She shook her fringe out of her eyes. "Not coming back, are you? Not ever." I glanced over at Kirsty, but she was saying goodbye to Ryly. "She knows, all right," said Ziz sardonically. "There you go, underestimating women again. *She* told *me*. Well—if you must leave us with that pig Simoneau—" She wrapped her arms round my neck and kissed me hard enough to draw blood, doing a slow-motion writhe at the same time. She felt slim and hard, totally unlike Kirsty, and for a minute I had a feeling of being torn in two. But the moment my arms tightened around her she pulled free. "There!" she said, in a tone of brisk satisfaction. "Coming, medman? Walk you into town!" And she scooped up Ryly and went stomping across the fields without a backward glance. Kirsty stood in the lock of the 'spacer, eyeing me very coldly. I ignored her and went across to the zep.

It was 07:50 by now, and a little unnerving to be inside the cockpit just then. I'd wedged the door, but it could still take off, I'd have to jump. Whether I was too high or not. I couldn't risk being caught. The cabin was full of things I didn't want to leave, and I kept finding them as I worked. At 07:58 I finished, by which time Ziz and Ryly weren't out of sight. I stood at the zep door and watched them climb over the low fence of the field, where sheep would soon be grazing. There was no such thing as unused land in Europe, even on the scrubby clifftops of Brittany. It was only the weather that stopped people building into the cliffs themselves.

I crossed to the airspacer and clambered in beside Kirsty. The heater was doing its best to banish the outside air, but the atmosphere was still frigid. "Kirsty!" I protested. "She's one of my best and oldest friends—"

"Then maybe she should've come away with ye, then!"

"She would have. If it hadn't been for you."

I warmed up the motors, and flicked on the zep's slave circuits. It trembled, and I saw the grass around it flatten under the lift motors. As the buoyancy increased it gave an unstable shudder and lifted, buffeted by the wind. I gunned the airspacer's lifters, which chewed at the grass and spattered it to one side. Then I, too, was fighting the wind and the ground was sliding away to one side. I caught a glimpse of a road, two figures on it looking up. I couldn't be sure who they were. Then we were high enough to catch the sun, and gold mellowed the grey light. I leaned over to watch the zep. It was circling slowly beneath me, banking and heading out to sea.

"Off to South America," I explained. Kirsty radiated silence. "A blind. They'll pick it up long before it gets anywhere, of course."

Silence. I found myself following and overtaking the zep to find the nearest corridor. It didn't matter, being tracked now. I wouldn't be back to answer questions. We spiralled up and away, and the sea and the zep dwindled beneath, turning to a racing white dot on featureless grey-green. And then, suddenly, I saw it lurch, bank, and sweep back in a wide circle towards France. Then there was another, sharper, lurch, and a puff of flame as the chemical detonator I'd left on the controls set off the small charge from my jacket lining. Trailing smoke, the zep wobbled sickeningly towards the shore, to where waves and wind had sculpted great arches and pinnacles out of the cliffs. 08:12 by my procom. Within my parameters, but close, a low inefficiency factor, probably. I remembered how pleased, and even proud, I'd been when I'd first been allotted the little craft. I piled on the lift and saw no more of it.

"They'll waste time looking for bodies. Not much time, but it all helps."

"My folks'll think—I couldn't even call them. She wouldn't let me."

"She was right, as I'm sure you know. Come on, g—Kirsty. It's only for a short time, till the first storm blows over. Then they won't dare touch you. They'll have no real reason to, either. You'll be all right."

"And you?"

I hadn't been looking forward to that. "It's not the same with me. I've shed blood. Far worse, in their eyes, I've betrayed—not a trust, exactly. More like tribal honour. A cult, maybe. I'd have to spend the rest of my life dodging vendettas, little unexplained accidents. However much I might be pardoned and feted on the surface. There'd be a knife in one of the backslaps. My life down there's over. I've shed what I was. That means leaving a lot behind—even some things I valued as much as my life, or more. You never did change your mind about leaving Earth, did you?"

Silence, and the sky grew darker. I poured on the power, and the acceleration became giant hands that clutched me back. But the fusor was far stronger, and we arrowed upward into the infinite chill of night.

I kept us on high acceleration. We had no time to spare for lovemaking, even if we'd felt like it. The zep had bought us less time than if it had come down in the open sea. The airspacer was not officially in my name, but that would hold them up only so long. In two or three hours there'd be a beam questing for my license transceiver, ready to twist the controls out of my grasp and send us hurtling back down to Earth. After two centuries of automation no man could call his transport his own. We sat and endured the acceleration in silence at first. It was Kirsty who spoke.

"You had tae kill them, didn't you?"

"You told Ryly why yourself."

"Aye, but that was different."

"All right, yes, I had to—though I didn't kill Yermolov deliberately."

"I know." She didn't say anything for a minute, then "Ziz was tellin' me about you—"

"Oh, hell. *Hell*. Kirsty, she's just a linespinner, you know? Experienced woman trying to shock daylights out of little girl, you know? That's how she'd see it, anyhow—"

"I know. Some of it was nice. She thinks the world of ye, really. But the rest—was it no' true, then?"

"Exaggerated. Out of context, probably. Look, Kirsty," I reached over and put my hand on her leg, affectionately. It was taut, tense, the muscles quivering like a startled deer's.

"Kirsty—"

Her voice was quite steady. "You scare me, Mark. No matter

what else I feel about ye, I'm still scared. I can't help it . . . what ye'd do . . . Oh, I'd've deserved it, I'd've given ye cause . . . But what ye'd do—"

I clutched at her. "Kirsty! Hell, I'm not some kind of sadistic—I'd never hurt you!"

"Ye're hurtin' me now!"

The shadow of Earth hung over us like a pall. Rising from west to east, we had slid from dawn back into night. The blackness ahead was like a detached fragment of the night, budded off or split like a cell to spread and multiply. And soon it was stretching out to draw us in, till there was only the vast golden nucleus spinning before us.

We emerged from D-Con damp and blinking and in an uneasy truce. Kirsty gave me an uncertain smile and took my hand as we stepped out to face Flight Deck and the impact of Whittaker's greeting. Sure enough, he began woofing all over us, but stopped almost at once, looking at us narrowly.

"It's serious, is it? Something you can tell me, or—"

"You, yes. But I think the Captain had better hear as well."

"Easily done. He particularly wants to meet you. We'll go down to his office right away, if you like."

We made our way out into a brightly lit area of Flight Deck, where the side-doors of one of the massive docking bays stood open. Workers, human and waldo, swarmed over an equally massive shape inside. Preoccupied as I was, I couldn't resist a closer look. It was only then I understood just why Flight Deck was the size it was; the bay extended a good two hundred metres back into the hull, and the craft inside more than half filled it.

"And we've got a dozen more of those," said Whittaker. "Ship's boats, you see. Incredible antiques, half-a-century old. But they're in mint condition, they were mothballed new; we're just stripping down the last of them now. They're space-to-ground tenders, mostly hold—see the big doors there? But really they're a little bit of everything; four of them have even got limited underwater capacity, so we can play submarines without waiting till we can build our own. Superb design— pity they're really museum pieces."

"Don't knock them just for that, Rev. You'd be surprised how little we've advanced in fifty years. And it's been more in quantity than quality—airspacers, BC toys, that kind of thing. Sure, they'd be outclassed, but—hey, isn't that a war-beam director there? And those'd be retracted gun turrets?"

"Light armaments, yes. Nothing the BCs mind us having. One gunship could breakfast off the lot of them, Liang says—"

Yearning flickered across Kirsty's face at the mention of breakfast, and I realized I was feeling pretty hollow myself, it being midmorning by our body time. But up here it was late afternoon, and I was getting impatient to see the captain and get a few things settled. Soon enough there'd be a dragnet out for me through every orbital station, manned or unmanned, and it was bound to come here. By then I had to know exactly where I stood, and Kirsty too.

For all Whittaker's disclaimers, Bridge Deck still had an aura of luxury about it. The captain's office was just one door among three, but they were the only three in a long corridor, and panelled in the same dark wood as the rest of the Deck. Whittaker didn't bother with the doorcom, just poked his head around, whistled and ushered us in.

It still felt like a royal audience from one of Kirsty's old plays. The room was light and airy, and empty enough to look slightly austere. But at the back there was an enormous crescent of a desk in reddish wood, flanked by two huge palm-like plants in wide tubs, ceiling-high and arching over it. They did not dwarf the figure that stood up between them: he topped even Whittaker by a centim or so, though he was slender by comparison. There was only the minimum of gold trim on his immaculate jet-black uniform, the same colour as his skin; he looked like yet another fragment of night. I recognized the face from the medcasts of a few years ago, smoothly handsome; the smile on it now, as then, was coolly professional, baring no teeth and not spreading over the high cheekbones to the narrowed, unreadable eyes.

"Mister Bellamy, Miss O'Neill, *M. le capitaine* René Joseph-Desiré Ekkela." Whittaker grinned. "Mark and Kirsty, Réné." The hand I shook was long, thin and limp, but heavily calloused. He could have played Chaka or any other Zulu emperor, though I knew he was Senegalese, a Fulani aristocrat and son of one of their BC princes. Probably not full-blooded, though; his name was an Africanization of the Afrikaner name Ekelaar. He'd risen to become one of their top test pilots before disgust with the Junta regime led him to defect, taking along one of their newest and fastest airspacers. Since then he'd lived all over the world, found none of it much more to his taste, and muscled his way into this command. Not that he wasn't an ideal candidate; few men of his calibre had the urge to emigrate.

We sat, and he looked at us for a second; the smile grew fractionally warmer. "So," he said, "I'm very glad to meet you both at last, after all I've been hearing." His English was odd-sounding but precise, tinged with the antiquated drawl they teach in African schools, making his resonant voice sound higher than it was. "We owe you quite a lot, for clearing up the business with Mr. Ryly, and with Mr. Whittaker here also. And now I'm told we may be even deeper in your debt—"

"Scrub that last one. I was wrong, I've found out. But there's still a lot you should know—"

Neither Whittaker nor Ekkela interrupted my story, though Whittaker was anything but silent. He rocked from side to side, bunched his fists, held his breath and let it out in great whooshes. But as it went on he grew grimmer and calmer. Ekkela remained impassive, leaning on the desk with his hands clasped lightly in front of him, until I mentioned the aliens, and where I thought they were. And when I described the fracas in the office his features set hard and grim, like a carved ceremonial mask. When I finished, the office was silent for a few moments. Ekkela stared across at Whittaker.

"Aliens! That close to the Colony! Of all the—That's all we needed, the devil's own luck! Danger from two sides—" He caught sight of Whittaker's face and corrected himself. "Potential danger, anyhow. They're *aliens*, Rev—think what that means! They could appear as friendly as pie and still be foreign to us in a million ways we'd never dream of! Ryly was right, we could never afford to trust them for an instant, ever—"

"How often can we trust our own kind?" grunted Whittaker. "If we survive their kind of attentions, I don't see that aliens need worry us much. I trust you weren't thinking Ryly right about anything more?"

"Well . . ."

"About that missile being a good thing, after all? Don't be an idiot, Réné!" Whittaker's voice was quiet, but it had a definite whipcrack to it. He leaned forward, stabbing out a heavy finger. "Every argument Mark used applies to the Colony as much as it does to Earth. We could hardly help getting caught up in this, if somebody did find out; we're unmistakably Earth humans. We'd have to lie low and watch everything we'd built up wither, or come scuttling home for shelter. Just what the BCs want, in both cases. Do you?"

"I just want to keep the Colony safe—"

"Well, the bloody missile willna do that!" Kirsty burst out. "Or have ye no' been listenin', cloth ears or somethin'?" Ekkela, taken mightily aback, blinked at her as if he hadn't noticed her before. "And even if it did, d'ye really want tae buy your safety at that kind of price? A whole bloody *world*, man, a' its lifeforms, its intelligences? That'd be a fine soil to put your roots down in, that'd really get your wee Colony off tae a grand start!" She ran out of breath and tilted back in her chair, eyes blazing.

"Good point, Kirsty!" murmured Whittaker, mouth twitching. "The means decide the ends, as always—eh, René?"

Ekkela spread his arms in a wide helpless shrug. "All right! It is out of our hands, anyhow. I just wish all this could somehow not have happened! It was bad enough as things were, but now—"

"They could be friendly," I pointed out. "Some help, even."

The mask settled over his face again. "In the meantime, I am faced with the problem of what to do about you. I do not like what you've done—"

"He'd no choice!" shouted Kirsty. Ekkela held up his hand sharply.

"That is arguable. I have heard only your story, Mr. Bellamy, and as a Security man yourself, you will excuse me if I neither believe nor disbelieve it. But I do know that by coming here you endanger the Ship, its people, the Colony itself—"

"In a damn good cause!" barked Whittaker. "And he's laid his neck on the line for us already, when he'd no reason to."

"I was coming to that," said Ekkela unhurriedly. "It is no small risk. We can hide you both, and your craft, so thoroughly that they would have to tear the Ship apart to find you. But suppose they struck lucky? We are caught hiding fugitives, somehow involved in political assassinations—that might give them sufficient excuse to tear the whole venture apart. I say this to be sure you know what you are asking. I am not prepared to order the Ship to accept it. The Council meets tomorrow; they should decide. If they agree, you may stay till we leave, some time around the end of June, or come with us then."

"They'll agree!" roared Whittaker, tossing his heavy hair out of his eyes. "Now let's find some food, eh—"

"Oh, aye, please," said Kirsty.

"—and get a look at this 'cast of Ryly's. I'm looking forward to that."

"So am I," said Ekkela with a hard smile. "Come back and watch it here. 18:00 EST, you said? Until then." We shook hands again. I resisted the temptation to crush the limp fingers to pulp. It would be just what the arrogant bastard was looking for, some lapse of control that would prove me dangerously unstable. Hence the insulting manner, though it probably reflected his real feelings. I couldn't blame him for not wanting a habitual killer on his ship; what I could and did object to was the way he was prejudging the issue. What would he have done, in a trap where the only way out was to kill? Tried, probably, and failed, because he hadn't been taught how. I was paying the penalty of success.

So I refrained from crushing him again a few hours later, when we came back to his office. It was easier, because I was fed and rested, and because Owen and Liang were there, and obviously glad to see me, despite Ekkela's open disapproval. We had eaten in the Bridge messhall, then slumped into comfortable chairs in a quiet corner and dozed till Whittaker came to fetch us. He was rubbing his hands with anticipation, looking up impatiently at the wide screen over the desk.

"Aliens!" he chortled. "All my life I've wanted to see aliens. How I was envying you today, Mark! Talk about green! Nearly turned into a little green man myself—"

"Never *little*, Rev," I said. "Don't expect too much. All I got were those ships, remember?"

"They'll do, oh, they'll do all right—ah!" The Free Agencies joint program menu was flickering up a choice of new programmes as the slot changed for the early evening peak.

"You know we've got a whole ruddy comcast set-up on board here?" remarked Owen. "Nobody with time or experience to run it, though. Maybe when we're underway—" The menu stopped. Ekkela looked at it and stabbed a finger at one of the items. The screen flicked to another menu, headed NEWSCASTS.

"Now what *would* the headline be?" mused Ekkela abstractedly. "Bellamy, there's no item here . . . *Mais que diable*—" He stabbed at a small line, and the screen jumped again. INVESTIGATOR DRUGDEATH, the headline read.

"—Ryly, Chaz, long-time investigative media reporter for the Chicago-World Free Media League, found dead in League's Praha offices this PM. Czech capital cops say medman long-term suspected tobacco addict, death due to cancer, circulatory disorders, gangrene. No third party involved. Tribute to Ryly from League supremo—"

The machine voice's idiot staccato rolled over me like a blanket, blotting out everything else. Up there on the screen was Ryly, looking younger and healthier than I'd ever seen him, and beside him film of what had to be his office, a desk drawer open to reveal a large flat tin of dark fibres and a smoking-pipe. Just visible beyond it was a hummocked shape under a glossy white sheet, only the familiar black hair visible.

"Bellamy," said Ekkela's far-distant voice. "You'd be the expert . . ."

"No way does tobacco kill you that quickly. They didn't even find out about the circulatory bit, and gangrene, till enough people began living past eighty. They were dying of other things first."

"So?"

"At a guess, the Free Agencies aren't as free as we've all been led to think—even the people who work for them. Ryly told me only his boss would see the stuff before it went out. So we know who shouted cop."

"Poor Ryly," sighed Whittaker. "All that doggedness, and he was just shadow-boxing. Acting as the BCs' safety-valve. A titillating illusion of freedom . . ."

"And trap," muttered Liang. "For just this kind of thing. Turn it off, sir, before I vomit."

Ekkela nodded, and flicked the screen back to the menu again. Then he looked at it more closely. "Something new . . . Bellamy, this looks like—"

The new headline read SECURICOP DEFECTOR?, but the voice-over was human and without the ridiculous journalese:

". . . wanted on charges of conspiracy to obtain classified information and pass it on to a hostile power, the Sea Station's chief security officer for twenty-one years, Bellamy, Mark."

They hadn't even got my length of service right. Dossier pictures of me were dotted all over the screen, superimposed on film of a crowd at some kind of official ceremony. A white ring settled around one person, me.

"Hellfire, that's the Maintenance Complex opening! And

there I am being introduced to fashing *Thorborg,* by . . ." I was feeling very strange indeed, lightheaded, nauseous, and suddenly overwhelmed by guilt I couldn't explain. Then I understood. "Slow that thing down, Ekkela! Right down to single-frame!"

He looked oddly at me, but pressed the control. One frame, another, another, perfectly innocent, and then—a white frame with screaming red capitals:

BELLAMY! SEE THIS! YOU'VE FAILED! IT'S USE-LESS! ALL YOUR FAULT! YOU CAN'T GO ON! YOU CAN'T LIVE WITH YOURSELF! YOU'RE GUILTY!

"Subliminals," I said weakly. "They're using subliminals. Probably something on the soundtrack, too, with the film to create associations—"

Ekkela was looking at me keenly. "It got to you, certainly. But subliminals can't create feelings, just reinforce them. Do you really feel like that? Well, don't. You did what you could. And I think the Colony could use you, if you're in the market for a new life." The other men made agreeing noises. "Feel strong enough for the rest?"

". . . Deputy Inspector Friedhofer, in charge of the investigation—"

A new voice: "No important breach of security, as far as we know, and the man himself is not considered dangerous. He may have taken refuge abroad"—by which everyone would understand Africa—"but we have indications that he may be hiding out on an orbital station. Our investigations are proceeding, but frankly we're not too worried, provided he commits no further offences—"

"As clear a warning as I ever heard," grumbled Owen. "We know where you are, we'd have a job getting you out, so's long as you keep your mouth shut we'll let you be!"

"And sail off in month or two!" added Liang. "Bastards think the Colony's finished anyhow, so what difference?"

"Shut up!" barked Whittaker. "Look!"

Another face filling the screen, shockingly young and yet the same face that had smiled up through the fog only a few months before. The time between had aged her. "Also wanted, for questioning only, O'Neill, Kirsteen Catriona, believed travelling with Bellamy . . ."

I swung my chair round, and understood why we'd heard nothing from her through those terrible few moments since the news about Ryly. She sat bolt upright, staring wide-eyed at a face hardly recognizable as her own, now ashen with shock. She shivered uncontrollably.

"Medical station," said Whittaker. "At once. Mark, how about—"

"I'll manage. I could use a drink. *And somebody shut that bloody thing off!*" For, keyed with my name, its hidden venom had had its effect on Kirsty, as, no doubt, it was intended to. It was a relief to see she was able to walk by herself when Whittaker led her out; I stayed in the background. With those subliminal reproaches screaming around in her head she'd be better off without me for a while. But I found myself wishing that Ziz or I had let her call her parents, dangerous as that would have been. Because Kirsty, who had so much hated the idea of leaving Earth, must know now that she could never go back.

Ekkela was saying something. "As far as I'm concerned, Bellamy, you and she can stay. But come to the Council tomorrow anyway; they should hear all this from you. For tonight you stay with Liang in his village. They're good people, half of them his relations, and there's an inspection hatch in a hill nearby. You can lose yourself between the hulls before any searchers get within a kilom of the Ship. The girl will stay with the medics tonight, they won't move her unless there's trouble. Right? Liang'll find you that drink, I don't keep any here."

Liang found me several drinks, and vast quantities of blazing Sechuan food that jolted me right out of my decline. We travelled to his village by the network of railcars that ran between the hulls; there were a few zeps on board, used only for urgent business, but airspacers couldn't be used in the enclosed space. The village was at the far extreme of the Ship, not far from the towering cliff of South End, which housed the main power generators for the Ship—fusors and antimatter—and most of its heavy industry. Like the other villages, it was a replica of a real Earth community, in this case Chinese, made up mostly of original buildings rescued from the path of progress Down There. It suited the Chinese emigrants very well, though there was nothing racially exclusive about the community. Liang's family made me welcome, and he and I got on well. Owen, too, when he dropped in after his watch ended. We sat under a massive magnolia tree and drank somewhat, talked more. It could have turned gloomy, with them brooding over the Ship's crippling supply problem, and me over my failure, and what I had brought on Ryly, and on Kirsty, and perhaps on others too. But it didn't work out that way. Anger and resentment whipped us from brooding to brainstorming, and the answer to my problem was suddenly obvious. And with that weight lifted from my mind I could see one more solution, staring me, all of us, right in the face. Round about the third bottle I plucked up the courage to suggest it. Liang fizzed and tore at his whiskers, Owen whistled incredulously, but within minutes they were hammering out the details between them. So the BCs were telling me I'd failed, were they?

The next day dawned on schedule, and with the sunlight that Weather Control had predicted. "Not always that way, to begin," said Liang. "Ever see snow in midsummer? I forget, you're British. But they get the hang of it now."

I meant to go and see Kirsty before the Council meeting, but Liang and I had our work cut out getting ready in time, especially as we had to spend ages kicking sense into his house data terminal, a brand-new antique like so many other things up here. As it was, we left rather late, and promptly got lost when we arrived. The Council was meeting in Whittaker's home village, which was a reconstruction of somewhere very Olde English called Stratford, complete with the authentic winding mazy street-plan. I felt that was carrying authenticity a bit far; why couldn't it be on a normal grid-plan like everywhere else? Liang, who'd been here before but was doing no better than I was, suggested they'd made it this way to confuse invaders. Still, we arrived at the village green just as the Council was settling down at an enormous table—of rough solid wood!—at one edge. Whittaker waved us in and passed out beer, introducing the councillors as he went.

They were a motley bunch, but impressive. Most were older than me, and two were absolutely ancient, well over their centuries. One was a gaunt, dignified old Sikh called Singh Gupta; the other was a short, dandified figure in white, with a crushing handshake and wide glittering eyes.

"Domenico Barbieri," said Whittaker dryly. "Known as the Brigand. Ask him why."

"I don't need to," I said. "His organization enlivened the first few years of my job. Operating out of Naples, everything from co-ordinated pilfering to piracy."

"Till I retired," he said with a charming smile. "Delighted to meet you at last, sir. Do you know you were a heading on the balance sheets for our sea-to-space operations? Accounting for a significant proportion of losses."

I found myself wondering why such old men were bothering with such a long voyage, with only a few years to enjoy at the other end. But then I remembered that they hadn't been born into the world as it was, that they'd been my age when the first Ship left. There was room to spare in this one—why deny them the chance they missed so long ago?

Among the rest were a Japanese engineer, a Greek politician, a physics professor from Tel Aviv, and a woman I couldn't place at all, with golden skin and lank black hair. She turned out to be a Jivaro Indian, a doctor of some standing who was emigrating with what was left of her tribe, now Brazil's rain forests were mostly a red dustbowl. She was about my age; Ekkela and the officers, the only nonelected members, were the only ones younger. The other eighteen or so councillors were less immediately distinctive, but they all shared a certain look, a mixture of serenity and determination, that I found encouraging. These were people who'd woken up from a bad dream. Now they could make their own lives, and they were determined to. They'd be fertile soil for my plans. Ekkela gave me a distant, neutral nod; he still didn't like me much. Well, in a few minutes he'd probably like me less, if I guessed aright. It was Whittaker who gave me qualms. My butcher's bill must have shocked him even more, yet I'd had nothing from him but help and good sense. Now, though, it might be different.

The probe came first on the agenda, after a few routine administrative measures, since it involved a non-member's presence. Not that that mattered much in this literally open forum. A few children were playing on the other side of the green, and nearby a young mother and child were scattering food for the few small birds around; their population, like ours, would take time to build up. Habit made it hard for me to talk loudly enough in such an unscreened, unsheltered place, but the Council were good listeners and seldom interrupted. Ekkela added one piece of news; an astronomer on the Navigation staff remembered hearing rumours years ago about some odd microwave mush from 40 Eridani, though there'd been nothing to suggest it was a signal.

"Hardly surprising," observed Owen, "if the thing's some

kind of encoded hologram. What kind of idiots sent a first signal that way?"

Whittaker smiled. "If that's how they see, it's only natural. Our first attempts to communicate were crude dot drawings, two-dimensional images of things we see in 3-D. How much would that mean to these people?"

The worst reaction I got wasn't to the probe or the killings, but to the news about the "free" agencies. The three American councillors wouldn't believe it at first, and bayed fury when they did. It was one of them who broke the silence when I'd finished. "Son, that was a good try. Mite bloody, but you hadn't much choice." A general murmur of agreement; not too grudging. "But now you've failed—"

"I haven't failed. Not yet." That caused a stir. Ekkela looked astonished, and then angry. I raised my voice a little. "The BCs think so, because I've got no proof now, nor any way to get it publicized. They don't mind being rid of me, because they think there's no more I can do. But there is—"

"Not from this Ship!" shouted Ekkela, on his feet. The birds fluttered off, the children stopped their play. "The BCs are just itching for an excuse to tear us apart! If you endanger us with your meddling—"

"The BCs need never know!" I shouted back. "Think! Suppose I'd succeeded, how could the probe have been stopped? They'd have sent a ship after it, an Infall-drive ship, the only one with the range! And what are we in now?"

Ekkela stared. "But we can't go haring across the Galaxy—"

"We don't have to! I've worked it out." Liang had, really, but I had reasons for not mentioning that just then. "We'll be parallelling its course in the early stages, overtaking it just over a year out, Ship's time. We'd only have to look around for a little, three weeks maybe, and—" I reached out and swatted. "Or would you rather just wave as we go by?"

A great tide of argument surged up, crested by Whittaker's massive voice struggling to maintain order. He succeeded; there was less actual disagreement than I'd expected, perhaps because I'd underestimated Ekkela. He was content to remind everyone that three weeks early in the voyage could be three weeks trimmed off our safety margins at the end, when we'd be running for the Colony with a seriously declining ecology and low energy reserves. "One good emergency and you could be missing that time badly. But I've no objection to spending *some* time on this—a week, say?" But it didn't take long to push him up to three weeks, though there he stuck, insisting it was the absolute maximum. The Japanese was worried that the BCs might suspect what we were planning, but I pointed out that we wouldn't actually be going near the probe till we were a lightyear away, far beyond their reach or vision, and anyway they probably didn't realize we knew its course. Ryly could have told them, but it didn't look as if he'd lived long enough to be interrogated properly. Someone must have overdone it there, which was common enough.

The vote was unanimous, and I sat back satisfied. We could worry about Ekkela's maximum when the time came. I made as if to get up and leave, and Liang sprang to his feet. "Mr. President! I ask that Mr. Bellamy remain as advisor for the next item! He has valuable suggestions to offer on the problem!"

"Seconded, boy," said Owen lazily. Startled, Ekkela glared at his junior officers, who met the look firmly. He growled his objections, throwing in comments about things going on behind his back, and undue influence exerted by newcomers and unknowns. Whittaker retorted that I was a proven friend of the Colony, and the Jivaro woman remarked that personally she'd heard no new ideas for weeks, and it was obviously about time to hear from a newcomer. So I ended up staying, watching Ekkela argue with Owen and Liang in furious undertones. Whittaker moved hastily on to the item itself.

"It's undoubtedly the most important problem still facing us. And it *is* a single problem, because the response to poor Ryly's report leaves no doubt in my mind that the serious shortfall in our supplies is deliberate BC policy. To sum up the latest report of the Supply subcommittee, we are wholly without usable hardware in a number of categories specifically laid down as essential in the original Colonization plan and urgently requested in the First Ship's Presentation. We need machinery for mining, smelting, and forging metals under low gravity; we need properly-equipped satellite stations for monitoring weather and resources; we need up-to-date agricultural machinery, greenhousing, maintenance, feeding and harvesting equipment; we need plant-mutation equipment to keep up with the changing planetary ecology; we need various kinds of industrial plant, mostly for microelectronics and heavy-duty robotics for space and low-g use. But most of all we need life! Plant and animal! We need stores of embryos, fertilized ova,

clone cells, anything! But we must have more than just the few
species in this tiny subset of an ecosystem of ours. In other
words, we need more or less exactly what we needed six months
ago. The BCs have kept us running on the spot."

"May I remind the Council of something," murmured Barbieri. "Despite the so-harsh emigrant forfeiture rules, many of
us retain little nest-eggs Down There, for a few last-minute
purchases. It goes without saying that these are at the Ship's
disposal . . ."

"You've said that before, *banditto vecchio,*" grinned one of
the Americans. "An' we're grateful, you know that. But I
costed the mining gear alone, and we can't afford more'n a
fraction of that."

"I've a little myself," I said. "No use now to the person it
was meant for, so the Ship's welcome. Won't make much
difference, though. But I do know where there's some mining
gear."

"Where?" demanded the American, eyes gleaming.

"On the Sea Station," I said. "In bond until it's needed on
the Moon in September."

His face fell. "So? We still can't afford it."

"Depends what you pay," I said, and met almost unanimous
blank stares. "You still don't understand, do you? Well, think.
These supplies are life and death to the Colony, aren't they?"

"Of course!" barked Ekkela. "Without them we're back to
the Industrial Revolution, raping our own planet for resources—"

"Just like Earth in a couple of centuries—"

"Making the same fashing mistakes and *knowing* it—"

"Stick a species in the Life Banks so it's technically safe
then wipe out its habitat—"

I had to shout over the clamour. "Well then—if you need
it, *take it!*" The birds fluttered up and away, and the children
faltered and looked around at us. "You're never going to get
anything any other way, that's obvious! Without that stuff the
Colony's dead before it's properly started. You might as well
not go, just sit here till the ecosystem comes crumbling around
your ears!" I waved up at the blue overhead, and the almost
invisible mirror-land behind it. "All those things you want—
the mining gear, the agricultural equipment, the factory machinery—it's lying around all over the world with hardly a
guard on it. It could be picked up by anyone with the means

to get it away quickly! And you—we!—we've got the means!"

"What?" gasped Whittaker.

"Those boats of yours, those tenders—"

"B-but Liang said—"

"One gunship, yes!" barked Liang. "Burn the lot! But how many gunships are there in the sky today? I can tell you! Two, over the whole world! And they're *slow!* First must catch their targets. Our boats—outshoot airspacer, fighter, outrun a gunship! No good for war, but for surprise raid on non-military target—"

"This is completely mad!" bellowed Ekkela.

"Worse!" grated Whittaker, like rasping ice. "It's evil. It means at least some fighting, Mark, gendarmes and security men like yourself—killing people who're only doing their jobs—"

"Yes," shrilled a little Indian woman, "and getting our own people killed—"

Barbieri spat. "We're fighting now!"

"And losing," added an American voice.

"That's right," I said. "Life and death, remember? A minute ago you were all clamouring to tell me that. And I agree! Death of an ideal, death of hope, maybe even death of a species. And death for every colonist! Proven rebels, anti-state elements, what'll our welcome be if we come home? Something to stop us infecting other people—labour camps, penal battalions which you mayn't have seen, but I have."

"I've seen them," said Whittaker evenly. "And I still will not fight or kill."

"You personally?" demanded the Greek, Paskalis. "Or your followers?"

"No need to worry, Rev," growled Ekkela. "None of this is going to happen, the question won't arise. I have a veto on anything that endangers the safety or well-being of the Ship and its inhabitants, and I'll—"

"You'll what?" raged Owen, leaning over the table. "You'll leave us high and dry and call *that* safe? The man's right— we're dead if we don't do something! Of course it's desperate— so's just sitting around."

That wasn't the kind of agreement I wanted. "No!" I called out. "Listen, damn you! There's nothing desperate about this, not if we plan it properly! Liang and I have worked out the broad details, the rest can be filled in later, modified if necessary. First, we strike just as we're leaving; that way we can up-fields and run like hell the moment we're done." Ekkela and Whittaker, they were the two to convince. They still looked stony, but they were listening. "We shouldn't need more than ten boats, of which two run very little risk—one lifting a couple of satellites, the other automated gear from the Moon. Then two for the most up-to-date agricultural training centres, probably European or American. Four for some of those prefabricated factories they've been scattering around the backwoods where the farmland's given out—a new robotics one in the Papua-New Guinea highlands, I think. One for Peking—the most dangerous one, I think—for the university lifebanks, supposed to have the best collection, and the plant mutation stuff. And one for the Sea Station, for the mining shipment."

"I'd have said that was the most dangerous, boy," drawled Owen.

"It's got the heaviest defences. But I think I've a way through them—"

Ekkela was beginning to look positively interested, and Whittaker was definitely on the defensive. "Over my dead body," he breathed, and meant it.

"Hold it, Rev!" I said hastily, before the row broke out anew. "You're thinking of fighting in terms of war. I don't. I'm a cop, not a soldier. There are other ways of defending ourselves, forcible, yes, but not lethal. If we can produce some of those, maybe use some of that money to buy what we can't make. And unarmed combat, I can teach that, so can others—"

Ekkela frowned, shook his head. "Sooner or later the shooting'll start."

"Yes. Hopefully later, if we can spread enough confusion beforehand—we've ideas about that, too. And, Rev, at least we won't have started it." Now I let the discussion take its course, a muted buzz instead of the row of a minute ago. It rapidly became obvious which way it was turning; Whittaker's supporters, including the Jivaro doctor, were outnumbered, and he himself looked torn in two. It would be a disaster if he resigned over this. "A feasibility study," I said. "That's all Liang and Owen and I are asking for. Maybe it's just a pipedream—"

"A nightmare!" said Whittaker, rising so he towered over the Council like an angry demigod. "Listen to me! Do you want me to resign, to lead opposition to this, civil disobedience throughout the Ship? Because I will—"

Everyone else was on their feet, rocking the table, shouting.

"—*unless*," thundered the priest, "unless you agree to two conditions! First, the vote's ratified by Ship's plebiscite at once. Secondly, that if we must go out on this venture we risk our own lives before those of others. The raiders may use only non-lethal weapons—" He paused and looked around, daring us to contradict him. My heart sank till he went on "—except in bluff, warning, or the last extremes of self-defence. Anyone going against this to face charges on his return. Well?"

"Suicide!" bellowed Liang. "Lunacy! Hand tied behind our backs!" But the roar of agreement wasn't universal.

Ekkela shook his head slowly. "That's how it'll have to be," he said. "That way, or no way, or find yourself another captain. Do we vote?"

After the vote I was sitting staring at the ground when it was suddenly darkened. Whittaker loomed over me. "Well?" he growled. "Aren't you satisfied?" He waved at Barbieri and the others dancing on the table, chanting *Fight! Fight! Fight!* "Why aren't you with them?"

"It's too much. It's a good idea, but when it suddenly starts becoming—so much of it's mine—hellfire, I'd have thought *you'd* understand!"

His fingers bit into my shoulder. "Be careful, Bellamy. Just be what you were, what you've always been. Or you'll end up thinking like me yet." He let go. "And talking of responsibilities, Kirsty was asking about you—"

In the months that followed she spent a lot of time doing that. There was so little time to prepare that a million and one different tasks fell onto my shoulders, and sleep and food became things I only took when I couldn't function without them. Once or twice I had an enforced holiday when the dragnet search parties arrived to make a show of searching this country in orbit, and then I usually shared a hiding place in a hollow hill with Kirsty. We crouched among the network of beams between the inner and outer hulls, in dim light and silence broken only by the distant whine of transit cars. The first time in, the first thing Kirsty asked me was if she could be taken back to Earth. I just stared at her as if she were mad.

"Not for good," she protested. "Just... Tae see my folks,

to say goodbye. That's not so unreasonable, is it? Just . . . Ye know I never wanted . . . You could get us in an' back safe, if anyone could—"

"Could I? I'm not so sure, love, not now. But that's not the point, unfortunately, or I'd at least try. But now . . . I know too much about—what we're planning. If I were caught and interrogated, it'd be the end. For the Ship, everybody. It's not just me. It goes for you, too." I heard her snuffling in the miserable dimness. "It's hard, I know. I never got to say goodbye to my family, either. African attack on Corfu Base, when I was at Staff College. Maybe a message 'cast when we're leaving, eh?"

A month later she asked me once again, and got the same, the only sensible answer. Security agencies all over the world were primed for me, and would stay that way even after the Ship departed, just in case. I had no time to worry about it, swept up in a whirl of combat classes, planning meetings, runthroughs, exercises, timed simulations and administrative snarlups; many of those were caused by Ekkela's frequent absences, keeping up a pretence of negotiation with the authorities. When the workload threatened to swamp me, it was Whittaker who bailed me out, as he did many other people. He still didn't like what was going on, and could easily have held back or become a serious obstacle. Instead, he helped—the people, not the project, as he put it.

Weeks later, I was on Flight Deck with him, discussing a logistics problem, when we heard Ekkela's airspacer being brought in. We lay in wait outside D-Con to get him to settle it, but we were startled to see Kirsty come out first. Something like Kirsty, at any rate. Her hair was chopped and dyed blonde, contact lenses changed her eye colour, inserts reshaped her nose and coatings her skin texture and prints—all the amateur trappings of disguise, which even some machines could see through. The voice was well disguised, and that was all. They'd have tagged her from the minute she landed, of course, left her in the hope that she'd lead them to something else useful; her parents were probably being grilled right now. Ekkela arrived, looking sheepish, and I was tempted to brain him for the risk he'd taken. But Whittaker understood as well as I did, and after a dumbfounded moment he began to tell them just what he thought of them. He was doing it better than I would, and from him they'd take it more readily; I was needed elsewhere, urgently. Why should I waste time on anger? Wilting in her unattractive shell, Kirsty looked more funny than anything else. In fact, she looked hilarious. I turned on my heel and walked away.

SEVEN

THE night lay heavy on Peking. At midnight the flood lights on the Tian An Men gate had been turned off, and the millions of glowing windows in the outer city and Baijing Shi, the metropolitan suburb, began to blink out. Only the clear pallor of the street lighting remained. A century ago Peking had been the lively hub of Asian Bloc power and culture, the focal point for a ring of client states such as Japan and Vietnam. Now it was fading into sleepy complacency again, its night undisturbed by such vulgar intrusions as holopic slogans on the low cloud that was gathering, as it was doing over our other targets. Owen and I, at the helm of his boat, watched the peaceful scene through the eyes of Liang's craft, the only boat in the atmosphere so far.

Not far beyond it, though, another hung motionless and six practised atmosphere landing approaches, the official reason for our presence. Liang alone had to land at a heavily defended spaceport; we would risk nothing that might arouse suspicion until he was safely down.

The Ship now sat, wrapped in its shadow-cone, in a new parking orbit beyond lunar apogee, about 500 megametres out. Our scheduled departure time was less than forty-eight hours away, and we'd announced that the move was needed to carry out some essential interference tests on the drive further out of Earth's gravity well. This wasn't too far from the truth; Infall interference effects could be spectacular. Take, for example, the insubstantial fingers that were even now reaching back across space to stir up the atmosphere like cloudy broth. The manned weather stations parked over North China and the mid-Atlantic would begin to find this suspicious a few moments before more and stronger fingers—call them field intersections if you want—scooped them gently out of their orbits into the arms of the waiting boat. Since, unknown to many, those stations monitored other things than weather, their disappearance would open temporary gaps in the local early warning systems, through which would come other boats. About then the disturbed atmosphere would begin to demonstrate why nobody had ever managed to harness Infall for real weather control; its objections would have a literally electrifying effect. Violent storms with attendant atmospherics, up to and including ball lightning, would further confuse detection systems around our targets. Not enough to panic people into letting loose Armageddon, though; just enough to be sure that stray craft weren't easy to track or challenge. As long as we did nothing aggressive while still airborne we should get through. Liang had actually identified his craft and obtained emergency landing clearance, as per regulations; the Peking spaceport officials would be puzzled, but as we'd hoped they were saving their questions till he was down. Then it'd be too late.

His boat was gliding low over the Imperial City now, and for an instant I saw its black shark-shape reflected in an ornamental lakelet. The boat hulls were beam-resistant, mirror-finished under their night-dark radar absorbent, but there were vicious little missiles nested in grassed-over pits around the spaceport boundary. Something of the electric atmosphere seemed to be loose in our small cockpit as we watched the boundary slide by beneath Liang's cameras. The ground surged up to meet them, there was an instant of shadowy confusion, and then the howl of the boat's battle alarm. The vision link cut out as arranged. Owen hunched forward over his controls. All we needed now was the word from our satellite hunters, and—

"We're away!" rasped the voice link, and cut. I could hear Owen whistling through his teeth as he tapped at his controls.

On the command screen I saw the whole flotilla sweep forward in a smooth scything curve behind us. Three boats tailed us towards the Atlantic, the other four dipped and peeled off towards the other gap over China. In less than a minute the atmosphere was a hot thin shriek around us, there was an instant's blurred glimpse of blue sky floored with stormcloud, then we plunged down through it and, still decelerating, nose-first into the green Atlantic.

Even though I was expecting it, even though the impact wasn't so very bad, that headlong dive left me sweating and shaking in my inertia web. Muscles voluntary and involuntary didn't want to respond properly, my heart boomed in my ears, my breath came hard. Owen, by contrast, was slumped comfortably back in his chair, watching his preprogrammed sequences steer us through our dive and click on the ballast pumps to level us off at about a hundred metres down. The gurgle of incoming water sounded very loud. I devoutly hoped it was all going into the tanks.

The thought pulled me back together. It was my job to look out for that. I quickly ran through the line diagram of the boat on my control screens, flicking up details of damage wherever spots of colour flashed.

"You came in far too goddam fast!" I complained. "We've got buckling in the bow—and we've lost some of our anti-radar coating! The seawater's stripping what you left!"

"No matter!" grunted Owen. "As long as the bows hold—" He opened the jet intakes and warmed up the motor, an eerie howl that reverberated through the boat. "Must be deafening the poor buggers in that echoing empty hold! Ah well, it's not for long . . . I brought her in very nicely, thank you!" He flicked on the steering jets, and began to swing the boat round. "If we'd come in much slower, you Cardiff tart!—turn—we might not have fooled anyone. As it is the Station's probably chalking up a serious crash right now!" He cut the jets and dropped the motor—an appallingly powerful steam jet produced by feeding seawater through the fusion shield—to a hissing idle.

"Any sign of it yet? Or did they move when they heard you were coming?"

"Encouraging bastard you are!" I commented. "I got something while we were turning, but these scopes are antiques . . . ah!" I had what I wanted, and flashed it up on the command screen. The old instruments took a second to adjust the image size, and it came tromboning up towards us like the last brick wall you ever see.

"What the hell's that?" demanded Owen. "Weed?"

Out of a blur of greenish-grey shadow emerged a thicket of dark lines, interlaced with thinner ones, that rose more or less vertically across the screen, without visible beginning or end.

"Very heavy weed," I said dryly. "Doesn't so much as stir in the current, does it? Let's have a look at the leaves on top." I'd got the pic under control at last, and I tracked quickly up the mooring cables towards the palely glinting surface. I wasn't prepared for the complex of feelings that started seething around in me when I saw the familiar shape at the top, the ringed kraken outline. I sat on them heavily, all the same. *Business, boy. Market day, remember? You're shopping for lives.*

"That's the Station?" murmured Owen. For once even he seemed impressed.

"That's it. Moored to the northeastern slopes of the Mid-Atlantic ridge. Give me a minute or two."

"Take your time," said Owen quietly. "Long as you need. It's an investment. I'll spread the word." He clicked on the shipcom. "Owen here," he said, in a newly crisp and resonant voice. "Despite rumours to the contrary I've got us down with an intact hull, so we'll have less of the *leek* jokes, *if* you please! The moment Mr. Bellamy's ready we move in. I'll sound quarters at that time. Remember—as soon as the motors stop Sergeant Beriosova's in command, so don't waste time looking for me, right? That's all. *Lwc-dda* to the lot of you!" He clicked off the com. "Means good luck in Welsh, but none of them'll know that!"

I found myself grinning. I'd caught some of the confidence Owen had been exuding, and the hairs that had begun to bristle on the back of my neck had subsided. For all Owen had said, though, I had to work fast. The Station would have detected us by now and in a few minutes even Simoneau would realise he wasn't looking at a wreck. I'd been carefully pulling the image closer and closer in, studying the lumpily irregular silhouette as it came. I could see the calm area within the seawall now, looking as if a circle of green glass had been laid down on the surface. Outside it was definitely getting choppy. I twisted the image carefully about, hunting for the vital points. It was made harder by the extra accumulation of marine growth since I'd last seen this view. *Maintenance getting careless*—I almost became hysterial at that. A thief criticizing his victim's house-keeping? But this had been my house once ... There was a point! And another! The more I found, the quicker I found others by reference. In less than a minute's scanning I had eighteen out of twenty possible places tagged in thin red circles on the target screen on my console. I locked in target instructions, range and firing sequence, which took a century or two, and slumped back, dripping perspiration.

"It'll do. It'll have to—"

"Good. Sound quarters, then—"

I touched a contact patch, and the whole boat rippled to the drumroll rhythm. Owen's fingers danced out a quick arpeggio on his console keys, then he started the jets again, wincing at the sudden howl of superheated steam. Only four of the boats had underwater capability; of those, two were held in reserve and the third was the satellite snatcher, the safest job. Ekkela knew how to husband his resources, all right.

I dropped the magnification from the command screen as we began to pick up speed. The Sea Station was an indistinct blob at top centre now, still stuck with minute red target markers. I was staring so hard at it that I jumped when an indistinct metallic shape bulleted across the screen directly in our path. Even as Owen grabbed at his manual helm, though, it wheeled without checking and dissolved into arrowing flecks of silvery-green light. A couple of light collisions sounded at the bow.

"You've lived out here," grunted Owen. "What was that, then? Cod?"

"No, more likely mackerel," I reasoned. "Cod are still rare. There must've been a predator chasing them or they'd have noticed us sooner."

"Well if any got into the jets he can have 'em steamed! Serve the dozy buggers right. Hope nothing gets in the way of your guns ..."

"They'll have to watch out for that. They'll only fire when they've a clear shot—"

Which had better be soon. I watched the figures reel off on my console screens—past 4000 metres and closing, 3800, 3700 ... At 2500 metres the Sea Station's automatic defences would issue a polite challenge, and at 2200 a warning shot. After 2000 metres all hell would break loose, turning the whole affair into a messy shooting match instead of the clean piracy we intended. I expected the guns to fire at 3500, but nothing happened. Owen was doing his best not to look worried, but he couldn't keep it out of his voice.

"When d'you think—"

"I don't know! We just never had enough time to practise with these old sighting systems. Especially not underwater— there may be limitations..."

"This antique bloody boat!" moaned Owen over the rising howl of the jets. A deeper whine joined them, the old hydrogen motors which powered us in the atmosphere where the fusor was too dangerous. "It's ridiculous! It's like attacking the *Bismark* with Nelson's *Victory*—"

3300, 3200, 3100. I fought off the temptation to take over manual control and start sniping myself. I might hit one target more accurately, but hardly eighteen at once, 3000 metres, 29—

The obsolete command screen began belatedly dimming when the firing alarm keened out. It was too slow. The streaks of violent green that sliced across and across it left a fascinating network of red-purple after-images on my vision.

Owen was past being encouraging. "Well?"

"Wait a minute, fash it! I'm trying to make sense of the target stills."

Murky images, close-up shapes of shadow and weed, were popping up on my console screens. I had to squint through my ruined vision like prison bars, searching for the tell-tale puff of bubbles in the cloudy water.

"Owen, there's one hit! And—three, dead on! No, four—"

"Good enough for me!" he rasped, and snapped on the com again. "Landing party, hang on to your hats!" He pounced on his controls with a wild yell, something about Harlech.

I was kicked viciously back into my web as the boat leapt forward and up, and half-deafened by the roar of blowing ballast. The mad Welsh bastard was feeding it out through the jets! One way of getting rid of it in a hurry, provided the system stood the extra steam pressure... Provided. And the close-ups came placidly in.

"Five hits! One miss, bugger—six hits! Seven! We're in business!"

Owen didn't answer, he knew I wouldn't expect it. He'd buried his face in the curving console, forehead resting on a bar folded out from above a control screen. The boat had the reactions but not the intelligence we'd need, so he was steering it by retinal reflection—not as good as a modern neural link, but good enough. It had to be.

There were horrible noises coming from the jets, and telltales on my damage screens began flashing crimson. I ignored them. If they held for another thirty seconds that would be enough—who needed them anyway after this?—so sit back and enjoy the ride and forget you and the crew being boiled alive if a pressure line goes and concentrate on that great greenglass sea window you're about to break—

The grey sky exploded into my vision as we leapt to meet it, like a huge flying fish. A slamming roar of atmosphere jets, let loose as we left the water, sent my stomach up to compound the blockage in my throat. We hung suspended for the vital second of orientation Owen needed, while the steam boiled in a cloud around us. He'd brought us out at the right angle, into the right lagoon, so that below us lay the wide air-landing stage that was the Station's southern arm. Owen swung us round a degree or so, then we dropped smoothly towards the landing area. Two broad and vicious warbeams intersected like a triumphal arch where we'd been an instant before. From the guard towers on the seawall, of course. They wouldn't hurt something this size much, of course—not at first—but all the same I felt an idiotic pride in my guards, who'd taken just about six seconds to react to this sudden appearance, swing their guns round from seaward, and fire. That was the reason I'd never allowed the guns to be automated or remote-controlled. I'd drilled a sense of personal responsibility into my guards—and by the holy bureaucracy they weren't going to make it a pushover for us!

There was thunder beneath us as the atmosphere jets swung round into landing position and lowered us. Owen was landing the boat on the airpad in exactly the place we'd worked out. The guard-towers' fire was blocked now by the buildings around it, and our guns were hissing and sizzling, taking out the small missile-firers on the pad before their peabrain firing systems could adjust. We had more than just surprise on our side. Multi-role craft like our boats were bad economics in normal circumstances; the power and space taken up by multiple drive and control systems, plus the cost of balancing them, could be put to other more productive use—more firepower, more speed, greater range or capacity. Only the colonizing expeditions had had a use for them, half a century ago; I'd not heard of any others being built since then. So I, in my former life, hadn't paid much attention to amphibious attack; I'd kept undersea and surface defences separate. I'd never done myself a bigger favour. We'd got in where other attacks would have been cut to shreds. The water defences had been alerted, but we were beyond their reach before they could act; the air and surface defences hadn't been alerted at all. We were already below the lowest firing angle of the beam cannon on the roof of Central Control. The Station hadn't any heavy missiles or shell-firers because they might cause more damage than they prevented; light ones the boat's own guns could handle.

"We're in with a chance!" I called to Owen as the landing motors gave a final bellow. Even before our landing skids jolted down onto the airstage he'd hit the emergency release on his harness, and I wasn't far behind him. Both of us slapped on gunbelts, and I had that bulky handbeam as well. Sprinting down the narrow mesh-floored catwalks, we could feel as well as hear the hold doors grinding open; our guns crackled on again, and then there was a deep gonging thud. What the hell were we fighting now? All became clear, though, when we burst into the hold and saw the first carrier rev up and rumble out and down the ramp formed by the lower door, barrel across fifty metres of open space and into the gaping, smoking hole in the wall of the warehouse opposite. We'd planned to blow its door open, but Beriosova had had a better idea. Until it passed the wall the first carrier met no resistance, but from inside the warehouse we heard shots, shouts and the popping of our patent gas grenades. The men in the second carrier still kept their heads down as they'd been trained to; it was just as well, as a hail of small-arms-fire—large-calibre autoguns, mostly—went sleeting past their heads the moment the carrier left the ship.

"Snipers on the Terminal building, Berry!" I called into my procom.

"I see 'em!" came the laconic reply. One of our autoguns hawked and spat, and the shooting stopped.

"You did shoot to miss, didn't you?" asked Owen anxiously.

"Yes, sort of," drawled Beriosova. "They could still run well enough, anyway."

Owen and I piled onto the third and last carrier, and acquired all sorts of nice new bruises as we went jolting out into the daylight. But the worst ache to me was the sudden gust of sea air—today, the last time I'd breathe it!—and the harsh cries of the gulls. They seemed to call me back to everything I was cutting myself free from. But then we were lumping and bumping into the warehouse, and all was shadow, stench and gunfire. Gas got me by the throat and I hurriedly pulled on my facemask.

The place was in chaos, with sprawled, choking guards being hauled off into corners and taped securely. One boy was flat out beside the first carrier with a ragged hole in his leg. One of our men was patching him up.

"Who shot him?" I demanded.

"Did it himself," said the first-aid merchant cheerily, "in the heat of the moment, eh?" The boy nodded shamefaced agreement. Then I saw his face twist in puzzlement, not pain. He'd recognized my voice, but not placed it yet. Between the smoky triangle of my face-mask and the month-old beard beneath, he'd some excuse. I saw him safely stowed, then went to join Owen. Perched on one of the big ground-effect load pallets, he was putting some order into things. In the corner of the warehouse a squad of marksmen were holding the main entrance from Central Building, against rather desultory fire from the corridor. There weren't half as many people about as there should have been, and from that and the slight list to the floor I was sure my scheme had worked. I'd always had some doubts about the Station's submergence protection, basically the same as a spacecraft or sub. The whole hull was divided into sections, separated by water- and pressure-resistant bulkheads that sealed themselves at the first sign of flooding. There was always plenty of food and oxygen to keep anyone trapped alive till rescue came—so what was the objection? My sharpshooting act on the way in had demonstrated it—seventeen hits out of eighteen. Seventeen sections, too cramped or too irradiated for humans, where only waldos and robots ever went—workshops, computer rooms and so on—had found themselves pierced by beamfire and flooding fast. Their mindless safety systems had immediately slammed the bulkheads in the area—and so blocked half the main corridor systems in the Station. Over half its staff were cut off in or behind the sealed areas, in no danger but out of the action altogether. Years ago I'd suggested this could happen, and been overruled—wasn't staff safety paramount? And anyway, what attacker would know just which sections to puncture? I was glad nobody had thought of the obvious answer. The Department architect had joked that anyone attacking that way would need the complete blueprints, *plus* x-ray eyes. I'd neither. But a good eidetic memory, plus two decades of combing the whole Station bit by tortuous bit for stolen, smuggled or otherwise illegal goods, had done just as well. So now the only ways out into the airpad and its surrounding buildings were either sealed or covered. We could get on with our raid in relative peace.

Which still meant absolute bloody pandemonium. Our searchers soon managed to trace the consignment of mining machinery to the third floor down, where nobody normally needed to go in person; the warehouse computers handled loading and stacking. They weren't feeling too cooperative, though. They would answer questions, and inform you that loading was in progress, but nothing happened. It didn't take long to dawn on me that we'd asked for this; it was an unfortunate side-effect of shooting up computer rooms. I hurriedly got a party together, and we went down to fetch the stuff ourselves. And who should be down there but a few guards who'd struggled in through an airshaft? Before the gas bombs took effect they'd shot one of our party in the stomach and smashed another's hand. We put the guards aside, trussed like turkeys, and rammed a bale of heavy plastic packing into the airshaft. Then we got down to business. Each floor of the warehouse ran the entire length of the airstage arm of the Station out to its right-angle bend—nearly a kilom—and we had our work cut out. The searchers had got the floor and consignment number out of the addled computers, and little else. Owen reckoned on a maximum of two hours, even with signal jamming and artificial bad weather, before someone came to see what was the matter on the Station. An hour after that the scheduled ferry was due in, anyway, and they'd spot something was wrong before they got within jamming distance. If we weren't in the air by then their landing motors could squash even our boat flat; they probably would, too, assuming we were suicide terrorists or something. We sent our carrier scudding along the narrow alleyways between heaps of featureless metal and plastic containers, all standard spacefreight packing sizes. I had to keep my eyes open as I was the only one who could sightread the loading codes. Perched on the cab of the carrier I gave myself a sore neck twisting this way and that. I turned round so sharply when

I did spot them that I almost fell off. I managed to twist to the side and land on my feet, though, making it look like mere impetuousity.

The mining gear consisted of five enormous containers and two heavily laden mobiles, their motors uncharged and meant only for lunar gravity anyway. Seven loads, and we'd only three carriers. We sent up for some of those big pallets and began getting the loading cranes going. All this seemed to be taking a century of leapyears, but my procom informed me we'd been in the water twenty minutes ago. The main power supply to this section hadn't been turned off, which meant nobody in Central Control was using their heads. They'd failed to realize the specific object of the raid. Probably Simoneau was maintaining his military presence up there, chivvying on his unfortunate underlings from a distance. Rash courage wasn't among his many faults.

The cargo elevator came hissing gently down with a carrier and a pallet. Some genius had improvised a towing hitch, so we'd only four trips to make—three double loads, one single.

"Hotting up, up there," remarked the carrier driver, pulling off his mask to wipe his face. It was Owen.

"How so?"

"One of your guard tower boys seems to have gone berserk!"

"Let's get that pallet shifted under the crane—yes, like that ... What's he doing?"

"Taking potshots at the wall of the building next door to us here. Don't suppose it ever did him any harm, did it now?"

I developed a sinking feeling. "The green building, with the flat roof? Oh brother. It's just a shed, you know? Used for on-field zep repairs, that kind of thing. It's big, but it's just four walls and empty space—"

Owen grabbed me by the shoulders. "You mean he could cut through it? Like we did with the wall?"

"If it's empty, it wouldn't take him long to demolish it completely ..."

"Then we'd better get loaded while we can!" snapped the Welshman. "It's the only thing cutting us off from his field of fire, you know? When it goes he's got a clear shot at the pad—and the boat!"

"Keep on loading, then—I'll go up top and take over!"

"Right!" gasped Owen, as he jockeyed the carrier under the jerkily descending crate—our crane operator wasn't too sure of himself yet. "Send another pallet—and watch out for any other troubles!"

It must have been his Welsh second sight. I stepped out of the elevator just as a concerted attack on the airstage was at last launched from three sides. There were only about a hundred people in all, though, and not many of them guards. The boat used its gas sprayer to drive off the main bunch, and then deployed our secret weapon. Half the boat's firefighting gear had been sacrificed to make it. I sent a party forward with two large hoses, which they managed to get into the last open corridor on this side of Sea Level. The former Police Dep chemist who'd made up the foam for us said it would fill a crowded street in three minutes. The corridors were a far easier proposition. It was non-toxic, you could breathe well enough under it—but you couldn't see a millim in front of your nose. It beat fog any day. Sound became muffled and directionless, and light vague and diffuse. It also made polished surfaces incredibly slippery. All in all it created a psychological effect of isolation and insecurity that was worth all the other effects put together. We drove back the attack with no serious casualties on either side—which, considering they were out for blood, spoke highly for us—except one crew member who was carried away moaning about this bitch who'd ruined him for life. I thought I recognized the fair hand of Ziz Brazda there. It was good being proud of both sides, but all the time I could hear the crackle of the guard-tower beam, and following it the crash of fallen metal. Luckily it only fired hundredth-second beams with a two-second recycle time, or we'd have been carved up in minutes, like cheese. As it was, we'd only just got the first load to the hole in the wall when a horrible crackle, screech and hiss of hot metal falling into the lagoon heralded the collapse of the zep shed.

Owen brought the nose of the carrier tentatively out of the impromptu door, like a timorous dragon peeping out of its den. For a second I thought nothing would happen, then a bar of green light stabbed neatly into the space between us and the boat. The surface of the landing area blistered, bubbled and flared for an instant before its fireproofing composition activated itself and slathered obscenely over the spot. Cursing a green streak, Owen kicked the carrier into reverse. The bar flicked by again, nearer.

"Letting us know we're pinned down, the sod!" he snarled,

wiping his forehead with a greasy hand. More demolition sounds came from our right. I peered cautiously round the wall, and saw the beam carving up the last standing wall of the shed. With that gone—

"Berry!" I yelled. "Beriosova, close the hatch! He'll have a clear shot!"

Owen was audibly grinding his teeth. "One beam in the open doors and he'll cut us to shreds! Sheesus, there he goes!"

The bar winked into existence again, striking just below the lip of the rising door. The bright metal scattered it into harmless sparkles, but it couldn't do that forever; sooner rather than later it would heat up, discolour and absorb more heat . . . The beam struck again, just an instant after the hold doors clanked shut in its face. That was something, at least, but it left us stuck here. Nearly an hour of our time had gone now. Our policy of minimal violence had its limits; it was the life of one man in that tower against those of the crew, and by implication the whole life of the Colony—Beriosova as boat's commander didn't need to be told. Answering fire was already spitting out at the guard-tower. We waited, and jittered, and gunned the motors of the carriers, ready for a dash. But the green beam didn't seem to be slowed down at all.

"Owen! Mark!" crackled Beriosova's voice in my procom. "I can't bring the guns to bear from this angle. Not meant for ground fighting, after all. And handweapons won't reach. Could we lift off and swat him from the air?"

"And get downed by the other towers and the roof cannon while you manoeuvre? We've not got speed or surprise on our side any more—just keep him busy, Berry, try to put him off his stroke. We'll do what we can from here—"

Owen waited till I'd clicked off contact before adding, "Whatever the fash that might be! At least those beams weren't made for stuff our size."

"Right. The roof cannon are the air defences. The towers protect the surface, and the sea wall—Owen! The wall! There's a causeway of sorts on it! And just about passable when the damping field's on and there are no heavy seas—"

Owen looked out at the lowering expanse of sea beyond the wall. "They look pretty heavy to me now, those waves . . ."

"Landsman's eye. They're a bit high, but nice and regular. As long as that lasts—"

"I can't really spare a squad," he protested, looking at the besieged back door of the warehouse. "There won't be much foam left, and the Station boys may find a way to clear it soon . . ."

"Two heroes should do—"

Before I could finish he'd grabbed one of the men beside us, a tough youngster in the regular Ship crew uniform.

"Mark's idea—you heard? OK, go with him, he knows the way—oh, *hell!*"

Just for a change the beam had stabbed at a man who'd incautiously poked his head round the corner of the warehouse, as I had a few minutes before. It didn't quite touch him, but he was blown off his feet, and lay where he'd fallen, writhing slowly. I felt queasy, and not only at that; there's a big leap between just thinking of something and putting it into action on the spot. I hadn't actually cast myself as one of the required heroes, but of course I was the obvious choice.

Owen was unbuckling his pistol and giving it to the crewman, who'd only been carrying gas grenades.

"Mark, this is Charlie, from Engineering—good man! Beat it back here the moment you can, both of you! We'll start loading the moment the firing stops." He paused for an instant. "Whatever happens, we'll wait as long as we can. Good luck!"

"We'll fashing need it!" snorted Charlie as we edged out of the far end of the hangar. "OK, whadda we do, sir?"

"Run like hell round the other side of the boat to the terminal building!" I was already running, and Charlie loping after me. Somebody sniped at us from an upper window, missing by kiloms; the tower beam kept on hammering at the boat. We made it into the Terminal building, deserted except for the hanging clouds of gas droplets that had driven its occupants back into Central. Gasmasks hadn't been readily available, and nobody had got to firemasks and scuba gear in time. They'd be digging them out now, though, and when they had enough they'd come pouring out at us again—and more than a hundred this time. We pounded through the familiar narrow halls, shooting open the occasional inconvenient door or barrier, until we stood in the open once again, looking at a strangely peaceful scene. We'd crossed the southern arm of the Station and were looking out at the other quadrant, and its wide landing lagoon. It, too, had a guard tower, so we slunk along very carefully towards the outer end of South Arm, hearing nothing except beamfire from the other quadrant.

"Nobody about?" inquired Charlie.

"Maybe not even in that tower. I think most people have bolted for Central . . ." I fought off the feeling that I ought to be there too. I pointed out over the quay at the end of the arm.

"See that? It's one of the cables anchoring the seawall; they carry any extra power the damping field or the towers need, as well—"

"Hey, suppose we cut it—"

"No. There are four main cables and at least thirty smaller ones. And besides, it's more than a metre thick. No, we're going in the water, Charlie boy—"

My coveralls were light and tight enough not to get water-logged, but halfway there Charlie had to stop and pull off his uniform top. It sank at first, but bobbed up an instant later and drifted away across the calm lagoon, floating spread out on the surface like a flag.

"If anyone sees that—" I called to him, but got cut off by a mouthful of seawater.

"Thought it'd sink! Felt like bloody lead!"

"Can't be helped!" I called back, spitting out half the Atlantic. Was the lagoon beginning to get slightly choppy? "Come on!"

Hauling ourselves along the cable was quicker than swimming and used less valuable energy; it also hid us from one side. It was festooned with smaller cables and wires, and we grabbed at trailing loops and projections, kicking out to help ourselves along. Occasionally we'd grab a weedstrand instead and sink spluttering. Beyond the wall the sea was definitely rising, but still running smoothly enough for the field to cope.

"If the fields weren't on," I shouted over the rumbling churn-sound of the wall units, "the wall'd shake itself to bits. D'you see that junction unit there? We'll climb up on it. And for Crissakes don't fall between it and another unit, will you?"

Like the others, the junction units contained wave-power generators and damping-field set-ups, but they also had communications and surveillance installations and the stress-monitoring system that protected the wall. On four large gyro-stabilized junctions sat the guard-towers, one to each quadrant of the Station. The one we were after was thirty units away from where we crouched, behind a peculiar antenna on our junction. The air felt slightly thick in the field, and the spray of waves breaking against the wall slopped and ran like thin grease around our feet. If you stayed in the field for a day you might find your blood doing odd things, but it was strong only at water level. Up here we were safe—relatively, at least.

"You mean we gotta walk on those bloody churning things, sir?"

"Run, if we can. It looks worse than it is. It's hard to see, but because they're turning eccentric cams the tops of the units are always more or less level whether they're being lifted or lowered by a wave. You just have to hang on, is all; it's crossing between units that's dodgy. Fall between and you're smeared like paste."

We ducked down as the guard tower swung slightly, and the beam flashed brilliantly against the dark cloud. It wasn't at us, though; we saw part of the warehouse wall buckle and smoke.

Charlie snarled and leapt out boldly onto the catwalk of the neighbouring unit, poised there for a second as it rode smoothly up on a wave crest, then sprinted down its length, dropping to a crouch at the far end. I was right behind him, ready to grab him if he overbalanced, but he'd have to look out for himself when he jumped. UP again, and he sprang for the next unit. DOWN again, and I followed. Most Station ears learnt to tune out that distant creaking rumble from the wall, but this close— UP again!—it sounded like the legendary quern grinding out salt without end—DOWN again!—amen. The wind was whipping at my wet hair, chilling it painfully. UP again! and leap! Run forward in a half-crouch—hold on. As each unit sank the next one rose. And leap! Charlie was getting the hang of it, we were making great speed. We needed to; the sea wasn't getting any lower. That weather business had seemed like a good idea at the time. Ahead of me Charlie stood poised for his next leap, not so far now from the apparently oblivious tower. Owen and Co. were keeping it fully occupied, and what raider would be able to cross the wall? The next unit lifted, Charlie launched himself—and then all hell broke loose. The air lashed like a burst cable, the sea smashed at the wall and shook it. A gigantic wave burst over me as I hung on blindly, tons weight of water battering at my senses. It passed, I rose with giddying speed on a wavecrest no longer gentle, but vast and black, a mighty wall down whose other side the unit tilted and crashed as the monster raced on to strike at the Station. The rumble had changed to a gritty scream. Someone in Central

Control, alerted perhaps by Charlie's jacket, had spotted the figures on the wall. And had turned off the field in the middle of Charlie's leap. The sea was breaking white over the causeway he should have been on. He was nowhere to be seen.

I went on—what else was there to do?—timing my leaps with care, waiting an eternity before plunging out to another wildly bucking unit. Time ceased to mean much; it was, always had been, a wait, a leap, a crashing of torrents over my head while I clung to the catwalk, and another staggering run in the icy wind. I leapt, again and again, but in mid-air I saw suddenly that the unit coming up to meet me looked different. I landed, clung, and tried to gather my wits while the next wave washed around me. The deafening crackle overhead and the strong ozone smell helped me to realize I'd reached the tower at last. Somewhere under my feet there was a whine, straining gyros, perhaps; at any rate the unit was staying more or less level, though it was rising and falling more than it should. It didn't seem to be giving the gunner much trouble. Green bars still imprisoned the boat, and the warehouse wall was looking very sick indeed. Soon—any minute now—somebody might realize something was wrong with the Station, and send help. Those beams would show up to a satellite even through cloudcover, if it knew what to look for. I pulled myself painfully to the companionway ladder leading to the tower, and looped tired arms over it. Slowly, and as silently as I could, I climbed.

I'd been up these ladders often enough, on my rounds, but never with the fields off. Near the top I took a second's rest to give my heart a chance to slow down, and just hung there with the wind hurling stinging spray at me, blessing the gyros. Was it my eyes or was the Station itself rocking slightly? The seawall noise was even louder now, and blended with an occasional ominous squealing crunch among the grind and clang. Something lashed up suddenly out of the water between me and the Station, like the neck of some extinct sea monster. It whipped up in a serpentine curve and fell back into the waves. Whatever genius had offed the fields had left them off just a little bit too long; the cables were breaking now, which meant that in a few minutes the whole wall, guntowers included, would begin to go. My journey had been wasted; I hung there, watching the shots from the tower begin to go wild as the gyros failed to cope, and wished I'd never been born.

Then the bite went out of the wind, though it still flapped

at my hair, and the sharp lift and plunge of the passing wave-crests slackened to a longer, slower motion. I was flaming with fury at the incompetent chancer in Central Control who'd left it this long to put the field back on; now the waves had built up too much momentum to be damped easily, and the damage they'd already done would open the way for more. I fancied I could put a name to that chancer. But then a huge wave broke against the base of the unit, sending a great spearhead of spray up to the height of the tower. The field slowed its falling slightly, so that its summit seemed to fade into a hanging net of droplets that slid away to reveal a wide rain-curtain on the horizon, herald of a tremendous storm. What would that do to the wall now? I'd more immediate worries. I drew my gun, and wearily, almost automatically, pulled myself up the last few rungs and onto the platform. The gun-turret was being swung and swivelled here and there by its compensation systems to provide a steady firing point, and a yellow warning light flashed above its door. After that nightmare on the wall, though, the leap looked easy. I landed on the slippery metal step and clutched wildly at the safety rail, almost dropping the gun in the process. Above me something large screamed over-head, not as far as I'd have liked it to be; a light two-man airspacer with NavDep markings, a patrol came to investigate the Station's communications problems. Our gunners, probably foaming at the mouth with frustration by now, sent a fearful tracery of fire up at it. It stood on its tail and climbed skyward, no doubt yelling for help with all its might. Our jamming would give it problems for a while, though.

I steadied myself, wrenched at the catch, and swung inside. The man at the gun jerked his head round in alarm—I heard a shot boil into the sea—then exhale with a sigh of relief, half turning back to the gun. Then he did a magnificent neckbreak-ing doubletake.

"Chief!" he shouted. "I mean Mr. Bellamy—" It hadn't occurred to me I'd know the man at the gun, but of course that was almost inevitable. I'd had other things to think about. I brought up the pistol, and saw his face harden as the impli-cations sank in. The weapon felt heavier than usual, but I managed to keep it steady.

"What the fashing—"

"Away from the gun, Peters. Right out of your seat, yes! I'm aiming at your arm, but this is a handbeam. It's unpredictable. And hands away from your own pistol—you know the drill!"

He stood, slowly, with a twisted, disgusted expression on his face.

"First you vanish, then there's all this crap about you defecting. I never half swallowed that, but here you are with the Africans now! Never figured you'd be the type to—"

"I'm not—this is different, no Africans or any other country involved. But it's life or death for thousands of people. We don't want to kill, but it's your life against theirs. So move! I won't hesitate to shoot."

"I believe you," he said wryly. "OK, I've moved. What now?"

"Against the wall. Going to tie you up. Hadn't planned to— a friend was going to keep an eye on you, but he got swept off—" I hadn't much tape left from the other guards, but my own training manual had emphasized that a little well-used can be more effective than swathing someone in the stuff. "Take it from me, Peters, I don't like this, but I've got my reasons—"

"Save it," he muttered, but he didn't resist as much as he might have. "That stupid shit Simoneau told me you'd both gone off the wall, thanks to his brilliant little trick!"

"So it was his idea! He'd have done better to turn it back on sooner. All that spray made good cover."

"Yeah! Nearly bust the whole show up, didn't he? Hey, listen, you just going to leave me trussed up?"

"No choice. But I'll call the Station and tell them you're here—"

"Well, do me a favour then, and tell them a small army got through, eh? 'Cause I'm going to need something to throw in Simoneau's face."

"It'll be a pleasure. I'll make it convincing." I turned to the gun. It left me at a bit of a loss. I knew well enough how to dismantle this model, but only with the power off—that was done by a security switch that only Central had the codes for. And with enough power around to vaporize the whole tower you cut no cables. After a moment's thought I tilted the gun down till it pointed into the lagoon, stuck my handbeam against the great mounting gimbals and fired. I'd angled the beam away from electricals; the heat-resistant bearings took a while to melt, but on the fifth shot they responded messily with clouds of black smoke and stench. Emboldened, I examined the trigger unit and found it had a plastic safety cover which could be melted into place behind the compression lever that was still the best way of activating guns. I clicked the cover into place and fired. That could have been a bigger mistake than it was, because the entire trigger unit exploded out of the casing and hit me on the foot, then clattered away across the lurching floor. Thick, stinking foam came oozing out after it.

"You cunt!" snapped Peters. "You've triggered off the fire failsafes! Leave it before you blow us both off the map!"

I'd forgotten the failsafes—too long since I'd worked with one of these guns—but I'd done what I came to do. The gun was overhaul material now.

"Thanks for the advice," I said. "I've finished. I'm going. Thanks for not making me kill you—"

"No sweat. You always wiped the deck with me in combat classes, anyway. But those reasons of yours had better be good or I'll come calling and stuff them—"

"You'll be lucky! Kick Simoneau's ass for me, will you? Bye!"

Going down the ladder was far worse than up. We were only about ten metres up on that damned tower, but it felt like a thousand with the sea heaving us merrily about underneath. Also I seemed to be carrying somebody about my size. When my feet hit a solid surface instead of another rung it actually worried me at first. I stumbled over to the edge of the tower unit, looking for the little electric canoe the guards used to come out here. I couldn't see one until I noticed a cord running from a power outlet apparently into the sea. The little boat had been swept off the recharge rack, but it was mercifully undamaged. The lagoon was positively rough now, and dangerous to swim in my state. There was too much of the Atlantic underneath it for comfort. I disconnected the charge cord, picked up the little canoe and leapt in. It buoyed me up while I scrambled aboard, floating full of water just under the surface. I baled out as much as I could and sent the canoe ticking its way over the uneven water. It was a bouncy ride, though the sharp prow cut cleanly through the small waves that made rapid rhythmical splashes underneath as we passed. Suddenly there was a bump, a lurch that nearly threw me out, and a slithering beneath that ended in a frantic rasping as the little craft's propulsor cut across something. I brought her about to look.

A vaguely human outline wallowed face-down in the grey

sea. I hauled it up and over by the shoulder, almost overturning the canoe in the process. It was Charlie, of course, the face still more or less recognizable. The grinding of the units had messed him up badly below the waist, though; the legs were gone completely. I tried to haul him on board, but the canoe overturned. In this rough water I couldn't tow him either; the drag made steering impossible. I managed to remove his pro-com and rings—there might be someone on the ship who should have them. It went against the grain to just leave him like that, but there was nothing more I could do. I hoped someone would pick him up soon; I'd seen enough bodies the sea had got to.

One of our men took a shot at me as I climbed shakily onto the airstage. Fortunately we were still shooting to miss; I was too exhausted to dodge. I slumped down against the warehouse wall and let Owen pour drink down my throat. He was in great form.

"Began loading the moment the shooting stopped!" he burbled. "Oh, boyo, it was beautiful, just beautiful!"

"Sorry I took so long," I said.

He stared. "Long, boy? What're you on about, then? Three-quarters of an hour, maybe, there and back!"

I sighed and lay back. My facemask was still lying on the other side of the Terminal Building, and the gas hanging around, even in the storm-tossed air, made my eyes water. We'd had quite a few casualties, but only one other death besides Charlie. My old strategy classes had called a ten per cent death rate on any dangerous operation "acceptable." Why was I so worried about two per cent, then? I'd hardly known Charlie, the other man I'd met only at the briefing sessions. Their deaths paid the ransom for a thousand lives—"acceptable" enough, surely?

I felt as if I wanted to be sick. I clambered to my feet and staggered over to the edge of the airstage, but when I got there I realized I wasn't going to be. Something had been digging into my guts as I sat, that damned handbeam. The HQ guard, Thorborg, Yermolov—the rights and wrongs of the world were blurring a little. All I was sure of was that death was a final thing, and a heavy one. Too many deaths weighed around my shoulders, threatening to overbalance me, tip me over the guardrail into the heaving black turmoil beneath. The first, the earliest four—they'd died here, hadn't they? On board this Station. I had to shed some weight, fast, or I'd sink. I pulled the handbeam out of my belt, dangled it down to the rising waves. One of them slapped icily at my fingers, and it was gone. There was an arm under mine suddenly, scooping me up, and then another under the other arm, Owen and a middle-aged woman who'd been on the first carrier. They bundled me back along the scarred warehouse wall—which had luckily been much more resistant than the zep shed—across the air-stage and in through the hold doors. I could feel them rising under my feet as we went.

By the time I'd been dumped back in my chair and inertia web I felt far better, even like singing—

> Gonna lay down my sword and shield
> Down by the riverside . . .

—but I saved my voice.

"Owen back aboard. Berry!" I heard him snap. "And resuming command. The jets are a bit buggered, so we'll take extra advantage of that gun being knocked out."

We'd barely lifted before Owen sent us skimming across the lagoon at what looked like millims above the waves. A fusillade from the roof cannon raked at us as we rose above the lurching sea wall, but we were still too low. The guardtower swayed horrendously as we passed, smashed this way and that with appalling force by the angry Atlantic. Enormous drifts of spray broke over it as it swung. If the damaged wall gave—I reached wearily for the com controls. *There were responsibilities, responsibilities* . . . Would they get to Peters in time? We rose above the clouds into the sunlight.

EIGHT

"The huge bay down there is the Huang Hai, the Yellow Sea," I told the Ship, watching the rear scope view scroll slowly across the command screen. "The coastal area's Hopeh province. That swirl of cloud from the sea to the mountains is the biggest damn storm I ever saw—looks like you lads overdid it a little there—and Peking's right under the heart of it. There's aircover buzzing about, but not a spacecraft in sight. So Liang hasn't taken off recently. It's just possible he got away about the time we did, and has headed a long way off course to dodge pursuit, but if not—well, there'll be more gunships coming up any minute, from the Pacific or Caspian military stations, or one of the Chinese bases. And the Brazilians have at least one fighter flotilla tucked away in an orbital station. Liang and the other stragglers could run into trouble . . ."

We'd had none ourselves. The only other craft in sight as we cleared the exosphere were civilian, the incoming ferry among them. Getting no clearance from the Station, it was already sheering off towards the emergency lagoon in Magilligan Bay, Ireland. All the patrol ships had gone haring after the first boats up, one that had gutted an electronics plant near Gangtok in the Himalayas and the two that had gone after farm machinery. They were outrunning their pursuers; one lumbering gunship had dropped back already and been drawn off by the next factory raider. Another was being chased by Texan revenue airspacers, still under fire but leaving them behind. The last factory raider, K-boat, had lifted after us, but was racing for home with a badly injured Barbieri on board, sprayed with bullets by some overzealous local gendarme while directing the stripping of a chemical plant in Kalimantan. That left only Liang. China was on the other side of the planet from the Ship, so we were relaying pictures—with, at Whittaker's earnest request, a commentary for all the waiting masses on the Ship. Flight Control chimed in just then to tell us that the satellite snatcher had encountered no opposition—rather the reverse, when the crews found out what was going on—and, already unloaded, was heading back to cover the retreat.

I stared. "Just the one? Why isn't Ekkela sending all the reserves in? What'll happen if more than one boat's in trouble?"

Owen shrugged. "He's being a bit overcautious."

"That's one word for it! Hell's teeth, he's so great at taking stupid risks, why's he balk at taking a sensible one?" I flicked on the voice link again. "Flight Control! We could use some support down here. Even for the early boats. What if there are gunships further out—on maneuvers, maybe?"

"Then they're a threat to the Ship, too!" said a familiar voice. "The fields are down, remember?" Owen grinned and swigged at a flat green flask. I'd tried it, and accused him of drinking distilled leeks—unjustly, as it turned out to be rubbing alcohol from the medikit. Being twice his age, I'd stuck to more orthodox battle stimulants. A maximum dose had restored me to life, but done nothing for my temper.

"Ekkela! What chance has the Ship without the raids?"

"Bellamy! What use are the raids without the Ship? Circular argument, so—*que diable?*"

But I had already seen the glittering pinpoint in the lower left of the screen, and scrolled the image across before it swelled and faded. Another blossomed briefly at screen centre. Owen tried to jump up and was yanked back by his inertia web, swearing blue murder. He beat a brief tattoo on the controls, still swearing, and the screen image heeled and wheeled away faster than I could scroll it. I shifted to forward scope as acceleration began to weigh me down, and it held. Unable to make out the details, I keyed my scanner maps into the image; glowing outlines picked out the shapes that traded missiles thousands of kiloms away.

"Mark!" bellowed Whittaker, causing digital peaking in the voice link, a deafening crackle. "What's happening? Is it Liang?"

"Keep your voice down! Yes, it must be."

"Well, tell the Ship! I can't bother Flight Control now!"

"Who's nearest?" I heard Ekkela ask in the background.

"The satellite boys," somebody answered. "And S-boat, they're turning back to help."

"What *ahu'i* gave them permission?" Ekkela barked.

"Nobody!" retorted the controller rebelliously. "But I would have—"

"You'd have been wrong," said Ekkela with sudden mildness. "Risking that many lives is my business, not yours. As it is, *tant mieux*. They know their own status best. S-boat, what's your ETA?"

He didn't get an answer. The screen image was fast resolving, and the sheer drama of it was arresting, with the great southern arc of the Earth, half in shadow, as a backdrop. Without the scanners the darkened hull of Liang's boat was visible only as a shadow-tip on a spearshaft of bluewhite flame, foreshortened by distance. Behind it—*hellfire, that close!*—at least fifteen smaller flames rode in an uneven wave, metal arrowheads gleaming.

"Pursuit fighters," I told the Ship. "Easily fast enough to catch one of our boats, if they can do it within their limited range. It's limited because they're the only kind of craft designed for dogfight tactics. They're just enormous multidirectional motors in a spheroid hull with one pilot at the centre and a few missile tubes scattered between the motor vents. Fast maneuvering in space means killing momentum one way as well as building it up in another, so there's murderous acceleration and deceleration every few seconds, with the motor blasting in all directions, eating up hydrogen and putting incredible stress on the pilots. Even with all the aids—liquid suspension cocoons, special suits, body reinforcement, fieldshields, the lot—it takes years of training to stand it for more than a few minutes at a time. The Americans call fighter pilots Globetrotters, for some old game where you had to bounce a ball all the time. I've been in a fighter simulator once—I came out black and blue, and they say the real thing's worse. And that's our hope—that Liang can hold them off, make them maneuver so much they'll have to give up, or just outrun them.

That's what he's trying to do now, but he's got to be careful. They mustn't box him in and stop him maneuvering, that'd let them swarm over him like hornets, killing the boat or crippling it till the gunships catch up—"

Owen nudged me and pointed. A large bright dot was swooping idly out under the South Pole. I flicked the scanner in again.

"Those are big—gunships from the South Pacific station, by the look of it—twenty at least! There's overkill for you! But they're too far away, no one's in danger except Liang— if he can only keep moving—"

"And if *we* can!" said Owen somberly. "The *gwraig hen*'s getting cranky, and small wonder after the way we've worked her today. Didn't the skipper want an ETA? Tell him not less than thirteen minutes, and what's to say it won't all be over then? Where's that bloody satellite boat?"

"Ship—" I began, and stopped. Behind Liang's boat the ragged wave-crest flared suddenly brighter. Some of them were pouring on the speed, shooting out to the sides, spinning and tumbling like firework sparks. For a moment I thought they'd given up, then I heard Owen slam a fist onto the desk and swear softly. He'd recognized the tactic; a trap was closing, and the dogfight only just begun.

There was cool order in the breaking of the wave, though the fighters darted here and there with bewildering agility, sprouting flames from innumerable vents till they looked like sea-urchins. It became clear that their mayfly dance was just to keep them safe from Liang's guns while they blocked off a narrow cone of space around the boat. Now they hung around it, pacing it almost mockingly, and every second or so one would peel off and tumble inwards across a segment of the cone to deliver its deadly sting. These didn't seem to be getting through, but the loose, mobile cone formation hampered the boat's maneuvering terribly. Every slight deflection it made to fend off a missile or strike at a fighter laid it vulnerable to a tormentor from a different direction. It was the next best thing to being boxed in. And, slowly but perceptibly, as the fighters got their opponent's measure, the cone was shrinking inwards.

"How long can they keep this up? It's got to be killing them—they've got to give up soon—" There was an almighty flash, and one of the fighters went spiralling clumsily out of its attacking arc, firing wild braking blasts. A beam from the boat, invisible on the screen but traced out on the scanner, had detonated a missile far too close to its launcher. In space that couldn't do much damage, but it could thoroughly rattle the pilot. Sure enough, that fighter didn't return to the dance, but headed homeward on a very gentle squirt of flame. Which still left fourteen rolling like blazing tumbleweed around the embattled boat.

Caught up in it all, I was gabbling away over the voice-link and bringing my sights to bear all at the same time. I'd done something like this during wargames at staff college, battle commentary for crews who had to work in isolated areas of a ship or sea-vessel, an essential morale technique. But against pictures there was no way to put an optimistic slant into what I was saying. A better gunner than I might have managed to lock onto those fighters and try some long-range shots, but I couldn't manage it. Three more fighters had fallen back, but none of them had been hit directly. It looked as if they were actually too fast for our antique sighting systems. Which meant they only had to keep trying . . . And with all the pilots nearing the end of their endurance now, they'd be going flat-out for the kill.

The missile trails were clearly visible now, little seeds to grow into such huge blossoms. Owen squealed suddenly as one spread over the boat's stern, a glancing hit. We couldn't see what damage was done, but one hit on the fusion shield would be enough. The Flight Control link·was full of cursing in a weird blend of languages and religions, apparently including Marxism. I bit my tongue, swung in the missile sights and fired.

The screen crisscrossed with streaks, too many to be all mine, and then it was ablaze with bursts of light, fading to shining halos and vanishing. A single missile burned out towards us; I caught that with a beam when it came into range, and in that instant the fighters broke and peeled off every which way, reminding me of that panicked shoal of fish beneath the Station. I worried at them with beams, though the range was extreme; I only wanted to keep them off Liang. Then I joined in the general roar as more missiles burst on the other side of the combat area, still too far away but impressive nonetheless; the satellite boat must be somewhere in the offing. When the screen cleared again there was nothing but Liang's boat, battered and limping, and an uneven row of firetrails, diminishing.

"The traditional view," I said, "of the losers—"

There was a hellish red spark right in the nose of Liang's boat, and the last fighter went streaking through the spreading glow of his shot. A brave chance, but it took him too close, right into the path of a beam from the wounded boat. A new star blazed briefly in its wake. It must have shone like a nova in Earth's night, and thrown new shadows on the Moon.

"Fusion shield," whispered Owen, eyes bleak. That was the pilot's greatest nightmare; I'd seen it once before, but he was young. Some idiots somewhere actually began cheering, and I rounded on them.

"Belay that! What's there to cheer about? This isn't a war, what'd we gain by killing him? Think he knew who he was fighting? He was just doing a hellish job well—same as us!"

"That's telling 'em, boy," murmured Owen in the silence that followed.

Pacing Liang's boat back was a nerve-wracking business. The only communication link still working was the direct navigation computer hook-up; it could have been modified to carry voice, but evidently nobody over there had the time to spare, so conversation was by keyboard only, and brief. The boat's self-monitoring told us most of what we needed to know. Damage was extensive; the hold and cargo were untouched, but there were growing irregularities in the fusion shield. Sooner or later these would defeat the fail-safes, enough heat would escape to destroy the generator and the dying reaction would consume the boat in a lick of starfire. They didn't dare slow down; all they could do was shut off every inessential power drain—life-support included—and race for home. But what then? Ekkela didn't want to take the boat aboard; if the shield went in dock it would make a mess of Flight Deck and maybe even open the end of the Ship like the overgrown can it was. Normally the shield could be sustained with Ship's power, but here the damage was too bad; even the sudden power surge might blow something. He wanted the satellite boat, now empty, to take off cargo and crew in space, but it soon became clear that couldn't be done without depressurizing the holds; life-bank material, already much shaken about, might not survive the transfer.

I hated that thought. All the missions were essential, but to me Liang's was the most vital of all. He was carrying the whole richness of a living world, a host of plants and animals we had cauterized from the Earth. Without that stock there would be no reborn redwoods and whales; we would only be exporting sterility.

"Right," said Ekkela at last, as we crossed the track of the Moon. "We've no alternative, we'll take the boat aboard. But the minute the cargo's clear, back out it goes; we daren't keep it a second longer."

"Well, what about the crew?" demanded the satellite boat's skipper. "There'll be casualties, maybe cut off behind bulkheads. You'll need time to put a rescue team in—"

"Can't risk it," said Ekkela firmly. "We'll have to put someone on before docking. That means you, S-boat."

"What?" yelped Owen. "We're all half-dead—"

"We'd help if we could," said the other skipper, "but—" He didn't have to go on. He had only thirty men aboard, a skeleton crew and few if any with rescue training. Well-qualified men had gone on dangerous missions, like ours. In fact, we had three or four of the Ship's best rescue team aboard, including their emergency marshal. And, of course, there was me.

We suited up in the corridor behind the forward lock, twelve out of the ninety-eight, each with a back-up to check over our suits. The boat's rescue suits were appallingly crude by modern standards—rescue gear was one area where real progress had been made—and it only had four; most of the team were in ordinary space armour. Not me; I had brought my own tailored suit along, the latest design with lots of extras. Which probably meant that if hell was opening anywhere I'd be the first man in. Great.

The marshal took us quickly through the drill, while we all stood around trying to shuffle in our unwieldy suits and enduring terrible gas pains until their internal pressure stabilized. The nose of Liang's ship was worst hit, sealed off entirely by pressure bulkheads; there could still be survivors, though, staying alive on emergency air supplies. We would go in via the midships lock and work our way through the torn nose, arriving back at the hold before the boat docked and taking out casualties and cargo together. If we couldn't get through in time, we'd be ejected with the empty hulk—not that we'd have long to worry about that. I stopped wondering if I'd overdone the stimpills; what was a little thing like brain damage right now?

Suddenly someone grabbed my arm, which wasn't bright;

I heard the clang, but didn't feel a thing. I turned ponderously.

"Berry! What's up?"

Like many long-term spacecrew, Beriosova was more than a little overweight. Now her face glistened in the yellow light, and she was panting so hard she couldn't get her words out properly, and just kept on hauling at my arm. "Screen—Owen said—the Station—from the Ship—come *on!*"

"Berry, what the hell—are you nuts? Can't you see—" But then the lockside screen lit up, and Owen appeared.

"He's there, Berry? Good! Mark, a couple of minutes after Berry took over your coms the skipper came on, frothing at the mouth. Something they'd picked up from Earth. I don't understand at all, you'd better see it. We've a few minutes yet before we can close in on Liang." The screen blanked and faded into a heaving grey blur I recognized before the focus resolved.

"It looks very rough—" ventured Berry.

"Landlubber's eye. Just a nice stiff breeze, we get worse in winter."

Then the commentary came on. "—surviving staff say savagery of attack clearly aimed at destroying Station—"

"What, with a few little punctures? The seawall's the worst damage and they did that themselves—*surviving* staff?"

"—casualty listings not yet complete as several bodies not yet recovered. Among known dead are Station Commander Herincx, Louis, seventy-three, Belgian; Deputy Chief Security Officer Brazda, Zdzislawa, forty-one, Czech—"

The sickening monotone, human but machine-like, proceeded to read me the roll-call of my best and oldest friends—Khalid, Dubuq, many others. I stood there, helpless in armour, and saw each one fall at my feet as if I cut them down myself. It was Ekkela's voice that snapped me into life.

"Well, Bellamy? Couldn't have miscalculated your shots a little, could you?"

"Don't be so fucking stupid!" somebody with my voice told him.

"Well, they couldn't have killed that many as a reprisal."

That many? Somehow they all seemed to be Ziz, poor Ziz who'd been so afraid of getting involved, who didn't want to know. And who never would, now. I could see her as I'd last seen her, a dwindling figure on a dull road. Or as we'd last shared a bed, sleepy and blinking in the morning light. Only now the eyes were sunken, empty, in a sea-ravaged face...

"—acting Station Commander Simoneau has promised full investigations to root out Colonist sympathizers among Station staff without whose help raid would have been swiftly repulsed—"

"Colonist sympathizers?" gabbled Ekkela.

"There's your answer," I told him. "The bastard moved quickly, for once. The way he mishandled the raid—" It must have seemed simple enough to him. On one hand, shattering evidence of his incompetence, enough to sink him for all his connections; on the other, evidence accounted for, contrary voices stilled, and several obstacles to his promotion out of the way. All for the price of a few lives, easily taken in the riot and confusion, with most of the personnel sealed away below decks. A simple choice—if you thought like Simoneau. He'd screwed up his honest chance—he'd have to take this one.

Which I'd handed him on a plate. I couldn't run properly in armour, and Berry and the marshal caught me before I'd gone four strides. I threshed an arm, but Berry hung on just above the claws.

"Where—what are you..."

"Lay off, Berry. Back to the Ship with Owen, that's where. Then pick up my 'spacer and back—"

"In that little toy? We're out past the Moon now, remember? You'd never make it back alive, you'd have to take days and run out of air or build up so much speed you'd never decelerate—"

"I could still come down on their heads! On the Station, on Simoneau, smash the murdering bastard to pulp and sink the place—like one of their own bloody missiles—" I swung my arm and sent her sprawling. But I didn't move on. I could see how hopelessly mad the idea was; the sky was alive with warships by now. I'd be picked up or off before I'd gone halfway. Or miss such a tiny target at high speed, or just ablate away to nothing on reentry. A million things could abort my revenge. There had to be something better.

There was. The idea seized me with an electric, almost sexual thrill, contracting back and neck muscles so the hair rose and prickled. I'd need resources, and people, and time. Well, I had the Ship, and the colonists, and the rest of my life. I dimly heard Beriosova babbling something about Simoneau not getting away with it, but I knew better. The BCs wouldn't be fooled, but they'd follow his line because it suited them—as, no doubt, he intended. He'd probably be confirmed in his post, and prosper. I hoped so, in a way. The fall would be harder when it came. I found myself smiling, though my face felt tight, as if something had dried on my cheeks. Hadn't Barbieri once quoted some old Sicilian proverb, about revenge being a dish best eaten cold? That suited me well. And, best of all, stopping that missile would be an essential part of it—

"I'll come along," I said, and clicked my visor shut. Several approving slaps clanged onto my back armour; I clacked my claws amiably. Let them give me credit for sticking to the job if it suited them. Popularity, too, was part of my plan.

The rumble of attitude motors echoed tinnily in our helmets as we crowded into the lock with our stretcher trolleys and cutting gear; Owen was matching velocities and edging us as close as he dared to the other boat. Sound died with the outrush of air, the door opened, and we were startled to see how close that was. All the jagged rips and tears in the darkened metal seemed to reach up to us like bright claws, just inviting us to make the jump. That, for me, was over in an instant's disorienting whirl that made me think I was back on the seawall; luckily there were more experienced spacemen to guide me. Last man in, I turned to wind the lock door closed and glimpsed our boat, scoured bright by seawater, streak away and ahead at a punishing acceleration; Owen would need to have it well docked before we arrived.

The whole forward end of Liang's boat was smoky chaos, lit green by the biochemical emergency lighting. According to the first men we released from a blast-sealed compartment, it had taken a hammering on the ground and then been hit by a small missile as it was lifting off.

"That was when Liang got it," one of them gasped. I almost dropped him off the stretcher.

"Liang? He's dead?"

"Yeah. Just pulling a straggler in through the forward lock, we were only a couple of metres up. Then—" He gagged in the thin smoky air, and I fed him more oxygen. "Outer lock just isn't there any more..."

I got him into one of the trolley compartments and hooked up to its air supply, and we moved off along the catwalks. The flooring was the usual thin metal mesh on frames, and in normal gravity the weight of our armour might have broken through. Now its elasticity bounced us along at a good pace; from time to time we paused to squirt foam onto one of the worse outbreaks of sparks and flame. The heat expanded and hardened the foam into a mass that stifled the fire and insulated the fault. Every so often we would come to sealed bulkheads and group together to lever, cut or just plain rip them open. Sometimes we found life on the other side, more often death, blasted, cooked or stifled past reviving. The butcher's bill for this operation would be terrible.

In the last few minutes we combed the bows for any survivors we might have missed, but we needn't have bothered. I had three others with me, one girl with a cutting beam, and we had taken a hefty dose of radiation in the area behind the nose. The fighter's last shot had vaporized the entire nose installation, shield and all, laying it open to space. Through the gap we saw something, distant and gleaming, disturbing me somehow.

"Ship looks odd without the fields, doesn't it?" remarked the girl. That was it! Without its shadow-cloak the Ship looked deserted, vacant, lifeless, like a roofless house—or a fleshless skull. Just the way it had through my telescope when I was young, and it was no more than the tombstone of a dream. Now, with all its field power still stirring up Earth's weather and communications, it hung there vulnerable as a naked child. I still didn't agree with Ekkela about the reserves, but I could certainly see his point.

On our hurried way back we came to the remains of the forward lock. City defence installations don't carry nukes, for obvious reasons, but in a direct hit on an open lock even a chemical warhead had bitten deep, a three-metre gouge either side of where the lock had been. Old-fashioned battle plastic had boiled into the gap at once, sealing and strengthening the hull, but it had spilled out into the corridor behind, gruesomely trapping a blast-dismembered body. It wasn't Liang. He and his straggler must have been blown to atoms in an instant.

Liang's boat—we'd all been calling it that, tagging his name onto our fears and our hopes. He hadn't been on it; someone else, maybe Sussmeyer, his relief pilot, had fought that duel with the fighters while Liang's dust was mingling with that of his ancestors. He'd brought my plans to life once; he could have done so again. Now I felt more alone than ever.

We had to cut through the foam to get out, an exhausting business which opened the gap again. Beyond it we saw, not space, but an endless golden waterfall. It took me a minute to realise what it was; we were already passing along the tumbling flanks of the Ship, across which the sunlight was striking low, throwing long, deep razor-edged shadows, a kind of constant evening. Here and there in the shadow sparkled bright pin-points, echoes of the warmer world within. Below us passed a brighter streak, Owen racing for home, in a fit of bravado passing through the wide gap between the forward torus and the hull, timing the passing of the support girders to a nicety. We took a more conventional route, sliding past webs of an-tennae, conduits and the intricate maze shapes of the field generators, ringed with blazing red lines to warn off Welsh maniacs.

The Ship's beam had hold of us by now, and before we were through the plastic barrier we were floating, without even the sense of weight the slight acceleration had created. Once through we hung there an instant, panting. But then the lighting dimmed and flickered, scaring the hell out of us even though we had suit lights and image intensifiers. It wasn't a place to be alone in the dark, and we kicked out along the corridor, squirting suit propulsors and bouncing off the walls and each other with clangs that were deafening in the suits. But in an instant we were swept gently up to what had been the ceiling, then dumped less gently onto the floor. The boat had been spun around its gyros and was now matching the Ship's rotation, so we had weight again. And in another minute or two it would be docked.

We scrambled up and ran, through corridors empty of every-thing except debris, sparks and the odd body; our teammates had gone ahead, and we didn't blame them a bit. There was nobody here to be rescued now. But there were other problems. Not far from the hold we rounded a corner and found a team at work on a huddled shape, cutting beams and torches flick-ering and darting. Overhead, as weight now was, there was a gaping hole in another walkway. An overladen stretcher trolley had burst the mesh and plunged through, carrying its occupant with it. The trolley had protected its occupants, but had landed on the operator and driven her legs through the walkway we stood on. The marshal sent everyone aft with the trolley except myself and the girl with the beam.

"If we kin get 'er out," he gasped, "Jus' pick 'er up an' run! Alarm goes, run anyhow! Don't stop ta play hero—" I stooped and dug my claws into the mesh, ripping it away, until an ill-aimed cutter beam severed part of one pincer. We were all very tired.

And only an instant later, when one leg had been freed, there came an insane high-pitched keening in our helmets. We all stood. Nobody ran. The marshal gestured in despair, seized the cutter and brought it slicing down across the inert form. The leg fell free below.

"Well?" he screamed. We were already snatching up the woman, whose suit was oozing sealant, not blood; the beam had cauterized the wound. We clattered on down the swaying walkway, almost falling through sometimes ourselves, jagged edges clawing at our armour. I couldn't see for the sweat that streamed into my eyes faster than the dessicator could remove it; I could only hope someone knew where we were going.

If we'd been further from the hold we'd never have made it. But there it suddenly was, empty in the rectangle of light that fell in through the doors. A narrowing rectangle. It didn't stop as we pounded towards it, and we found ourselves running up a curving incline that steepened under each step. Then we were at the lip and toppling over in a heap, twisting so as not to land on the body we held. We fell about two metres; the marshal, coming last, scrabbled through the tight gap and crashed down four. I heard the soft snick as it shut very clearly, despite the bellow of the alarm klaxon. Then I felt the rumble of the docking cradle in my bones again, and the werewolf howl as air was spilled heedlessly out of the opening bay drowned even the klaxon. There came bulky shapes in bright light, and I thought I was trapped in the aliens' film. But suited hands seized me, hauling me upright to face the screen by the bay doors. The rumbling ended in a low solid thump, and I watched the dark shark outline tumble away against the stars, looking too small to have held so much life and death. For an instant it was silhouetted against the crescent Earth, like an arrow on a bow, and then an awful glare filled the screen, blotting out the image.

Against it I recognized the face of the man who held me up, even through his suit visor and mine, sallow and hawkhard.

It was Sussmeyer, who'd flown the boat back.

"You did a good job," I croaked at him.

"We got the stuff," admitted a listless voice over the suit link. "They say it's all right. You heard about Liang?" I nodded. The marshal hobbled over to order me profanely into D-Con, where assorted medics leapt on me and filled me full of all kinds of antirads, told me I'd keep hair and gonads and that the woman we'd got out would live, just, and might even grow back her leg with a little assistance. And time, of course; she'd set that foot on a new world. Owen and the rest of our crew came through from their bay à minute or two later, having been supervising the unloading of the mining machinery; they were full of high good humour which even the news about Liang couldn't entirely damp.

"Look at it this way, boy," said Owen. "He knew what he was about, same as you, same as me. Nobody lives forever, so better to go out doing something useful—that's how he thought about it. And where better than China?"

We stumbled through D-Con in any old order. I went through the showers with two women, Beriosova (who kept thumping me on the back) and a pleasant girl who'd been a mobile driver and crushed a finger loading; now it was stiff with surgical foam which the decontaminants were staining a strange ghastly green. Foul as they were, though, the welcome heat of the sprays soaked some of the fatigue out of me, and the last stimulants the medics would allow took care of the rest; by the time I was dry and in fresh coveralls I felt almost human. Owen had had his uniform sent up, and looked godlike as he led us out of the doors.

We couldn't complain about our welcome. Half the Ship seemed to be there, and the impact of the cheers and shouting and music left us dazed—none more so than Owen, whom they tried to carry shoulder-high till he found the ceiling was just too low. All the earlier-arrived mission commanders had been smaller. Streamers flew about our ears, our hands were pumped and our backs slapped till they ached, and hugs and kisses flew thick and fast. Some fool was playing the Valkyrie Ride over the com at deafening volume, and speech was impossible. Suddenly into the midst of the melée came Whittaker, trampling and trumpeting, and more or less snatched up Owen and myself.

"Magnificent show, magnificent!" he panted when he could be heard. "Welcome back, both of you, welcome! Sorry to tear you away, but we've got to talk, urgently. Then I've got to get my hands on Sussmeyer, same reason. There was fighting on your mission, wasn't there? People killed—"

"If you believe that bloody medcast—" I began, furiously, but he put me off.

"Of course I don't, and I'm sorry; I think I can guess what happened. No, I meant our casualties. You see?" He waved a hand at the crowd, dissolving now and flowing by us, full of the boat crew's happy reunions—wives, lovers, children, pets and so on. Beriosova was half crushing her girlfriend and shouting exuberantly. But two women stood stock-still like rocks in the stream, an older and a younger. In the midst of so much celebration tragedy loomed almost visible over them both.

"Paru Raiy and Blanche Pulasky," said Whittaker, who seemed to know everybody.

"Right," said Owen. "Bill Raiy hit by a beam, Charlie was with Mark when—"

"Don't tell me," said Whittaker quietly. "Go and tell them. That's part of the job."

Owen went pure white. "*Iesu*, Rev, I can't handle this—the skipper—"

"Er-no," said Whittaker hastily, "he's taking a couple of hours off, till the last boat's in. There's not much he can do till then, and he's been on watch since early yesterday. He's right to rest while he can—"

"Sure," I said, thinking of the long voyage ahead. "His troubles are only just beginning."

Whittaker looked at me a little oddly. "How about you, Mark? Do you feel up to—you must've had to do something like that in your job."

"Sure, but it was easier with an official face to shelter behind. Not much easier, though. I'm no good with words."

"I don't agree," he said severely. "That commentary of yours was electrifying—you had the Ship hanging on your words. Not so much what you said as how you said it. You talk to Blanche, I'll go with Owen."

And he left me to it, moving aside with the older woman, leaving the young one alone, looking at me. As I walked over to her in the lowered weight of Flight Deck I was suddenly

back on the seawall again, with the procom and rings in my
pocket a ton weight, dragging me down.

Somehow or other we got through it all; I took the girl down
to the North End transit station and left her there. Her own
village would look after her. The car hissed out and away, and
left me standing on the empty platform, startlingly alone. Nobody needed me now. There was nothing screaming to be done.
Months of manic preparation were gone in an instant, made
irrelevant in the instant of their success. I'd never once looked
past that moment of fulfillment, and now it had washed up and
fallen back, leaving me stranded high and dry here, alone with
my past and my future.

Right now I couldn't face either. Such home as I had was
in Liang's village and I couldn't face them now. There was
only one place I wanted to be, only one face I wanted to see,
one voice to hear, almost the last one close to me in my old
life the last few hours had spared. I took the next car along,
out into the Ship's cloudy night.

Rain had passed over Stratford village by the time I stood
outside her door, leaving the air cool and clean and vastly
refreshing. The silence, though, was a little unnerving. No
town Down There was this empty, even at night, and nowhere
so dimly lit; the understreet lighting was phosphorescent and
eerie, with very few lit windows to help it. I thought one of
them was Kirsty's, the only one in the house, but I wasn't sure.
I'd only been to her rooms here once—she had a huge suite,
separate living-room and bedroom—and that had been ages
ago. I hadn't had time to talk to her before the raid, though
she'd kept trying to get in touch with me; I'd found a good-
luck message in my procom memory the night before we left,
too late for me to reply.

I pushed open the street-door—nobody locked them here—
and climbed the ridiculously low-roofed and rickety stairs. There
was music coming from somewhere, something old and rich
and sensuous, Strauss or Mahler or Wagner; for all Kirsty's
coaching I couldn't tell. It was oozing out of the room door,
also slightly ajar; people just weren't paranoid enough here.
Being so goddamn authentic, the door had no com or any other
signal. What was it people used to do? Knock with their
knuckles? But the door was *wood*, and I was afraid of damaging
it. My first inexpert pat swung it open. The living room beyond

was a clothes-strewn mess, empty except for the glutinous music. The bedroom door beyond was open, and I was about to call out when I heard the chirrup of a procom. Kirsty didn't have one, or I'd have called ahead. Was I in the right room?

In the open gap of the bedroom door an arm appeared, slender and muscular and dark, reaching across to scoop a procom out of a discarded shirt. "Captain here."

"Sorry to bother you," said a tinny voice, "but you wanted K-boat's ETA the moment we were sure. The voice-link's back, he's decelerating and'll be in about two hours from now."

"Fine, thanks. I'll be back on in an hour, then; sooner if you need me."

The procom dropped softly back onto the shirt.

Something was pressing suffocatingly over my face, the music maybe, though the roaring in my ears drowned it. Somehow it was hot, burning my face like the vent of a furnace. I stepped back, almost stumbled by the doorpost, and pressed my blazing forehead against the cool corridor panelling. I caught at the bannister that stood out from it and heard it creak in torment. Kirsty's scent seemed to pour out of the room, cloying and sweet. Inside me something reared and plunged, aching to be let loose—

The things you could do. The ways they taught you. Taught, assessed, tested, scored. And then mercifully forgotten. Till now . . . The hard course, the one only the right students took. Things that would have sickened a medieval witchfinder, academically presented. Visual aids, incomplete bloodstreaked images, intimate nakedness of flesh and bone projected onto Kirsty, mewling and writhing in terrible parody of love. The visions came seething and boiling up before me as the stimulants bucked and goaded in my blood, as if they needed only the flick of a hand, the tightening of a grip, to make them material, actual, *real*. What was it that sobbed now under my hands?

I reached the foot before the bannister could creak.

Laughter, mocking the death it had flirted with, followed me down. Beyond the door the night was everywhere, and darkest of all behind my eyes, where all was empty and dark. Blind, I ran and then strode to the heart of it, or in no direction at all, hearing but not understanding footfalls and a voice. But when a hand fell on my shoulder it was the purest, the most natural relief to strike out hard at the source of it. There was a surprised grunt, and then the night erupted into starry agony, hurling me through something that raked at me. Then my face was flat against rich sweet earth, with what had to be a bush over my head and a mighty agony in my left cheekbone. I'd no urge to move, but I was grabbed by the shoulders and yanked bodily to my feet, and propped against a wall. Cool silver light, the suntube in night mode, spilled through the ragged clouds, turning Whittaker's face to an angry statue's.

"Have you gone mad?" he barked. "Didn't even look—that could've been my throat, not my ribs, if I'd been shorter—if it had been Kirsty—" He stopped, looked over his shoulder at the lighted window, and shook me till my teeth rattled. "What've you done? You haven't—"

I grabbed at his arms and forced them down and away. "Of course not!" I snarled. "They never even knew I was there. What d'you think I am?"

Whittaker rubbed his massive arms where I'd gripped them. "A very deadly weapon," he said. "I know the kind of things they teach security men." He looked puzzled. "But then why did you go there, if it wasn't to—you didn't know?" I shook my head. He exhaled sharply. "I see. She wasn't—there was nothing underhand about it. You were neglecting her, maybe even avoiding her. Ekkela wasn't. And he ran that risk for her—stupid, I know, but not as she'd see it. And that day, when you just gave an irritating sort of laugh and walked off—"

"Hell. Laughed aloud, did I? She did look so damn silly ...No wonder she thought I knew. And she kept wanting to talk to me."

"I thought you knew, too. That remark tonight about Ekkela's troubles just beginning, it sounded snide—"

"Right, right, don't push it..." My anger had gone whistling off into nothing like air from a punctured suit. I felt like the suit. "You know, for a pacifist you hit pretty hard. With a touch more technique you could've ripped my head off!"

"Then I'm glad I don't have it," he said crisply. "I haven't your self-control. That I admire. I was really afraid you'd done something terrible..."

I didn't feel like telling him how close I'd come. Or had I? "I was angry, sure. Not so much the sex thing, just being made such a goddamn fool of. But ripping them apart wouldn't have changed anything. And now you tell me I haven't even got that. What's left, then? It's all in my lap. If I'd just found a couple of minutes to *talk* to her..."

"You'd a lot of responsibilities," rumbled Whittaker. "Too many."

"Yeah, and she was one! She's barely nineteen, she's just a kid! I whipped her away from her home and her family, dumped her into this, just left her adrift—"

"Bullshit!" rumbled Whittaker, startling me. "Face it, that's just you dressing up your possessive instincts. She's old enough to look after herself, I know, I've talked to her. She was desperate to get away from home. When you came along she found a way—" He must have seen the thunderclouds forming as I thought back to some of the things she'd said that first night, because he added hastily, "Don't be an idiot, you were more to her than just that..."

"I know, damn you! What business is it of yours? Any of this?"

"None," he answered quietly, "except that you're both my friends and I'm caught in the middle. Hard," he added, rubbing his chest ruefully. Just about throat height for Kirsty, right enough.

"Sorry," I said, "not intended. I'm paid in full. I can feel my face going up like a crash-balloon."

"Mmn." Whittaker flexed his huge paw with something suspiciously like satisfaction. "Well, people will think it's an honourable scar from the raids. Which it is, really. They were your creation, you had to give them all the time you could. And you also had to pay the price of that..."

"I know. I could stand that, I suppose. But Kirsty's paid it, too..."

He stared. "Why? She's all right, believe me—"

"All right? Caught up with that son of a bitch Ekkela?"

"You don't like him much, do you?" murmured Whittaker.

"All right, I don't, I never have, and why the hell should I? Ever since we met he's treated me like some kind of un-aborted psychopath! Standing in judgement on everything I've done—how'd he have managed in my shoes? But he'd never have risked that, not him! Too fond of his own skin. He'd have sat back and let the whole thing just go on festering, he's so—

overcautious! And *he* condescends to give me gracious leave to foul up his private paradise by staying! That damned military aristocrat manner of his—born to rule the lesser breeds and doesn't he know it! Even when he smiles he's spreading his superiority like slime! Know who he reminds me of? Simoneau, that's who!"

"I've met him, remember? I wouldn't say there was much comparison. In fact, you know who Réné really reminds me of?" He chuckled throatily. "You."

"He what?"

"You!" Whittaker was enjoying my reaction for all it was worth. "And not only me! Kirsty said as much. She likes the type."

"What bloody type?"

"Oh, the heroic mould, you could say. Romantic kind— mysterious, strong-willed, a loner. You and Réné both fit the bill. And the two of you are stubborn as blazes, weighed down with responsibilities, fanatically dedicated—"

"Well, so's half the Ship or they wouldn't be here. Even you."

"Touché! Even fossilized me. But I make a better father-figure. Not that I've given up love of any kind, but I just don't have the time—and at my age one needs it." He smiled to himself, and added, "I'm not saying you and Réné are iden-tical—just very alike. For example, he's more Kirsty's intel-lectual type—"

I winced. "Him intellectual?"

"Well—yes, very. When you get to know him—"

"It'll be a cold day in Hell before I do *that!*" I stared up at Whittaker for a moment, then I spun on my heel and stalked away. Right then I'd had enough of him, of anyone else. Maybe Kirsty would be better off with Ekkela; what had I ever brought my friends, after all? I might be spared the trouble of avenging her, at least. The village slipped by, and the open fields were around me. Moonlight came as if it were real, sparkling on the rainstorm that came spiralling down the axis of cloud towards me. I preferred its chill to human warmth, the indiscriminate kind of a Whittaker or an Owen who'd be friends with all the universe if they could. I didn't trust it enough.

The nearest hilltop suited me better. I sat and watched the shimmer of the distant lake under the passing cloud shadows, past warming even by vengeful fantasies, feeling nothing except empty. I vaguely knew I had reached that stage of exhaustion where sleep itself is impossible, and I hardly cared. But I began to dread the coming of dawn.

I don't know how long it was before the feeling of tension came, a faint thrilling hum in the air, more felt than heard. Then a voice like Whittaker's god rang through the failing night.

"This is the Captain." For all its immense amplification his tone sounded less arrogant than usual. "Our dangerous quest for supplies has been successful beyond hope; the last of our boats is now safely docked. We have lost many good and valued friends, the latest of them Councillor Barbieri—but not in vain; the purpose we all shared has been accomplished, and we are ready to leave." I realized they must be modulating the field that contained the clouds. What would that do to the weather? "Look to the future too! Because now it's in our hands." Ekkela paused, and there was a sound like a great bell. He added, less formally, "A spectacular send-off. The old mass-driver on the Moon is slinging small mountains at us! But the fields rise to drive mode in just one minute from now. At dawn!"

It was better than any trumpet fanfare. The long suntube, its moonlight dimmed to smokiness among the clouds, reddened slowly and then blazed golden, raining down brilliant light the length and breadth of the land. It was Ship's autumn, and the scattered woodlands flamed in scarlets and bronzes and gold, like spreading banners. Blinding halation danced on the lakes, and the rivers shone silver in great arcs around the Ship, rushing upwards into what I saw as the sky. There was more birdsong in the air than I expected, and, astonishingly, I saw a pair of gulls sweep up and wheel, grey against the dazzling cloud. Distant cheering and shouting rose from all directions. Beyond the hulls the energy-devouring blackness of Infall sundered us from our native space and time, but in here it was held at bay, a kernel of life in the cold shell.

From the open-air auditorium by the lake I could hear music rising. That was the last thing I wanted, it reminded me of Kirsty. Slowly I began to trudge down the far side of the hill, staggering as the warm light fell on me with almost physical pressure. With each step the planets of the Solar System were dropping away behind us; to them, all this, from the terraced cliffs of North and South Ends to the dew beneath my feet, must seem an infinitely thin line of heat-radiating darkness with an attenuated wave-particle somewhere along its path. I laughed aloud at the thought, and then stopped. No wonder I knew that music; Kirsty had played it, often. I heard a chorus that had stuck in my mind, a powerful jagged rhythm—

> *Dispossessed,*
> *Aside thrust!*
>
> > *Chucked down*
> > *By the sheer might*
> > *Of a despot's will!*
> > > *Of a tyrant's frown!*

I sympathized.

> *The mind bold*
> > *And independent*
> > > *The purpose free,*
> *So we are told,*
> > *Must not think to have the ascendant—*

There was something in that; it was the way I was always feeling. Then I remembered the work, and who it was singing— the demons, from *The Dream of Gerontius* . . . I laughed again, and wandered off to find a quiet tree to sleep under. So I was a demon, was I? I could still be comfortable under an old transplanted oak, sprawled in the warm shade with nothing but the odd buzzing insect to bother me. A lazy demon, then, chucked out of hell for incompetence, and falling, perhaps, at least part of the way to heaven . . .

NINE

In the dim light of the room three people watched my face as I spoke. And one of them was me.

"There you have it. Our time is limited, and we've almost reached the limit. We've been on our way now for thirteen subjective months, and if we lowered our drive fields now we'd find ourselves at rest in normal space about a lightyear out from Earth. And somewhere, not so very far away in astronomical terms, would be that so-called probe. But where? That's the problem. Our detectors can't pick out something that small at any great distance. We've got to hunt along its possible courses. Now, at a certain historic council meeting nearly a year and a half ago, Captain Ekkela agreed to give us the minimum necessary time to search for that thing and destroy it. And, by diverging as far from our course as he feels he can, Captain Ekkela has kept his word. For the last three weeks he has spared no effort to track it down."

Privately I wasn't so sure of that, but I wasn't fool enough to make an issue of it without proof.

"In less than two days, though, our time is up. Then it will actually become significantly dangerous for us to stray from our course any further. Yes, dangerous. I don't dispute that.

But—" I paused for effect. "—not *very* dangerous. And Captain Ekkela doesn't dispute *that*. But he's opposed to putting us, the Ship and its inhabitants, into any danger at all! He'd rather let that probe go on unchallenged, stand back and watch it carry out a purpose he must find as horrible as all of us do." I wasn't sure of that, either. But said that way it put him on the spot. "And there I can't agree with him. And I never will!"

I smiled ruefully. "Not that I don't understand why he feels that way. This Ship, you, me, everyone in it, rests ultimately on his shoulders. That's a terrible weight. He's taken it on himself to get us through a voyage that's already long, difficult and dangerous enough to scare off the average man or woman. Completely!"

I grinned, and it looked positively wolfish. "But we're not average! If we were, we wouldn't be here! We're special. The Captain, you, me, every last one of us. We've had the determination, the guts, the sheer goddam nerve to fly in the face of our self-appointed masters, of our fellow citizens, of the whole infinitely dangerous universe—to do what? To prove that we can make a fresh start. That the human race isn't bound to go the way it did on Earth, that it's capable of better things when it hasn't got the past like a millstone round its neck. And if we can't do that—better never to have tried. Better to have sat at home, bowed our heads, forgotten our hopes and visions and faith and everything else that made us *special*. Right?" I remembered how the com operators had nodded.

"Well, then. Isn't this probe, this missile designed to wipe out a whole race of alien beings who've never shown us anything but friendly interest, isn't that a good contender for the worst thing Earth has ever done? And it's out here with us! The evil we left behind, sent out ahead of us. What are we, if we can just sit back and pass it by? What are people who do that to a drowning man?" Pause again.

"Make no mistake about it, these aliens are people. On the little I've seen of them they're closer to us than whales or dolphins ever were. They build things, they ride groundcars, they're curious about life on other worlds. They're unlike us physically—so what? That only makes them less likely to be our competitors, safer to treat as friends. So, tonight I'm asking you to do some very hard thinking. Perhaps the probe will be found before the Captain's limit expires. I certainly hope so. But if it isn't, what are we going to do then? Captain Ekkela thinks that's already been decided. He thinks we're going to forget all about the terrible destiny prepared for these *people* by our own kind. That we're just going to push on to our brave new world and never look back. But I don't recall him ever asking you and me about that! Asking us if we can enjoy the safety he's kept for us, when we know how we've sacrificed someone else's. I know what I'd tell him—what I'm going to tell him, when the time comes. And I'm asking you to tell him too! He claims he's protecting us. But surely it's our right to decide just how much protection we want! And if it isn't— well, what the hell did we leave Earth for, anyhow? Thank you all, and goodnight."

My face faded into the stylized outline of a Ship's boat silhouetted against the solar corona that was the insignia of the broadcasting service. Lately it was also coming to symbolize something else. Maurya leant forward to turn it off. Faint thumps and giggling from upstairs became audible. She smiled. "Those two! I'd better go up soon and chain them down. I'll make some tea, then—or would you like coffee, Owen?"

"Mm, tea for me, please. I'm acquiring a taste for luxury fast. Anything hand-made!"

"Oh, you're just as bad as Mark—see that jacket of his?"

"Blinded by envy, I am. Is that real sheep's wool?"

I stroked it complacently. "Loom-woven, hand-made *and* made to my own peculiar measurements. Think about that! Like a bloody BC prince!"

"It was a gift from that Australian community," said Maurya. "They wanted it to be a surprise—I had a terrible time getting those measurements!" She laughed, looking more like somebody's harvest goddess than ever. The sari she wore heightened the effect, blue as her eyes and baring her right shoulder and breast. Some interesting new fashions were springing up on the Ship as the reaction to Social Morality set in, and Maurya had the figure to take advantage of them. She'd still been in coveralls when we'd met again, three months out from Earth, pushed together by matchmaking busybodies at a winter party. Of course, we wanted to sink through the floor at the sight of each other, but that gave us something in common, at least, and, eventually, something to laugh about. I was badly in need of that just then; I'd found nothing better to do than potter around as an agricultural labourer in the torus units, pleasant enough work but ultimately boring. I badly missed the sea, and began to get claustrophobic. And though I wouldn't admit it to myself, I was lonely. Maurya was no better off. All she'd been able to do was housekeep for Whittaker and some other old Council buffers who were too busy to manage for themselves, and that hardly stretched her mind. She'd been a court clerk before she'd married a young Finnish merchant marine officer; in the two years before he went down in a submarine collision they had little enough time together. In reaction to his death she'd applied to emigrate—and found herself having to fight to keep her children. It was even suggested that she'd not been entitled to have the usual quota. Whittaker and his people had helped her, and with her legal background and friends in the tribunals she had won through. She was glad enough to be aboard, but, like me, she had found that there was little market for her skills; law enforcement was a local community affair on the Ship, and likely to stay that way. We talked and talked and talked, and the party retreated into the distance around us. Then it began to snow quite heavily, and someone suggested snowballs; we spilled out laughing into the snow and belaboured each other and everyone else with a will. I happened to mention how long a trek I'd have back to where I was staying, and that reminded her how close her home happened to be, and before the first fall had quite stopped we were on our way, catching each other as we stumbled through the low drifts, feeling ready to melt them around us.

In the early hours of that morning, as we huddled exhausted together under a warm insulator, I had a dream, and clutched her to me so tightly that my fingers left bruises. Even after she woke me the image of it still hung before me, a dagger-like talon of fire that cut a ragged swathe through endless rows of human forms, unrecognizable, but somehow vastly important to me. Only the last had a face I could see, and it was Maurya. By my own light I saw it as I swept down on it, for although in the beginning it had been far away and something else, now the blade of fire was me.

Maurya got up and made us hot chocolate—a new product of the torus farms. It was the first time I'd ever tasted it. We laced it with brandy and sat naked together under the cover watching the winter landscape beyond her window. It was hypnotically still in the cold light, but in the distance another storm was moving down the Ship; the flakes seemed to be spraying downwards, sideways, upwards in a great ring outwards from the suntube, dimming the starlike lights above and turning our little world into glittering caverns of ice. I reached down across the warmth of her back and closed my arm around her.

"Maybe I'm afraid," I told her. "Of hurting what I touch. My friends haven't done very well out of me——"

I remembered how she'd nuzzled my shoulder then. "If I do no worse," she'd said softly, "than that little bitch Kirsty, then I'll have no cause to complain. And I'll help you any way I can."

She already had. Talking to her, telling her all about the probe business and the night of the raids, revived the germ of an old idea that I had been busy burying alongside the painful memories. The very next day, feeling fresher and fitter than for weeks, I took some time off to look over the Ship's com facilities, and found, as Owen had once told me, that the original designers had included everything necessary for a small but effective public com-casting service. I reported on this to the Council, presenting a plan for activating it. There was a huge store of suitable library material buried in the Ship's vast databases, old but all the better for that; the hands of State bias and censorship had fallen on it relatively lightly. We could use that to start with, easing in homegrown material—amateur entertainment, education, community news and views. The Council jumped at the idea, and as an unemployed coms expert I was the natural choice to implement it; also, almost everyone seemed to remember that commentary of mine. Within a week I was supervising test 'casts, and within another week I was running the Ship's one and only media network. And by then I had moved in with Maurya. She had helped me with the administrative work, an ideal job for her because she could do most of it from her home terminal. Her children, Arvi and Juha, were marvellous, and I only had to be careful not to spoil them. With her my life began again.

There were more thumps from upstairs, and a loud wail. Maurya gestured mock despair, rose and swept out. Owen's gaze followed her, and lingered as she went. "Oh, gorgeous woman that," he breathed. "Lovely she is . . ."

"I saw her first," I chuckled, topping up his beer stein.

"Just as well you did," he said bitterly. "Oh, if only I had! Fat chance of that, though, on Officer's Row. My sex life's damn near nil up there."

"Move out, then, right out of North End, into the Ship—"

"Would if I could. And will, when I can stop doing two men's work. That's why you've seen so little of me this last year. It's murder without Liang there. Hard bugger he was, but he kept the Bridge running smooth as a baby's bum. Not easy to fill his shoes."

"No more than it would be yours."

"Well," he sighed, "maybe not yet, not till we've trained up a few. Sussmeyer's the best, of course—and Beriosova, but she's needed to take charge of South End. Maybe when some of our teenagers grow up a bit . . . You wouldn't feel like having a go, would you? You're not a pilot, but that doesn't matter so much as long as we've got Sussmeyer. His trouble's running things, he's not a staff college man like you—and command college as well, isn't it? There you are. He could be master pilot and you second officer."

"Under Ekkela? No thanks. Anyway, I'm too busy."

"Oh yes," muttered Owen. "Pardon me for forgetting. Too busy with this political lark of yours."

"It isn't politics! Not really. And it sure as hell isn't a lark! I wouldn't be running this campaign unless I had to. I don't trust Ekkela over this probe business. I think he's still got some sneaking hope that it'll get through!" I'd expected Owen to object, but he didn't, just stared moodily into his beer. "At the very least, he'd rather not find it so far away that he'd have to go far off course to reach it. I may be wrong, but I can't risk leaving it all in his hands. And when something this important's at stake, you've just got to defend it with every means you can find! And when that includes informing people who've got a say in the matter, and enlisting the support of the ones who agree with you—"

"It sounds a lot like politics to me. That's a hell of a snake to let into the garden, Mark. Or bring in. Speeches like that one, banners, public discussions that are beginning to look more like rallies. And you at the middle of it all, the best-known face aboard, everyone treating you as if the suntube shone out of your—"

I thumped my beer-stein down on the table. "Owen, what is this? You know me—do you think I like that? Of course I get some of it, of course I'm well-known! I could hardly help that, what with being five places at once in the raid preparations and then on everybody's holocom for the last eight months! But I don't bloody court it!"

"I know, Mark, I know," he said quietly, watching the beer I'd spilled curve away across the smooth wood surface. "Wonder what makes it run all funny like that, mmh?"

"I don't know," I said wearily. "Coriolis force, maybe..."

"Maybe. All right, then, it isn't politics, it's just this one issue, the probe. On which, by the way, I couldn't agree with you more, in case you were forgetting. So, when that's all over, you'll just be wrapping all this up, no doubt. No more *campaigns*. The com service goes back to being just a com service—"

"What else is it now?"

"You know as well as I do, boy. Well? Does it end there?"

I took a minute to consider my answer. "I hope so," I said, trying not to sound guarded. I didn't like the idea of lying to Owen. "But when did politics ever really end? They're just human nature in action—every time more than two people disagree, you get politics creeping in—"

"Maybe, maybe. But it's a matter of degree. Me, I don't like the effect politics has on people; it's like a tobacco habit, it sticks and it grows. Look at you, boy. If I'm not wrong, you've just told me you'd revive the whole damn business the next time you and Ekkela don't see eye to eye."

"What if I did?" I threw back at him, beginning to get genuinely angry. "I suppose he, the pure innocent, wasn't playing politics when he sent you down here tonight to offer me that post which'd get me nicely muzzled up in the chain of command? Well?"

Owen writhed. "There's more to it than that, boy. It was half my idea. We said, well, if you're feeling your oats and want to try running things, good luck to you, we need people and we'll give you the chance! But *responsibly,* Mark! In a way that won't break down what we're building up."

"Yeah, Ekkela's banana republic. No, sorry, I know there's more to him than that. But he's too much the politician himself—African style. And that means dictator, benevolent as hell, yes, but dictator all the same. He can't let people rule their own lives. Whether he knew it or not himself, he'd mostly got muzzling in mind when he sent you down here tonight!"

Owen laughed in pure delight. "Oh, whether he knew it or not, that's a good one! Well, I know him better than you do, and I wouldn't say you're a hundred per cent wrong. But you're not right, either. It wasn't the only reason, see? Not even the main one, *bach*."

"Well, what the hell is?"

"Oh, nothing so important. Just we've found the probe, that's all."

Some part of me heard, understood and snapped me upright like a puppet on strings. The rest of my mind held me there, swaying, and struggled to understand. Owen fielded the heavy table as it teetered over.

"You've—" I must have been a sight worth seeing. I shut my mouth and started over. "It's true? And you've just sat here gabbing all through dinner, with *that* to tell me—"

"Hardly gabbing," said Owen coolly. "I wanted to make you that offer first."

"Well, what the hell are we sitting here for now, then? Maurya! *Maurya!*"

She swept in from the kitchen. "You'll wake the children!"

"We've got to go, now! They've found the probe!"

Her face lit up, and she flung her arms round my neck. Owen shook his head. "There's no need to go rushing about, you two. Anything to hurry about and I'd have told you earlier, wouldn't I? All we've got is a few read-outs that add up to a spacecraft that fits the probe's description, at maximum range. We won't be near enough to make out much more than that till midnight. Captain's compliments and would you both like to come up to the Bridge then. Now can I have my tea?"

Maurya looked up at me. "I'd better stay here with Arvi and Juha. I'll watch it on the com—"

"Ah, that's another thing," said Owen. "Captain requests no live coverage, says there could be some tricky work and he doesn't want medmen cluttering the place up and his staff worrying about their public image. I agree."

"Fair enough," I said, thinking about it. "It's his Bridge. As long as we can have pictures afterwards."

"You can," grinned Owen, "if I can have my tea."

At 23:30 he led the way out to his zep, resting in the field behind the house. Maurya jammed herself into the doorway with me, clinging. "Will this be the end of it, then?" she whispered. "Will this satisfy you?"

It was even harder to lie to her. "For the moment," I told her. "Maybe for good."

"Maybe?" There was the glint of tears in the moonlight, but I caught them before they'd gone three freckles. "I said I'd help you, and I will. But I don't want to lose you to guilt and hatred . . ." She stood looking after me.

Owen's zep was a mess. I heaved a pile of rubbish off one seat, and heard more of the same, empty cans mostly, go rattling and clonking to the rear of the cabin as he jerked the nose up into a swift banking turn. He went on carolling about how lucky I was.

"Great home, great kids, lovely lady! Come on, man, how'd you do it? Let's be having your secret, then! Where'd you meet her?"

"Well, the *first* time was when I hit her with an electric goad. When she was trying to scratch my eyes out, you see."

"Wow, how romantic. I'd never have thought it of her. All these violent women you seem to get off with, Mark. Now Kirsty . . ." He trailed off, embarrassed.

"Kirsty? She's not violent!"

"Not with you, maybe."

"What, with Ekkela? Funny, I was told he was more her intellectual type."

Owen's reserve, never great at the best of times, broke down. "*Iesu,* boy, you should hear them! I live next door now, and I do. Should have thought you could hear them down South End. Screaming matches every second night, most of the night, things smashing and I don't know what. And then they make it all up, and that's even noisier, and both fresh as bloody daisies in the morning and the rest of Officer's Row dead on their feet! Sussmeyer went round and kicked the blazes out of their door last time and they never even heard! I reckon you're well out of it there, boy."

"I'm sure you're right," I said a little coldly, to cut him short. Kirsty was more than I could cope with just then; I was too caught up in what Maurya had said, and why. I'd never told her or anyone else about my long-term plans, and yet she seemed to suspect something. I hoped I hadn't started talking in my sleep or anything like that. Because, though what I'd said about the moment was true, tonight was just the first essential step in something I'd begun long before.

Right from the beginning, from the moment of Carlsen's murder, I'd seen the whole thing as an ideal lever for reform, a cathartic scandal I could turn to my own advantage. A series of inquiries and purges in SpaceDep, triggering off others in other departments, headed by people like me—there had to be hundreds of thousands who felt the same way, and only needed a lead. But the scandal had become too large, and the BCs constantly ahead of me. In their own world I hadn't been able to outmatch them. But now I was beyond it, on my way to another—or, more correctly, two others. Reaching the Colony would be just another step, however important, however long. Sooner or later I meant to go on, to contact the aliens.

I'd seen their ships and I'd seen the potential in them. Primitive, yes—but the sheer size of them! By themselves they were nothing, of course. A single fighter could run rings round one. But the drives were something else. Nobody these days thought much of fusor drive-flames as weapons; they were satisfactorily destructive, but the focus was too narrow, and in maneuvering to align them on a target you sacrificed your ability to get out of the way of simpler weapons. But with a drive flame half a country wide these considerations might change a little—if it was used only as a weapon, mounted on an Infall ship. With three of those drives I could sweep every warcraft out of Earth's skies. I could melt the polar caps or boil the Atlantic—I'd have a planet hostage. And then there would be a real day of reckoning—and first and foremost for my murdered friends.

I wondered if the idea had occurred to any of the BCs, or their tame experts. Probably it had, and was dismissed as impractical. The aliens didn't seem to have Infall, and they'd no reason to think anyone from Earth would go a-borrowing—not before that missile struck, at any rate. And it might also have counted that none of these experts was on board an Infall ship, facing death from a fusor and half mad with the need for revenge.

For a while that idea had been the only comfort I could find, a future into which I could drain the pain of the present. And even when Maurya and the children came along I went on working towards it, laying the groundwork for the years ahead. To carry it through I needed a following and a powerful voice in Colony affairs; with my hero status from the raids as a basis and the media service as a platform I was beginning to command both. The campaign to stop the probe, essential in itself, was also a useful practice run for the greater struggles ahead.

In all this I'd had so many immediate concerns that I'd been able to let these longer plans slip away ahead of me into an indeterminate future. Now they seemed much closer again, uncomfortably close. For the first time I found myself wondering about them; what would carrying them through do to the Ship, the Colony, the people in it closest to me? Politics, dissension, distractions which could hamper the building of a new world, perhaps fatally. But always in the back of my mind I saw a night of storm and secret murder on the Station, people cut down in the traps I'd prepared for them, faces I'd lived half my life with ruined and blank under a pall of smoke. I owed them more than I could ever repay—but all of it could never bring them back.

The Bridge Deck corridors were more crowded than usual, but Owen and I had no trouble getting through. Except, that is, for the backslaps and handshakes I was getting. By the time we got to the doors I was aching.

"Popular lad you are," grinned Owen. "Must be something in this political lark. I'd try it myself, only I'd be no good. Not devious, me."

"No, really? When you were careful not to tell me about the probe till my speech had gone out? So its effect would be halved—"

He made a face. "Didn't bloody work, though, did it? You'd covered yourself in the text."

"Naturally."

The Bridge itself, normally fairly quiet and calm, was buzzing with activity. It was the first time I'd ever seen every desk manned, and sometimes double-manned; the section that saw to Infall was jammed, each desk occupied and what looked like a team of experts moving up and down between them, exchanging occasional urgent whispers. The main lights were dimmed, intensifying the glow from the desk screens and from the images of space that scrolled ponderously across the command screens overhead. Many of the faces in the glow were very young.

"Trainees' night out," said Owen. "Skipper thinks this'll be good experience for them. And so it will, if it doesn't scare the daylights out of them. Close maneuvering's hell when your position's just a shifting probability."

The control tower was up already, looming over all the toiling masses. Figures were clambering nervously up the flexing metal stairway that spiralled up its flank, with a certain amount of chaffing and heckling from those already up. When I appeared this changed to a good-natured shout, echoed from the Bridge floor. I waved, but didn't linger. I'd seen a tall slender form move to the stairhead, and I was looking forward to a word with Ekkela. He looked as fit and smart as ever, but I was interested to see traces of grey in his hair that hadn't been there before. Was it the job, I wondered, or was Kirsty to blame? I got the usual cool smile, but the handshake was less limp. "Welcome aboard! My tower, that is. Glad you could come!"

"Glad you could find room," I said.

"What, for you? Didn't you hear the shouting? You're a celebrity, man! And we wouldn't dare start this without you!" He added in an undertone, "In case you didn't believe we'd done it!" I laughed, and he ushered me in. Whittaker was already there, and most of the Council; the rest were swaying on the stairs behind me. And so, unavoidably, was someone else.

"Hullo, Mark. How're you keeping?"

"Oh—hi there, Kirsty. Settling down, thanks. Keeping busy."

"So I've seen," she smiled. "Never thought of you as the medman type, really."

"Neither did I. But I quite enjoy it. It'd have amused poor old Ryly, wouldn't it?"

It was stilted, embarrassing conversation. I'd seen her only once, from a distance, in the last year, and I had to fight down the inclination to stare. She'd changed. Her face was less rounded now, and none the worse for that. One or two of her lusher curves had smoothed down a little, but nowhere too much. In fact, she'd gone from just pretty to thoroughly beautiful. And yet it wasn't all improvement: she'd lost something, more than just weight and a little of her bouncy energy. It was something more obvious, but I couldn't pin down what. She leant back against the rail and looked at me. "Maybe you're keeping too busy," she said softly. "You've more than a touch of strain about you. You should look after yourself, Mark. Supposed you cracked up, how'd Maurya manage without you?"

"I'm not going to crack up, Kirsty."

"Be careful, all the same," she said softly. "You're not that easy to manage without."

She left me staring, and drifted off into the gloom. I turned and leant on the springy rail, staring out at the activity below, doing my best not to think certain thoughts. *Not that easy* — and then I heard what was missing in the echo of her words. Her accent! She was speaking pure Standard — or stilted — English now. Her own musical lilt gone so completely that it must have been deliberate. Was that Ekkela's doing? Probably. It would be just like him, bullying everything around to fit his idea of perfection. It was a cheap, unpleasant idea, like rearranging a folksong. It annoyed me so much I hardly noticed the dimness beneath me deepening, the glow of the Bridge lights fading and coalescing into sharper, more brilliant points. I was startled to find myself staring down into a well of stars.

It was a dramatic sight. The simulator graphics had been tinkered with since I'd last seen it, and much improved. The stars stood out fine and sharp, and the sense of depth was far greater. The effect was not so much natural as supernatural, like some medieval cosmology that fixed the stars onto a crystal sphere. With us, perhaps, as titans bestriding the flat planet at its centre. I leant out and looked, but there was no trace of the roots of the tower; we floated like fish in a bowl. Somebody tapped me on the shoulder — Owen. "Up here, boy," he said, very quietly. He pointed, and everybody moved to follow.

Over the rim of the tower rose a minute point of intense red light. It seemed to hang exactly halfway between us and the stars. In front of me I saw Ekkela settle himself into the massive chair behind the command desk "Bridge Coms, can't you get it better than that?"

"I'm doing my best!" snapped a waspish voice. "People expect instant fashing miracles, I don't know . . . It's like Welfare stew out there — ah!" The point held its position, but like a plant seen in time-lapse it swelled and grew, spreading to a thin streak that spread and intensified into a great jagged line, blazing sultry red. As it swelled it seemed to arch over towards us, and for an instant it looked like the talon in my dream. I knew the colour was coincidental, chosen by the simulator for contrast; the real colour of the driveflame would be a glaring stars-and-lightning white, if anything. The body of the craft riding on it was just becoming visible, foreshortened by distance; the simulator showed it in a solider version of the same angry colour. I heard a murmur rise from the little knot of people around me. Ekkela swivelled his chair and beckoned me over.

"You're the one who knows exactly what this beast looks like," he said. "Would you care to make a formal identification?"

It occurred to me that I had never actually laid eyes on the thing, not even on film. All I'd seen before was the same kind of computer diagram I was seeing now. All the same, I knew.

"That's it," I said. There was a general sigh of relief from the dimness around, in which Ekkela joined.

"I'm glad you can be sure. There may be other races around here able to build probes—or missiles. I'd hate to set back someone's research program."

"Or get caught in an interstellar crossfire," I said.

"I don't know," murmured Ekkela. "I'd be less worried about the probe if that kind of thing were going on. It would be hard to pin on Earth, more easily written off as a stray . . ."

I stared at him in disgust. "You just don't give up, do you?"

He shrugged. "What worries you? We're here, aren't we? And there's your probe. What do you want me to do about it?"

"How about a missile?" suggested Whittaker cheerfully, padding up behind us. "Or maybe a nice warm beam?"

Ekkela smiled and shook his head. "We're in an Infall field, remember? Nothing would get out, except maybe as heat dispersed randomly along our path. And if we drop the fields we've only the velocity we started with—effectively, we'd just be sitting there."

"With that thing accelerating away from us at a high percentage of c," I added. "Several hundred millions kiloms an hour. Out of range before we could aim a beam, and no normal missile could catch it."

"Admirably put, Mark." Ekkela's grin glinted up at me. "So I'll ask you again—just what do you want me to do with it?"

"All right," I said patiently, "I'll play your little game. Overhaul it and drop something in front—a few tons of debris should deflect it, at least. Or a couple of warheads—"

He shook his head again, grinning hugely. "No, sorry. At that speed the debris wouldn't count for much against it. It's come a lightyear since it was launched. Do your sums on the mass increase already! The warheads might be better, but it's got a guidance system, remember? It could easily navigate around something that small, and we haven't many to spare. You'll need something more certain."

"Overhaul it, turn in front and let it run into the field?"

"Close," he laughed, "but no cigar!" I'd never heard that bit of drug-culture slang. Either Ekkela had hidden depths, or it was an old expression. He hauled himself up in his chair, and looked around at his audience. "You see," he said, with great gusto, "whatever Mark's been busy telling you, my staff and I haven't been entirely idle. We've considered all the options you've heard, and rejected them. It's a very pleasant idea, letting it smash itself up on our fields, but there are problems. First, the small exterior area of the fields would make it a very delicate maneuver; the impact of any large mass over a small area of field creates imbalances. Not dangerous, really—that would take ten times the mass—but a strain on the generating systems I'd rather avoid." He grinned. "But there's another alternative. You're speeding along in a groundcar, Mark, with your arm out of the window. It catches on something solid. What happens?"

"Torn out by the roots."

"Yes, I thought you might like the analogy. Well, that's what we'll do. Run the fields along as near parallel to the thing as we can manage. In relation to normal space the field surface isn't moving at all, remember, just fading away behind us and appearing ahead as we move within it. So—" He broke off, peered at a couple of read-outs and tapped a control key. "Owen, Sussmeyer, to your places, please. And anyone else who isn't already. Take us in when you're ready, Owen, and give me an MMD soonest. Sussmeyer, hook up to Bridge Power and Bridge Field Controls, please!" Those were the responsible divisions below. I saw Owen hunched jacketless over the main screen of the first pilot's desk, his bared arms thrust elbow-deep into slots on either side of it. I realized he must be steering by direct neural link, probably by induction from implants in his ulnas, and metacarpals, giving him very fine control but requiring fiendish concentration. Ekkela nodded to him and turned back to us. "So, as I was saying, all we need to do then is extend the field a little, just enough to snag onto part of that thing. The stress on the field will be similar to an outright collision, but for a much shorter time. The merest twitch should set up enough stress in the missile to shatter it, without exceeding our tolerances. Does that meet with your approval, Mark? It's almost rash enough for one of your ideas!"

"Almost," I grinned. "Sidelong maneuvers are more your speciality—"

"Drop it, the pair of you!" ordered Kirsty from behind us.

"Hear, hear!" grunted Owen. "I'm trying to think over here! Both on the same bloody side, aren't you?"

I looked down at Ekkela. "The kids have a point."

He nodded. "Quite bright for their ages, really. Distinctly promising. And there was something I was forgetting. Bridge Coms?"

"What's it now?" said the waspish voice.

"Show us the field margin on the simulator, please."

"Was wondering when you'd ask. Here goes."

The image of the probe hung below us now, a little to the right of the tower-top; it seemed very little larger than when I'd first seen it. Between it and the tower a wavering line the colour of the full moon appeared, its ends narrowing and fading to apparent infinity. It ran parallel to the probe; I was just beginning to wonder about the distance when an illuminated scale sprang up in the simulator, like a glowing bridge linking the two craft. We were only two and a half kiloms from the probe, and closing fast. The appearance of the scale could have destroyed the simulator's illusion, but didn't. It looked like some extension of the field, a tentacle pulling its prey in towards that pale line, whose wavering was almost hypnotically regular, so that your breathing kept trying to keep pace with it. The whole thing was a heightened reality; no matter that what it represented was cut off from us by a gulf of chaotic spacetime. The real battleground was here.

"Minimum Marginal Distance, Captain!" barked Owen. So that was what MDD meant. "Holding at five hundred metres!"

"Thank you, Owen. All right to keep her there for a while?"

"Fine, fine! If my arms start smoking I'll give you a shout. . . ."

Low chuckles spread across the tower, but Ekkela's clear voice cut through the background noise. "B-Field, begin final survey. Sussmeyer, monitor them, but be ready to relieve Owen if he needs it."

"Monitoring," came a curt voice from the other side of the tower. Sussmeyer was his usual dour self despite all the excitement, or more likely because of it. "B-Field, report when ready."

Silence fell on the tower as we waited. Kirsty, leaning on the command desk, began drumming her fingers until stopped by a sizzling glare from Owen; it wouldn't do for *him* to start. "Come on, B-Field!" snapped Sussmeyer. "You've run all your checks, I've monitored them. What's keeping you?"

"Sorry, Suss," said a puzzled Australian voice. "All checks clear, ready to go as far as we're concerned. But we've spotted something funny. You'd better have a look." I moved over to Sussmeyer's desk to see, but he was already transferring the details to someone else's screen.

"B-Coms, what d'you make of that?"

"What's it look like to you?" answered the snappy voice. "It's a maser beam, of course, tailing the probe. Point of origin, Solar System, probably Earth."

Ekkela blinked. "Well, I'm—can it affect the attack sequence? Is it any kind of threat to us?"

"Down There can't be tracking with it, if that's what you mean, Captain. It hasn't half the power it'd need at this range: it's even on the weak side for communications. Not that it's carrying anything right now."

"Then we can worry about it later," said Ekkela firmly. "Right now we're in a hurry. B-Field, go when ready."

"Proceeding, Captain."

I half expected the line to waver and break, or spout branches like lightning, or rise up like a cresting wave. None of that happened. One side of it squashed outwards like smudged chalk, thinning and fading from the centre as it went. Ghostly whiteness flooded slowly along the distance scale, an amoeba reaching hungrily out to pluck at the darting thing in its path.

And then the sky erupted, as if oil had been poured over the crystal. A great wave of rainbow iridescence swept up from behind, with darkness at the heart of it and leaving pure blackness in its wake.

"Coms!" roared Ekkela. "What's *that*?"

"Not a fault! It's *there*—"

"B-Field! We've aborted attack sequence—our instruments have gone nuts—"

"Hold on, B-Field!" instructed Ekkela, as calmly as if all this was a drill. "Keep on doing your sums, be ready to restart when I give the word. All stations, attend. What are we seeing? Any ideas?"

The intruder was settling into shape now, or perhaps it was

turning and showing us a different angle. Now it was a black teardrop, irridescent at the rim, apparently hanging a little above and beyond the probe. Its sharp end pointed in the same direction as the probe's drive flame, but narrowed down to an almost invisibly thin filament stretching off into the distance; I could almost make out another, from the blunt end. It looked like an absurd caricature of a snake swallowing prey, like—I leant over Ekkela's shoulder. "I've seen iridescence like that before. So have you, I expect. When you bring an airspacer in through the fields—"

Ekkela snapped his fingers. "Between shieldfield and Infall, right! B-Field, B-Coms, is the simulator trying to show us another Infall field?"

"We're just checking that out, Captain," said B-Field distractedly. "On the results so far, I'd say yes. But—"

"What?"

"Well, look! The size of it—" The voice tailed off. I didn't blame it. The simulator blurred ideas of size a little. But if that thing dwarfed the probe to that extent . . . Almost everyone stared, open-mouthed.

Almost everyone. "Wake up, all stations!' barked Ekkela. "So it's big! How big? And what else can you give me on it?" The details came tumbling in, but they boiled down to very little. Huge as the mass in the other field must be, it couldn't be more than half our size. The iridescence was caused by peculiar irregularities in the surface of the other field, which were still being checked out.

"Mark!" Whittaker tapped me on the shoulder, whispering so as not to disturb Ekkela. "I thought Earth had no other Infall ships—"

"Only the old experimental rigs, that I ever knew of. And they're not nearly that size, and they haven't the range to get out here—"

"Nor the power to overtake us," another Council member, an electronics engineer from Poland, pointed out. "Smaller masses travel faster in an Infall field, but even so—it would need considerable extra power . . ."

"Well, we'll soon find out," announced Ekkela, swivelling round to face us. "My turn to make a lucky guess now, Mark. Coms have just confirmed it—there's nothing irregular about the way that field's pulsating. It's being modulated! And it looks like binary—"

"A signal!" exclaimed Kirsty.

"Of course!" hissed Whittaker. "How else could two Infall craft communicate? Can we reply?"

"Well, we've got the software to do the same thing, if B-Field and B-Coms can implement it—ah!" He swung back to his desk, peering at a screen. "Voice link ready? Very well. This is Captain Ekkela of the Second Colonial Expeditionary Ship speaking. Do you understand me?"

Nobody expected an instant reply. Even Ekkela jumped. "Hi, Ekkela. Will you please stand off from that spacecraft?"

Ekkela took a deep breath. "Identify yourself!" he said coolly.

"Don't suppose my name'd mean much to you," drawled the voice, in perfect English with a faint nasal twang. "Stand off and we'll talk."

"No I will not!" shouted Ekkela. "Who are you? Earth didn't have any ships the size of yours—"

"Will you stop shouting? Nearly blew my eardrums out! This tub just looked like another orbital bucketshop while they were putting the bits together. Horrible sloppy job they made of it, too. Just stripped the drives out of the little old ships and stuck 'em in here. All of them. That makes it a little crowded, what with the power plants and all. There's only fifty of us in here, stuck in a rotten little lifesystem. Rest of our hull's full of Infall gear. And that's why we think you should stand off like we want you to. We're a warship, you see."

"A *what?*" laughed Ekkela. "My dear fellows, what are you going to do? Fire a broadside? Board us, perhaps? With grappling irons?"

"Something like that," answered the voice, just a trifle nettled. "You'd better take us seriously. We're not just something stuck together to go after you. They've been planning this tub for a long while now. Your Mister Bellamy there, by the way?"

"Nobody of that name on board," said Ekkela casually. "What if there was?"

"Oh, couple of things," said the voice laconically. "Thought he might show a bit more sense. Given what he dug up, he should've expected us."

I leant over Ekkela's chair. "Why's that?"

"Oh, hi, Bellamy, thanks for the voiceprint. Got a friend of yours here, our pilot. Says he met you a couple of years ago in Scotland, at some farmhouse or other. Wishes he'd known you'd be such a celebrity. See, Bellamy, you must've realized that little feller out there's a pure one-off surprise weapon, no second chances. So what happens if it misses? Ten to one your target'll try an' return the favour. How d'you stop his little probe? With an Infall warship, of course. The probe was the sword. We're the shield, the backup, the second installment, us and a few more they're building. It's all one project, with a sky-high budget. But you fellers gave us a surprise, you see? Only one hull finished, and none of the drives ready, so we had to turn cannibal. But don't make any mistake; it's crude, but it works. We can do just what we were built to."

"I believe you," said Ekkela. "Bluff."

"Now how do you work that one out?" inquired the voice genially.

"Well, what can you do to us? We've had enough trouble working out a way to get at the probe. And you can't use that against us, because we're under field too."

"Uhuh. Not as powerful as ours, though."

"So? And you can't chase us, because with only a life-system you haven't a quarter of our range. Less, if you ever expect to get home."

"True. We're very near our limit already—I tell you that free, gratis and for nothing. It's getting very very stinky in here, huh, boys?" There was just a tinge of hysteria in the laugh. I began to remember the material I'd read on the psychology of close conditions. These must be unquestioningly loyal men, MMs probably, and yet their overlords had chosen to inflict that on them rather than trust them with a shred of interplanetary capability. "Which brings us to what we want you to do."

"I know, stand off from—"

"That, Ekkela, and more. About turn, feller, and go home where you belong."

"What?"

"Back to Earth, like I said. Oh, personally I think it's better off without crap like you, but I've got my orders. Why else d'you think I'd spend so much time bullshitting? And my main job's to protect the probe; I can't let you go and come back again outside my range, can I? So I take you back, or—"

"Well?"

"Squash you here. Which I can do. Field on field, inter-ference effects—your power boys ever heard of those? In a vessel that gets its pseudogravity from rotation? Ask your Power boys, I'll gladly wait. But not too long, Hamfisted Heinz here's getting just a little tired. And I know he's worthless, but your boy can't be doing much better..."

Owen muttered something, probably a Welsh oath. "Take all the bloody time you want, Skipper!"

"You hear?" said Ekkela complacently, and cut off the voice link. "All stations, on your toes! B-Power and B-Field in particular. What can he really do to us?" He listened to the discussion for a moment, then turned and opened another sound channel, one he had never used since the day we sailed. "This is the Captain!" The cloudfield rolled his voice thunderously around the hull. "I am sounding an alert, although there is no immediate danger; this is simply a precaution. When the alarm sounds, go at once to your nearest shelter if you are not on any listed duty. Please be inside within ten minutes, following all emergency procedures. Emergency marshals and village watches will advise you if necessary. I repeat, this is purely a precaution—so far. So—*move your asses!*"

Whittaker's laughter almost drowned the alarm drumbeat. "Wouldn't something on the lines of *Damn the torpedoes!* have been more fitting?"

"Ach, they probably dreamed that one up afterwards," said Kirsty, with just a trace of her old astringent voice. "Like all those speeches the Roman emperors were supposed to make before battles—" And she and Whittaker were instantly deep in an argument about famous sayings I'd never heard of. *Intellectuals!* I thought, and left them to it. Around me Sussmeyer and other reserve personnel were scrambling into pressure suits; someone was scuttling around with airmasks, so I helped myself to one. With its little rebreather I'd be all right in anything but hard vacuum, and for a little while even in that. I wanted desperately to call the village shelter to check that Maurya and the kids were all right, but knew I shouldn't be tieing up coms at a time like this. The village watch would look after them. Kirsty hooked a mask around Owen's neck, and I saw beads of moisture gather at its edge and run down. Ekkela would have to make his move soon.

"Captain, they're calling again. Getting pretty restive..."

"Stall, stall, stall," muttered Ekkela, opening the link again. "Listen," he pleaded, "You've got to give us more time. This isn't an easy decision—"

"Yeah, well, it's not so easy where we are either. And sharing a lifesystem with these unwashed goons does nothing for my patience, I can tell you—"

Ekkela left the link open, but turned off his microphone. "B-Field, are you ready?"

"Still recomputing, Captain—a minute or two—"

"Don't wait to be told, then. Go when ready."

"You're sure they're bluffing, then?" asked Whittaker anxiously.

"Nobody's sure," said Ekkela. "Infall research has been languishing in recent years—published research, anyway. It seems it's theoretically possible to induce some sort of effect, like a mild gravitational stress, but only with really vast amounts of power. Doesn't sound very effective to me, but a few strained hull seams might be awkward. Hence the alert. But anyway, what choice have we got? I don't suppose anyone's exactly anxious to go trotting off back home—"

"Home!" hissed somebody. "D'you call *that* home?" There was an angry rumble of agreement. In the background the voice droned on, something about hating to mess up our pretty little ecosystem, so why make it hard? Ekkela grinned, as if he was enjoying himself.

"Well, then!" he said. "Since we can't outrun him, and he's not the patient type, as well be hung for a sheep and have a stab at that probe!"

Again the line smudged outwards, spreading.

"I warned you guys," said the voice.

And suddenly my own weight pressed smoothly down on my shoulders.

My arms fell to my sides, and I could feel the blood pool in my fingertips. The air around me seemed to thicken, so my lungs laboured to expand against the pressure. My eyes felt swollen, my feet pressed flat in my shoes. Kirsty swayed, grabbed for a desk to support herself and fell with a solid crash that sent the air whistling out of her. I stooped to help her, and almost fell myself.

"They're speeding up our rotation," said Sussmeyer, as if he didn't believe himself. He tried to stand, overbalanced, and slapped painfully back in his chair. Something more than weight made it hard to stand, and blood swirling around in head and eyes blurred my vision further. I had to leave Kirsty where she was and grab onto the back of a desk for support.

Owen cried out suddenly. Then weight seemed to fall off for a second.

"I had to pull back!" he shouted. "The weight—distorting my arms—affecting the controls—"

"All right, Owen!" hissed Ekkela, eyes suddenly and alarmingly bloodshot. "Take us out of—"

The weight returned in full and frightful measure. Terrified of falling but unable to stand, I found myself sliding down the side of the desk, scraping my knees against its side, clinging to the rim as if it was a handhold on a rockface. Everyone else on the tower was sitting or lying by now, except Whittaker; the old man's shoulders were hunched with effort, but he still stood upright, glaring at the simulated stars, the angry red scar across them and the pool of oily darkness beyond. Then I saw what he did. The sphere image was beginning to flatten out, distort, as if it too was succumbing to the pressure.

"Can we stand this?" Whittaker muttered.

"Not if it gets worse," gasped Sussmeyer, chewing the words out as if they were tough. "The hull will hold, but we will not. And there is delicate equipment that may be damaged—"

It was as if the Colony's giant waterfalls were beating down on my back. I shook my head to clear it, but that was stupid; my semi-circular canals were as bad as the rest of me, my balance was gone and I crashed sideways onto the floor. Because it was soft I was only slightly stunned. I saw the simulator sphere distort grotesquely, and thought the blow had affected my sight. But then the image, stars, probe, warship and all, vanished like a pricked balloon, and the Bridge burst in around us.

There was a sudden sharp report, like a distant concussion grenade, and cries of alarm from below. I hoisted myself painfully up on one elbow, and saw a crack flicker like lightning across the great window.

"Battle plastic!" I heard Ekkela snarl. "If that's going—"

It was. There was another loud crack, the fragmenting line spread and branched, then there came a crisp smashing sound and the window became a crazed network of fine lines, white and opaque, and exploded inwards with an awesome crash.

"Réné!" Whittaker was gasping for breath,, like the rest of us. "Call them—say we'll go back—"

"What good'll that do?" snarled Ekkela.

"Stall them, you idiot!" bellowed the priest. "Tell them

anything—to give us a minute—so we can at least try to get clear—"

Ekkela tried to nod, slapping at the microphone contact. "Warship! Warship, d'you read me?"

"Oh my god," breathed Kirsty, "What'll it be like in the shelters?"

I was doing my best not to imagine that. What use could I be? How could I help? I had to do *something* . . .

"Warship, come in, damn you! You've got to stop this! We'll do what you want, we'll go back—anything, but stop this! Come in, you fashing crew of fascists—"

"You had your chance," said the voice unexpectedly. The weight on us never slackened. "Now you might try and make a break, mightn't you? Offer withdrawn. But I'm not unreasonable. Drop your fields and I'll make it quick. Clean. Never feel a thing."

"Bastards!" whispered Owen. "Why make it easy for them? For all we know they're about to overload their drives—"

"—or their power plants!" I added. "We might at least make some company in hell!"

The warship commander may have heard that. He didn't sound amused.

"Well, have it your own way. No second chances! We'll rip your fucking guts out—"

Weight eased so suddenly I almost fell over again, and wheezed the air out of my lungs unnecessarily hard. In the same instant came a lurch that dislodged some people from their handholds, and brought me tumbling to my knees by the stair platform.

Then I began to feel I was going insane.

My uneasy balance told me that something was changing, as if the ground—the tower—was sliding out from underneath me. Perhaps in the most savage earthquakes—but they would have noise and fire and violence. This had the smooth inexorable silence of tectonic shift, but over seconds, not millennia. The seabed became a cliff, the mountainside a plain, the direction of fall surged gently around through ninety degrees until it lay along the axis of the Ship.

I thought something had finally given in body or mind, until, clutching at the rail, I looked over the tower edge and saw, on the Bridge floor, crew clinging to and hanging from their desks, small objects slipping loose and tumbling past them. Behind me Whittaker slid down against the rail with a bang, then swung himself effortlessly back up against Sussmeyer's desk; he reached out and grabbed Kirsty as she slid past. It was as well he did; I saw one woman on the Bridge floor lose her grip and slide screaming along the increasingly precipitous surface, gathering speed until she smacked into the side of a column of screens and lay draped across it, twitching. There was a growing sound in the air, a low, almost subliminal bass note, like a titan groaning.

"Hull stresses—" began Ekkela, but was cut off by a tearing shriek. A man in crew uniform slid among jagged fragments of window, slithering inexorably towards the space where it had been. Hands clawed out at him, but he was torn from them by—*not* by gravity. By an interference effect that sent him howling on until he slammed first into the light safety railing and then the saw-toothed standing fragments beyond, snapping off their tips in his path out into the churning air. The cloud field was bunching up its contents into weird grey-green sculptures shot blue with angry lightning; a flash silhouetted the falling figure for an instant, then it was gone.

Reflexive horror clamped my fingers hard onto the railing, and that alone saved me. I was flung in the air as if by a giant, and then smashed down hard on the stairhead platform, so hard I felt the metal dish under me. Mercifully nothing broke, but I lay there bruised and fighting for breath, watching chaos trample across the Ship outside. A rain of procoms, note-recorders, drink-beakers, and anything else imaginable, plus the lighter fragments of window, came spraying back down around the Bridge, bouncing and scattering. I saw what looked like another such shower beyond the window opening, and then as it suddenly changed direction and flung itself towards us in a low spraying arc I realized the size of the debris. Only one bit of it reached the Bridge, a massive tree that whistled over our heads and smashed at the angle of the ceiling, missing the command screens by millims.

Nothing they showed us had changed; probe, field and stars were just as the simulator had last showed them. But they couldn't show us the vast tendrils of energy that were twisting and warping the very space around us, so that up and down lost all meaning in a frantic dance. One instant you hung by your hands as a vast ponderous invisibility plucked at you and your heart battled with the sheer weight of your blood, then you weighed so little that the howling tornado beyond the window threatened to dislodge you like a withered leaf. And all you could do was hang on, when the world outside you was in such a state of flux that every other action, reasoned or reflexive, betrayed you. Was I really seeing a high hill half the length of the Ship away bulging up suddenly as if some great blind thing burrowed and wriggled beneath? Was I seeing the stretch of green field beyond rippling and blurring like heat-soaked air? Far away I saw a whole lake empty from its bed in a split second, rising in one smooth-silver thread to dash itself at the flickering sun-tube and exploding before it reached it in a starburst of superheated steam, slicing and scattering the cloud-castles around. Sheet lightning blasted right across the Ship, and whirlwinds wavered in and out of existence, adding to the rising moan of the tortured hull. In horror I watched a whole detached circle of earth rise slowly and evenly as a dream, floating only metres from the Bridge window-space before sinking equally gently from sight. The tormented hull moaned agony that blotted out all other sound except the shrieks of the winds; the voices of men were drowned.

Another wave of sudden weight and lightness passed like a whipcrack down the Bridge, with a great boulder on its crest that smashed into the tower itself a metre below me, crushing half the stair. One hand tore loose, spinning me round to face death. Across the tower I saw Ekkela whipped up out of his seat, and Owen, reaching up to catch him, flung awkwardly aside in an absurd cartwheel of limbs. Ekkela fell lightly and slowly for an instant, then as weight returned he slammed down back first across the railing. The impact almost jarred my other hand loose. He lay sacklike across the rail as I began to struggle my way round it to pull him in. But before I was halfway there Whittaker, who had been anchoring Kirsty and one of the Bridge crew with his massive arms, shouted to me to grab them, shook himself loose and made a fast lunge at the unmoving body. He slid Ekkela back into the tower as gently as he could, then almost toppled over the rim himself as the floor lurched beneath us. The crewman wrapped himself in a foetal crouch around the base of Sussmeyer's chair. Two Council members were trying to hold onto Owen, sprawled limply out with a great streak of blood across his face. The moan rose to a howl, and with the onrush of the wind and Kirsty in my arms I was suddenly back in the field where an aeon past my madness had begun.

I brought us all to this. . . .

From Kirsty, from my handholds, a convulsion shook me loose, and the death I ached for flung me right up and out into the face of the great screen, whirling down in hatred on the red-taloned night.

It erupted in white fire to meet me.

And the blaze passed, and the dark closed around me, and I was still falling, a silent plummet into infinity. There was no sound at all, and then there was the soft sea rushing that had filled half my life. Sea rocked me, waves washed around me and through me as I lay there unresisting, content to drown and dissolve the calm.

Then, as I turned, the unreal stars lit up and wheeled majestically about me, as if I were the centre of a construct sky. The searush was my breathing, and I turned in air, feeling it play across my face. A feather's touch on my hand startled me so much I pulled away, then just as automatically snatched at it. Jagged metal sliced into my palm, and I almost let go.

But then, with a single mighty flicker, the sun blazed out.

I was hanging, or rather floating, in midair over the devastated floor of the Bridge, clutching at the edge of a ruined stair, around which drifted tiny red globules, my blood. In that moment I sensed a ghostly movement downwards, growing gradually stronger. I pulled myself in hastily, sprawling on the few remaining stairs. They creaked under me as weight returned, and I clambered painfully upwards, unable to control my slashed right hand. At the top I knelt, only half aware of the warm spurts of blood between my fingers, staring stupidly up at the screens, at the stars. Nothing obscured them, no iridescent night appeared as they scrolled slowly by. Nothing— until, as I struggled desperately to focus, a thin red streak swam into view, dwindling and fleeing down a dark tunnel into endless depths. I cried out and sprang up to claw after it, but that brought agony and a different kind of darkness roaring up to meet me.

Bright light was sleeting down on my closed eyelids, and all I could do was groan and turn my head aside. But someone was holding it, and bent over to shade my face. I mumbled something grateful, and tried to shift a little. There seemed to be a massive pressure on one side of my chest, and my right forearm was so much dead weight. Startled, I opened my eyes, and looked into another pair, large and dark and anxious like a seal's.

"Does it hurt?" asked Kirsty quickly. "The doc said it shouldn't—"

"No," I croaked. That explained the pressure; it was a common enough symptom of severe pain damped by drugs. The light still bothered my eyes, so I lifted an arm to shadow them. From forearm to palm it was encased in stiffening splint-film, reeking of acetone still. I stared stupidly at it.

"Ye ripped two arteries," said Kirsty softly. "Leakin' like a sieve. The doc topped ye up wi' cultured stuff an' left me tae glue the bits back. It was easy wi' the machine."

"You?"

"Yes. I've been studyin' paramed last year, didn't ye know? I couldn't just do nothin'. And it's a fine old Scottish tradition. I did your side as well—bad internal bruisin', two big muscle tears under your arm, and three cracked ribs. Ye should be able to move a bit now, though; doc told me tae keep ye out for a few hours till the glue set—"

"Hours?" Suddenly I was thinking a hundred things at once. "Kirsty—got to call—the probe—the shelters—"

Kirsty held me down with no trouble. "Will you lie quiet a minute? I called your place half an hour back. They're fine, Maurya and the kids. Just a bit shaken, mostly worried about you. I told them ye'd be all right an' home soon."

"Kirsty," I sighed. "Thanks a million. I—" A sudden inrush of memory stopped me short. "And you—the skipper—how is—" I followed Kirsty's gaze, gone suddenly bleak. I found I could lift myself on my right elbow if I was careful, and found that I was still on the tower-top, laid out on the floor between the control desks. Beside me was a small knot of people, bustling round something. To one side was a discarded uniform top, and as somebody moved I saw an outflung dark-skinned arm.

"They say he'll get better," said Kirsty quietly. "Nothing that can't be regenerated in a year or so . . ." The crush parted a little, and I made out the prone form in the life-support stretcher, a mess of cables and tubing taped down onto his back. The little Jivaro doctor was crouched over him, seemingly adding more. Beyond him Owen stood, or rather leaned, against a desk. Dressings and soft film covered his forehead and left cheek, and what showed of his face was ashen. But he managed a lop-sided smile when he saw me, and came hobbling around at once.

"Glad to see you back, boy! Feeling all fit, are you? Nothing but a little brain damage, eh, and who'll ever notice that?"

"Nobody, with you around. Owen, what happened? Why are we still here?"

He looked at me. "Bloody great chunk of rock smashed into the tower, smashed the stair and jammed it so we couldn't lower it. They got ladders up, though, and they're working on it with cutters—"

"No," I said patiently. "You know perfectly well what I mean. Why did the attack stop? What happened to the warship? And the probe?"

"It got away," said Kirsty bitterly. "And good riddance, after a'the misery it's made . . ."

Owen avoided my eyes. "There's no going after it now. We'll be lucky enough to get where we're going, after all this . . ." He helped me up, and I managed to stand, despite Kirsty's protests and the pain stabbing past the analgesics. I saw what he meant. The Bridge below, and the Ship beyond it, were a mess. And yet, appalling as the damage was, it was relatively superficial in terms of the ship. It was concentrated in a central band, as if a pair of giant hands had closed around the hull and twisted. The internal disturbances were side-effects, of the kind we had used to wreck Earth's weather patterns, but far stronger. A great strip right round the inside hull was ploughed up; all the debris had come from there, and most of the other damage had been done when it fell. Some wide burnt scars puzzled me, until I remembered the lightning. All in all, we had got off very lightly, according to Owen and Sussmeyer, presently in command. The toruses, source of our food supplies, had hardly been affected, since they rotated independently, and we could rebuild the ecology from them— just.

But it had been close, so very close. The suntube, running the length of the Ship's axis, had been twisted by stresses its fail-safes were never designed to cope with, especially when the Ship had been spun laterally. Its shielding, much lighter

than a normal fusion system's, had been within an ace of going—
would have, if it had been on full sunpower, rather than moonlight. When the stresses were relieved, in the moment of my
fall, the fail-safes had been able to shut it down; hence the
sudden darkness. Then, as rotation began again, they'd started
it up to emergency daylight power, which they wouldn't have
if it had been seriously damaged. A tech team were working
on it now.

The people of the Ship had come well enough out of the
trouble, too. The shelters were well-designed and tough, and
only one, in the gripped area, had actually been damaged; there
were plenty of long-term casualties, but no deaths. The crew
on duty, and other staff outside shelters, had been less lucky;
casualties at North End totalled ninety-two serious injuries and
ten deaths, plus two who might yet be brought back. It was a
terrible blow after our raid losses. Three hundred was considered a bare skeleton crew for the Ship, and for the next year
we would be lucky to have that.

"And Ekkela will be out of it." No matter what I felt about
him, I knew we'd have our work cut out to find someone as
capable.

"*Quand on n'a que f'acassé un peu f'dos?*" It was a weak
and weary sound, but it was Ekkela's voice.

"Messed up your back a leetle?" snorted the doctor. "You
have crack-ed seex vertebrae and rupture-ed the spinal cord.
A year or more to grow eet back, and more before you are
ab-el to work."

"Well, I'll still be able to lie around handing out useful
advice," grinned Ekkela. "Power without responsibility—marvellous! Just the kind of holiday I need—*aie!*"

"You feel that? Good, lumbar breedge is operating. Soon
you feel worse . . ."

Owen and I moved tactfully aside. "That's one mercy, anyway," I said. "But you still haven't told me what happened to
that goddam warship!" He looked at me for an instant, then
turned to the desk beside him, ignoring a smear of blood across
one side of it, and punched a few numbers. The screech of a
power saw joined the buzzing cutter beams below. The largest
desk screen lit up with an image of space, evidently from the
simulator's memory. There in the middle of it hung the blackness that was all we had ever seen of our enemy, and for a
minute I thought there was nothing else. Then I realized that

the stars in a small area were oddly bunched and distorted, as if a whirlpool was forming.

"The light's being distorted," Owen told me. "Look at the next frame." For a minute I thought the attack had damaged our detectors. It seemed to be just an insane jumble with no relation to the last image—a few thin streaks of light twisting in towards an indistinct smoky shape, impossibly bloated and foreshortened, that loomed like a malevolent genie over the warship. "Not very informative, that," sighed Owen. "No time to scan it properly before it hit . . ."

"Hit?"

"Yes, boy, hit. Ran smack into their fields, it did. And hardly noticed, I daresay. It's not that big, but the speed it was coming in at it must've massed like a small planet."

The impact of any large mass over a small area of field . . .
"It blew their generators?"

Owen nodded, sombrely. "And their power plants, probably. Field hysteresis contained the bang just long enough so the thing didn't get caught in it. It just went on its way, a blur in the next frame and then out of our detector range, like that!" He snapped his fingers. "The speed, boy, think of it . . ."

I was doing just that. Fast, massive, following a course with mindless determination—the thing sounded all too familiar. "Owen—where did it come from? And where was it headed?"

"We don't know, yet. Not with half the Bridge out of action or up to their ears in damage control. We'll find out soon enough." There was no disguising the uneasiness in his voice, and it found an echo in me. Ransom, especially at the eleventh hour, may command a terrible price.

It was only a minute or two later that the strange hush settled over the tower-top. It was so noticeable, even against the screeches of tormented metal from below, that my skin prickled. I looked up from the corner where I'd slumped, brooding, over to the command desk where Sussmeyer now sat. I sprang up, horrified. There were tears trickling down his harsh features, though they were as impassive as ever; it was like seeing a statue cry, or a river in the Negev rock, Whittaker, beside him, I could hardly recognise; he looked his age and more, shoulders sagging and back caved in, face taut with grief and anger. The knot of people round them were equally upset, in floods of tears, or just staring, horrified, at something on the desk screen. From the Bridge floor came a sudden hysterical wail of anguish;

I saw someone run madly towards a door, be stopped and gently led away. I heaved myself up and stumbled over to the desk. One or two faces turned my way, and then hastily away again; I didn't like what I'd seen in them. They parted to let me through, and behind me they began to murmur.

When I reached the desk I didn't look at the screen, but turned to Sussmeyer. "It's another missile, isn't it?"

If he was surprised there was nothing in the dead eyes to show it. "It is. Of around three times the general size of the one disguised as a probe, but otherwise remarkably similar. Do you also know where it has come from?"

"I can guess. Somewhere round 40 Eridani."

"Yes. And by now it has accelerated to a tremendous speed and a proportionately enormous mass. Unlike the probe, this one is relatively near its journey's end. That is how it came to destroy the warship."

"The maser—"

"The tracking maser, as you say. The probe was a little off-centre, as you would expect at such a distance. But the warship, guided by the beam, was naturally sitting at its exact centre. And the other missile was at that point in its course where it was casting around for signals to home in on."

"Just now?" I breathed. "Now, of all times?"

He shrugged wearily. "No coincidence. It has probably been lurking out there for some time. It could fly, say, in a flattened spiral to delay its arrival—give it time to search. So when the maser came on—"

"It picked up the beam," muttered Owen, from the other side of the desk. "And came thundering right down the centre of it—"

Sussmeyer nodded. "With the results we saw. And there it still continues, no doubt, unless it has found a stronger signal leading earthwards. Because Earth is unquestionably its target."

I closed my eyes, but found the stars rising behind them, a negative afterimage of the command screens. I did my best to feel shocked or even surprised, but I couldn't; I only felt burnt out and empty, a furnace extinguished. Everything I'd done, everything I'd tried to save and to destroy—it was all irrelevant now. The lives I'd ended, one way or another—I'd robbed them of a few months, no more. And the vengeance I'd longed for would soon be the most meaningless thing of all.

I couldn't join in the hysterical little arguments that flared up and fizzled out around me. It was all too obvious that there was nothing we could do. Any message we sent would arrive at most a few seconds before the missile. So would we, if we went after it under Infall.

"But couldn't we destroy it?" begged Kirsty, eyes huge and distraught. "The way ye were goin' tae stop the probe—"

Owen looked at her bleakly. "Saw what happened to the warship, didn't you? This thing's far more massive than the probe, and we've not got a half of the warship's power. Even a flick from it would send us up in a puff of gas. The most we could do is ram it, but I don't think we'd even deflect it—not that we'd live to find out, of course—" He wound his fingers together till the blood drained out of them. "It's so bloody maddening! Those things shouldn't be hard to stop!"

I rubbed my forehead wearily. "The warship could have done it, if it hadn't been so preoccupied with us. Tried our trick with more power, perhaps, or just dumped a good-sized planetoid in its path; all sorts of things they could have done. It was what the warship was designed for, the man said. And built with the probe's huge budget, no doubt. But the BCs wasted it safeguarding their own murky little murder weapon. Ironic, isn't it?"

Whittaker clutched at his hair in agony. "But *why?* I don't understand it, I can't accept it—why should those aliens launch that missile?"

I shrugged. "Why did we?"

"No," said Ekkela weakly. The stretcher encased him now from the neck down, but with head and shoulders supported so he could see and swallow more easily. "It's different, the Rev's right. They opened communications, not us. Our people, our rulers, panicked when they were contacted. But the aliens could've laid low and never contacted a soul. *Enfer*, Mark—you should see that! That's why you assumed—very reasonably—that they were friendly! They'd nothing to gain otherwise! You're not trying to tell me they'd just send out those messages to flush out potential targets, are you? It's inconsistent—"

Whittaker shook his head despairingly. "Maybe they're just too unlike us, too alien—"

That did it. Laughter bubbled up inside me, welling over in tears and bringing new pains to sides that didn't need them.

I was practically doubled up, face streaming, unable to get breath to speak.

Then I was straightened up sharply, and kept on going till my feet dangled off the ground. There was a deathgrip on my less injured arm, and another bunching up the front of my jacket, forcing my head back so a pair of freezing eyes glared into mine. The fingers ground in like glaciers, but for all the pain I couldn't stop laughing.

"I don't suppose you'd mind sharing the joke?" grated Whittaker. His fist tightened chokingly in my jacket.

"You're the joke!" I spat at him, still wheezing. "Too inconsistent! Too alien!" He released my arm and slapped me across the face, not especially hard, and stood me on my feet again. I met the contemptuous stare. "I'm not hysterical! At least not the way you think. Too alien? Hellfire, Whittaker, if only they were! You know what I'm wondering? If out there there isn't some poor stupid bastard just like me, who went ploughing through everybody and everything, trying his best to stop that missile—and failing miserably, of course! *That's* how like us they are! Inconsistent? Well, wouldn't you say," I went on, more calmly, choosing my words carefully, "that going to the enormous expense of setting up an interstellar colony, and then abandoning it—actively trying to stifle it—was pretty damned inconsistent?"

That hit Whittaker harder than I'd expected; his lips trembled. "B-but times changed—they were different people—*oh my God!*"

When he said that, of course, he meant it.

"Now d'you see it?" I said, to him and to the others around. "Two races, close both spatially and culturally! Both cultures going through a prosperous period, expansive, outgoing, a bit wasteful. Both looking to the stars, and so likely to encounter each other. But they're different, so they do things a little differently. One happens to discover a viable interstellar drive, so it founds a colony. The other sends out massively powerful messages. Both of them huge expensive projects, tying up time and resources. And so swallowing up a lot of the prosperity—in search of long-term returns, of course. But that looks bad on a balance display; it's a gamble, a matter of confidence. And for the moment the prosperity's gone; confidence suffers, the boom becomes a slump. And new people gradually come to dominate the government, people identified with active opposition to those projects—vultures on the carcass—"

"Yes," said Whittaker tonelessly, "vultures." Nobody else spoke.

"So. Their message arrives just in time to hit the tail-end of our period of prosperity, between forty and fifty years ago. So our government keeps it a secret, but does send an answer. But by the time that answer reaches 40 Eridani, more than thirty-three years have passed—probably longer, given the time taken to decode the message and prepare the reply. And by then the alien government is no longer the one that sent out the message. The vultures have gathered. Insecure, petty, ingrowing characters who thrive on intrigue and betrayal; xenophobia's as natural as breathing to them when they can't even trust each other! So when they find there really are intelligent aliens out there—well, you remember the arguments. Keeping people's eyes on the stars. Widening horizons. Making the cage harder to endure. And maybe easier to escape—by helping dissidents, arming them, even . . ." I savoured the bitter taste of *that* one, and was startled to see Ekkela smile faintly. What at? I hurried on. "Meanwhile, our vultures are gathering, too. So, in terror of each other, both governments—both sets of BCs—come to the same conclusion. It just takes us a little longer. And off go the missiles. Ironic, isn't it? Frightened by their own reflections, like birds at a mirror."

"Iesu," murmured Owen. "I think the boy's right . . ."

"It's possible," grunted Sussmeyer. "Given that thing's speed—yes, the timings work out. I can't think of anything better—but then I'm no politician . . ."

"Neither am I!" I said fervently. "Not after today. Never again!"

"Dieu soit loué!" croaked Ekkela. "Much as I hate to admit it, Mark, I think you've got the general idea. Ever study any space-flight history? That boom-slump business has happened before, on a smaller scale—"

Owen snapped his fingers. "America! In the 1950s—or was it the 1990s? Some time around two and a half centuries back, anyhow—just after Apollo, before orbital industry began to pay off . . . Space research was so underfunded it almost died before it was born, hardly."

Even allowing for Owen's exaggeration—everyone must have realized they needed *some* way to get at off-planet resources, even that long ago—I was impressed. "Sounds as if our BCs aren't just a modern invention, then . . ."

"Fools!" said Whittaker quietly. "Damned, damnable, pitiful fools. All of them, the aliens and ours. Ruled by greed and fear and hatred—pitiful!"

"They've signed their own death-warrants now," said Owen grimly.

"And those of millions of innocents!" grunted the old man. "May God forgive them, because I'm not sure I'll ever manage to—" He choked and turned rapidly away to look out at the stars. Many people were doing that, as if they were trying to catch a last glimpse of all the faces they'd left behind, the people they could not take with them, and the places that gave shape to their memories. These were things everyone on board had never expected to see again, and yet despite that—or perhaps because of it—it had been a comfort to know they were still there.

Whittaker raised his head sharply, as if at a distant sound "Is it possible the aliens have another planet, a Colony? They didn't tell us, of course, but then we didn't mention ours—"

"For which you can thank your god."

"I'd something of the sort in mind," he said mildly. "But it occurred to me that—if the two races have so much in common, if their rulers think alike—well, maybe their colonists would think more like us. Where it counts, anyway."

"And they sure won't be able to feel morally superior, if we run into them one day. That's a damned encouraging thought—"

"It grew out of a very harsh one. That those missiles might be agents for good—like a surgical beam—slicing away what had grown corrupt in both peoples, leaving the healthy free to grow again—the disease curing itself—"

I stared, horrified. "You rationalize it any way you like, Rev. You're a braver man than I am. I'd have nothing to do with a god that thinks like that." I turned away and saw Kirsty, standing alone and weeping for the family and home she'd wanted to escape from, and instinctively took her in my arms. After a while she was able to speak.

"Th-thanks. How is it with you?"

"It's easier for me, I suppose. For me there's only the places. Everyone I loved back there is dead already . . ." She was warm against me, and more welcome than I would have thought possible. I knew well enough by now how different an experience every woman is, and yet there was no escaping it, there was something special about Kirsty, or perhaps about Kirsty and me together, a kind of unity I'd never felt before. Or since, though I loved Maurya not a fraction the less. And for a year, or two years, Ekkela would be crippled, disembodied almost—brain and body raced at the thought, and I looked up hastily in case he was watching. He wasn't, but Whittaker, in the little group around him, caught my eye. I released—or rather detached—Kirsty as gently as I could, and strolled over.

"Ah, Mark," said Ekkela from where he lay. "I was just thinking—I'm going to be not much more than a talking head for the next couple of years—"

I still refuse to believe in telepathy. "I'm sorry," I said, and meant it.

"Thanks. You may be even more sorry in a minute. I'm going to need a replacement, or rather the Ship is. That offer Owen and I made you—"

"Well," I said, "as things stand now I might accept it. As second officer, after you've promoted Owen and Suss—"

"No," said Ekkela cheerfully. "Owen's not got the drive, and Suss, by his own admission, couldn't organize an orgy in a *bordel;* admin's a torture to him. No, we want somebody—" he gave a mock-modest simper, "say, more like me. A natural leader who can command people's confidence, an experienced administrator, a single-minded courageous fanatic with enough sheer drive to get this ramshackle ship to Epsilon Eridani if he's got to get out and push!" His grin widened. "The kind of man they end up building statues of—"

I panicked. "Ekkela, *no*—" But we were a long way off the ground.

"Oh yes!" grinned Owen. "Don't slide out of it this time, you bastard!"

"That's right!" chuckled Whittaker. "After the hammering you've been giving Réné these last few months you don't dare refuse."

"No!" I said, awash with anguish. "You don't understand—you don't know—what I almost *did*."

"At a guess," said Ekkela coolly, "you were thinking of getting some help from the aliens, some of their big fusors maybe, and going back Down There to settle some very heavy old scores—don't stare like that, man! That's been your prob-

lem all along, assuming nobody else thinks like you. I'd have
thought along the same lines myself, if I'd been hit as hard as
you were. But I'd have got over it eventually, and I think so
would you."

"That's right," said Whittaker. "Everyone makes mistakes."

"Like that? How do I know I won't do it again, something
just as stupid? If the warship hadn't come along I'd have gone
blissfully on with it, probably got the Colony wiped out too!
I'm not safe to trust."

"Then neither am I," said Whittaker. "You only thought
about destroying the Colony. I actually tried to."

"You—"

"Me. I sat on the committee that originally agreed to aban-
don it." I could only gape. Owen and Sussmeyer and Kirsty,
who had joined us, looked much the same, but Ekkela only
smiled. Whittaker shook his head sadly. "I was very young,"
he said, "Though that's no defence. Power comes early in
autocracies; one of the greatest English prime ministers took
office when he was twenty-six. I was about that age. I'd applied
to join the first Ship—you know how oversubscribed that was—
and I was turned down. Family pressure, of course, though it
was well hidden from me then. I suppose I was rather a spoilt
young man, not used to being refused. I was piqued, I was
jealous of the Colony, I managed to convince myself that it
was impractical and wasteful and so on. I became one of your
vultures, Mark. For nearly ten years I was as bitter an opponent
of the Colony as anyone." He smiled. "My fall from grace
occurred before the aliens' message arrived. I was spared that,
at least. And I wasn't the prime mover or casting vote—it was
unanimous—or anything like that. Just an important cog in
the machine. But I still share the responsibility . . ."

"Ye've more than made up for it!" said Kirsty fiercely. I
joined in the chorus of agreement.

"I told him that ages ago, when he first told me," smiled
Ekkela. "He's not given up, has he?"

"Well, to some extent, maybe," said Whittaker, scratching
his head. "But there you are, Mark."

"Sure," grinned Sussmeyer, which was a terrible shock in
itself. "You think you've got problems? Better that you should
do something about them."

"And remember you'll have us to look after you!" said Owen
solemnly. "Best back-seat drivers in the known universe, us!"

"And," said Ekkela with gloating satisfaction, "you'll have the benefit of my helpful advice! After so much of yours this year, it'll be a real pleasure—"

"What he means," said Whittaker hastily, "is that you might benefit from a spell on our side of the fence. Though there's no denying we might sleep a little easier, too," he added with a grin. "But we wouldn't have mentioned it if you weren't the obvious person for the job—"

"The *only* obvious person," rasped Ekkela. "You *can't* refuse. You're needed, damn you! Do I have to waste my voice making that any clearer?"

Not even in Thorborg's office had I felt quite so trapped. And I wouldn't have, if I hadn't known they were right. I was the obvious choice, in many ways the only one. "I've got to think it over—"

"Not for too long," said Whittaker. "We've got to let people know. It's going to be hard enough to keep up morale as it is."

"You're telling me? What about *my* morale? I tried to kill myself back there, you know. I still half feel like it—"

There was a screech of metal from below, and a clang. "Almost there, tower!" came a distant voice. "Ladders away! We're bringing you down now." There was a grinding sound and some kind of ratcheted mechanism began a slow, regular clanking. Millim by millim, jerkily at first, then more smoothly, the tower began to descend.

"You want to punish yourself?" said Sussmeyer wryly. "Then you don't take such an easy way out. But I think you're worrying too much."

I watched the Bridge come up to meet us, wishing I'd escaped down the ladders, arm or no arm. Now I couldn't get away. Kirsty was watching me, and I thought how little attention she'd had for Ekkela. And she'd said I was hard to manage without . . . And Ekkela, Whittaker, Owen, and the others, looking at me the way I'd looked at some of my more appealing rogues, about to get what they deserved at last. Friends and less than friends, but certainly no enemies.

"Well," I said tentatively. "If it's what you want . . ."

"It certainly is!" barked Whittaker.

"Hear, hear!" said Ekkela. "This'll fix you! Congratulations, *Captain!* Maybe you'll get that statue yet . . ." And he closed his eyes with a sigh of absolute bliss. Kirsty's eyes were shining—at what? Who for? She was looking at us both. I knew now that if I wanted her back, I'd get her. But if not now, like this, then never. We could stay friends, maybe even occasional lovers. But that special unity would be lost.

"Congratulations!" she breathed. "Ye'll do fine, Mark!" Everyone else echoed her, till I held up my hand.

"This is all a bit premature. First, we don't know if we can survive the next year, whatever I do or don't do. Secondly, I haven't accepted yet." Their faces fell as I turned and looked over the rail. Two metres to go. "Not for at least—twelve hours, say. If you're going to make me so bloody responsible, I'll start by getting my priorities right. I'll be with Maurya and the kids."

And I vaulted the rail with ease, and landed running. Some responsibilities are worth the trouble.

At the mouth of a green valley, opening onto a wide ocean, a statue stands. Oddly unheroic, short and square, it looks out across the expanse of water, facing the sunrise. It has stood there through storm and calm—watching the gulls and the whales and as undisturbed as they by the sea and air craft that pass—for a thousand years. And the inscription on its base reads: *For behold, I create new heavens, and a new Earth.*

THE ORBIT SCIENCE FICTION YEARBOOK 2

The best short SF of the year

Edited by

David Garnett

Plus articles by

Brian Aldiss and John Clute

WORLDS OF TOMORROW

Rolling and tumbling from the typewriters of the world's best Science Fiction writers, here are twelve gems, as different as diamonds, emeralds and rubies, but with the flawless glitter that denotes the perfect artefact.

J. G. BALLARD, PAUL DI FILIPPO,
SHARON N. FARBER, STEVEN GOULD,
JAMES PATRICK KELLY, KATHE KOJA,
IAN MCDONALD, JACK MASSA, RUDY RUCKER &
MARC LAIDLAW, HOWARD WALDROP,
IAN WATSON, ROGER ZELAZNY

The second volume of the ORBIT SCIENCE FICTION YEARBOOK also features articles on the best SF novels of 1988 and a review of the year in Science Fiction, by BRIAN ALDISS, JOHN CLUTE and DAVID GARNETT.

"The anthology to buy first . . ." INTERZONE

"By far the best anthology . . . a stunning collection"
THE INDEPENDENT

"John Clute . . . makes me grit my teeth with envy"
David Pringle, WHITE DWARF

FUTURA PUBLICATIONS
AN ORBIT BOOK
SCIENCE FICTION
0 7088 8316 8

All Futura Books are available at your bookshop or
newsagent, or can be ordered from the following address:
Futura Books, Cash Sales Department,
P.O. Box 11, Falmouth, Cornwall TR10 9EN.

Please send cheque or postal order (no currency), and
allow 60p for postage and packing for the first book
plus 25p for the second book and 15p for each additional
book ordered up to a maximum charge of £1.90 in U.K.

B.F.P.O. customers please allow 60p for
the first book, 25p for the second book plus 15p per
copy for the next 7 books, thereafter 9p per book

Overseas customers, including Eire, please allow £1.25
for postage and packing for the first book, 75p for the
second book and 28p for each subsequent title ordered.

interzone

SCIENCE FICTION AND FANTASY

Bimonthly   £1.95

- *Interzone* is the leading British magazine which specializes in SF and new fantastic writing. We have published:

BRIAN ALDISS	GARRY KILWORTH
J.G. BALLARD	DAVID LANGFORD
IAIN BANKS	MICHAEL MOORCOCK
BARRINGTON BAYLEY	RACHEL POLLACK
GREGORY BENFORD	KEITH ROBERTS
MICHAEL BISHOP	GEOFF RYMAN
DAVID BRIN	JOSEPHINE SAXTON
RAMSEY CAMPBELL	BOB SHAW
ANGELA CARTER	JOHN SHIRLEY
RICHARD COWPER	JOHN SLADEK
JOHN CROWLEY	BRIAN STABLEFORD
PHILIP K. DICK	BRUCE STERLING
THOMAS M. DISCH	LISA TUTTLE
MARY GENTLE	IAN WATSON
WILLIAM GIBSON	CHERRY WILDER
M. JOHN HARRISON	GENE WOLFE

- *Interzone* has also published many excellent new writers; graphics by JIM BURNS, ROGER DEAN, IAN MILLER and others; book reviews, news, etc.

- *Interzone* is available from good bookshops, or by subscription. For six issues, send £11 (outside UK, £12.50) to: **124 Osborne Road, Brighton BN1 6LU, UK** Single copies: £1.95 inc p&p (outside UK, £2.50).

- American subscribers may send $22 ($26 if you want delivery by air mail) to our British address, above. All cheques should be made payable to *Interzone*.

- -

To: **interzone** 124 Osborne Road, Brighton, BN1 6LU, UK.

Please send me six issues of *Interzone*, beginning with the current issue. I enclose a cheque/p.o. for £11 (outside UK, £12.50; US subscribers, $22 or $26 air), made payable to *Interzone*.

Name _____

Address _____

_____